# The
# Provençal
# Tales

The great affair is to move; to feel
the needs and hitches of our life more nearly;
to come down off this feather-bed of
civilization, and find the globe granite underfoot
and strewn with cutting flints.

RLS

# The Provençal Tales

## MICHAEL DE LARRABEITI

PAVILION
MICHAEL JOSEPH

First published in Great Britain in 1988 by
PAVILION BOOKS LIMITED
196 Shaftesbury Avenue, London WC2H 8JL
in association with Michael Joseph Limited
27 Wrights Lane, Kensington, London W8 5TZ

Designed by Jillian Haines
Map by George Galsworthy

British Library Cataloguing in Publication Data

De Larrabeiti, Michael
The Provençal tales
I. Title
823'.914 [F]

ISBN 1–85145–211–7

Typeset in Garamond by
Wyvern Typesetting Limited

Printed and bound in Great Britain by
Billing and Sons Limited, Worcester

*This book is above all for Jean Renoult who*
*was the first to show me the roads of Provence.*
*It is also for the shepherds of Grimaud who*
*allowed me to walk those roads in their company:*

*Marius Fresia et Huguette, Leonce Coulet,*
*Paul Graziani et sa fille, Milou et Lucien,*
*et la Famille Martel-Jules,*
*Joseph, Jean et Jeanette*

# CONTENTS

◦◦

# | INTRODUCTION |

I saw Provence for the first time in the summer of 1957. I was travelling by train, overnight from Paris; a travel guide escorting five hundred people to a holiday village at a place called St Aygulf – a tiny resort on the Mediterranean a few kilometres to the west of Frejus. Somewhere south of Valence I awoke, leant out of my couchette, raised the blind that darkened the window and found myself in a different country to the France I had gone to sleep in. The sun was fierce, the colours were a thousand years old and the roof tiles were rounded and pale.

By the early spring of the following year I was the assistant manager of the holiday village with a staff of thirty or more to look after. I supervised the restaurant, I organized excursions and I was the master of ceremonies for the soirées that were held on the terrace. There was no dance that I dared not tackle, no partner that I feared to approach. I could rhumba and I could cha-cha-cha; I could fox-trot and I could tango. In my lightweight mohair suits and white Italian pumps I was the nattiest of fellows.

This promotion had been brought about not so much by my talents but rather by the temptations that went with the job. In the three years since it had opened Les Auberges au Soleil, as the residence was called, had lost the same number of assistant managers. One had run off with the cash; another had succumbed to the lures of the flesh and the third had drunk himself into hospital. I was engaged to put a stop to this decadence.

The manager of the 'Auberges' was a podgy little ex-maître d'hotel with suspicious eyes and a button of a nose set in the middle of a round and heavy face. His thin black hair was smarmed in streaks across his skull and contrasted nicely with his red complexion. He looked choleric and was. He disliked most people, trusted no one and had married a woman with a face as narrow as a knife. His name was Garreau and there was only one thing to recommend him – the moment he saw that I was halfway competent he handed me over to a man called Jean Renoult and then left us to rub along exactly as we wished.

Jean Renoult had been at the 'Auberges' since the day the first tourists had arrived to leave their footprints in the wet cement and to sleep in the roofless chalets. He had emigrated from Normandy, where he'd been raised, to live in the sun and along the way had decided that work of any serious kind was a waste of valuable time. He had married a girl from Toulon, sailed a canoe along the Mediterranean coast, been a soldier on skis, patrolling the Italian frontier in 1939, and a forester in Brittany during the German occupation. He had no home apart from his books and not many clothes either. He loved love, the sun, the rolling hills of Les Maures, all women except Madame Garreau, reading, the sea, his wife and children, pastis, the Provençal language and the oddities of human behaviour. He disliked only one thing; working for money.

On his arrival at St Aygulf Jean had done his best to hide his understanding and intelligence and had taken up the job of gardener and odd-job man. It hadn't come off. A succession of managers had seen through his disguise and when I met him he was living with his wife and children in one of the chalets and had been made responsible for the forward planning of the restaurant and the general maintenance of the whole set-up; plumbing, drainage, gardens, everything.

Jean taught me my duties within a week or two and we buckled down to the long season, March to October. We worked together every day and ate at the same table when we could. As the weeks went by he talked about Provence and told me where it lay and who lived there. I learnt some of its history and some of its poetry. The sensation I had felt in the train that first day had not misled me. I had entered a different country indeed. Provence, as I discovered through Jean's words and the books he gave me, was a wide and empty land of lonely peaks and windswept plateaux. Not France, not Spain, it was a country of extremes; cool forests and bleak hills that burned in the sun; waterless plains and deep torrents – a cruel land.

But there was magic too. There were Saracens in the woods and castles on the mountains; deserted villages where the ghosts of wise and beautiful women still listened to the songs of troubadours. And there were archbishops and sorcerers, forever searching for power and happiness. Above all there was the language – the Provençal that sounded like a song.

While it lasted my job was good enough but there was no working with Garreau for long. A hot-tempered man he was jealous perhaps of the strong friendship that grew up between Jean and me. In any event he was certainly irritated at being both ignored and disliked and he soon made my life at St Aygulf unbearable. By the March of 1959, and as the result of a flaming row, I found myself packing my trunk.

Without having given the matter much thought I decided to return to London but Jean came to my room, a rather pleasant one looking down to the sea through eucalyptus trees, and convinced me otherwise. He was right; I had money in my pocket, Provence lay before me and there were books to read.

What was more, he said, I could stay with his mother for as long as I liked. Two hours later I was standing, over-dressed in a pale blue suit, at the end of a track in the middle of a vineyard, halfway up a stony hill, somewhere behind the town of Grimaud. Two peasants, a man and a woman, their heads only just visible over a bank of broad vine leaves, were staring at me. I was surrounded by suitcases, the sun was hot and I was sweating.

Bonne Maman Renoult was as remarkable as her son. Her husband, an artist turned engineer, had died only a couple of years previously. Now all she had to live on was the minutest of pensions and, after moving from one rented shack to another, she had finally settled in a two thirds derelict farmhouse halfway up the hill of Rascas.

Like most Provençal farmhouses Rascas was tucked into the hillside in order to protect it from the mistral. Extensions had been built on to it at various times but they were now in ruins. Bonne Maman lived in three rooms in the middle; one down and two up. There was of course no electricity and water came from a well a hundred metres away. Brambles grew up to the door and in through the ruined windows. There was no lavatory either and the track from the valley was a vertical path by the time it reached the little plateau on which the house stood.

Bonne Maman's living room was a treasure trove. All round the walls were scores of her husband's paintings, showing, as far as I could tell, undeniable talent. There were one or two fine pieces of furniture from her great days in Paris, books, silver oil lamps and, above the fireplace, there hung a portrait of her husband painted by his cousin Raoul Dufy, all in dark browns and yellows. She was, when I met her, about seventy years old.

Bonne Maman had no idea I was coming that day, just as I had no idea that I was leaving St Aygulf. It didn't matter a bit. She showed me where the wheelbarrow was and I brought up my cases and installed myself in the third room, happy to begin a visit that was the first of many and which was to last three months.

Our social life, or rather her social life, was a fairly busy one. Though she lived on her own there were often ten or fifteen people at her table. Visitors came from everywhere; there were priests, peasants, sculptors and painters, relatives and strays like me. She held court up there on the hill of Rascas and I was a fortunate onlooker. I threw away my suits and my sea-island cotton shirts and cut back the brambles. I found a broken bike in one of the nearby ruins and mended it. Now I could cycle down to St Pons les Mures, on the coast road between St Maxime and St Tropez, climb a gate, cross a vineyard and come to a deserted beach and picnic alone; there where now the holiday apartments of Port Grimaud stand with their security gates, their breeze-block 'Provençal' towers and their plastic boats at the door.

It was at Rascas that I met Marius Fresia, the shepherd. Bonne Maman had gone to visit friends at Avignon for a few days and I was left in charge of the house. Quite early on the second morning I was awakened by strange sounds; a kind of rustling by the door, a shout or two and the clanging of small bells.

I got up, put on my dressing gown and went out into the sunlight to find myself surrounded by about five or six hundred sheep. In the middle of this flock, with two savage dogs at his heel, stood a man some fifteen years older than me, leaning at his ease on a stout staff. He was clothed in a rough flannel shirt and heavy corduroy trousers of dark brown. On his feet were big solid boots with soles an inch thick. On his head he wore a broad brimmed hat of olive green felt, while tied across his back with a piece of cord was an enormous blue umbrella. Over his shoulder was slung a large leather bag, the musette, containing his food and drink.

The man's face had been darkened by the sun and the wind but his expression was cheerful and bright, like the sound of his voice, though that was so coloured through with the language of Provence that even when he spoke French it was, at first, difficult for me to understand him. This then was Marius, the man I later cajoled into taking me with him on the transhumance, a trek of about two hundred kilometres, from Grimaud to La Colle St Michel and beyond, from the coast to the mountains with three thousand sheep, away from the burnt out grass of the coastal plain and up to the high pastures of the Basses Alpes.

❈

There have been shepherds in Provence since pre-Roman times and Marius, as well as those who travelled with him, were little different, I imagine, from their forebears. They herded their sheep towards the mountains during the cool hours of the night and chose always to begin their journey at a time of full moon. When the sun got up they rested in the shade, leaving the sheep to lie exhausted under the trees while around them the dogs slept, panting. But the shepherds never slept. Instead they stretched their bodies on the ground, propped themselves on an elbow or against a tree trunk and talked the day away, drinking from time to time or tearing chunks of bread from a loaf to eat with the saucisson that they hacked at with their knives.

What they spoke of at such length was not, at the beginning, easy for me to discover, but after a while, and little by little, I managed to pick up just enough Provençal to follow the burden of their conversation: sheep and their illnesses; what had happened on the road in previous years and who were the best drovers to hire. But there was another thing. There was an on-going, everlasting discourse that, I suppose, had been kept up for generations, and it was spoken in low murmurs all the way down the long road.

The greater part of this talk was devoted to the misfortunes and adventures of other shepherds, both alive and dead, ancient and modern. But I heard stories too and fragments of stories, legends of Provence not told in any literary way, but recounted in an offhand, outdoor fashion. And more tales, only touched upon, casually, as we threaded our way through a ruin or camped under the trees and the ghost of the place reminded a shepherd of something he had heard or seen.

These more oblique references intrigued me and, when I could persuade the others to speak in French, I would worry them with questions as we walked along: 'Where did these stories come from and were they true? – but all the answer I ever got for my pains was a shrug of the shoulders or a shake of the head. And so my imagination was set free to wander from the track we followed and I encouraged it to range over the whole country, searching by night for castles and sorcerers, and by day for troubadours and the ladies they served.

And of course I must have dreamt as well, fighting against sleep at each bivouac so that I could listen to the shepherds, but often tired beyond measure, especially during the first two days, I would sometimes doze through the lazy hours and not come fully to my senses until Marius shook me awake at the very moment it was time to march on.

The ground, I remember, seemed as soft and inviting then as a quilted mattress but I knew I had to open my eyes and force myself to my feet. Even as I stood the shepherds were calling in the dogs, hitching up the mule and throwing their cloaks into the cart. All I had time for was a swig of water and I was off again, stumbling along, still half-asleep on legs that ached to the bone, not daring to look over my shoulder lest the people of my dreams still lingered beneath the trees or slumbered on their coats by the embers of our fire.

∾

The shepherd, constantly on the move, has always been feared by the sedentary peasant. In the popular imagination he was a stranger from beyond the horizon. He had seen many things, he was many things; doctor at best, magician at worst. He garnered and kept knowledge; he knew the names of poisonous plants and could make potions; he knew the spells to ward off the evil eye. Some said he was a descendant of the wandering gypsies and weren't they, if the truth were told, the Saracens who had failed to return to Africa and Spain after the fall of Fraxinetta? Whatever the reality behind these legends it was certain that the shepherd was the repository of much dangerous learning, and it was best not to cross him in case he pronounced the words that could do you harm.

But there was one thing the peasant could not help admiring in the shepherd, and that was his power of story-telling. The shepherd's ancestors had been closer than anyone else to the ancient troubadours and they had been accustomed to welcome such travellers to their camp fires, happy to exchange meat and wine for ballad and song. Over the years, subjected to this influence, many shepherds had become troubadours, and, in bad times, troubadours had often been forced to become shepherds.

This alliance, enduring for some two centuries, had made the shepherd the guardian of a quantity of stories and this was, perhaps, his most curious gift. If you could induce him to tell his tale then it was bound to be both wondrous and enchanting. Unfortunately it was something he would rarely do beyond the confines of his own narrow society. He held the peasant in contempt and scorned the stranger; in a word the shepherd kept to his kind.

I soon found this to be true. For the duration of the transhumance, Marius, with a flock of about six hundred, had joined forces with four other shepherds who possessed flocks of a similar size. Herding three thousand sheep, not to mention half a dozen spare mules and thirty goats, is hard work. Marius's companions did not know me nor did they want to – I was a nuisance. On that first night of the trek they ignored me completely, except to swear roundly when I got in their way. For the next three days they continued in the same vein, more or less, and I was on my own. Marius could not be expected to help me, he had work to do and, after all, it had been my idea in the first place. He had said that it wouldn't be easy and it wasn't.

The food Bonne Maman had given me ran out after a day or two; I didn't have a cloak to keep me warm and I didn't have the enormous blue umbrella, the mark of the shepherd, to keep off the sun and the rain. And, in those first three days, I wore through the soles of my gigolo shoes and there were blisters on both feet. I was on the point of giving up, just as everyone had said I would, when one of the hired hands fell ill and left us. He was the man who walked behind the mule cart, transporting the food and drink, the spare clothes and the new-born lambs when there were any.

It was the most despised job of all and he who had it walked forever in a cloud of dust and horse-fly, on call at every moment to run the length of the flock with whatever was needed; cloaks, leggings or a bottle of wine.

I welcomed this opportunity with open arms and proposed myself for the vacancy and, from the moment I showed that I was not a fool come along to gawp, everything changed. Someone lent me a spare cloak, ragged but warm. Someone else told me that I could buy a pair of the best shepherd boots ever made at Bargemon and yet a third person gave me a broken umbrella. I was no longer a tourist.

❧

Six years later, having in the interim read for a degree at Trinity College, Dublin, I was offered a twelve month scholarship to the École Normale Supérieure, Paris, so that I might look round for a suitable subject for a doctoral thesis.

What I did for most of the tenure of that scholarship was visit the Cinémathèque, the theatres and art galleries and sit in cafés arguing with friends. Occasionally, however, I would spend a day or two in the Bibliothèque Nationale – a huge, imposing library where the quiet echoed between old wooden desks and which was lit by row upon row of table lamps bearing dark green shades.

It was a good place to work and I whiled away many hours in it, browsing through volumes that dealt with Provence and its history, hoping, in a vague way, to find something that might link the shepherds and troubadours in some common tradition.

I did not take this work at all seriously but gradually I pieced together a theory which was substantiated here and there by references that did indeed indicate a bond between these two groups of men – Doctor Michael de Larrabeiti, how well it rolled off the tongue.

It was not to be and my thesis never saw the light of day. The two or three stories I had been told in French and the fragments I had heard in Provençal would not leave my thoughts. As I attempted to press on with my research I began to unearth allusions to the shepherd stories and to the past of that wild country I had trekked across. Gradually my interest in a doctorate waned and I read only where the imagination led me.

Now it so happened that during my time on the transhumance I had made a point of keeping a notebook. I had written down the distances walked and the names of the places where we had camped. I had also kept a brief record of conversations and these notes reminded me of nearly everything that had been said. I made use of this detail and slowly, at my desk in the Bibliothèque Nationale, I put together the scaffolding for a collection of stories, half-imagined and half remembered and all to be set against a background of what I had read and observed.

But the stories went the way of the thesis. The attractions of Paris were too strong and too many. The original enthusiasm slipped away and before I realized it the wonderful year had ended and I took myself off to do other things. It was not until recently, while emptying a trunk, that I rediscovered the sketches for 'The Provençal Tales' and came to the conclusion that they were still worth working on.

I have decided to remain faithful to the original structure because that was the way the transhumance happened, though now, after a gap of twenty years, it is difficult for me to distinguish between what I overheard and what I invented. The shepherds were always telling anecdotes of one kind or another; forever reminiscing and wondering out loud. 'There is no place without a story,' Marius used to say, 'and what is more, someone has to tell each and every one of them for the very first time, sometime, someplace, so why not me . . . or you?'

I have often been reprimanded by my friends for not going on with my research: I should have persevered with the troubadour connection, they say, and even prevailed upon the shepherds and their families to divulge more of what they knew. I don't know. It was a rare invitation I received that June to walk the road and that experience can, perhaps, be best conveyed by these stories and their setting. Besides it is too late to begin again. Most of the shepherds I went to the mountains with are dead; they were well into their sixties then, though I am told you can still see Marius and Jean Martel in the plain by Cogolin, and at eighty-five Jules still leans on his staff and counts his sheep above Peyresq.

But nowadays those sheep are freighted to the high pastures in lorries and the shepherds follow in their cars. Even if I should take to the road of the transhumance I would not find men like the men I knew beneath the trees near Bargemon or down by the river at Castellane – characters in their own mythology with stardust clinging to their cloaks. Nor are the ruins of Rascas ruins any more, for they have been rebuilt entirely and the Parisiens who own them can drive to within a yard of the entrance. Bonne Maman has gone and so has her son, Jean Renoult, to whom I owe so much it cannot be told, but this book is for him – and the shepherds too of course – I know that's what he would have wanted.

OXFORD, 1988.

# LE COL DE
# GRATTELOUP

**M**arius came in the middle of the afternoon, right up to Rascas through the heat. 'It's tonight,' he said, 'it's decided. Be at la Queste about midnight.'

I was pleased. 'Have a drink,' I said.

Marius laughed and turned to go back down the path, his head already level with my feet because of the steepness of the hillside. 'There's too much to do,' he answered, 'much too much.'

I was eager to set off and had been for days. Everything I needed was in a large white duffel bag that had belonged to Bonne Maman's husband. There was a sleeping bag, several changes of clothing, a map and a note-book. That evening, after dinner, Bonne Maman and I talked until it was almost time for me to leave, then we stood outside the house for a little while and the moon came up as big as a melon, illuminating the ruins of Rascas and the narrow terrace that I had cleared of brambles. Bonne Maman walked to the edge of it with me and we embraced. 'Come back when you want,' she said and I went down the path.

It was only two or three kilometres from Rascas to Notre Dame de la Queste and I soon covered the distance. In front of the chapel, by the side of the road, I sat on the duffel bag and waited. Opposite was the black bulk of a farmhouse and all around me the silver fields. Midnight Marius had said. I glanced at my watch. I had an hour to go.

The air was still and I might have been the only person alive in the whole world. I looked towards the castle of Grimaud where it stood like a ghost against the sky. I could hear nothing save the trickle of the fountain a few metres away. Then, a moment or two before one o'clock, the noise came, distant to begin with but growing louder with each minute. I got to my feet.

I distinguished the cries first, the voices of men, tense and angry, shouting at the barking dogs. Next came the bells, heavy ones that boomed and lighter ones that rustled more than rang, each one made by a shepherd's hands and each one with a different tone; scores of them filling the night with sound. Now I could hear the rattle of twelve thousand hooves on the tarmac, the bleating too and soon I saw the hurricane lamps being waved

15

from side to side to warn those who drove cars at night of the dangers that lay before them.

At last came the flock and the backs of three thousand sheep caught the moonlight and sent it rippling from place to place like the shadow of the wind on water. Dark shapes of men went past me. I stepped forward and swung the white bag to my shoulder. Plainly visible I was ignored until Marius ran by, his two dogs leaping beside him. 'Throw your bag into the wagon and get moving,' he shouted and then he too was gone. I did as ordered and followed the lamp that swung from the tailboard of the mule-cart. 'Don't get so close,' a voice said, 'you block that light and some stupid car will drive right into us.'

I moved to one side and we marched on; all along the coast road, through Beauvallon and into St Maxime. Here the dawn came up as we passed by the grey sea and the sheep filled the streets outside the dead night-clubs and the sleeping restaurants. We went deeper into the town, crossed the bridge and turned left, heading upwards and inland. Now the noise of the shouting and the bleating and the bells brought people from their beds and they came to their balconies and rubbed their eyes as we went by. Children ran out into the street in their night-clothes, dragging their parents with them, their faces all smiles because the passing of the sheep meant that summer had arrived. And some families walked with us to the very edge of town before they fell away and waved and went back to their breakfasts.

But the shepherds could not stop and the long straight road continued northwards and the sun came up and the air began to creak in the heat. The heads of the sheep drooped and they slowed their pace; the dogs padded behind in silence and I began to limp, not knowing if I could finish the day's distance. It was not until ten o'clock, nine hours and twenty kilometres after leaving Grimaud, that we arrived at the Col de Gratteloup and the sheep were guided from the road and pushed in under the trees. Then the mule was unhitched and the cart manhandled into the shade of a ruined chapel. There we found another shepherd, with his flock, waiting to join us, and this was Leonce Coulet.

Leonce was at his ease, both fed and watered, and he started talking immediately. I was beyond anything. I pulled my belongings from the cart, climbed into my sleeping bag and fell into a deep slumber, too tired to eat or drink. A few hours later I was awakened by Marius. The shade of my tree had shifted from me and I was lying in the full strength of the afternoon sun.

'Best move,' he said, 'your brains will fry in this. You ought to eat something, and drink too.'

I rolled back into the shade. The shepherds lay around me, their limbs sprawled in comfort, their hats tipped over their eyes. Leonce Coulet was still talking. His voice was rough, like stones on a shovel, but it was full of mirth and compassion too. He was a tall man dressed in a soft grey shirt and a waistcoat and trousers made from black corduroy. His hat was black also and had a wide brim.

But it was his face that I found remarkable; framed as it was with iron grey hair and lined with dark creases where he grinned or frowned. It was a face that stopped you in your tracks and made you want to know the man and listen to him. Under well-marked brows his eyes were mischievous and when they rested on you they made you feel glad to be alive and when he spoke his huge hands moved and wove a spell. Troubadours must have looked and sounded like Leonce Coulet; perhaps he was a troubadour, one who had been lying in ambush at Gratteloup for centuries, just waiting for us to halt there so that he might tell his tale before we went on with our journey.

# The Troubadour and
# The Cage of Gold

There was once a young and handsome Prince and he lived in that most beautiful part of Provence which people have always called Les Maures. This young man had been born and brought up in a fine castle built halfway between Collobrières and La Mole and in due time, that is to say on the death of his father, he came into his full inheritance. The Prince had loved his father and grieved for him deeply, as was only right, but as soon as the proper period of mourning was over the Prince looked about him and set his mind to the future and to the responsibilities he bore.

The Prince had come into possession of a paradise on earth and the loveliest part of it all was the castle. Called the Château of La Verne it nestled into the side of a gently sloping hill and was surrounded by splendid trees. Their branches gave a welcome shade throughout the long days of summer, and under the broad leaves the traveller or troubadour could always find somewhere to rest and refresh himself. There were trees of all sorts; chestnuts, pines, cork-oaks, fragrant eucalyptus and even palm trees that had been brought, so some said, from Africa by Abd al-Rhaman in the ancient Saracen days of war and pillage.

Inside the walls of the castle was a wide hexagonal courtyard and in the middle of the courtyard was a large fountain fed from a spring so deep that it never froze in winter or ever dried in summer. Growing high over the fountain was a ring of tall and leafy plane trees and it was here, in the dusk of the evening, that the inhabitants of La Verne, from the richest to the poorest, would meet to talk together until night fell and it was time for sleep. Around the perimeter of the courtyard, at intervals, flights of steps rose to the apartments of the castle while the largest entrance led to the Prince's quarters and the main dining-hall.

Beyond the fortifications and all along by the banks of the river that gave the castle its name, were to be found the farms and fields and vineyards that gave the Prince and his courtiers their sustenance. As chance would have it the Prince was not a greedy youth and his father had seen to it that he grew up to appreciate his good fortune and, as part of his upbringing when a boy, he had been made to help with the harvest and the grape-picking every year. He had even wandered the hills in all weathers with the rough and ready shepherds who tended his father's flocks. Now everything was his and his peasants and servants were happy to come under his rule for they knew that he would manage his lands to their best advantage. The people of La Verne were completely happy but the Prince himself was not – and the reason lay in the past.

As part of his education the Prince had travelled from one end of Provence to the other, visiting many castles and every large city. Because of this he knew that although his father had been content with the simple life of La Verne he himself entertained very different expectations. He had no wish to change the way the ordinary people on his estates lived, quite the contrary, but after all, he had seen dancing, heard music; he had read books and discussed philosophy. What was perhaps more important was that he had listened to troubadours and had been deeply moved by the stories they'd told him and the ballads they'd sung. But there was nothing to be learnt at La Verne; his father had discouraged it; no poets came to exchange verses with other poets and no troubadours came to tell stories to other troubadours – yet that was where the Prince's desires lay. He was possessed by a powerful and irresistible ambition. He wanted to transform La Verne into the most renowned of all Provençal castles, and by doing so he dreamed of making himself the most renowned of all Provençal princes.

The Prince knew that this would not be an easy task. Troubadours and minstrels and travelling magicians were very special people. They were free and untrammelled. 'They blow where the wind listeth,' the proverb said. They might tarry in your company a week and write wicked lampoons about you; or, if they fell in love with your lady, they might serve her for months, making poetry and telling stories and the music and words would carry her fame, and sometimes her husband's, from one end of Europe to the other. It was the best gift the world had to offer; Immortality in a song.

So it became obvious to the Prince that he was missing a lady to grace La Verne and to be his wife. Nor could she be any ordinary lady. She would have to be descended of a princely blood. She would need to be excessively beautiful and she would need a keen and kindly intelligence. Such a paragon would not be easy to find and the Prince knew it. In all of Provence at that time there was only one princess who even approached these requirements and she had been sung of by every troubadour who had enjoyed the good fortune of seeing her. She was still unmarried and about the Prince's age but she was much sought after and possessed a mind that was independent and robust. She was not a fool and certainly not the type to collapse in a swoon at the feet of the first prince who appeared before her. She was a princess who desired a full life and would do her best to see that she got it. She lived, under the protection of her father, in a castle just above the town of Callas, and that was her name – the Princess of Callas.

The Prince felt that he had little chance of persuading the Princess to make La Verne her home and him her husband, but he was no coward and decided that he could but try. Many princes, he knew, had asked for the hand of the Princess but none had ever been accepted. It was not that the girl was over-weening or spoilt, it was that the men who had come for her had all seemed boastful and pretentious, as if she were the lucky one; and they had spent most of their time talking about themselves and the feats they had performed at hunting and fighting. The Princess wanted the man she chose to be brave, of course, but she knew that there are more things in life than sticking swords into enemies or spears into wild boar.

As soon as he had made his decision the Prince set off on the long journey from the valley of La Verne to the town of Callas which is situated on a hill not far south of Bargemon. He travelled quite simply with only a dozen archers for protection and no great retinue. On his arrival at Callas he presented himself to the Lord of that place and after the requisite compliments and presents had been exchanged he asked for permission to see the Princess. This permission was granted, under certain conditions, and the Prince and two of his noblest companions were led by a servant to the terraces where the Princess was to be found.

The Prince was impressed by everything he saw at Callas. In almost every part of the castle were troubadours and minstrels singing, or in company with the ladies of the place, composing songs for the next day. The Prince's heart swelled to breaking point. This was his heart's desire.

At last, in the shade of a great silken awning that fell in folds from a stone balcony the Prince discovered the Princess sitting with her ladies-in-waiting and several men of letters. There was also a minstrel playing his lute nearby but as the Prince and his companions appeared all conversation stopped and silence came over the terrace.

The Prince blushed for the Princess was as beautiful and as regal as rumour had said and suddenly he was aware of how inadequate he was. How could anyone dare to ask for her hand in marriage. He bit his lip. He felt uncouth and awkward. He and his companions had not even bothered to change from their travelling clothes so impatient had the Prince been to present himself. He hesitated, halted, but then, summoning up all his courage, he advanced towards the Princess, trying to ignore the fine and accomplished courtiers who stood near her.

For her part the Princess was struck by the young man's appearance. His life in the forest of La Verne had given him a fine constitution and he moved with a natural grace even when he was embarrassed. His clothes were covered in the dust of the roads, it was true, but she looked beyond that and saw that they were simple and straightforward with no excess of fashion on them. His face was open and honest. A good face. His manners were not polished in the way of the courts of love but he looked kind and sincere. He was certainly different from most princes who came to ask for her as if she were a horse they wanted to buy.

The Prince bowed. 'Princess,' he began. 'Forgive me, I have come from La Verne, in the hills of Les Maures, to the south. I should, I know, have changed my clothes but I wished to see you . . . without wasting a minute.'

The ladies-in-waiting lowered their heads and laughed and the minstrel plucked at the strings of his lute and made a discord but the Princess raised her hand and there was quiet. She liked the reason the Prince had given and she thought it did him, and her, credit. She smiled and the full power of her smile bore upon the Prince and he felt his heart weaken and his task recede further from him. She was so stately.

'Well, Prince from La Verne,' she said, 'what is it you have come all this way to say?'

The Prince looked about him, at the ladies and courtiers, the men of letters and the minstrel and he said nothing. Everyone was staring and waiting for him to speak, but he could not: not in front of so many. The Princess understood and rose from her chair and taking the Prince by the hand she led him to the end of the terrace where, though still in sight of the company, he and she were out of earshot.

'Well, Prince from La Verne,' said the Princess once more, 'what is it you have come all this way to say?'

Then the Prince began to speak of the range of hills that is called Les Maures and which the Princess had never seen and he told her how restful it was there, how dark and green was the shade beneath the trees and how cool was his castle of La Verne. And he told her about the fine estates his father had left him; how his parents and his parents' parents had already made his inheritance into a paradise for the body and how he, the Prince, wanted to make it a paradise for the mind as well. He could see, he said, just by looking at the castle of Callas, what a court of love should be but he had no real idea of how to begin. The Princess's reputation was already known over most of Provence. If only she would agree to be his wife her intelligence would guide him and her beauty would be reflected in song and verse. She might become immortal, she might not, but at the very least she would be mistress of the endeavour.

The Princess turned to look out from the walls of Callas, across the plain to the crossroads in the distance. Now it was her turn to be troubled. What should she answer? It had been easy to refuse all those who had come before – they had not been worth accepting – but this suitor was different. He was not someone who had simply asked for her hand in marriage so that he could squander her dowry and father children on her. Nor did he ask her just because she was beautiful, though it was obvious that he found her so. He no doubt desired her for all the usual reasons but he also wanted her for something more; he wanted her to take a part in his life and in the life of his castle.

'We must speak further,' said the Princess and she commanded chairs to be brought, then a table with food and drink and she and the Prince sat down at their ease and the young man began to talk.

The Prince's companions and the Princess's suite sat at a distance and waited. No longer did the minstrel pluck discords from his strings; never had he seen anything like this.

All that afternoon the Prince spoke of his castle and the plans he had for it. And the next day he talked again, and the next day, and always he spoke with eagerness and sincerity, asking the Princess for her ideas on all manner of things. And gradually, as they talked, his plans became their plans and they decided, after a while, on what those plans should be. And a week of walking and talking went by and at the end of it they looked into each other's eyes and kissed and knew that a strong and proper love existed between them.

As soon as they had discovered this love the Prince went to the Princess's father and formally demanded her hand in marriage and as the Prince de La Verne came of an excellent family, and his estates were known to be in excellent order, the Lord of Callas gave his permission and the young couple were married the very next day.

The wedding was a splendid affair and for several days following there were great celebrations in Callas, but the Prince and the Princess were both impatient to begin the work they had set themselves and as soon as the revels were over they made preparations for the journey that would take them to La Verne.

So admired and loved was the Princess that many people from Callas wanted to accompany her, but she resolved to take only a few followers. Two of her troubadours and a favourite minstrel begged to go with her but she smiled at them and refused. 'You scoffed when my Prince came for me,' she said, 'and now I must be loyal to him. Perhaps in a few years, when you are the best troubadours in all Provence I shall send for you. We shall see.'

In this way the Princess left her birthplace and journeyed southwards and she was joyful that she had found her Prince, and joyful that life offered her an important thing to do. What was more the people and the courtiers of La Verne were delighted with their mistress. When she went into the fields and farms of her husband's estate she brought comfort and serenity to all those who saw her. 'It is like having another sun in the sky,' they said.

It did not take long for the happiness of the Prince's castle to become known and the Princess too had carried her reputation with her. Soon troubadours and men of learning began to appear at the gates of La Verne, asking for admittance. The Princess and the Prince received everyone with cheerful hospitality and all equally. The Princess set high standards for conversation and demanded the same of her courtiers and their ladies. Music and poetry were played and recited every day. From all over Provence, and even from Italy, people came to see and sing. The Princess was adored and the Prince admired; they were a perfect couple and had created a paradise that everyone desired to visit – everyone that was except Bertrand de l'Avelan.

ॐ

Bertrand de l'Avelan was the most acclaimed troubadour of that time and it was said that he was known throughout the whole civilized world. He had sung in Austria and told stories to Saladin. If he stayed in a castle for a month then that castle was honoured. If he wrote a song for a woman, no matter how lowly, then she gained immortality. And so the Prince believed that if Avelan could be tempted through the gates of La Verne then its reputation would be assured and his dearest wish fulfilled. But Avelan never came, nor was there any news of his coming.

This state of affairs did not perturb the Princess in the slightest. Her castle was perfect and so was the life she led there. She loved her husband as much as she had on the day of their marriage and, in the seven years since, she had presented him with two handsome and talented sons to ensure the succession. She had more than enough troubadours to amuse her and she never gave a moment's thought as to whether or not the great Avelan was aware of her existence.

But for the Prince this absence was an insult and it poisoned his life. It was as if he needed to extinguish in his mind the fame of all other castles of courtly love before he could enjoy that of his own. This preoccupation was a deadly one and the Prince fought hard to conceal it; none of his courtiers knew of it and nor did his wife. He saw to his estates and his servants and entered into all the culture and learning that La Verne had to offer, and yet, underneath an appearance of joy, his heart became more and more envious.

The Prince himself hoped that his envy would gradually disappear but to his horror, he found it increasing as time went by. Seven more years passed in this way and it seemed that the more perfect La Verne became the stronger was the Prince's obsession with Avelan the troubadour and the reasons, real or imagined, why he had never come to sing before the Princess. In the end the Prince began to fall into black moods of despair. At times, so as not to disturb his wife's happiness, he locked himself away in his own apartments. There he would bury his head in his hands and wonder what was to become of him. He should not have tormented himself. One day, in the early evening, the finest troubadour in all Provence simply appeared at the castle gates. There was no warning, no messengers, no servants and no companions; just Avelan.

Avelan was a man of good looks; not too tall and not too broad. No longer in his first youth, his hair was cut short and bleached a great deal by the sun and not a little by the years. His face was scarred by the wind and the rain and the things he had seen, but it was a compassionate face and one that understood the world. He wore the simplest of tunics, held at the waist by a wide belt with a silver buckle on it, a shepherd's belt. His legs were bare and brown and his shoes were old and covered in the dust of the roads he travelled.

Over one of his shoulders hung a lute, and over the other a goatskin bag containing songs and poems. That was all that Avelan carried with him.

With no ceremony at all he strode through the open gates of the castle and entered the wide hexagonal courtyard where the plane trees grew. Here, weary from his journey, Avelan sat and took his ease at the fountain, resting his feet, shoes and all, in in the cool waters.

Those servants and courtiers who were standing nearby were much taken aback for the stranger's manner was direct and outlandish and they had no idea who he might be. He did not, from his appearance, seem to be a person of note but, nevertheless, one of the castle servants ran for his master and, finding him quiet in his room, went instead to inform the Princess of the strange new arrival.

The Princess came immediately to the window of her apartments where she had been avoiding the heat of the day, and looked down at the courtyard and the crowd now gathering there. She saw the troubadour with his feet in the fountain, arms straight behind him on the wide stone coping, and his head flung back to the sky while his eyes were closed so that he might better enjoy the sensual pleasure of tired limbs. Something plucked at the Princess's heart and she caught her breath. This was no ordinary man.

'Stranger,' she called, 'you will soil the water with your dusty feet.'

Avelan straightened his head and opened his eyes. He gazed at the Princess for a moment and then smiled. 'It is good honest dirt from the roads of Provence,' he said, 'and it will soon wash away . . . but if you knew, lady, how far my feet had tramped so that they might bring my eyes to see this castle and contemplate your beauty you would not begrudge me this luxury, for I deserve it. And if your castle pleases me I might make it immortal – you, Princess, I certainly shall.' And with this Avelan rose and bowed, where he stood, in the fountain.

The Princess smiled and leant against the side of her casement and Avelan took his lute from his shoulder and there and then he sang the Princess one of his most beautiful songs. As he sang the shadows of the day lengthened and the evening sunlight turned the castle walls to gold and not a single person in the courtyard moved. The Princess stayed at her window and was entranced. Never had she heard music like this, or a voice like this or words that grew so well the one out of another. She felt bewitched, spell-bound in bonds she could not break.

At the end of the singing the silence lasted a long moment and the courtiers turned towards the Princess and waited for her to speak and at last she did, leaning forward and saying: 'Are you a troubadour or a magician?'

Avelan laughed and leapt from the fountain. 'To be the first, my lady,' he answered, 'is to be the second, though to be the second is not always to be the first, but being one or both leaves me, none the less, weary and hungry.'

The Princess nodded and, gesturing at her servants she gave commands. 'Your chamber will be prepared,' she said, 'and you shall dine with us. Will you sing again?'

Avelan slung his lute to his shoulder. 'After food and drink,' he said, 'I will do anything,' and with this remark he turned to follow the servants into the castle but the Princess spoke again.

'Your name,' she called, 'you have not told me your name.'

The troubadour looked up to the Princess on her balcony and his eyes burned into her and her heart stirred again. 'Why,' he said, 'I am Bertrand de l'Avelan, the troubadour, and you are the Princess of Callas and as many leagues as I have walked to see you I would walk ten times over for the merest glimpse only.' And everyone in the courtyard laughed at the compliment and its exaggeration, but they admired it also, and so did the Princess.

❧

During this time, in his own chambers, where the shutters were closed to keep out the sun, the Prince had been sitting alone in one of his sombre moods. But his apartments too overlooked the courtyard and he also had heard the song of Avelan, just as clearly as everyone else. The music and beauty of that song had been wondrous and it had stolen into the Prince's heart and banished the gloom that lay there. It had raised his head from his hands and made him more content than he had been for years. It was as if all his ambitions had been realized and his whole life fulfilled; as if he had been on a long quest and at last found the thing he had searched for. In his dark room he stood and stretched his arms to the ceiling – now his name, and the name of his wife would live forever.

In the hall of the castle that night there was great rejoicing. The Prince and the Princess had dressed themselves in their finest clothes and so had every courtier and servant. The happiness of the Prince was visible and the sight of it made the Princess happy and when she was joyful the whole world was. The tables were crowded and some of the villagers from the valley pushed into the room and stood around the walls in groups and stared. On the right hand side of the Princess sat Avelan himself, washed and revived and looking splendid in apparel that the Prince had presented to him, celebrating this arrival after so many years of waiting.

Those fortunate enough to be sitting at the top table hung on the troubadour's every word. Between courses he drank the good wine of Pierrefeu and told one story after another. He told sad ones and humorous ones; some of hate and some of love and his words were a spell and no one present so much as dreamt of interrupting him.

And the Prince leant back in his chair and smiled at his wife from the heart, like he had not smiled in a long while. He touched her face and kissed her and they both thought of the day, fourteen years previously, when he had ridden into Callas to ask for her hand in marriage. And they both looked back down the years and saw how everything had grown into what they'd wanted and how this night was the best of all nights. With the coming of Avelan the good had been made perfect.

This brief glimpse of perfection led the Prince to believe that all those moments of envy and despair he had seen in the past were exorcised from his heart for ever. He imagined that now his ambition would fall away and wither and leave him content for the rest of his life. But he was too hopeful too soon. Already another desire was stirring in his breast. Here before him was beauty and music, story and poetry such as he had never heard, but how, the Prince began to wonder, could he seize that perfection and keep it. Surely such a thing was not beyond human wit. There must be a way to possess this gift eternally – there must be a way.

It was as these thoughts entered the Prince's mind that Avelan reached for his lute and started to sing a song for the Princess; a song of such charm that it cheered the Prince immeasurably, and he raised his cup of wine to the company and everyone present drank a health to the troubadour who had no equal and who, they hoped, would stay with them and never leave.

At first it certainly seemed that the troubadour had no intention of quitting the hills of Les Maures and the castle of La Verne. From month to month he was there and the news of his whereabouts spread through Provence as if carried by the birds of the forest. The reputation of the castle and its lord and lady grew and minstrels hastened to the place so that they might learn from Avelan. Everyone knew that this time at La Verne was a blessed time – but they also knew such wonders could not last, and they said so. Even the lowliest shepherd in the valley was aware that however much a troubadour might love his lady it was in his nature to journey on when the spirit moved him. All too soon Avelan would think of saying his farewells. After all he had served the Princess for more than a year; more months than he had ever served anyone.

The Prince grieved deeply when he heard these rumours of the troubadour's impending departure. He went in search of Avelan and found him leaning on the battlements, gazing into the blue haze of the hills beyond Gonfaron. It was high summer and the forest below the castle lay at the very point of incandescence and Avelan was thinking that in the mountains the air was cool and the water in the streams there tasted like wine.

'Avelan,' began the Prince, 'stay with us a little longer. Everyone loves you so, it will make us sad to see you leave.'

Avelan turned and smiled at the Prince. He leant his back against the wall, resting his elbows on the flat top of it. 'I have been happy here,' he said, 'perhaps too happy. It is not easy to take to the road again – but troubadours must. If I do not leave I shall die. The memory of the stories I sung you, that is my gift, it is all I have and I give it you with all my heart. But I must go, there is no changing it. I must feel the earth beneath my feet, the grass under me when I sleep and the hard edge of life cutting into the palm of my hand. If I dwell too long in castles I am not a troubadour and if I am not a troubadour I cannot sing and I shall wither. Believe me, Prince, this is the way of it.'

The Prince of La Verne sighed and gazed between his feet at the flagstones of the terrace. He understood but did not want to understand. He nodded, opened his mouth to answer but then said nothing and went to ask his wife to speak to Avelan so that she might add her entreaties to his and beg the troubadour to stay if only for a short time more.

The Princess did as she was commanded but again Avelan smiled his smile and shook his head. 'Never have I served a lord and a lady so full of grace,' he said, 'but I have new songs in my pack now, songs that sing of you and La Verne, and all the world will know them. Perhaps, when I am too old to walk the roads of Provence, perhaps then you will give me a corner of the castle where I may keep warm in winter, but now, while I can, I must go. There is only one way for me to live and that is the way of the troubadour.'

The tears trickled down the Princess's cheeks and she was moved as profoundly as she had been on the first day. 'Troubadour,' she said, 'I trust that your songs will be immortal, but even if they fade from the world they will stay forever in my heart.'

Avelan looked towards the horizon. 'It is only in your heart that I can live,' he said, 'and whether your husband sees reason or not, I still have to bid you farewell.'

'Yes,' said the Princess, 'I know.'

When the day of departure came there was a great melancholy felt throughout the castle. Avelan felt it too and for a yea or a nay he might have stayed a little longer, but deep within him he had no doubt; he had to journey on. So, with only a brief 'Adieu', Avelan strode through the castle gates and took the track that led northwards to the mountains of High Provence, the shepherds' road to Castellane and beyond. He looked exactly as he had done on the day of his arrival, for all his fine clothes, those presents from the Prince, he had left behind in his tiny turret room.

'You cannot travel with possessions,' he had once said. 'How can you sleep by the roadside if you are fearful of being robbed, and how can people invite you to their table if you have more to eat than they have?' And Avelan crossed the valley and disappeared into the forest with only his lute on one shoulder and his bag of songs on the other. The moment the troubadour was out of sight the Prince fell into the blackest mood he had ever known. With a gloomy face he rushed to his apartments and locked the doors, swearing that he would see no one, not even the Princess.

Concern for the Prince, coupled with the effect of Avelan's absence, made everyone in the castle morose and the quiet of death fell over what had been, only twenty-four hours earlier, the happiest court of love in all the kingdoms of France and Navarre. That evening, when courtiers and servants gathered at the fountain, they scarcely spoke and those troubadours still present were subdued and despondent, not caring to sing even one song.

This silence continued and no one thought to break it until at dusk, when the red sun came to rest on the rim of the horizon, the Prince reappeared dressed for the hunt and, in a fierce and angry voice, called for his best horse and six of his archers. When all was ready he led his men from the castle at a gallop and took the road to the north; the road that Avelan had taken.

The people of La Verne were much perplexed by the Prince's behaviour but they were not kept in suspense for long. That very night, before the moon had risen very far, the Prince and his archers returned. Their horses' hooves clattered across the drawbridge and the Princess opened her casement to stare at the scene below. There, in the flickering light of the burning torches, mounted behind an archer, his hands tied behind him and his face covered in dust from the tempestuous ride, was Bertrand de l'Avelan.

No one spoke. Quickly the archers dragged their prisoner from the back of his horse and hustled him away to the room he had lived in before and where all his fine garments and possessions awaited him. But this time his door was locked and a guard was set at it. As for the window, it was high in the turret. Anyone attempting to climb from there to the ground was sure to meet death on the rugged cobbles below.

Strange as it may seem there was very little criticism of the Prince's action. Most inhabitants of the castle had been made so unhappy by the troubadour's departure that they were only too pleased to see him again, no matter how his return had been accomplished. Even the Princess, who still loved her husband as dearly as ever, managed to find excuses for his conduct and, with only a little effort, persuaded herself that no damage had been done. That very night the Prince came to the Princess's bedchamber and told her what he was setting out do do, and why.

'I have no intention of keeping him long,' began the Prince, touching his wife's hair, 'a month or two, that is all. I love him and you too much to keep him imprisoned. It is that my people were so downcast, we must give them time to get used to the idea of his not being here, time for other troubadours to finish learning his songs. I have explained this to him, he understands. It did not take many words to persaude him to come back to us.'

'You did him no harm?' asked the Princess.

'My love,' answered the Prince, 'as if the man who is your husband could do any such thing.'

'He will be free, he may go where he likes?'

'Of course,' said the Prince, 'though there must always be an escort of archers with him. You understand that?'

With this the Princess was content and when, next morning, she met with the troubadour and talked with him she was delighted to find that he appeared not at all put down in his spirits. The Princess smiled and took the troubadour's hand.

'You must forgive us,' she said. 'It will only be for a little while. We missed you so and my Prince was so unhappy. I promise, Avelan, that you may wander where you will and it will be just like before. Be patient.'

And so things at La Verne went on as they had done previously. Avelan made light of his captivity and told stories and sang songs at table and in the courtyard every day. He donned his rich clothes again and talked to the Prince and the Princess without giving any sign that he was angry at being held against his will. In fact rarely did he stray beyond the castle gates, but when he did he was always accompanied by three or four archers, each with a bow in their hands and a quiver of arrows at their back.

This state of affairs continued for some months. It was as if Avelan had always lived at the castle and had never dreamt of leaving. The Prince quite forgot that he had ever ridden out after the troubadour, and the Princess no longer remembered that she had promised he might leave after a few weeks. From time to time Avelan would try to discuss his captivity with anyone who would listen but when he did the courtiers shook their heads, saying that they couldn't possibly do without him and, what was more, the Prince certainly would never let him go. Everyone urged Avelan to be patient: 'Only be patient,' they would say, 'only be patient and you will soon be back on the open road.'

It was no good. Avelan could not wait forever. He saw his life slipping away and he always a prisoner.

One day he was not at his usual place in the great hall; he was not in the courtyard. From his room his lute, bag and tunic had disappeared. There was no mistaking the evidence. Avelan had escaped.

This time the Prince rose from his table in a towering rage and called all his archers and soldiers and servants to him. Hastily they mounted and the whole company set out to scour the length and breadth of the countryside. All that night, the next day and the following night, they searched and it was not until the morning of the second day that a small group of the Prince's men came up with the troubadour on the road to Montferrat. Although Avelan was well beyond their master's jurisdiction, they took him anyway and bore him back to the castle of La Verne, and Avelan wept.

'Do not weep, troubadour,' said the Prince when his captive stood before him. 'You have my promise that you will not be here much longer. Believe me, I only wish to do what is right. Here you are loved, everyone admires you. All this time you have been with us your renown has grown and people come from all over Provence to sit at your feet. My only wish is to increase your fame and to make a collection of your songs . . . and then you shall leave us. All down the centuries people will remember Bertrand de l'Avelan and the castle of La Verne.' And when this speech was done the Prince commanded that Avelan's door be double locked, that bars be set at his window and that sentries should guard him all night and never sleep.

Now things were greatly altered. Avelan kept to his room and rarely showed himself, never touching his lute or singing. Sometimes, when quite alone, he might touch his bag of poems or even whisper a song into the loneliness of his soul, but nothing more. Almost all his waking hours were spent at his window, staring at the bright countryside by day and at the starlit forests by night.

Slowly the heat of the summer diminished and the evenings became shorter and colder until at last the shepherds and their flocks came down from the mountains, passing through the valley on their way to the pastures by the sea. The troubadour raised his head and heard the sound of sheep bells in the dark.

At dawn he saw the shepherds resting on the river bank, and the sight filled him with sorrow for this was a true sight of the open road.

Soon Avelan became ill, taking to his bed, and the Princess went to him immediately, grasping his hand and pressing it to her lips.

'Oh, my love,' she said, 'be not so sad. Only let my husband make this book of your songs and I promise on my heart that you shall leave us, but do not keep yourself alone like this. Remember we love you.'

'Yes,' said Avelan, his voice lifeless, 'such a love is a cage of gold,' and he said no more and even though the Princess kissed him yet still he would not sing.

Then the Princess knelt before her husband and begged him to release the troubadour at once. 'This,' she said, 'is not part of the bright dream we once dreamt of together.'

It hurt the Prince to see his wife kneel and he raised her from the ground and spoke with kindness, asking that she bear with him only a little longer. He had no desire, he said, to do Avelan any harm, but the troubadour could not leave now that he was ill, but as soon as he had recovered his spirits he would be released – meanwhile the Princess must look after Avelan and make him happy. He must be made to sing again for the Prince had conceived a new ambition. Not only did he want to copy into a book every song that Avelan knew but now he wanted to copy the stories and poems also. Above all he wanted to learn some of the troubadour's skill; how he composed, how he planned his stories and what were the mysterious gifts that lay behind the telling of them.

'And you must help me,' said the Prince to his wife. 'To me Avelan will say nothing, but to you he will tell all, I am sure of it. A scribe shall sit behind the door, writing down everything Avelan says, and you will spend your days with him . . . learning his secrets and when you know them you will tell me. He shall be well again and I shall become the most talented lord in all Provence.'

In spite of herself the Princess was persuaded by her husband's idea. It was obvious, as the Prince had said, that the troubadour could not leave the castle as he was. She must nurse him and during that time the Prince could learn the things he wished to know. The sooner he was satisfied, the sooner the troubadour would be free and she would have made both men happy. The Princess smiled and embraced her husband: 'Yes,' she said, 'I will help you.'

As soon as this conversation was over the Princess went directly to Avelan's room and, ordering the guard to open the door, she entered the sunlit cell, sat by the troubadour's bed and told him of her husband's latest plan, and of her part in it.

'Madouneto!' he said. 'What your husband asks is madness. He does not have enough life and nor do I,' but the troubadour stopped speaking when he saw the Princess's face fall in disappointment, and even though he wanted to say more he did not. Instead he glanced away at the horizon for a moment and then looked back at his lady. His eyes flared with a new idea and a smile of cunning touched his lips. The Princess mistook the smile and answered it with one of her own.

'Will you do it?' she asked, breathless.

Avelan glanced at the horizon again before answering.

'Yes,' he said at last, 'but you will have to spend long hours with me, work hard and note everything I say . . . then you may carry my words to your husband. It might succeed. I have never attempted such a thing before . . . but, do I have your word that you will release me on the day when I can tell you no more.'

'Oh, Avelan,' said the Princess with tears of happiness on her face, 'of course you have.'

ᘛᘚ

Avelan's scheme was to teach the Princess with all the craft he possessed for he knew that his very freedom depended on it. He was convinced that the Princess would release him from his captivity if she could, but he was equally convinced that her husband would not. His ambitions would go on growing and he would always find a reason for keeping the troubadour at La Verne. But Avelan also knew that once the Princess had learnt all there was to learn about the way of the troubadours she would no longer be the person she had been. Then she would understand the life of a minstrel and would set him at liberty no matter what her husband commanded.

Now Avelan called on all his powers and sang the Princess songs of great beauty and told her stories of great passion; stories of lovers separated, of dungeons and cruel husbands and lovers triumphant. Day after day the Princess listened and every day the scribe sat at the door and copied down all things but he could not copy what was in the Princess's heart. Soon Avelan taught the Princess to string the lute and his hands touched her hands on the strings and they sat close upon the bed and sang songs and read poems and, without realizing it, the Princess was happier than she had ever been at any previous time in the whole of her existence.

It was not too long before Avelan discovered that the Princess was revealing a remarkable gift for all things relating to the way of the troubadour and she sang and played as if trained to it all her life. Seeing this Avelan began to take real pleasure in his teaching and taught his pupil other mysteries; how to invent stories from a nothing and how to tell them; where to pause and where to smile; where to break off and where to pick up the thread. Never had Avelan seen such an eagerness to learn and he became determined to discover how accomplished the Princess could become. And there was something else that intrigued him – could a woman learn all the skills necessary to a troubadour?

Because of this new interest Avelan's spirits revived entirely and occasionally he even sang at the Prince's table. The light in his eye brightened and when he looked at the Princess that light clouded with tenderness. The Prince was delighted with his stratagem and could hardly believe his good fortune. It would take years for the scribe to copy out all that Avelan knew – the rest of the troubadour's life perhaps – but in the end, what a jewel of a collection it would be and how great the reward for such toil . . . immortal renown. The Prince's heart felt like it would burst with happiness and he looked back to his youth and saw how fortunate he had been. In his wildest dreams he had never thought to achieve so much.

In this manner life at La Verne went on into the winter and the Princess soon felt confident enough in her knowledge to begin instructing her husband in the techniques and principles she had learnt from Avelan. The Prince was eager to learn and together he and his wife read through the poems and stories that the scribe had collected – but the Prince could not learn them or retell them in a way that brought out their magic. The Princess did not despair but encouraged her husband and placed his hands on the strings of the lute but his voice could not warm to the burden of a song and there was no life in what he sang.

A chill seized the Princess's heart; the man she had loved all these years was in reality different to the idea of him she had carried in her imagination. For all his dedication to the art of the troubadours he now seemed coarse to her. He was like a man crowding his garden with statues to show how rich he was, leaving no room for the grass to grow. The Prince wanted only the glory of possession – story and song in themselves meant nothing to him.

The Princess was dismayed. Why had she not noticed these things before? But she knew the answer – Avelan had done this. He had shown her how to be a troubadour and the revelation had cleansed her; now her heart was like a prism new-cut and the light passing through it would never illuminate in the old way again. She was no longer what she had been and in that same instant she realized that she loved Avelan with a love that was not the love of a lady for her troubadour and she knew it certainly.

Just as soon as she could the Princess left her husband's side and went straight to Avelan's chamber and he looked at her and he also knew. He took her by the hand and together they went to the window and gazed at the horizon.

'Now you understand,' he said and the Princess nodded.

Then there were more weeks and Avelan began the last part of his teaching. He told the Princess of his own life, right from the very beginning; how he had run wild as a boy; how he had gained a precarious living as a shepherd, paid only by the day or with scraps of food. And later, how a troubadour had sat by his fire one night and talked. 'Those words were enough,' said Avelan. 'I put on my shepherd's cloak and I followed that man for two years and learnt all I could. I have never stopped learning. I have been to Italy to see the great painters. I have slept in silken beds and in ruined barns. I have been loved and I have been despised. I have read all the poets and sung all the songs. I have had children and I have left them. I have wept and laughed. Without all these things I would never have been a troubadour. To be a troubadour is like having the sesame that will take you to live in a tapestry of a thousand flowers – but you cannot stay there long, for you will always wake to find that you have been sleeping under a hedge, but even so, only troubadours travel in that country of flowers and magic, only troubadours.

'And I,' asked the Princess, 'will I ever travel there?'

Avelan nodded. 'You will,' he said, 'you have the gift. From me you have learnt, but from others you must learn also and one thing only you can do, and that is to cross the world and see and sing alone. Your husband thought he could take all this, imprison it, make it his, own it, show it. He cannot. There are two things, the gift and the crossing of the world. You have the gift already. The Prince has neither. Even the finest troubadour alive is not permitted to keep the gift. It is something we borrow for a while, use, and when we die it is left by the side of the road for someone else to find. By trying to possess what cannot be possessed the Prince will lose everything, including that which he loves the most.'

The Princess lowered her head at this for she knew that what Avelan said was true and there was no denying it, but Avelan put a finger under her chin and made her raise her head again and after only a second's hesitation, they kissed.

When the kiss was done the face of the Princess shone with a radiant light and she knew that she had finished with the past. 'We must leave this place,' she said, 'I can no longer live here, it no longer means anything to me, nor my husband nor my children. It is as much a prison for me now as it is for you. All I can think of is escape.'

❧

Escape was not easy. The Prince was a determined man and, since the troubadour had already tried to get away once, stern measures had been taken. Although Avelan was relatively free during the day, at night there were at least two guards at his door; half a dozen more were on duty below his window, while the main gate to the castle was barred at sunset every evening. There was a small postern gate also but that too was watched. It seemed that there was no way out for the lovers, but then Avelan was a poet who had seen and done much.

'We need a potion,' he said one day, 'a sleeping draught, something that we can put into the wine the guards drink at supper . . . and something that you can put into your husband's drink also . . . for you will have to betray him.'

The Princess placed her arms around the troubadour's neck. 'It will not be difficult,' she said. 'In the woods below the castle wall lives a witch. I have never seen her but my servants talk. She has powers, they say. Next time I go riding I will see her.'

Some days later the Princess dismounted outside a cave in the valley of La Verne, entered it without fear and discovered an old woman, covered in cloaks, sitting in a wide wooden armchair, warming herself by a low fire. The Princess was surprised at the benevolence that showed on the witch's face. It was the face of someone who took pleasure in aiding those who were in trouble and curing those who were diseased. She had never used her magic for the purposes of evil.

The witch smiled at the Princess. 'The Princess of La Verne,' she said. 'I have heard much about you and you are as beautiful as they say . . . but what does someone who has everything need with me?'

'My husband does not rest,' answered the Princess. 'He has an ambition, he is obsessed by it. He needs to sleep deeply so that he may wake with clear sight. He would be happier then.'

The witch, whose face was lined and whose hair was a dirty grey, folded her arms where she sat and stared at her visitor. 'And while the Prince sleeps, what will the Princess do?'

The Princess's voice faltered. 'Why, I shall care for him, see to the castle, and the estates. If I know that his mind is healing then I shall be content enough.'

The witch sniffed. 'Would that all wives loved their husbands as much as you,' she said.

'Who can tell?' answered the Princess, 'perhaps such is the case.'

The old woman questioned her no more but, dragging her cloaks tightly round her shoulders, she went to a cupboard at the back of the cave and took out a small green bottle which she gave to the Princess. The Princess took it and held out a gold coin but the witch shook her head and pushed the money away.

'This potion,' she said, 'not only brings deep sleep but when those who have drunk it wake they find that they perceive the things of life more clearly. After his sleep your husband will see his obsession for what it really is and with you to care for him he will be a wiser man. But you . . . you will never be happy, not like before.'

The Princess dropped her eyes to the bottle she held in her hand. 'The happiness I once had I no longer desire,' she said. She shook the bottle. 'Is there enough here?'

The old woman went back to her chair and sat in it. 'One drop,' she said, 'will make a man sleep for a week. Two drops and he will sleep for two weeks. The whole bottle and he will sleep forever.' She watched the Princess closely and the Princess's face reddened at the idea of murder.

'I do not want to make anyone sleep for ever,' she said.

'No,' said the witch, 'I don't think you do, and if you are only patient then one day we shall all sleep forever.'

'I know that only too well,' retorted the Princess, 'that is why each of my days is as precious as a diamond,' and with those words she turned and left the cave, hurrying back to the spot where her attendants waited for her.

✄

The Princess lost not a moment in putting Avelan's plan into action. That very night, as she sat next to her husband in the great hall, she poured two drops from the witch's bottle into his goblet of wine and held it up to him.

'Since it is you, my wife,' said the Prince, who had already drunk well, 'I will raise this cup to our love and the renown of our castle of La Verne.'

'Yes, my love,' said the Princess, 'drink.'

And while the Prince drank the Princess called her favourite servant to her, and gave him a gold piece and a bejewelled belt so that he might take a jug of her husband's strongest wine to the guardroom, where the sentinels of that night were at supper. And she gave him also the potion, instructing him to pour into the jug twice as many drops as there were guards. The servant bowed and did as his mistress ordered.

No sooner had the Prince drunk his cup of wine than he fell forward onto the table in a deep stupor. This was by no means a usual occurrence with the Prince but it had happened once or twice before so the Princess commanded those courtiers dining with her to carry their master to his room. The Princess accompanied the courtiers to see that the Prince was safely and properly laid in his bed and, as soon as she was alone with her lord, she took from his neck the chain that bore the key to Avelan's quarters.

For the last time the Princess gazed at her husband's face. 'Sleep,' she said. 'You gave me love for fourteen years but now it is not enough, and nor are you. I hope your heart does not break when you find me gone. I fear that mine may, husband, but not for you.'

And with this farewell the Princess hastened to the turret where Avelan waited for her and there, sprawling across the stone steps, the guards slumbered. Quickly the Princess slid the key into the lock of the prison door and it swung open. Avelan stood ready, smiling, and the Princess ran into his arms and they kissed, free of everything now save for the love they bore each other.

Then they lay together on the bed and waited for the middle of the night so that the whole castle should be asleep; and when it was they arose and the Princess took some boy's clothing and dressed herself as a page, and in this disguise she went with Avelan down the turret stairs and out into the courtyard.

There too the guards slept and by the castle gates also. Without a word the two fugitives slipped across the flagstones and made their way to the postern. The witch's potion had done its work well. Here the sentinel sat against the wall, his head cradled in his arms, and on the ground by his side lay his pike. Avelan drew the bolts; the door creaked open and in a moment he and the Princess were following the path that led into the valley and to the road that ran north and south.

'Let us hurry,' said the troubadour, 'tomorrow we shall be pursued.'

'Nay, let us tarry,' said the Princess, 'the Prince will not wake for two weeks, nor will his soldiers.'

Then Avelan laughed and took the Princess in his arms and in the starlight he looked into her eyes. 'I shall make such a song about you,' he said, 'and it will be sung forever, but come, let us walk across the world and into the tapestry if we can.' And together, side by side, the man and the woman set out along the dusty road towards the horizon but long before they reached it they had disappeared from view beneath the dark trees of the rolling hillsides and what became of them was never known. Some say that Avelan only used the

Princess in order to escape and that once she had served his purpose he deserted her in the forest. Then, when she found herself forsaken, her heart broke and for the rest of her life she wandered, crazed and demented, until at last she died of the cold one winter, starving and in rags.

Others say this tale is a nonsense and that Bertrand de l'Avelan could never have done such a thing. They say that after his imprisonment at La Verne his reputation went on growing, and it is further said that wherever his name is written in the ancient books there is also written the name of the Princess, and their love and talent lasted until they died.

There is yet a third tradition, more believable it is thought, which tells a different story. However much Avelan loved his lady he wooed her to be free. Certainly they would have stayed together for a while, a year or two even, but one day she would have woken in a castle room, stretched out a hand and found nothing. Being what she was the Princess journeyed on and became a troubadour in her own right, continuing to disguise her womanhood beneath men's clothes. This person is famous in the histories as Mellano de la Queste and her poems are still read wherever Provençal is spoken. But although this story has the ring of truth about it nothing is known for sure.

As for the Prince when he awoke it was into a life of sadness. Just as the witch had said the potion gave a clearer awareness of things and the Prince knew as soon as his eyes opened that his wife had left him, that she had taken to the roads like a troubadour and that she loved him no longer. He knew also that it was pointless to search for her. He could see now how foolish he had been in his attempt to possess another person's gift and experience. He saw too his lack of talent and his wife's abundance of it, and he lowered his head into his hands and wept like a child.

For the Prince there was nothing left and from that day his castle was avoided by everyone because of the great sadness that abided there. No troubadours came by, no music was sung or stories told. Then the courtiers and servants took their leave, singly and in groups – after all Provence was wide and full of song. And the Prince's sons grew to manhood and rode away, disdaining their inheritance and preferring to take their chances in the world as their mother had done.

When the Prince died, many years later, the castle was abandoned and not even the grazing sheep would enter its ruined gates. Eventually the spring beneath the fountain ceased to flow, the castellated walls crumbled and, piece by piece, every last stone was taken by monks to build a monastery which still stands, itself a ruin, on a hillside some miles away. So of the castle nothing now remains to be seen; all is overgrown and vanished and only the fox and the wild boar can find their way to the place where once a princess listened to the songs of Avelan, the finest troubadour that ever lived.

# THE ROAD TO
# LE MUY

**W**e set off as the shadows lengthened, but even so the ground and the air smelt scorched and baked and the evening flies and mosquitoes hovered over us. I threw my duffel bag into the cart again and followed on, my legs aching, my feet sore and my head throbbing from sleeping in the sun. The pace was slower now; partly because we had left the busy coast road but mainly for the benefit of the sheep. If they were not allowed to feed sufficiently they would refuse to advance.

The countryside around us was dull and sterile with scant grass to be seen and what grass there was sprouted without hope from a dirt soil that lay only thinly on the bed of rock underneath. Here the pines grew tall and straggly like weeds and the cork oaks were stunted and disfigured – their bark stripped from them by sharp knives and greedy hands.

From time to time a car would come up behind us. After all this road was the only link between St Maxime and Le Muy and must be kept open. This was the most tiresome work of all and it seemed never ending. As each vehicle approached my companions would swear and force themselves to run along by the side of the flock, scaring it out of the way by shouting like savages and cracking the whips they always used when on the march. They were known to be expert with those whips, the shepherds, and had they wished they could have blinded an enemy with a simple movement of the wrist.

A shepherd had only to reach for this weapon and the half-wild dogs that travelled with him would cringe on their bellies; and the moment the sheep heard a leather thong split the air like a bullet they picked up speed no matter how jaded they were. In the old days, so it was said, disputes had been settled with whips, and I was often told the story of the short-tempered tourist who got out of his car to berate a drover from Cogolin and only got back into it after several weeks in hospital. The shepherd is generally a placid man but it does not do to abuse him.

∞

The road to Le Muy wound on across a low plateau of small hills rising gently along the way until, suddenly, it bore to the right and the ground fell away from under me and I could see all the wide valley of the Argens and, beyond the valley, in the purple dusk, the dark and imposing shapes of the mountains we would have to cross within the next few days. Steeply now the road fell to meet the river and the brake was tightened on the cart. In another hour or two we would be able to rest.

At the rear of the flock that day was Joseph Martel and his hired man. The hired man led the mule and Joseph plodded beside him, a heavy staff on his shoulder. Already old, though not as old as his brother-in-law, Coulet, Joseph came originally from the mountains and for him Grimaud was not home. He was a solid man, short and square with forearms as thick as my thighs. His face, like Coulet's, was deeply lined, weathered dark as a gypsy's and brightly flecked with silver stubble. He wore an old peaked cap and I never saw him out of it but once, even when he slept. Joseph talked in short bursts only and hardly at all when we were on the move. Amongst the others he had a reputation for 'la gourmandise' and whenever we stopped to eat and brought out the big wooden box containing the provisions I noticed that it was his hand that fell on the jam-pot first and the same hand that relinquished it last.

At eight or nine that night we came to the river and camped about three kilometres from Le Muy. The road passes close to the Argens here, though high above it, and the sheep were suddenly fearless and threw themselves like suicides over the edge of an almost vertical slope, knowing of nothing but the quenching of their thirst. There was hard work for a while, containing the madness, but once all was settled the mule was led out from between the shafts of his cart and the shepherds carried their provisions down to a wide shore strewn with boulders. In less than half an hour the moon appeared and the sleeping sheep and the large white stones that lay everywhere merged in the unmoving light and became one flock.

Near the stream's edge I removed my shoes and socks and bathed my burning feet. A few metres to my right was Joseph Martel. Carefully he placed a flat stone in the shallows and knelt upon it. Then he bent and dipped his huge hands like a ladle into the water, raising them to his face many times, splashing and snorting so that the drops fell like coins, under the moonlight, back into the ground, disappearing in the very second they became visible. It was at this moment that Joseph knocked the cap from his head and never have I seen hair so bright. Silver in a silver beam it looked like a holy torch; some ardent grail that ordinary people should not gaze upon.

Quickly Joseph replaced his cap, as if resentful of my staring, and saying nothing we returned to the others and took our places; he in the centre of the group with his pot of jam; myself on the periphery, eating what Bonne Maman had prepared and taking from the shepherds only what they passed me. Now that I had a chance to rest I found that I was faint with hunger and trembling with fatigue.

At length Marius turned to me and placed the bonbonne of wine in my hands and I drank deep, glad to do so. 'You had better eat tonight,' he said in French, 'or you will fade away. And keep your ears open for it is here, by

37

the Argens at Le Muy, that Joseph tells the story of the Golden Goat, the best known story in Provence. . . .'

'I will,' I said, and drank again and filled my cup and handed on the wine. The shepherds had wedged themselves amongst the rocks, the food box with them, and the talk was beginning. I settled myself comfortably and determined to stay awake until the story was told.

# The Golden Goat

One cold night, many years ago, on a dark hillside in the country of Provence, an old shepherd knelt by a wood fire and shook his sleeping son awake. As the boy opened his eyes the shepherd prodded the fire with his staff and a bright flame leapt upwards, making yellow shapes out of the black trees and revealing crooked twigs which clutched like witches' fingers at the shepherd's silver hair.

'Pacorro,' said the shepherd, 'three of our sheep have wandered up the valley, I can hear their bells and you must go after them.'

The boy rubbed his eyes and stood, pulling his cloak up with him to settle it on his shoulders, then, with only one word of farewell, he left the firelight and stepped into the forest darkness.

Since early childhood Pacorro had run with his father's flock and he was as sure-footed as the nimblest goat alive and never had he slept under a roof or in a bed, for his father owned no pastures but grazed his sheep on the common land by the roadside and on the rocky hills by the sea. So Pacorro the shepherd boy was not afraid of the forest; he passed through the first of the trees, touching their uneven bark with his finger-tips, and followed a narrow valley that led away from the sea and towards the mountains. Above him in the sky was half a moon but it was prowling behind low clouds and gave no light. Every now and then the boy stopped to listen for the sound of sheep-bells but he heard only the trees around him as they scraped their branches together, sounding for all the world like rough voices whispering in the forest.

'May God protect me,' said Pacorro, 'but there are Saracens abroad in the woods tonight,' and he drew his cloak more tightly about his neck and walked on.

For nearly an hour he searched, sometimes hearing the faint sound of a bell in the distance, sometimes not, but however far he walked the sound came no nearer and he began to despair of ever finding his father's sheep. It was then, almost on the point of giving up his task, that he saw a light. It flickered through the trees and out along the sides of a dry river-bed like sunbeams on the sea. Pacorro heard a strange noise too, not the ordinary harshness of his own sheep-bells but a clear and simple ringing, like silver touching silver. The shepherd boy quickened his step; this brilliance could only come from a shepherd's fire, he thought, and the ringing would be their sheep-bells. He would talk with them and they would help him to find his missing sheep.

Suddenly the river-bed turned one last turn and Pacorro fell, throwing his arms up in fear, blinded by what seemed to be a burning flame. Never had he seen anything that hurt so – not the heart of an ember, nor the centre of the sun. Pacorro waited, wondering if his sight was truly lost. Minutes went by and when at last the shepherd boy lowered his hands from his face he saw that he could still see.

He had come to a gully whose rocky walls almost touched overhead, a gully made impenetrable by growths of sturdy thorn, strong and matted. It was one of these bushes that gave out the mysterious light and the sound of the silver bell, a pathetic jangling noise as an animal vainly struggled to free itself from the powerful grip of some unseen thing. Against his will Pacorro was drawn forward. He stared, and, deep in the thorn bush, in the centre of a cloud of diffused gold, saw a graceful and elegant goat, caught by her long ebony horns in a deadly trap. Slowly she turned her face to look at the shepherd boy, contemplating him with eyes of incredible sadness. She was beautiful and Pacorro gasped, holding his breath with the wonder of it.

The goat's fleece was long and touched her feet, it was combed and groomed but it was the colour of the coat that had made Pacorro gasp. The colour was the light that filled the gully and the light was more than golden; it gleamed and shone in a magical way, flaming with a fire that was not a fire and ablaze with a flame that could entice men to their deaths. Fear struck at the boy's heart and he knew that he was in great danger. He had found the Golden Goat of Abd al-Rhaman, trapped by her horns in a hunter's noose. On her head she wore the Caliph's seven pointed coronet of gold, a crown made of metal so soft and pure that a man might draw his name across it with the slightest touch of his finger-nail.

Pacorro drew his knife, it was broad-bladed and sharp. The old legends said that the Golden Goat was evil and dangerous. He who was unlucky enough to find her should slay her and seize the crown she wore on her head. The boy's thoughts went to his father and the fields the old man dreamt of buying for his flock, and a hut too where the shepherd might live in comfort when he was too weary to follow the sheep. Pacorro raised his knife to strike but, to his astonishment, the Golden Goat turned her lovely head and spoke to him in a voice that was as beautiful as she was.

'Do not slay me, shepherd,' she said, 'cut me free and I will show you all the treasure of the Caliph, Abd al-Rhaman, and you may choose from it three times and take from it all that you can carry. One ruby alone would make you and your father rich, and your son and your son's son rich also.'

Pacorro wound his hand into the goat's long hair. It was spun gold and yet softer to his touch than the wool of a rain-washed lamb. The goat still looked at him with her brown eyes and seemed as human as he. Pacorro did not answer; he stood still and remembered the old story as his father had told it to him, so many times.

Some hundreds of years before Pacorro's birth the Saracens had appeared over the edge of the sea in their war-galleys and had conquered Provence and taken it for their very own.

Under the orders of their leader, Abd al-Rhaman, they had built a castle on a steep hill and called it Fraxinetta. For years it had remained impregnable and the Saracens seemed ready to rule the land for ever, taking whatever they wanted, raiding and killing wherever they wished.

At long last the princes and abbots of Provence decided to win back the country they had lost so they raised a great army and fought the Saracens in many long and savage wars and after ten years of cruel and bloody fighting they forced the Caliph to take refuge in his castle.

The siege was long and bitter and Abd al-Rhaman, looking down from his battlements, came to realize that he could not win this last campaign. He begged his enemies to let him go in peace, promising never to return and, rather than see their soldiers slain in war the abbots and the princes granted the Caliph's request, but only on condition that the Saracens did not take their plunder away with them.

But Abd al-Rhaman was subtle and double-tongued and under cover of darkness he had his slaves carry his treasure into a deep cavern where they threw it down in haste and the entrance to the cave was shut fast by the spell of an Arabian sorcerer, the most powerful wizard that ever lived. The next day the Saracens slipped aboard their galleys and in less than an hour their ships had disappeared over the horizon.

Of course the Caliph's promise had been a false promise. He had secretly sworn to revenge himself on his enemies, to recover his vast riches and in order to prove to his followers that he meant to return the Caliph left behind a priceless possession, his only daughter, the Princess Suhar.

The Princess wept but her father was cruel and ignored her tears. He commanded his sorcerer to change Suhar into a superb mountain goat, sure-footed and speedier than the finest horse that ran. She was to guard the treasure and, should searchers ever come near the cavern, she was to entice them to their deaths or bring them to the brink of madness.

In return the sorcerer vowed that the Princess should live forever, just as long as she was not captured by hunters. To protect herself, should she be captured, she was given the power of gentle and persuasive speech. On the other hand, if she left the cavern to live the life of an ordinary mortal she would regain her former shape but she would become subject to age and decay as she had been before.

But the Caliph never returned to claim his riches and for centuries men had sought to capture the Golden Goat, believing that under the threat of death she could be forced to reveal the whereabouts of the cave of treasure. The goat had been seen often enough over the years, glimpsed between the dusk and the dawn, but no one had come near her and lived unscathed to tell the tale. All that was known for sure was that once or twice in a generation a poor witless shepherd was found, wandering far from his sheep, muttering crazily that he had met and talked with the Princess Suhar and seen her treasure.

Pacorro stirred himself, wound his hand deeper into the goat's long hair and thought of one other thing that his father had told him. The Golden Goat would lie, cheat and deceive, would murder and betray, would do anything to escape from whoever found her. He who wished to take her treasure would have to become as cunning and as evil as she. 'If you find her, kill her,' the old shepherd had said, 'before she drives you mad.'

Pacorro pushed his knife between the goat's horns and cut the noose that held her.

'There,' he said, 'you are free.'

No sooner did the rope fall from her than the goat leapt twenty paces along the river-bed, clearing bushes and trees in a gigantic bound. Pacorro was wrenched from his feet, dragged through the thorns and his legs were made bloody and his body was bruised, but he did not relax his grip on the goat's long hair. When he regained his feet, angry with pain and surprise, he raised his knife to the goat's neck and pressed the blade close up against the vein that throbbed there and only a thought kept the knife from the blood.

'My father needs a house,' said Pacorro, 'so show me your treasure as you promised or I will slaughter you as I have slaughtered many other goats, and skinned them too.'

'I only leapt for joy,' said the goat, 'I rejoice that I am free and will see my treasure again.' She nuzzled the boy's shoulder and said, 'Come, we have far to go.'

And so the goat led the shepherd boy across the slanting darkness of the hillsides, hoping to exhaust him, hoping that his grip on her fleece would weaken. As she ran she spoke to him, trying to deceive his senses with her soft voice but Pacorro only tightened his fist in the golden hair and ran pace for pace with the goat and as nimbly, gritting his teeth and thinking of the land he would buy for his father.

At last the goat rested in a deep ravine and Pacorro felt the full weight of her brown eyes upon him as she told of the great battles of the past, how many men the Caliph had tortured and slain for his pleasure. She told of the slaves he had captured too and the shepherd boy shivered as he heard the sounds of death and the clashing of weapons and the cries of the wounded. He saw the ghosts of dead warriors and he felt the touch of their breath on his cheek and fear crept under his skin like a maggot. But he was brave and again tightened his hold on the fleece and said; 'I swear I will slay you and steal your crown if you do not keep your promise.'

'I tell you stories of the Caliph,' said the goat, 'so that the road we travel may seem less wearisome,' and she led Pacorro into a cleft that was narrow and full of stubborn bushes carrying thorns of sharp iron-wood, but as the goat advanced the thorns swayed back from her though they clutched at Pacorro and brought blood to his arms and face. The noise of battle and the screams of the injured were louder here and the boy wanted to turn and run to his father but now he did not dare.

Suddenly the clamour stopped. The Golden Goat halted before a blank rock wall in which there was no fissure or crack. She lowered her head and spoke in Saracen words more than a thousand years old and the granite wall rolled aside and the goat stepped into a cavern whose roof was so high that it could not be seen. Pacorro was drawn in with her and the cavern door closed behind him. He was deep under the hillside, shut in with the Golden Goat of Abd al-Rhaman.

Now Pacorro released his hold on the fleece and stumbled forward. There was treasure all about him and the light from it dulled even the sheen of the goat's golden coat. Here in the cavern was everything that a man, even in his greatest greed, could desire. Everything that the Saracens had torn from the conquered land, stolen at the price of blood, death and slavery. The floor was ankle deep in precious stones, they overflowed from deep sea-chests, carelessly filled. There were ivory statues draped with gowns of silk and cloth of gold; here were orbs and sceptres, thrones and crowns, tapestries and gem-woven vestments, still stained with the blood of dying priests. It was all thrown down in disorder and it had lain there for hundreds of years, waiting for the Caliph to return.

The goat stalked proudly into the cavern and Pacorro followed, his eyes unequal to the task of looking at so much splendour. The goat went on and everywhere she walked there was treasure. At last she stopped by a huge throne of gold thickly decorated with diamonds. Across its arms rested a great jewelled sword in a scabbard of silver. The goat looked in disdain at the trembling shepherd boy and her eyes blazed up with pride and greed. 'What a mighty fellowship,' she said, 'was the fellowship of my father the Caliph. Stronger than all your princes, bolder than your kings and more daring than your knights. How they feared us.'

She touched the throne with a horn, 'This we took from an archbishop, those tapestries we took from his cathedral . . . those caskets of jewels we had in ransom for your most powerful king, and all you see is mine until my father returns . . . then I shall be a princess once more and I shall live with my own people.'

The goat moved on and Pacorro walked with her, his scarred and filthy feet stepping over rich silks and precious stones, but the boy did not forget his father and he thought of the little he had. Once more he showed his knife. 'And where is my reward?' he asked. 'Three choices from amongst your riches you promised me. I want them, remember that I saved you from the hunter's noose.'

The goat lowered her head and her eyes went dull. 'Shepherd boy,' she said, 'choose.'

Pacorro pointed to the jewelled sword on the magnificent throne. 'The sword,' he said, thinking that he could strap it to his body, leaving his arms free to carry something more.

'Oh choose some other thing,' answered the goat, 'for that was the Caliph's favourite sword. I would be disgraced if he were to return and find it gone.'

Pacorro pointed next to a caftan made of gold and silver thread, heavy with rubies and opals and pearls of matching beauty. 'That,' he thought, 'I shall be able to slip over my shoulder and leave my hands free to carry something more.'

The goat stamped a foot and her voice was angry. 'Fool, you cannot take the caftan of the Caliph, when he returns he will look for this caftan before any other thing.'

Pacorro felt pity for the goat in her trouble and cast his eyes all round the cavern for another treasure to bear away with him. 'I will have that turban,' he said at length, thinking that he could place it upon his head leaving his hands free to carry away something more. The turban bore a rich diamond at its front, a diamond as big as the boy's clenched fist.

The goat placed her head on Pacorro's shoulder and her brown eyes filled with tears as she looked at him. 'My father wore this turban on his wedding day, I dare not let you take it . . . he would punish me sorely if I let it go.'

Still Pacorro had pity and chose again but the goat made yet another excuse and bade him choose elsewhere. But whatever it was that the boy chose the Golden Goat refused and hours went by in this way and Pacorro grew weary and fell silent, realizing that the goat would allow nothing to be taken from her hoard, not the smallest diamond nor the meanest silver pin, and he began to fear that he would die amongst all that treasure. He felt a madness beginning to stir in his brain and he forgot about a field in the mountain and a field in the valley with a hut for his father. He longed to be out in the night air but at the same time sorrow rose in his heart and he wept, weeping for the Princess Suhar, abandoned, alone, loveless for so long. He knew, as every shepherd knew, that the Caliph and his sorcerer had been dead for hundreds of years and would never return to seek the treasure and to change the Golden Goat back into the form of a young princess.

Pacorro took the goat's lovely head in his arms. 'Princess,' he said, 'leave this horrible place, better to be a shepherdess in the sun than live a thousand years alone. Come away and you will sleep under the stars and listen to the sheep bells at dawn.'

The goat shook her head. 'How could I leave my father's treasure? The Caliph might return tomorrow.'

'Princess,' said Pacorro, 'your father will never return. He and his sorcerer are dead.'

The goat wandered a step from Pacorro and gazed steadily over all her possessions. 'I know,' she said, 'but the Caliph was not the man to let death defeat him. Besides, how could I leave? I am used to the feel of silk, the sight of gold and the glint of rubies. If I went with you I would become a woman again but I would lose the power of opening the cave. I could never live as you live, poor, dirty, a barefoot shepherd.'

Pacorro was angered. 'Living as we live is better than living as you live,' he cried.

'And dying as you die,' said the goat softly, 'and how is that?'

'Dying a shepherd is better than living a goat,' sobbed Pacorro and the tears ran down his face.

The goat came close to Pacorro and put her soft mouth into the place where his neck met his shoulder; 'Your tears are kind,' she said, 'and you are right, I will come with you but you must help. It will not be easy for me.'

'Yes,' said Pacorro and he brushed away his tears with the back of his hand. He put an arm round the goat's neck and he half led, half dragged her, half-resisting, to the doorway of the cavern and the goat spoke the word and the rock wall opened and Pacorro saw the pale starlight outside. The goat trembled and the shepherd boy held her tightly but, as they were about to cross the threshold, Pacorro thought of all the wealth he was leaving behind and he thought once more of his father and how one pearl only would shelter him from the cold nights of his advancing age. So Pacorro, hoping that the goat would not see him, squeezed the toes of his right foot around a small ruby that lay in his path, meaning to hobble with it into the outside air.

But the goat knew at once what he had done, feeling it in his touch, and she reared from his embrace. 'Oh, do not take that ruby ,' she cried, 'my father would search for it in the very moment of his return.'

Pacorro allowed the ruby to drop to the floor and went towards the goat, his arms outstretched but the goat retreated, back into the cavern.

'I cannot go,' she said, 'I cannot betray my father.'

'It is not your father that keeps you here,' said Pacorro, 'it is the treasure,' and he leapt forward, seized the goat by the head and by the horns and he dragged her, stiff-legged, through the doorway.

Suddenly Pacorro fell backwards and rolled into a thicket of briar and bramble; he pulled himself free with bloody hands. The goat had disappeared from his grasp and there in its place stood the slender form of the Princess Suhar, regal and beautiful. Her long dark hair was black and where it was darkest it was blue, like the midnight sky, but her face was sombre and sad with centuries of waiting. The gown she wore was the colour of sapphires and it was patterned over with the finest diamonds from the Caliph's store, each diamond purer than the last and carrying in its heart a flickering candle-flame.

Across the Princess's forehead glittered the Caliph's coronet of gold with the seven points.

The Princess looked about her. She raised her hands and studied them closely, moving her fingers. She touched her face, her arms, her hair, and then she screamed.

'No,' she cried, a dreadful moaning in her voice. 'How strange I feel, how horrible this shape, this cannot be beautiful. How long would I live in this body? I would grow old like you, die like you, unable to run, forever, sure-footed cross the hills.' And with these words she stepped back over the threshold of the cave and as the Princess Suhar disappeared the Golden Goat wheeled on its four fine feet in the doorway and spoke the word and the rock door of the cavern began to rumble and roll forward.

Pacorro, his blood still wet on his hands, leapt into the entrance and grabbed the goat's horns and fought with her. But the goat was decided now and she lowered her head and shook it hard and the shepherd boy was flung from the cave and his breath was knocked from him. The door rolled on and shut fast.

In a little while Pacorro recovered and crawled to the door and stood before it, but no opening could he find. It was dark again. The golden splendour had vanished with the goat and her treasure, only cold dawn light shone above the cleft now and that too weak to reach the ground.

Pacorro began to grope his way along the gully, his eyes uncertain after the sights they had seen. He felt before him and in those first doubtful steps his foot struck something which rang out with an ancient sound as it moved against a stone.

Pacorro knelt and his wounded hands searched in the dust until he touched the thing. He could not see what it was and so he raised the object above his head and held it against the stars. It was round and smooth with seven points – it was the golden coronet, fallen from the goat's head during her last struggle with the shepherd boy. Pacorro smiled to himself in the darkness; the dream of his father would come true after all; as much pasture as he wanted now.

As the boy smiled there came a terrible sobbing from the depths of the hillside; the great door began to open and there came the sound of that voice which no man could resist.

'And what will the Caliph say?' it called. 'What will the Caliph say when he finds his crown stolen by a shepherd? Return it to me and you may choose what else you will from this treasure. . .'

The great door of rock opened completely now and Pacorro saw the Golden Goat again, shining brighter than the brightness of the treasure behind her. And as the light grew stronger the goat stepped across the threshold once more and took the form of the Princess Suhar, holding out her arms and speaking in tones of great sadness.

'Will you leave me here like this for ever, without my father's crown? Return it to me, shepherd boy, and I will teach you the secret word that opens this cave and you and your father will be as rich as Abd al-Rhaman once was.'

Still clasping the coronet Pacorro raised his hands to his head and tried to shut his ears, but the voice of the Princess was like the voice of reason itself and the light from the cavern burned into his eyes and blinded him and he felt soft lips whispering of wealth and power beyond belief and gentle hands led him back into the cavern to choose what he would, and slowly the great rock door closed behind him.

And three days later Pacorro's father found his son lying on his back in a gully whose rocky walls almost touched overhead, a gully made impenetrable by growths of sturdy thorn, strong and matted. The old shepherd cut his way to his son's side and knelt beside him but Pacorro did not recognize his father and the man wept. The boy's mind had gone. He said nothing and stared at the sky out of unseeing golden eyes.

# LES GORGES DE PENNAFORT

A piercing whistle awoke me and when I rolled onto my back and opened my eyes I saw that the encampment was deserted though the heart of the fire still glowed red. A shout came from up above. It was Marius.

'You'll have to catch up with us,' he called, 'and make sure the fire is out,' then he was gone.

Shivering in the morning damp, down there by the river, I poured water on the embers, gathered my belongings and then scrambled on my hands and knees to the top of the steep embankment, sliding on the loose stones and gravel. There were sheep droppings on the road and I followed them across a bridge and into Le Muy itself.

Even now it was barely five o'clock and the town was deserted. I went past the church and through the square and saw that a long, straight road led to the horizon and halfway down it were the sheep, all neatly contained for once and held together.

As I hurried along, my bag bumping on my shoulder, the door of a café opened and the proprietor stood before me, wrapped in a dark blue apron.

'C'est toi, le berger anglais?' he asked. 'There's a cup of coffee for you in here, and a drop of cognac.'

Once inside the café I could see the cups and glasses on the zinc counter where the shepherds had come in one by one on their way past, watching through the window as the sheep went by. The café owner stared as I drank, his eyes travelling slowly over me, their scrutiny ending at my feet.

'You look like a tramp,' he said without emotion, 'you'd do well to get some proper boots.'

Within a kilometre or two I caught up with the others and loaded my bag onto the cart. We were at the bottom of a large plain now and what hills there were lay to our left. Close to us on both sides of the road were vineyards and the shepherds were hard pressed, making sure the sheep did not get into them and cause damage. Luckily it was Sunday and there were no cars trying to pass us; it was still too early for market and much too early for mass.

As we advanced, the ridge of hills came nearer to us and rose higher. Our route began to turn and twist, dropping a little and then, suddenly, we were crossing a long, narrow bridge of stone and entering a little valley, all green with spreading oak trees.

Under the bridge was a fast running stream and good green grass. Before us the ground was flat and formed a meadow and as I crossed the bridge I could look down and see that the greater part of the flock was already grazing and moving towards the water's edge to drink.

It was a beautiful spot, a favourite with the shepherds and, relieved to have reached it, there was a touch of frolic about the way they searched the cart, in amongst the cloaks and umbrellas, for a bottle of vermouth, and then poured large glasses of it so that we could raise them to celebrate the morning.

Marius wiped the sweat from his forehead with the back of his hand and nodded downstream. 'Follow that path,' he said, 'and you'll come to the cascades of Pennafort – clear water in red rock. Take care though, Micheu, it's just the place for the Golden Goat. If you see her don't go after her whatever you do.'

I crossed the road and followed the path that Marius had indicated. The stream below me was not large but here and there it spread into wide pools, sometimes shallow and sometimes deep enough to cover a man. The canyon itself was narrow and above my head the sides of it were sheer, leaning towards each other in places, broken and rugged with cracks and clefts where bushes and small trees grew. It was a wild and haunted corner of the world and for a moment I felt apprehensive about going on, intimidated by a feeling of loneliness. Marius could be right after all, who knew what might be concealed in this chasm? A Golden Goat to drive me mad or a magician to weave me into some irresistible spell.

I took enjoyment in these thoughts and clambered over a huge rock and came to a secret pool with sloping slabs of fallen cliff on either side of it. The river made hardly any sound here and the cascades of Pennafort were muted in the distance. The sun was high and had reached the rocks and they were warm. I took off my clothes and lowered myself into the cold water, a pagan giving thanks for the day. I was tense at first but then I allowed my body to float and drift across the surface of the pool, staring up to the rim of the canyon and beyond it to the sky. No matter how far I ever walked I knew that moment would make it all worthwhile.

∞

When I got back to the bridge I found a motorized bicycle on its stand by the side of the cart and there, sitting with the shepherds, was Jean Renoult. He had come to eat with us, bringing in his rucksack and panniers enough food for a regiment; pastis and iced water too, and in my absence the pastis had done the rounds.

Jean was a good-looking man with a strong face, like the portrait of his father that hung in his mother's house. Tall and elegant, slightly bowed at the shoulders and with hair prematurely grey swept back from a wide forehead. The first time I had seen him, in tattered shorts and frayed shirt, his skin tanned from the sea and the sun, he had reminded me of pictures I had seen of Pablo Picasso, but Jean's eyes were special and they touched you with an enormous love. He poured me a drink and placed it in my hands.

Marius was speaking with his mouth full. 'Shepherds are only shepherds,' he said, 'so that they can take to the road twice a year. They like to talk and gossip, and they are right for gossip comes before all books. Today talk – tomorrow literature. That is why shepherds like to hear the old tales again and again, and even a new one from time to time, it is only gossip retold and reheard.'

'I knew a shepherd from over by Avignon,' said Jean. 'Every summer I used to drive a lorry with his sheep in it up to the pastures. He came from Fontaine de Vaucluse, Petrarch's village . . . I got to know him well after two or three years. He told me a story once, while we were driving to the mountains . . . you might not know this one, though if you want to hear it you'll have to hear it in French.'

'Hmph!' said Joseph, leaning forward and reaching for the jam-pot, 'it won't be anywhere near as good.'

# *The Shepherd of Fontaine*

*I*n all the centuries of its existence the village of Fontaine has hardly altered. Little more than a hamlet it lies in a hollow at the foot of a vast and forbidding cliff that marks the southern edge of the great plateau of Vaucluse – a wild and empty land of hills and mountains lying between the lonely peaks of the Ventoux and the Lure.

The village is hemmed in on three sides by sheer precipices and the road that leads there dies there. In times gone by a castle stood upon the highest escarpment, the castle of the Bishops of Cavaillon, though now all that remains of it is a ruin of small stones that has nothing to offer the visitor save the view from its broken walls. Yet, in spite of all this, Fontaine is renowned throughout Provence and even beyond; it is a renown that derives its origin from the beauty of a river and the story of a poet.

The river is the Sorgue and its waters, mysterious and green, burst from the edge of the Vaucluse plateau with a never-ending energy and sound. This torrent first fills a deep pool that lies under the cliff itself and then, especially in winter when the rains and snows are heavy in the uplands, gushes from an arched grotto and cascades over a jumbled barrier of fallen rock, until at last it flows along a gully and into the village, its main current twisting and bulging as solidly as muscle.

The poet was Francesco Petrarch, one of the world's most gifted. An Italian, he served the Popes of Avignon as a diplomat and academic. He was also an antiquary and he studied archaeology. He rode into Italy on secret missions and wrote books and monographs in a Latin so pure that the sound of it rang across the whole of Europe. But for none of this is he remembered. Today his fame rests on the love he felt for Laura de Noves, a married woman who, so history says, was too virtuous to return his illicit passion. Ten years after their first meeting, his love still unrequited, Petrarch fled the temptations of Avignon and retired to the calm and beauty of Fontaine and began to write the songs and sonnets that were to bring him and his Laura a shining immortality. According to the records Laura was to take little note of these poems and to perceive no glimmer of the honour that was to be hers. While still a young woman she died of the plague and was buried in the church where she had first been seen by her lover.

Such prospects of literary brilliance were of no concern to the ignorant inhabitants of Fontaine; they could hardly be expected to notice the comings and goings of a mere scribbler. Learned works in Latin meant nothing to them, no more did Italian sonnets written for a fine lady of Avignon. What did a man want with another's poetry when he had words of his very own in his heart? What need was there to praise the virtues of some aristocratic beauty when you already had soft shifting limbs in your bed? 'We must look after ourselves,' the people of Fontaine would say wisely, 'for the rich won't.'

In this way the villagers were content to live their lives, taking no heed of the famous man who had come to stay amongst them. This was not surprising for they were only simple peasants; fruit-pickers, fishermen and shepherds – and the shepherds were the simplest of them all and the simplest of all the shepherds was a strange creature who went by the name of Paradou.

Paradou did not even own the flock of sheep that was in his care. He was hired by the year and paid, sometimes, in food. No one in Provence was poorer than Paradou. His clothes were ragged, like the meanest beggar's, and the cloak he wore to keep out the rain was so threadbare that his elbows poked through it. He ran shoeless across the craggy hillsides and at night, for he had no home or any family, he would sleep in the open with his charges, creeping right up close to them for the warmth of their bodies and wool.

It was said that Paradou knew all his sheep by name and could recognize them by their faces. He treated them as human-beings, talking to each one and caring for them when they were sick. He smelt like a goat, never washed and lived like a beast.

The villagers of Fontaine certainly thought of him as one. If he crossed their path they would beat him out of it. Even when disposed to give him scraps of food they would drop them down onto the ground as if to a dog, and the children were encouraged to throw stones at the idiot shepherd just as hard as they could.

There was, however, one person in Fontaine who, during the few short years since he had come to her notice, had treated Paradou with a certain amount of kindness. She, as the village gossips had it, was a widow whose husband had been a nobleman with large properties in Avignon. On his death his lady had taken up residence in Fontaine, eager to devote the remainder of her life to the memory of a man she did not wish to forget. Although long past her youth she was still beautiful, elegant also and generous. Whenever she noticed the gaunt figure of Paradou in the pastures she would bid her servants prepare food and drink and see that they took it out to him.

No one had ever treated Paradou in this manner and once, when the widow had taken the food out to him herself, he had been so overcome by her presence that he had thrown himself to the ground and hidden his eyes like an imbecile. From that moment on Paradou worshipped the widow with all his heart and with all his body. Not that he could give any form to this passion. There were not many thoughts in his mind and even fewer words to give those thoughts shape. All he could do was to love the woman as devotedly as a dog. If he saw her in the distance his heart leapt into his throat and threatened to stifle him. For Paradou she was an angel from heaven, except that he was barely aware of the existence of such a place and had no idea how to approach its creatures.

Like all shepherds Paradou did not graze his flock in the same pastures every day or at every season. In the heat of summer he would take to the high slopes of the mountains and wander at will. In winter he would bring his sheep down to the milder temperatures of the valley below the village. It was there that the widow's farmhouse lay, large and magnificent to the eyes of a shepherd, shaded by plane trees and protected in the north from the mistral by a row of poplars, stately and strong.

This was the vision of Provence that Paradou always carried in his simple mind; that for him was perfection – the green of the pastures merging with the green of the river and a cool bright blueness above, unbroken by a single cloud. All summer long he thought of it for he knew that once or twice at least, during the months he was there, he would see the widow and perhaps she would even bring him food which her own hands had touched. For Paradou there could be no greater joy.

During these winters the shepherd would graze his flock over a wide area, allowing his ewes to roam along the steep valley sides as well as down in the rich bottom land. Sometimes too he would follow the river to its source, leading his sheep through the village itself so they might clamber up to the jumble of rocks at the entrance of the arched cavern, and even higher to where sweet grass was to be found growing between huge, fallen boulders.

There Paradou would stand, his face turned upwards, watching the flock climb, his mouth open and his ears deafened by the ceaseless roar of the

Sorgue as it flooded out from the base of the precipice. He loved the majesty of this river and the continual booming of the waters always seemed to calm him. He felt at peace there, as if he were at one with the noise and had become a part of the very landscape.

So it happened one winter, as Paradou stood listening to the sound of the river, that he noticed one of his favourite sheep climbing higher than was usual along the side of a crag and, having advanced onto a narrow ledge, was then unable to return. Even as the shepherd clicked his teeth in annoyance and, even as he was still watching, the sheep disappeared.

Paradou blinked and stared. One second he had been looking at the sheep and the very next he had been looking at an empty ledge. Paradou shivered; was this magic?

Heedless of these fears Paradou began to scramble upwards. He could move and run like a mountain goat and he leapt from boulder to boulder easily, quickly crossing the cliff face above the mouth of the river. On the far side he followed a tiny track, edging along it, his body pressed against the wall of rock until he came to the ledge where he had last seen the sheep, and there he discovered where it had gone. He saw a slight angle in the path at this point and in that angle was a narrow fissure, very dark so that from a distance it looked like a shadow, but it was wide enough to take a man.

Paradou slipped into this opening and saw that it continued, heading as if for the heart of the mountain. There was also a faint path and the shepherd followed it and as the light from the outside dimmed he found that another light, glimmering from within, was showing him the way. Gradually the path widened and the roof of the passage grew higher and soon Paradou came into a rocky gallery high up inside the cliff, and from this gallery he could look down on the huge pool that was the beginning of the River Sorgue.

Here the thin rays of winter sunlight streamed in through the great vault of the entrance and shimmered across the surface of the water, beating up against the roof of the cavern in ripples of a golden green too bright to look at. Everything was bathed in the same flickering luminosity. Paradou looked at his hands; they also were golden green, like fish suspended above movement in the deepness of a flowing brook. And the sound of the torrent was reflected everywhere and was shattered like the light into tiny emeralds and thrown against the walls.

As the shepherd stared at the scene before him there came a noise to his right and the missing sheep bleated and pushed past Paradou, making its way back to the open air. At the same time it knocked against something set in the shadows of the ledge on which Paradou stood and an object rolled towards him. When it came into the light he saw that it was an old earthenware jar, half as tall as a man.

The shepherd started at first but as soon as his surprise had passed he knelt and examined the object and vague thoughts of Saracen treasure drifted into his mind. He hesitated, not wanting to put his hand into the receptacle for fear that some snake or scorpion might have taken up residence in it, but after a while he upended the jar and shook it until several square packets wrapped in goatskin fell onto the ground.

Paradou picked up the largest package and opened it. Inside he found a manuscript written in the finest black ink, in a scribe's hand, on the clearest of parchments. The shepherd was disappointed. Although he had a distant childhood memory of being taught to read, all his letters had gone and now he was hardly aware of the existence of language. It was only with a great effort that he could half-remember even that there was such a thing as writing and that some people could understand what it said. For Paradou the manuscripts he had uncovered might just as well have been the mystic spells of a magician. With a sigh he replaced them in the jar and, after one last look at the beauty of the waters below he went back along the narrow cleft and out onto the mountainside.

In spite of the fact that he was unable to decipher the manuscripts the discovery of them had a profound effect on the shepherd. For the first time in his life he had something that was all his own. Now he thought of little but the cavern and the strange writings he had found there; the beauty of the light and the sound of the waters. He returned to the source more and more often and at each visit he would gaze for hours at the golden greenness of the great pool, and then he would take out the manuscripts and study them, searching into his past for the power of reading.

When he was in the cavern Paradou always experienced a feeling of guilt. Was such beauty for the likes of him? Was this a treasure that really belonged to another? Should he not go to the shepherd who hired him and tell him what he had found; or the Mayor or to the school-teacher, men of great learning? But Paradou did not. He was convinced, without knowing how or why, that the very secrecy of his discovery made it sacrosanct. Only one other person had ever been to the cavern and that was the person who had hidden the jar there in the first place. For that there must have been a reason and Paradou believed that he was respecting that reason by doing nothing and saying nothing.

In this way the winter passed and the summer came and Paradou was obliged to take his flock up onto the plateau of the Vaucluse and live for a season on the high peaks and in the empty valleys, all alone, seeing no other human-being from month to month. And all the time he was away he thought of the cave above the pool and the writings in the jar, and he found that something wonderful was happening to him.

It was as if, although many miles from Fontaine, he could conjure up the cavern in his mind's eye whenever he wished. He could see the writings too and over the long summer they began to mean something to him. He saw the lines and letters separate and take a form. He learnt what writing was, and reading too. He had discovered language.

This feeling grew stronger and stronger in the shepherd as the days went by and Paradou longed for winter to return so that he might take his sheep back to the village. It seemed that the time would never pass, but it did of course and as soon as Paradou found himself once more at the source of the River Sorgue he clambered across the great arched entrance, went along the ledge and entered the cavern where the golden green light painted everything. For a moment he stared at the great pool and the surge of the water over the rocks and then he knelt, as before, and took one of the manuscripts from the jar which stood at exactly the spot where he had left it.

Carefully he opened the packet and taking up one of the parchments he stared at it and, with no effort, he understood all that was written there. He was looking at a sonnet in Provençal and he knew now what a sonnet was, and he knew too that Provençal was his mother tongue – a language that was accented like a song. Then Paradou read the poem aloud and his voice echoed round the gallery and mingled with the sound of the river and the colours of the light.

Paradou's heart throbbed as he read and his mind became clear as if an enchantment had been cast over him. He saw how ignorant he had been up until this point in his life, and yet he was happy to discover, in the same moment, the joys that had been denied him for so many years. But with this happiness there came a hatred too; a hatred for all that wasted time and the unknown reasons that had caused it.

From that time on Paradou visited the cavern at every opportunity, reading poem after poem, and there were hundreds. Line by line he learnt them, and so easily did they come to him that it seemed he was simply remembering them. On the days when he grazed his flock away from the cavern he would recite the sonnets aloud, from memory, waving his arms and declaiming the poetry to the sheep, laughing at their surprised faces. The rich Provençal rolled off his tongue and he revelled in it. He had been given a great gift and he was thankful; glad that he had perceived a new world and glad that he had been allowed to enter it.

And the magic of the poems did not cease there. Paradou no longer crept abjectly along the margins of village life; no longer could the inhabitants of Fontaine beat him from their path. The barefoot, ragged shepherd had gone forever. He stood upright now and could speak. He had confonted his master and had claimed the money that had never been paid him. He had a new cloak and it was warm and he wore sturdy boots. He valued himself and slept under a roof like everyone else. His hair was brushed and his beard combed.

The villagers were astounded by this change in Paradou. They shook their heads and said no good would come of it. Gradually the story spread all along the valley, passing from farm to farm, and so it was not long before it came to the ears of the widow herself and she became eager to see the effect of the transformation at first hand. The very next time she heard that the shepherd was moving his sheep through the pastures nearby she made up a basket of provisions and, putting on her hooded cloak and taking a servant with her, she set out to discover what truth lay in the tale she had been told.

To her surprise the widow found the shepherd even more changed than she had been led to believe. He was clean, properly clothed and his hair shone in the sun. When she offered him the basket of food he did not throw himself to the ground as he had done in the past, but on the contrary he inclined his head in a little bow, accepted the gift with grace, and smiled.

'You have always been kind to this poor shepherd,' he said, 'and I have little to offer in return, except my devotion, but,' he added, 'I can recite you a sonnet or two in the most beautiful Provençal you have ever heard. Here, sit on my cloak,' and as he said this Paradou spread the garment and the widow and her servant sat and prepared to listen.

Then the shepherd spoke and as his voice rang out the widow felt her cheeks pale and she pulled the hood of her cloak around her face, though she stared at Paradou as if seeing him for the first time. As for the servant woman, she blushed deeply and lowered her eyes; she had never heard such things. These poems were the songs of a warm and irresistible passion, devoted to one woman and praising her hair, her limbs and her breasts.

Soon the recital came to an end and the shepherd bowed again and the two women rose to their feet, hesitating, neither one knowing what to say; then the widow broke the silence.

'These are powerful sonnets,' she said. 'Where did you learn about such things? You could not write in such a way of love. Where do these songs come from, shepherd? Did you steal them? Did you read them in some ancient book? Were they purloined from the desk of some old man?'

Paradou pointed away down the valley. 'In a secret place,' he said, 'I found them, in a jar, and read them when before I could not read. You are the only person who knows and I shall tell no other.'

'You have already said enough,' said the widow. 'Come to this spot tomorrow at this hour. I will listen to you then, and speak to you as well.' With this the widow turned and, taking her servant's arm, she went with her to the farmhouse, never once looking back at Paradou who stood as still as a tree until the two women had disappeared.

The very next day at the appointed time the widow came alone to the pastures and found Paradou waiting for her. She brought with her, as she had before, some provisions and once again she sat on the cloak and then commanded the shepherd to sit opposite her.

'Shepherd,' she said, as soon as she was settled, 'how many of these sonnets do you know?'

'There are hundreds,' answered Paradou, 'and I know them all, almost without learning.'

The widow nodded at this and with a defiant gesture she threw back the cowl that shaded her face and stared at Paradou. He gasped. This was the first time he had seen the widow without her hood and never had he seen anyone so beautiful. Twenty years older than the shepherd himself the widow's beauty was unlined and unwearied. Her brow was broad and her glance was knowing and subtle. She shook her head and her dark hair, only lightly flecked with grey, settled around her face and softened its outline. Paradou cried out in disbelief. 'Why,' he said, 'you are the lady in the sonnets . . . you are Laura.'

The widow smiled archly but made no attempt to deny the assumption. 'Yesterday,' she said, 'you told no poem which mentioned Laura by name. Why?'

Paradou was troubled. 'I was saying them for you, madame, not knowing that you and Laura were the same.'

'You are honest,' said the widow, then she lay back on the cloak and closed her eyes. Her body was trembling. 'I am Laura de Noves,' she continued, 'and these poems were written for me. You say you know them all. Then recite them all for it is many years since I heard them.'

And Paradou obeyed and sat cross-legged and watched her face as he told the sonnets one after the other and his voice shook. As he spoke he felt an admiration for this woman growing inside him and even though the poems were carnal Paradou knew that the love he felt was not of that kind. His love was something he had never known before and he could not describe it. By the time he had come to the end of the last sonnet his emotions had so overwhelmed him that the tears were pouring freely down his face and he collapsed to the ground, exhausted by the feelings that had invaded his heart.

Laura de Noves left Paradou alone for a while but then, when his sobs had lessened, she sat up and wiped his cheeks with a handkerchief and poured him a cup of water from the flask she had brought with the provisions.

'Come Paradou,' she said, 'and do not weep. This was perhaps wrong of me. I was selfish and wanted only to hear those poems again.'

'Again?' said Paradou, and he put down the empty cup.

'I was only a young girl when he saw me in the church of Santa Chiara,' said Laura de Noves. 'Already married to another man, but Petrarch loved me.'

'Petrarch,' said Paradou, 'and who is he?'

'Petrarch the poet,' said Laura de Noves, looking deep into Paradou's eyes as if searching for something. 'For ten years I would not listen to his entreaties, and during those ten years he wrote me poems of unrequited love, such poems . . . in Italian those, and he smuggled them to me, at church, in the streets, at the Papal court . . . and I loved them, and through those poems I came to love the poet. I gave myself to him, in secret. There never was a love such as ours, never; and never was there such a poetry, until this.'

'But the poems I found are not poems of unrequited love, and they are in Provençal, not Italian.'

Laura de Noves turned her fine head and gazed away down the valley, looking towards her farm though there was no one to be seen. 'My husband became suspicious,' she said, 'and I was carrying a child that was not his. The plague came to Avignon, it often did, and many died so I died too. Bodies were easy to come by . . . the plague disfigures the dead you know. A corpse was dressed in my clothes and placed in my bed and buried in my name. I came here, to this farm, saying that I was the widow of a nobleman . . . dead of the plague.'

'And Petrarch?'

'Petrarch had made this hamlet his retreat for many years. When he was not on missions for the Pope or living his life in Avignon he came here and wrote his learned works and the poems in Italian . . . that is why I came here. We had years when nothing came between us. My son was born. We cared not a jot for what the world said but the world said nothing. No one came from Avignon to here and no one went from here to Avignon. I had but few servants and those I had were trusted. Ah, such a life it was.'

'And then?'

'And then . . . Ah then, Petrarch wrote the poems in Provençal and never wrote better. "I sung you in Italian," he said, "when you would not love me, but now that you do I shall sing you in Provençal, the queen of languages; every inch of your body, a song of flesh and blood that will surpass all my songs and all the pagan songs too and this will be my masterpiece. There will be nothing to match it. Let the world forget those simpering songs I wrote before. This in Provençal will be alive as our love is alive and the world will never see its like again." That is what Petrarch said to me,' and with these words Laura de Noves leant back on her arms like a young girl and stared upwards in a smiling trance as if her lover was actually there, high in the cloudless sky.

Paradou leant forward and gently touched the woman's hair. 'Endless songs have sung this face,' he said, 'and no matter how long the world turns no face will be sung more.'

'That is so,' she answered, and moved her head so that she might look at the shepherd, 'and sung by Petrarch too. The most beautiful sung by the most beauteous.'

'And then?'

'And then. Ah well, love is only love. A poet is only a poet and my body was only a body.'

'But the words remain.'

'Yes the words remain, but Petrarch did not. I discovered, afterwards, that during those ten years, when he wrote the Italian poems, he led a life of pleasure. There were other women and other children.'

'Other poems?'

Laura de Noves laughed but the sound was mirthless and saddened Paradou. 'I think not,' she answered, 'but once he had written the Provençal poems he tired of this place, and of me. He said I loved the child too much. It diminished him, he said, and our love. I threw myself on my knees: "Take the child," I said . . . after all it was Petrarch I loved and his poems were my children. So the child was taken and I never saw it again, at least not as a child. It made no difference. Petrarch was called to the Papal court . . . he was loved there. He was crowned laureate of all Europe . . . with green leaves on his head. He went to Italy . . . Rome . . . Padua. I hardly ever saw him again, and as for me, how could I return to Avignon? I was dead, incarcerated and entombed under the weight of those Italian poems. Petrarch had gone.'

'And the poems in Provençal. How did they find their way into the cavern?'

'Petrarch read them to me as he wrote. . . Those five years we had together.

How I loved them. How they made my body tremble, like they did again today when you read them in that voice like his.'

'Yes I saw.'

'Petrarch knew that his reputation as laureate resided in the learned works he wrote in Latin and in the stately verses he wrote for me in Italian. The world was not ready for the sonnets he had written in Provençal . . . me a goddess . . . the human body becoming divine . . . such things could have led him to the stake . . . and so, although he knew they were the best things he had ever done they were to be hidden until after his death. I never thought to hear them again.'

'How did he find the cavern?'

'Petrarch knew the shepherds, walked with them. He respected their way of life, it was close to nature, he said, though in reality he liked great cities and great men too much to stay here for long . . . he needed to be admired. An old shepherd showed him that cavern, and Petrarch saw that it was the perfect place to conceal his poems. He described it to me. Is it as beautiful as he said?'

'Yes,' said Paradou, it is. But how did Petrarch know that his poems would not be lost forever?'

'It has all been arranged,' said Laura de Noves. 'Someone will come for the poems when Petrarch is no more. He would never let them lie there, unread. More than anything else he knows that his immortality resides in them, and, you see, I know where they are also. I would not let them die . . . there is my immortality to consider as well as his.'

'He is still alive?'

'In Padua, very old now, as I begin to be.'

'Why did you not go to him, in Italy?'

'If Petrarch had wanted me he would have sent for me, or come for me himself. Besides, what would an old Petrarch have wanted with an old Laura. Did you not feel the fire in those poems as you spoke them? If Petrarch saw me now and if Petrarch could still write he would compose lampoons and satires about me . . . and if I could see him now I would pity him for his age . . . love does not want pity. No, this is better. When those sonnets are brought into the light I shall be beautiful again, desired again . . . forever lovely in men's eyes. Imagine . . . no poems like those and no woman desired like me since the topless towers of Troy were burnt for Helen. That is not something I wish to change or lose. My life for those sonnets . . . it was a bargain.'

'But it was not,' said Paradou suddenly. 'For ten years this Petrarch loved elsewhere and fathered his children elsewhere . . . and when at last you gave yourself to him his love could only endure until the sonnets were written. Then he grew tired of you and took away your child in jealous spite. He was a selfish man who loved nothing but his fame.'

Laura de Noves smiled serenely as if she knew a hundred things that Paradou did not. 'Of course he loved no one,' she said, 'but have you not read this Provençal. Are they not the most wonderful sonnets the world will ever know . . . will they not live forever. Think of the power of them . . . look how their magic has turned you from a savage into a man with a mind.'

'I know,' said Paradou, 'and I am thankful for it, but that same mind that Petrarch gave me tells me that Petrarch is hard and cruel. He is not a man I could have loved.'

The smile of Laura de Noves became more mysterious and she laid a hand upon the shepherd's forearm for a second. 'How can you know?' she said, 'after all, you are his son, and mine.'

There was a long silence then, broken only by the sound of the sheep stirring afar off, their rough bells rustling as they moved their heads. Paradou looked as sick as death and his lips tightened. The woman nodded. 'You are Petrarch's,' she said. 'That is why the poems worked their spell on you. I was the one who began to teach you to read . . . before he took you away . . . and the poems . . . you had heard them as a child.'

Paradou climbed slowly to his feet and stared at his mother. 'Why did you never tell me?' he asked.

Laura de Noves shrugged, almost unconcerned. 'Petrarch would not have wanted it,' she answered, 'besides I did not know who you were, not till a few years ago when I gave you food and saw your father's face in your face. I half-thought then to take you into my household but what good would it have done? Petrarch wanted me to love no one but him and you were happy, I suppose, in your wild life . . . it was better to leave you.'

Paradou's face reddened with anger. 'Happy,' he cried, 'better to leave me . . . you do not understand what I have been these thirty years . . . a beast, an animal, a hired servant who until last year lived as his sheep lived. I have been beaten by the villagers and their children have thrown stones at me. I have been cheated of my life . . . I too might have been a scholar and written in Latin and travelled into Italy. Petrarch has done this to me and you have let him. He does not deserve to live and nor do his poems.'

Now Laura de Noves got to her feet. The warmth had left her and all at once she looked more than her age. 'You fool,' she said, her voice sour, 'what do you know of such things? Petrarch had his work to do and that work has more right to live than you or I.'

At this Paradou beat his temples with his fists and wailed at the top of his voice and the old savagery and madness began to take possession of him. 'His work,' he shouted, 'his work, yes, and the best of his work is in my power . . . your sonnets. I shall destroy them as you have destroyed me. I shall cast them down into the deep pool.'

Then it was the woman's turn to look crazed. She glanced towards her farmhouse but there was still no one to be seen. She threw herself at her son and flung her arms around him in a vain attempt to hold him to the spot. 'You cannot destroy such a work of art,' she cried, 'you cannot. It is a crime worse than any other.'

'No worse than the crime committed against me,' shouted Paradou. 'I am worth more than any sonnet, and so were you until you forgot,' and then the shepherd struck his mother a terrible blow and she fell to the ground sobbing.

'But I do not matter,' she said, dazed, holding a hand to her brow and feeling the wetness of the blood, 'I do not matter. The sonnets are more valuable than me or hundreds like me . . . and yet I live in them, and every inch of my body lives in them – when I was beautiful and young and was loved forever. Oh, my son, do not destroy them, do not kill me twice.'

But Paradou had gone and did not hear these words and Laura de Noves fell back into the grass, unconscious. It was then that her servants saw the shepherd running down the valley, and they went out to search for their mistress and found her by the untouched basket of provisions, her hair all bloody. Gently they raised the injured woman and carried her to her bed and though she recovered her senses she remained delirious and could not cease her weeping for the lost sonnets.

She did however pass through one brief moment of lucidity and during it she told her own shepherd how to find the cavern above the pool and bade him go there to search for the poems and for a sign of Paradou himself. This shepherd did as he was commanded but he returned empty-handed. There was no jar, he said, and he had not seen Paradou, nor had anyone he had questioned. All he had seen were traces of footprints in the dust.

When she heard this news Laura de Noves only wept the more and became quite inconsolable. Eventually she lost consciousness again and a fever took possession of her. From that moment on her end was sure and three days later she died. Just before her death she cried out and seized the hand of the servant who was tending her: 'Send word to Padua,' she whispered, 'send word to Padua,' and with that Laura de Noves closed her eyes and breathed no more.

Later that day bands of men were sent out to apprehend Paradou for the murder of his mother but he was never found. In the years that followed, the shepherds of Fontaine often said that they had seen the criminal running in the hills like an animal, all naked and mad with his matted hair floating over his head like a banner. Some of them also said that they had felt his presence at night, on the rim of darkness which lay beyond their camp-fires, but none of this was ever proved and nor was any other part of the story.

In fact this tale of Paradou was never told by the troubadours and has come to us through the mouths of shepherds only. Nor is it written down anywhere and history tells us that Laura de Noves died of the plague in Avignon and that Petrarch never wrote in Provençal. But the shepherds of Fontaine, when you can find one who will talk to you, will always smile and swear on their lives that there is a secret cavern in the cliff and that they have seen it, but they will never tell you where it lies.

# THE GÎTE AT
# CALLAS

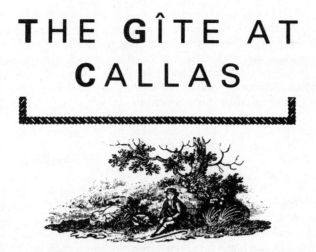

**B**efore we set off that evening Joseph's hired man announced that he could go no further. His feet were chafed and sore and he had been limping all day, but more than that he was running a temperature and needed to see a doctor.

Jules, the brother of Joseph, drove a Peugeot 403 estate and it was he who formed our only link with the world. Every day he went in search of fresh bread and fruit, returned, then walked with us a while before going ahead to make sure that other flocks had not stolen our grazing and other shepherds had not camped in the places we wanted. Jules was a hard man with a face like a rock and now he was angry. He did not mind taking the shepherd back to Grimaud but he was furious at being short-handed.

He looked at me, not a trace of humour in his expression. The others looked at me too and I knew this was the moment. 'Je peux te le faire,' I said. 'I can do it,' and that was it.

Nothing could have been simpler than the work I had volunteered for but it was infinitely more tiring than being a free agent. No longer could I wander off the road to rest whenever I wished or bathe my feet in a brook when I felt like it. Now I was obliged to keep the same slow pace as the sheep, waiting while they browsed at the side of the road; always struggling with the mule and never able to turn my back on it because I knew that left alone it would escape in an instant, pulling the cart and all our belongings into some deep ravine where it fancied it could see fresher and greener grass.

There were three new-born lambs being carried in the cart by this time and they bleated ceaselessly. Their mothers tried to linger near them but they were continually harassed by the pack of dogs that brought up the rear of the flock. Heat burned from the mule's body as it plodded forward and I noticed the horse-flies tucked into the folds of its skin, sucking. I tried to scare them into flight but they were all too gorged and lazy to move and so I struck them dead with the butt end of the whip that had been given me and streams of shining blood ran down the animal's side.

So we went on, the dust covering us. My clothes were engrained with it and I was as filthy as the shepherds and like them I smelt of sheep. We were still going north with the ground rising; the evening sun pale over the vineyards and the vine leaves beginning to stir in a freshening wind. Further forward there were fruit trees, and beyond, high on the edge of a hillside, its houses crowded carelessly along a ridge, I saw the town of Callas with its Roman roofs the colour of flame in the dying daylight, and its lamps gleaming from open windows. It was a landscape more dream than real.

And the wind rose as we climbed and the sky grew darker, but in the streets of the town the noise of our shouts and the clanging of the bells brought everyone to us, and they stood in their bright doorways and offered up glasses of wine as we went by.

Then the rain began to fall in drops as big as medals and a man stood under the dry of a tree and held the mule while I ran forward with the umbrellas. And then the road went steeply out of the town and I followed the flock into a kind of sunken field that in the dark might have been an old quarry. A hurricane lamp was thrust into my hand and I held it while Jules swore and struggled with the buckles and the cold, wet straps that lashed the mule to the cart.

Right behind us was a stark concrete structure about four metres square, its iron door standing open. Into it we carried the food box, the wine, the cloaks and everything else we needed. A tarpaulin was tied over the cart; the sheep were settled and we placed hurdles across the entrance to our camp. Then one by one the shepherds squeezed into the shack, each of them cold to the bone but glad to be out of the rain at last.

There was no furniture inside our shelter; there was nothing but four walls, a roof and a concrete floor. Jules hung the hurricane lamps from a rope and slowly our bodies warmed. We folded the cloaks on the floor and sat on them and someone found the brandy, drank from the bottle and it was passed on from one man to the next.

In that sickly light we looked like a gang of ruffians, the last dregs of a defeated army, our faces unshaven and dirty, our clothes ragged, our bodies smelling. Behind us were the dogs, smelling also, like wet dogs always do, lying with their wicked eyes watching everything, waiting to devour the scraps we threw away, catching the morsels in mid-air, moving their heads suddenly out of statuesque stillness, their jaws snapping like gin-traps.

Against the wall leant Milou, not sitting like the rest of us. He bent forward every now and then to take something from the box, a knife in his hand. Of all of us he was the most unkempt. A short man with a face full of cunning, the stubble on his chin yellowed by nicotine. His thick fingers were yellow too and his nails were cracked and full of dirt, rough ended and ridged. The teeth that chewed his bread were broken and brown.

Milou was another hired man but only hired for the journey. He wore two jackets, both torn, the good parts of one meant to compensate for the bad parts of the other. On his feet were open-toed plastic sandals that he'd scavenged from the St Tropez rubbish dump. Milou had the appearance of an old jail-bird who had come along for the food and drink, especially the drink. I had often seen him sneaking wine from the bonbonne in the cart when the others were absent, winking at me in complicity. His favourite meal was broken bread thickly covered with sugar, swamped in red wine and then eaten with a spoon.

He studied all our faces in turn and shoved some food into his mouth. 'Look at us,' he said, 'squatting in this hut like the poorest of the poor, smelling like cess-pits and only our breath to keep us warm. Is this a life?'

Outside the rain and the wind continued to beat against the side of the hut and Milou sat now and began to make his dish of bread and wine and sugar. 'I have always been poor and never expect to be anything else,' he said, 'and the poor have always lived like I live, I suppose. They have a hard life and a hard death for the most part. And, if you pass me that bonbonne, friend Jules, I will tell you the story that tells us so.'

At this Jules shook his head and, without a smile, as if he had seen all man's folly and Milou's was the worst, he handed over the wine and the hired man uncorked the bonbonne and filled his bowl to the brim.

# *Pichounetta and The Sergeant of Arles*

Once upon a time a dark forest covered the mountain slopes that rise steeply along each side of the river Durance, and in a gloomy clearing in that forest lived a woodcutter and his younger sister, and her name was Pichounetta.

Both brother and sister were artless and untutored in the ways of the world, never having lived in it, but in their own simplicity they loved each other dearly and were content to live out their lives in solitude, doing no one any harm. They never married or even felt the call to do so, indeed only rarely did they descend to the banks of the Durance to sell their wood and buy the things they could neither make nor grow. Those people who lived in the hamlets and farms of the region likewise never entered the dark recesses of the forest where the brother and sister lived and were, to tell the truth, too frightened to do so. They purchased wood from the pair each winter, stacked it in the dry and minded their own business.

Such a way of life was by its very nature uneventful and in that remote and uncivilized part of Provence only death disrupted the even course of the years, and so it happened that the woodcutter died suddenly and much before his time. This cruel tragedy left Pichounetta in a state of dismay verging on madness. Without warning or preparation she had lost her only companion; the only person on earth who loved her. She was completely distraught and at first ran here and there like a wild thing. She had not seen the death of a human being before. She could not remember the death of her parents; she did not even remember having any. Always there had been her brother, strong and kind – now there was nothing. Pichounetta's grief was acute but gradually she came to her senses and her simple mind saw that something needed to be done, but what, she did not know.

Lower down the mountain on which Pichounetta lived there was a ruined farmhouse, built into the hillside and inhabited only by an old woman, the last survivor of her family. Often, at the beginning of winter the woodcutter had left kindling for the old woman and she, in return, had made cheeses for Pichounetta. It was towards this farmhouse that the girl eventually bent her steps. The woman was old and wise, she thought; she had seen death many times and would surely know what to do.

When the old woman had heard Pichounetta's tale she sucked on her toothless gums and smacked her lips of gristle together. She bade the girl sit by the fire and pulled her shawl about her shoulders. Pichounetta trembled in spite of the warmth. The old woman looked like a witch; her hair was grey with wood-smoke and her skin was soft and creased like ancient leather. Her nose was a hook and one eye was blind.

'Sit down, Pichoune,' said the old woman. 'There is nothing to fear. I know I am not good to look upon but then beauty is not always wise, nor is it always kind.'

Pichounetta did not answer but stared at the smoke rising from the grate. She was used only to the company of her brother and the telling of her story had exhausted her.

'Here is what you must do,' said the old woman, 'and it is what the poor of Provence have always done. You must return to your cabin and you must wash your brother's body so that it is clean. You will then dress him in his finest clothes, however tattered they may be. Then you must take his saw and his hammer and you must make a coffin, a box to bury him in. Can you do this, Pichoune?'

The girl raised her head from her contemplation of the fire and spoke proudly. 'My brother and I made everything we needed,' she said, 'I watched and helped him all the time. Of course I can make this box and I shall make it well.'

'Listen then,' continued the old woman. 'You will lay your brother in the coffin and under his head you will place a soft cushion, if you have one, if not, a folded sheepskin will do, or an old coat. Once your brother is resting in his box you will take resin from the trees and make the lid water-tight and you will nail it down so that not the slightest drop of water may enter.'

'Water,' said Pichounetta.

The old woman held up her hand for silence. 'You must take at least four copper coins, or two of silver. Wrap them in a purse and the purse you must nail firmly to the lid of the coffin. Next you will take your sled, the one that you use for dragging firewood down to the farms, and you will place the coffin upon it. Then you must pull your brother through the forest and across the stony fields until you reach the very banks of the great river. Can you do this and are you strong enough?'

'All my life I have worked with axe and spade,' said Pichounetta, 'and never have I failed.'

'Good,' said the old woman, 'for you will need all your strength, and when you reach the river you must take the coffin from the sled and you will float it out into the middle of the current and there you will pray, if you can, and say farewell to your brother for ever, for the water will bear him away to the holiest of resting places, the Aliscamps in the city of Arles.'

'City,' said the girl, 'and what is that?'

The old woman laughed at the girl's ignorance. 'Arles is a city,' she said, 'and a city is full of houses, hundreds, all close together in narrow streets. Arles has turrets and castles, palaces and churches with high walls all around. There are huge caves under the ground for keeping wheat and there is a stone bridge too, the bridge of Trinquetaille. I went there once when I was a girl, and the sight of it still shines in my good eye. And there, in Arles, is the Aliscamps, the largest burial ground in the world. Every Christian in Provence desires to be buried there, for if they are they will go directly to paradise and, Pichoune, if you wish for your brother to escape eternal torment, he who never went to mass or prayed in his life, then to the Aliscamps he must go.'

The old woman did not lie in anything she had said. Since time without counting the Aliscamps at Arles had been considered the holiest ground in the world. Legend said that the colonists from Massilia had always honoured the dead there and that the word 'Aliscamps' was but the Roman way of saying 'The Fields of Elysium', which was the name the Greeks gave to paradise.

Whether this legend was true or not it was certain that from the earliest years of the Christian era the rich and powerful of Provence had seen to it that they were laid to rest in that holy precinct, entombed in massively carved sarcophagi which had been arranged to form wide and delightful avenues, those avenues made shady by tall plane trees and fragrant by the sweet-smelling eucalyptus.

As the centuries passed more and more sarcophagi were carried to Arles and the graveyard began to spread over several miles in all directions. Before long, both for convenience and to save space, the tombs were raised up, one above another, to a height of five or six at least, and the Aliscamps became a veritable city of the dead, a necropolis with hundreds of its own streets and a score of its own churches.

The legends multiplied also and were told from generation to generation: St Trophime, the first bishop of Provence, was buried there; Roland and Oliver too, the knights of Charlemagne, had been borne to Arles on their shields, all the way from their last battle at Roncevalles. Small wonder was it then that the dead arrived at the Aliscamps from everywhere in Provence, for to be entombed in such illustrious company was to ensure your eternal rest whatever your previous sins might have been.

For those with the means to extend their will beyond the grave the last voyage to the Aliscamps presented no problem. Richly caparisoned barges would float both corpse and sarcophagus down the wide waters of the Rhône, and sombrely dressed mourners would accompany the deceased to his or her last resting place, while on the banks of the river the labouring peasants would cross themselves and watch in wonder.

But it was not only the rich who were desirous of gaining paradise. The poor too wished for that ultimate reward. Unfortunately for them they were not possessed of that golden power that forces others to perform our wishes even when we are no longer present. Yet, in spite of this disadvantage they managed to satisfy the yearning of their souls and discovered a way out of their difficulty, compelled by their very poverty to become ingenious. All those who lived within a day or two's march of the river Rhône, or any of its tributaries, were, after their deaths, placed by their relatives in water-tight coffins and launched upon the swiftly flowing waters and given into God's care.

It was not only God of course who looked after these wandering souls. Anyone who found a coffin caught up in branches or reeds, say, or stranded on a rock, was bound, both by his duty and religion, to free it and relaunch it into the current. Nailed to the lid of every coffin there was always a purse and heaven help the wretch who stole the few coins that had been placed within it. The devil, the common people said, would drag him straight to hell for those coins were to recompense the good people of Arles for the labour of taking coffins from the Rhône and carrying them, on their carts or on their backs, across the city to a decent burial in the unfashionable, but still holy, areas of the Aliscamps. It was this tradition, already ancient at the time of this story, that prompted the old woman to advise Pichounetta in the way she had. In her wisdom she knew it would comfort the girl if she thought that her brother's soul was going to sleep forever in the Elysian Fields.

'Do you have enough money?' asked the old woman at the end of her explanation, 'enough money to pay the fee of Aliscamps so that whoever takes your brother's coffin from the river at Arles will treat it with respect.'

Pichounetta rose from the fireside. 'I have enough money,' she said, 'and more than enough. My brother was a careful man and over the years we sold much wood. I will send the coins with him to see that he is well buried.' The girl paused and her face creased with worry. 'How do I know that the coffin will end its journey at Arles?' she asked. 'It may go on and drift until eternity, or fall into hell.'

The old woman laid a hand on the girl's arm. 'Do not think of it, Pichoune,' she said. 'At Arles the great river bends wide around the city and there is the bridge at Trinquetaille and ropes are tied from one pillar to the next, above the water, to catch the coffins. You may depend upon it that the people of Arles are always on watch, for they have much to gain from their vigilance.'

With this explanation Pichounetta was content and, leaving the old woman with a word of thanks, she took the dark, steep path through the forest and returned to the cabin where her brother's body lay. Wasting no time she set about making a sturdy coffin, choosing good straight planks from a stock of seasoned timber that her brother had always kept in store, both for his own use and for selling in the valleys.

When the box was finished she washed the body and dressed it with care, placing it, as gently as she could, into the coffin, a pillow beneath its head. Then she took the lid and, painting the edges with resin, she nailed it firmly into position. This accomplished she dragged the heavy burden outside and inched it onto the wooden sled that waited there, and, without taking time to rest or eat, she slipped the leather traces over her head and shoulders and began the long journey through the forest and down the mountain.

Pichounetta was a sturdy young woman and her muscles had been formed and tested by years of hard work. Her determination too was strong and she made such good speed that within four or five hours she came to the banks of the great Durance. There the peasants in the field stood to watch while Pichounetta pulled the sled across the white and rounded stones of the river's shore and with one final effort pushed the coffin into the water.

As soon as the current of the Durance felt the coffin it seized it and bore it away with an easy violence. In a moment the rough box was speeding over the white foam and before Pichounetta had time to say a prayer, or even wish her brother well, the coffin had disappeared around the nearest bend. It was in God's hands now.

With tears in her eyes Pichounetta turned and began to make her way back to the lonely cabin on the mountainside. The peasants still stood unmoving and watched until the young woman, and the empty sled, disappeared in the distance, passing eventually between the trees and into the wild darkness of the forest. When the peasants were sure that she had gone for good they crossed themselves and bent again to their endless tasks.

∞

Pichounetta took up the threads of her life immediately and as best she could. There was no great difficulty for her in accomplishing her daily work for she had always been capable of doing anything that her brother had done. Her hands were broad and strong, her mind direct and uncluttered. She could wield an axe, slaughter a goat and plant and grow vegetables. She had chickens and a few sheep; she had all she needed except company and love.

It was this loneliness that preyed on her and from the very first day she began to talk to her brother as if he were still alive. Soon she became convinced that he was entering her conversation, aiding her to survive the solitude. By the end of the second week of her bereavement his presence had become real to Pichounetta. She could see his face and thought she could touch his hand.

He smiled; he seemed happy and content and this fact served to ease the pain in the girl's heart. Each night he came to her and, standing at the foot of the bed, he recounted his progress on the long journey to Arles.

All along the Durance he had gone, he said, and then out onto the waters of the Rhône, and even though his coffin had been stranded on the banks from time to time, always had there been some good person to free him and set him on his way. What was more, never had anyone tampered with the money in the purse which his sister had nailed to the coffin lid. Before long he would be at Arles and someone would take him from the river and bury him in the Aliscamps. There he would find the gates of paradise and, beyond them, eternal peace.

Pichounetta was, in her ignorance, borne up by the visits of this apparition and the tales it told. To her it was a good thing and she did not bother to ask herself whether or not the spectre was a dangerous temptation or simply the product of her own imagination. In any event such sophistication was far beyond the grasp of her mind and not something she could have thought of on her own. So it was that when one night the ghost appeared in grief, wringing its hands and silently weeping, not for one moment did Pichounetta question the truth of what she heard.

'Oh save me, Pichoune,' said the ghost. 'I have been sorely betrayed. He who found me on the river at Arles was an evil man. He came upon me in the middle of the night and making sure that no one saw him at his dreadful work he stole the money from the purse and then pushed my coffin through the arches of the bridge. And now the current of the Rhône has brought me down to rot in the Camargue and never shall I reach the Aliscamps but rather will I have a watery grave until the last day of time.'

Pichounetta sat upright in her bed and stared. Never, in life, had she seen her brother so distressed. 'Oh mercy,' she wailed, 'what can I do? I have never left this forest. I know nothing. How could I help you?'

'I have been robbed of my blessed rest and the glory of the Aliscamps,' said the apparition. 'I will not lie easy until you have revenged me. You must denounce this man. His sin is great and he deserves to die and his soul made to wander like mine. I must have revenge!' And with a low moaning sound and more wringing of the hands the brother disappeared.

At the very first light of day Pichounetta leapt from her bed, dressed hastily and went, as quickly as she could, to the ruined farm where the wise old woman lived. There was no one else to whom the girl could turn for advice; certainly her own experience would not be enough to counsel her.

The old woman listened to Pichounetta's story in silence but as soon as it was concluded she worked her lips over her gums and began to speak.

'It is probably true,' said the old woman, 'that you brother has been robbed of his deserved rest, and if that is so the villain who committed the crime should be punished in this world as well as in the next – but who is there to accomplish this task? I am too old and lack the strength. You are too innocent and lack the knowledge. The world is a wicked place, Pichoune, and full of wicked men. It is a great distance from here to Arles and I fear that you would have your throat cut before you got there. I counsel you to live with the sorrow of these tidings, Pichoune, for there is nothing to be done but endure all things until the day of your own death.'

Very slowly, and with her head bowed, Pichounetta left the old woman's house and returned to her cabin, more than determined to follow the advice that had been given her; but the ghost was equally determined and would not let her rest. Later that same night it reappeared and made such lamentations that the poor Pichounetta was driven frantic with guilt and fear.

'Spare me, brother,' she cried at last. 'How can I go so far, I who have never left the forest. How would I travel?'

At this question the ghost ceased its wailings and laid its head on one side, smiling. 'Why sister,' it said, 'you will travel as I travelled, what could be more simple. You will make yourself a coffin like the one you made for me, only this time with a lid that you may hold in place from the inside. Lay your box on the waters of the Durance and let it float until you reach a stone bridge. That is the city of Arles.'

'My brother,' said the girl, 'I am too simple for this task, and what would I do at Arles?'

'When you are at the bridge,' answered the ghost, 'you will go onto the land. You will place a few stones in the coffin to give it weight and you will hide and watch. In the night I will send you the robber and you will see him steal the purse. As soon as it is safe you will go to the town and make all this known to those in authority. That very day they will seize the villain and send men to search for my body in the marshes so they may bring it to the Aliscamps. Then shall I be satisfied, then will I find rest.'

The moment she had heard all this Pichounetta scrambled to her knees on the bed and held out her hands to the shape that stood before her. 'Brother,' she said, 'if all this is to happen as you say then I am no longer afraid. Ignorant though I am I will do anything to see you at rest in the Aliscamps.'

'You are truly my sister,' answered the ghost and it smiled again, more mysteriously this time, nodding too as if well pleased. A moment later it had disappeared and Pichounetta sat on the edge of her bed and wondered and wondered until it was dawn.

As soon as that dawn came and the first rays of sunlight spilled over the mountain tops Pichounetta broke from her reverie and began her work. She took out her brother's tools, selected the best planks that remained to her and by the end of the morning she had finished a coffin that was much better constructed even than the previous one had been. Inside it was room for a pillow and a blanket and enough provisions to keep the girl alive for a week or two.

When all was ready Pichounetta took the pouch that contained her brother's fortune, dressed herself in her warmest clothes and loaded her coffin onto the sled. Then, with never a backward look at the only home she had ever known, she drew the traces round her shoulders and once more set out in the direction of the Durance. Once arrived at the river Pichounetta dragged the coffin into the shallows and got inside it, lying down and sliding the lid across until it slotted neatly into the deep grooves she had made, blotting out all sight of the bright blue sky. The peasants, still labouring in the nearby fields, shook their heads, knelt and prayed and then went back to their work, convinced they had seen a miracle.

Pichounetta's craft immediately bobbed into the middle of the current and from there was carried forward at speed. Once or twice in the days that followed the coffin ran up against a sunken tree or a shifting sand-bank, but nearly always there was a Christian soul to come by and push the coffin back into the main stream again. And if there wasn't Pichounetta would wait until nightfall and free herself of whatever entanglement had impeded her progress. Also at night, when she felt secure, Pichounetta would push the lid back from her face and watch the stars rushing by overhead and listen to the surge of the waters beneath her. She had no idea where she was at any given time or in which direction she was going. All she knew was that there would be a bridge at Arles and there she would stop and creep to the river bank to watch for the villain who had betrayed his trust.

Pichounetta's journey was far briefer than her brother's had been. Much rain had fallen in the mountains and the waters of the Rhône were flowing fast and high. And so one night when the moon was on the wane, Pichounetta, who had been lulled into a long sleep by the noise and movement of the currents, was woken by the shock of her coffin striking a massive stone pillar. She had arrived at the bridge of Trinquetaille.

Round in a large eddy spun the coffin, scraping along the ropes that had been tied from arch to arch, and gradually nudging its way to the riverside where at last it grated to a halt on the gravel of the wide shore, for here the Rhône swung in a bend at the wall of the city and formed part of its defences.

As soon as she heard the noise of the gravel Pichounetta remembered her instructions and, first making sure that it was indeed the middle of the night, she lifted the cover of her coffin and slipped into the open. Quickly she found three large stones and put them in her place. That done she took hold of the heavy lid and set it firmly back in its grooves, afterwards creeping away, unseen, into the bushes that grew thickly at that point, right down to the water's edge. There she crouched and hid herself – for that was what the ghost had told her to do.

She did not have long to wait. As the first finger of light touched the furthest corner of the eastern hemisphere Pichounetta heard footsteps on the sloping strand above her. Turning her head, but not rising to her feet, she saw, against the skyline, a small hovel and from it had emerged the shape of a man. He had seen the coffin and was making his way, as silently as he could, down a narrow, winding path.

The man advanced and passed within a yard or two of where Pichounetta was concealed. Without hesitation he strode into the water, caught hold of the coffin with one hand and took the money from the purse with the other.

Without bothering to count the coins he thrust them into his jerkin and then waded further into the river, pulling what he thought to be a corpse behind him.

'By the devil,' Pichounetta heard the man swear, 'this is a mighty carcass by the weight of it. Best send it down to the marshes to rot.' And as he spoke the man eased the coffin under the restraining ropes and pushed it through the nearest archway of the bridge. There it was taken by the current and soon disappeared into the middle of the Rhône, well on its way to the empty wildernesses of the Camargue.

Pichounetta remained crouched amid the undergrowth, holding her breath in fear. The daylight was growing stronger now and the robber was anxious to get himself out of sight. Looking this way and that, to make certain he had not been observed in his evil work, he went ashore and scrambled back up the path to the top of the bank where he immediately disappeared into his cabin.

As soon as she dared Pichounetta crept from her hiding place and climbed noiselessly past the robber's hut and onto the short stretch of road that joined the bridge of Trinquetaille to the city of Arles. Never had the girl seen such a sight – a broad and paved highway leading to massive iron-bound gates which were themselves set in a towering wall of stone that bristled with battlements. So that was a city!

Pichounetta shivered in the early morning chill, but in spite of her fears she went forward bravely and in a very few minutes came to the eastern gate of the town just as it was opened for the day. Slowly the two huge portals swung back on their enormous hinges, and there, under the high arch, stood two men of the watch, leaning on their pikes. By their side, and in command of them, was the magnificent figure of the Sergeant of the gates of Arles.

Pichounetta faltered and then came to a halt. She did not know what to do; the two guards looked so fierce to her eyes, the Sergeant so splendid. He wore a gilded helmet on his head, decorated with a fine red plume. His breastplate was burnished and his black cloak was lined with a brilliant satin of crimson. The naked sword he held in his hand shimmered in the low sun of early morning. His eyes glinted with the hardness of rock and his fine moustache curled upwards with arrogance. When this officer saw Pichounetta revealed by the opening of the gates he turned to his two companions and smirked. Those same gates had shown him many a strange sight on many a morning but never had he seen anything so unkempt.

The Sergeant of the gate smirked again and strutted forward, his plume nodding as he walked. Pichounetta fell back a step but, remembering her brother's commands, she did not run away although she wanted to. A yard from the girl the Sergeant came to a stop and looked down at her. He smiled a smile of irony, a smile that was as near to pity as he ever got – a pity that other creatures were not as beautiful as he. 'Damnation,' he whispered to himself, 'she looks like a beast of burden, all misshapen by toil and burnt black by the sun and the wind.'

It was true of course. Pichounetta was ugly and she had no idea how she looked to people from the great world. Like an animal of the forest in which up until then she had spent all her days, she knew only that she was alive. Her body and its appearance was not something she was conscious of. Now suddenly, on seeing this splendid Sergeant, the poor peasant girl came to know that she was just as savage and uncouth as the officer thought she was.

What the Sergeant saw was not a human being at all, in his terms, but a barbarian. Pichounetta was clothed in rags which a beggar would disdain. Her face was flat, like a gypsy's and deeply lined. Her black hair had never been brushed or washed and fell in greasy ropes to her shoulders. Those shoulders were square and strong but bent like an old woman's from years of toil. Her thighs and calves were thick and muscled from dragging heavy loads through the forest and the knuckles of her fingers were swollen from knocks and cuts. To the Sergeant she was beyond redemption and below consideration, and by this judgement was her fate decided.

'And what do you want here?' asked the Sergeant and the sun shone from the centre of his breastplate and dazzled Pichounetta until she could not see. She droppped her gaze and stared at the dust between her feet.

'My brother's corpse has been robbed of the fee of Aliscamps,' she mumbled, 'and his soul has been left to wander across the Camargue. His ghost came to me and told me what to do . . . and so I too floated here in a coffin, more miles than I can tell, until I reached this bridge and with my own eyes I have seen the robber.' Pichounetta half turned and pointed. 'He lives in that cabin by the bank, there, under the great bridge almost. My brother's spirit cries for revenge and proper burial. He bade me come to you because you are a great man of the law and will know what to do. You can help me find my brother and take him to the Aliscamps . . . is that not so?'

The Sergeant took one more step forward and placed his hand on Pichounetta's elbow and guided her a little further from the city gate, out of earshot of the two guards who still leant on their pikes and idly watched the scene before them. Pichounetta's simple accusation had taken the Sergeant by surprise. He was only too well aware of the practice the girl had spoken of, and he knew the robber involved. In fact for many years he'd shared the villain's plunder and in return for half the proceeds he had ignored the thefts instead of exercising his legal powers and arresting the man.

There were even further complications. Of late the robber had refused to pay the Sergeant his proper share and, what was worse, had threatened to tell all if ever the Sergeant were to denounce him. For months now the officer of the law had felt unsafe. Not only that but he was much poorer than he had been. The money he had once received from the robber had furnished the best of his pleasures; evenings of drunkenness with his companions and careless nights with the ladies of the town.

The Sergeant glanced over his shoulder. The two guards had lost interest in Pichounetta and were now deep in conversation with each other. No one yet stirred on the road from the city and the early morning mist still hung low over the Rhône and the far side of the bridge of Trinquetaille was not yet visible. The Sergeant drew a deep breath and a plan formed in his mind. This animal from the hills would provide him with a way out of his dilemma. He moved his hand from Pichounetta's elbow and placed his arm around her hard shoulders. She leant wearily against him and felt protected for the first time since her brother had died. The Sergeant spoke to her, his voice newly kind.

'My dear child,' he said, 'you have made a serious accusation and though I do not doubt your word, others will. We must take this villain in flagrante delicto, as the law says, and we must have money. Do you have money?'

Pichounetta nodded, but she did not look up, too confused by this flood of words she hardly understood.

The Sergeant, satisfied, beamed down at the top of Pichounetta's head. 'What the law requires,' he continued, 'is indisputable proof. I have to see the robbery happen so that I may bear witness.'

'But,' interrupted Pichounetta, completely bewildered, 'the man has already robbed my brother and sent his coffin into the marshes . . . and me too he has robbed and sent an empty coffin after my brother's. How can you see these things? Will the man go unpunished and my brother never be buried in the Aliscamps?'

'This villain will not go unpunished,' said the Sergeant, and by way of comfort he clasped Pichounetta to him in the embrace of his arm. 'I shall see to it. What is more I shall see that you find your brother again, believe me. But you will have to aid me, my child. This is what you must do . . . just a mile or so above the villain's cabin, on the very edge of the river, you will find a little wood and you will wait for me there, today. I will give you my own provisions, a flask of wine too. Do not stir and do not talk to anyone. No one can be trusted in this world, my child, no one. As soon as it is dark I will send a servant to you and he will bring with him an empty coffin and on the lid will be a purse containing the fee of Aliscamps . . . and you will do what you did before. You will float in the coffin as far as the bridge and while you do I shall be hidden nearby, watching and waiting and ready to see everything. As soon as you hear the robber lay his hand upon the purse you will speak to him, as from the grave, and curse him for what he does. Then when he is amazed and terrified I will seize him and drag him before the Archbishop of Arles himself. I promise you he will be sorely punished – twenty years in the galleys, I'll be bound.'

Pichounetta moved her head. 'And my brother?' she asked.

'Yes,' said the Sergeant, 'he will not be too far away in the marshes and we will begin the search for him just as soon as we have taken the robber . . . but there is another thing, my child, though it hurts me to ask it . . . we do need money. You see there is the fee for me to place in the purse, and then I shall have to buy a coffin and also reward my servant for his work and for his secrecy, and at the trial of the robber there will be a lawyer and a clerk to pay, and afterwards, to search for your brother, we must hire a boat to sail the waterways and lakes of the Camargue . . . do you understand? The law is a costly diversion and revenge has always been a luxury.'

Pichounetta reached inside her ragged bodice and took out the large pouch which contained her brother's savings. 'I do not know,' she said, 'is this enough?'

The Sergeant took the pouch and opened the neck of it. Silver shone in the interior and his mouth moistened with greed; here was sufficient money for a year of sport. 'There is more, than I need, my child,' he said, 'enough to pay for all I have mentioned and some left at the end of things to send you home.'

At last Pichounetta looked up at the Sergeant and smiled and that smile came close to warming the man's heart but even a smile of such simplicity and beauty could not accomplish that. 'Thank you, my lord,' she said. 'I shall do as you command.'

With this the Sergeant took his arm from the girl's shoulder and hiding the pouch of silver beneath his cloak he strode quickly to the gatehouse, took up the basket of provisions he had brought with him for the day and, returning to where Pichounetta waited, he thrust it into her hands.

'Now go,' he said, 'and stay silent and secret all day. Look for my servant when night falls and do exactly as he says. Remember I will be waiting at the bridge, ready to protect you.'

Pichounetta did not hesitate but clutching the basket with both hands she turned and made her way along the river bank. The Sergeant stood and watched her go and as he did one of his guards, trailing his pike behind him, approached his officer and laughed aloud.

'I never saw such an ugly woman,' he said, 'and were you possessed by the devil to give your bread and wine to such a sorry vagabond? I never knew you strong on charity. Why on earth did you do such a thing?'

The Sergeant continued watching until Pichounetta had disappeared into the undergrowth that grew along the river bank, then he smiled at his colleague. 'Because,' he said, clutching the bag of silver beneath his cloak, 'it is written that if you cast your bread upon the waters it will be returned a hundredfold,' and with that he walked away.

The guard followed him, puzzled. He had never known the Sergeant quote the bible before, if that were the bible he had quoted, not in all the years they had kept the gate together. The guard shrugged, the world was a strange place, sure enough, and made stranger by the people in it.

❧

All day Pichounetta concealed herself in the deepest part of the thicket where the Sergeant had sent her. She ate the provisions from the basket and counted her blessings, happy because the very first person she had met that day had been in authority and had treated her with kindness, promising to help her bring the robber to justice. And what a fine person the Sergeant was; how handsome, how bright his armour, how splendid his cloak. Tonight would see the robber in irons and her brother's soul placated. And afterwards the Sergeant would search for her brother's coffin and find it too. All would work out as planned and when it was done she would take what was left of her money and journey home. It was perfect and the world was not as bad a place as the old woman had said.

Comforted by these thoughts and the Sergeant's provisions the girl lay, all afternoon, between sleeping and waking, her mind whirling with the sights she had seen; a bridge and a city; a fine officer and soldiers in uniform; and such wine too. Never had she tasted anything so delicate; strong as a magic potion it had warmed her body through and through, from top to toe, making her feel that she might sleep for days on end – but such a thing was not to be. Pichounetta was roughly woken from her dreams by the sound of a handcart being pushed along a stony track. The girl opened her eyes and shuddered. All around her it was dark and cold.

Quickly she crept to the edge of the trees and, in the starlight, she made out the figure of the servant. 'I am here,' she called. 'I am here.'

The rattling of the handcart stopped and a rough voice said; 'Are you the one who waits for a coffin?'

'I am,' said Pichounetta, 'was it sent by your master?'

'It was,' said the servant, 'if by my master you mean the Sergeant who guards the gates by day and lays siege to women by night, though who else would be sending you a box at this time I cannot fathom.'

At these remarks, though she did not fully understand them, Pichounetta emerged from her hiding place and approached the handcart. Resting on it was a well-made coffin. The girl looked at the servant; his expression was mean and his eyes were shifty.

'Let us do what we have to do,' said Pichounetta, and she seized the coffin, set it on her shoulders and carried it easily to the water's edge which was only a few yards distant. There she set it down and, after removing the lid, she clambered in. The servant had followed behind, amazed at the girl's physical strength and determination. He groped for the lid, found it and slid it into position, shutting out the sight of Pichounetta's face.

'Are you ready, girl?' he said, his voice harsh.

'I am ready,' answered Pichounetta and the water lapped at the foot of the coffin.

The servant hesitated for a moment and shook his head. He did not always understand the commands of his master but he was nevertheless obliged to obey him: there was no living else. The servant sighed loudly and took from beneath his cloak a hammer and a handful of long nails. Quickly he placed the point of the first nail on the lid and hammered it home. Then another.

'Why do you nail the lid?' asked Pichounetta, her words trembling with fear.

The servant placed another nail and began to strike it. 'Fear not, woman,' he said. 'My master ordered it and you may trust him. He will release you at the bridge, fear not.'

'But,' insisted Pichounetta, 'how will I breathe if you nail down the lid so tightly?'

'Be quiet, woman,' said the servant, 'or your plan will be discovered by the robber and everything we have done will be for naught. You go but a little way and stay but a little time. My master will release you. There is air enough and time enough, I promise you.'

Satisfied with this explanation Pichounetta said not another word and the servant continued with his hammering until with his last nail he affixed a purse to the coffin and then dragged it into the deeper waters of the river Rhône.

'Is all well, woman?' he asked and when he heard the muffled voice of Pichounetta answer that it was the servant crossed himself and let the coffin go. 'May God protect you, little peasant,' he said and he turned away and waded to the shore.

In the dark gloom of the bridge of Trinquetaille the Sergeant stood, wrapped in a black cloak, not a glimmer of starlight reflecting from his breastplate. For an hour he waited until at last he saw the coffin turning slowly in the Rhône's current. To begin with it struck against an archway not far from where he was hiding behind a stone pillar and up to his knees in the river, but then, at the urging of the current, it drifted along the ropes towards the bank on which the robber's cabin was built. The Sergeant drew his dagger. It would not be long now.

Nor was it. At the darkest part of the night the robber came. His footsteps sounded on the gravel path and he strode directly into the water until it reached his very neck. He stretched out a hand for the coffin, caught hold of it and stumbled back into the shallows, stopping only when the swirling tide had fallen to his waist. Then he reached out for the purse and tore it free of its nail.

'Praise be,' he whispered, 'this purse feels big and heavy – there'll be silver and gold here. It is a good night's work I have done.'

Suddenly the voice of Pichounetta came from within the coffin. It was muffled and weak but it was loud enough to be heard quite clearly.

'A good night's work,' she said, 'then you shall burn in hell for it. Where is my brother? Answer me that. Where is he buried? Why does he weep and wail instead of lying in the holiest ground on earth? You evil man. All the ghosts of the night shall haunt you now until you die of terror.'

On hearing these words the robber screamed, let drop the purse and fell backwards into the water, clutching at his heart where it thumped in his chest. He gasped for breath, only just managing to keep his head above the surface of the water. 'Mercy, mercy,' he cried.

'There'll be no mercy for you,' said the voice from the coffin and at that the robber whimpered and made a feeble attempt to crawl to the shore.

The Sergeant, who had been listening all this time, now came into the open and went to where the robber was lying near the edge of the river. The robber's eyes flickered in recognition. 'Sergeant,' he said, 'help me.'

The Sergeant laughed. 'Rob me of my share of the fee of Aliscamps, would you? Threaten to tell the Archbishop, would you? You'll get no help from me, you dog.'

'There's money,' gasped the robber, 'it lies beneath my hearth-stone. Take it, only save me.'

'I'll save you from yourself, that's all,' rejoined the Sergeant. I'll send you where you've sent so many others.' And he raised a foot and pushed the robber's face under the surface of the water and held it there. When the man was dead he released the body and watched it float away; a large black shape, half-submerged, it slipped beneath the coffin ropes and on towards the marshes of the Camargue – carrion for sea-birds and water-rats.

'So perish,' said the Sergeant and he replaced his dagger in the sheath at his belt, rejoicing in his new-found security. And there was something else too. He had only to search the villain's hovel and he would discover a substantial hoard of money.

Hastening in his greed the Sergeant began to move away but as he made to go there came a tiny voice from within the coffin which was now drifting back into the current.

'Oh, Sergeant,' called Pichounetta, 'release me now as you promised and help me find my brother's body. Oh hurry, I can hardly breathe. Oh let me feel the good air upon my face.'

The Sergeant cursed. In his excitement at the thought of the robber's wealth he had completely forgotten about the ugly peasant girl. Here was another mischief. She must for certain have heard the exchange between himself and his accomplice. Now she would know what the robber had known and, being as simple as the morning, she was likely to blurt out the precious information at any time. Once again the Sergeant saw himself in jeopardy.

'Oh, Sergeant,' came the voice, insistent, but weaker than before, 'please help me.'

The Sergeant cursed again. He went towards the coffin and seized it. 'I know where your brother is,' he said, 'and I shall send you to him. In but a little while you'll be together and never shall you trouble me.' And with these heartless words the Sergeant thrust the coffin under the ropes and out into the main current of the Rhône where in no time at all it disappeared into the wide night.

Without a backward glance the Sergeant returned to the shore and climbed the bank to the robber's cabin. There, under the hearth-stone, just as the villain had said, he discovered a mound of treasure – so much he could hardly carry it away. Thanks to Pichounetta the Sergeant had become very rich, very rich indeed.

∞

To celebrate his good fortune the Sergeant went that same night to his favourite haunt, a noisy tavern near the eastern gate of Arles. There he was in the highest spirits and bought pitchers of wine for all his friends and they slapped him on the back and drank his health, telling him what a good and generous fellow he was. A beautiful woman too ran her fingers through his hair and kissed him full on the mouth and told him that he was the handsomest man in Provence.

It also happened, by chance, that among his drinking companions that night was one of the guards who had been on duty with him at dawn. This man came and sat next to the Sergeant, spilling wine from his cup as he lowered his body onto a bench. He grinned stupidly at his superior and spoke loudly to make himself heard above the great noise of talking and singing.

'And weren't you the soul of kindness today, master?' he began. 'Do you know, friends, our brave Sergeant gave all his food away this morning, and his wine, for nothing mark you, for nothing . . . and to the ugliest, most stunted peasant woman you have ever seen. I tell you she was ill-favoured enough to make the milk curdle in the goats and all the wells of Arles run dry.'

Many laughed at this jest but the Sergeant's face grew dark and angry. He did not enjoy being ridiculed. He half rose as if to attack the guard but the beautiful woman pulled him back into his place and put her arms around his neck.

'You,' she said, kissing him again, this time on the hand, 'you, giving your food to a peasant woman, for nothing in return. Is this a side to the Sergeant we have never seen before – doing good by stealth and blushing to find it famous.'

'I could not help myself,' stuttered the Sergeant. 'Never have I seen anything so ugly, so like a wild animal. She was starving, you see. Heaven knows where she came from, she'd never even seen a city before.'

'Or a man like you,' said the beautiful woman, 'I'll be bound.'

'I told her to go back to her home,' continued the Sergeant, beginning to believe his own story. 'I told her that the city is no place for the innocent. I told her that here she would be enslaved, or worse. You know. I bade her go and gave her food, yes, and some money, so she could. I never saw anyone more ignorant of the world than she.'

'Well,' said the beautiful woman, 'you have done a praiseworthy act. The world is certainly not meant for the ignorant or the innocent. By the time they have discovered what kind of a place it is they have wandered into it is generally too late for them to profit from the knowledge they have gained.'

With this sentiment all the revellers within earshot agreed, and they laughed and shouted and raised their tankards and drank another toast to the Sergeant of the gates, praising him for his kindness and wisdom, and he smiled and accepted their compliments, lifting his cup as high as the rest and drinking to his own health until, at the end, there was no wine remaining in the whole tavern.

# LE CHÂTEAU DE FAVAS

There was little sleep for anyone that night. We were on our feet by three and on the road by four, glad to be moving so that we might walk the cold out of our bones.

The clouds were lying thick around us to begin with, rolling slowly across the hillsides to obscure our path. Even the dawn was reluctant to rise and when it came its light was gloomy and without warmth. Bringing up the rear I could see only a small part of the flock and, from time to time, one or two of the shepherds as they crossed a ridge and stood against the greyness of everything, magnified by the mist, looking like giants in their cloaks, their umbrellas open, big and black on their shoulders.

The morning seemed destined never to end and I became dispirited. Had a passing motorist offered to return me to Grimaud at that moment I would have gone with him like a shot, leaving the mule tied to the nearest branch – but apart from my companions and me not a soul moved on those wintry uplands. I consoled myself by halting frequently to rest, using the time to replace the pads of soggy cardboard and cloth with which I had attempted to mend the holes in my shoes. I was hobbling badly now and stealing rides on the cart whenever I thought I was unobserved.

'Where do we stop today?' I asked Joseph when he loomed close to me once. 'Bar-je-moun,' he answered and would say no more. We were following the contour of a huge hillside that climbed, under a covering of forest, to a height of two and a half thousand feet. Our road had been cut into the slope and although it kept level it wound backwards and forwards as if it hated the idea of advancing. Nor did the mist stir but kept everything cold, until suddenly, when hours had passed, the clouds soared away and there was the sun and a blue sky and the land began to steam and our clothes too.

To the right the ground dropped steeply while above us it was thickly wooded. On the far side of a broad valley was Bargemon, looking near enough to touch, but our road went the furthest way to its destination and it was gone seven that morning before I led the mule into the town square, which was empty save for an old man who stood with his arms behind his back to watch us pass.

In the middle of the square grow two huge plane trees and they shade a fountain that stands beneath, embracing it tenderly with their branches. There is a café here also and the chairs and tables were in the street when I arrived and must have been there all night. My coffee and cognac were waiting and as I drank Joseph appeared at the door of a grocer's shop, carrying a pot of jam. He slipped a bar of chocolate into his pocket as he walked by me.

'When do we stop?' I asked.

Joseph turned and tucking the end of his staff into his armpit he leant on it. He looked as fresh as a man who had spent the night in a four-poster. 'Only another couple of hours,' he said. 'Last night a gîte, today a château.' Then he smiled and told me his precious secret. 'But we won't be moving on for two whole days. Just imagine, two whole days.'

I never did see the Château of Favas and even now I am not sure that such a place exists. But there was a river, the Nartuby, and wide fields with good grass and rounded hills on all sides. So we unloaded the cart and spread our belongings under an oak tree where other shepherds must have rested for I could see that large stones, much blackened by smoke, had been set together to form a fireplace.

I managed to stay awake until Leonce had made a soup of water, vermicelli, butter and salt and pepper. The moment I had swallowed it I crawled under the cart and fell into the deepest of sleeps, not waking until five that evening, brought back to consciousness by the sound of a car door slamming. Dragging my cloak with me I came out into the open on my hands and knees in time to see a woman opening the boot of a small car.

The woman was Huguette Fresia, Marius's wife. She was on her way to the tiny hamlet of Argens where Marius owned a small stone-built house. She was to prepare it for him, seeing to it that there was a stock of food in the cupboards and clean sheets on the bed. High above Argens, on the top pastures at about six thousand feet, Marius also owned a shack and it was there, completely isolated, that he would spend the summer months.

Huguette glanced at me as I came, dishevelled and dirty from beneath the cart. She shook her head in disbelief. ''Garde-moi ça!' she said. 'You look worse than Milou. What would Bonne Maman Renoult say if we sent you home like that?'

It was like a brand new experience seeing a woman again. Her body looked so neat and clean and well-defined. She had scrubbed herself shiny and she smelt of soap. Her movements were quick and determined, as if she had thought of every gesture years before doing it. She unloaded a big jar of soup from the car and then a box full of provisions. It seemed so long since I had eaten a proper meal that my mouth watered at the very prospect.

Except for one or two who were absent, watching the flock as it grazed, all the shepherds lay in the shade of the tree, heads propped on arms as they stared at the woman now kneeling at the fire, her hands busy. There was going to be the soup, oeufs Provençaux, some meat, salad, and then 'les pains perdus'.

The smells of the cooking grew stronger. A vermouth was poured, then the wine. As I ate so the despair of the night and morning faded and I remembered with pleasure that there was to be no walking that night. We cleaned our plates with bread and Huguette shook the frying pan and sprinkled sugar into it.

Milou licked his chops like some old wolf and drank his wine. 'Les pains perdus,' he said, 'ever since I was a child that's been my favourite . . . my poor mother used to cook 'em.'

Huguette studied Milou for a moment. 'Poor mother is right,' she said after a while. 'I daresay you made her suffer enough and sent her to an early grave. But then you men are all the same.'

'It is the truth and I wouldn't attempt to deny it,' said Milou, holding out his plate for a second helping and getting it before I'd even had my first. 'But then again, if women weren't so foolish they would not be so easily hoodwinked. I told the story of Pichounetta last night . . . now there was one who was too trusting.'

'Pichounetta is a good story,' said Huguette, dipping a slice of stale bread into the mixture and then dropping it into the pan, 'and it shows how wickedness will always take advantage of innocence. But it was not Pichounetta's fault that she died the way she did . . . she was poor and ignorant . . . she knew nothing of the world – that is all. Yet even those women who should know better, women born into position and knowledge, even they are betrayed by men, and sometimes by those men who are nearest to them in love and should protect them . . . and if you wish I can tell you the story that tells us so. So listen, Milou, for once. Do you know, you who think yourself so wise, do you know how the ruins of the castle of Grimaud came to be ruins?'

Milou shook his head and the woman, her work finished, leaned back against the food box and began her story. 'Well then,' she said, 'I shall tell you, and for the benefit of this boy here I shall tell the tale in French.'

And as the sun had gone behind the hills, we put more wood upon our fire and pulled our cloaks around our shoulders for the evening was turning cold at last. When we were settled Huguette began her story and the first sentences were indeed in French but it was not long before she slipped back into the Provençal and I could only guess at what she said.

# The Ruins of Grimaud

*T*he town of Grimaud is situated on the southern edge of the massif of Les Maures. No further than four or five miles from the sea its houses crowd together on the slopes of a steep hill and command fine views over the surrounding countryside. On the summit of the hill stand the ruins of a tall tower and beside it the ruins of a smaller one, their stones blackened by flame and darkened by blood – they are all that is left of what was once the most magnificent castle in Provence.

Below the town, a small and sleepy place no larger than a village, there spreads a wide and fertile plain where vines and fruit trees grow and where the shepherds from the mountains graze their flocks in winter. Even today it is a beautiful corner of the world; indolent and full of the fragrance of pine and eucalyptus.

Many centuries ago this plain lay deep under the sea and the salt waves used to break against the very walls of Grimaud, then a much larger settlement and thought to be impregnable. In those far off days merchant ships would anchor as close to the town as possible, seeking the protection of its castle; and so they needed to, for although the Caliph, Abd al-Rhaman, had been made to abandon his fortress of Fraxinetta, the coast was still open to attack and often the Saracens would cross the Mediterranean, from Spain and Barbary, on the look out for plunder and slaves.

Sometimes, though, they came to buy and barter, bringing with them silks and spices and bright dyes from the East and, just as long as there were never too many war-galleys in sight at once, the inhabitants of Les Maures were as happy to trade with a Muslim unbeliever as with any Christian alive, especially if it were to their advantage.

On one such occasion a fleet of three large galleys, their oars rising and falling in unison, rowed into the Bay of Grimaud and hove to. A trumpet of parley sounded out from the leading ship. A small boat was lowered and began to make its way to the shore, and there, on the quayside of stone, a herald landed without fear or hesitation. He was tall this Saracen, with fine and noble features that told of an aristocratic birth. He was clad in the most sumptuous of Arabian caftans and on his head was a high turban encrusted with jewels. His belt too was studded with rubies and, as befitted a messenger, he carried no scimitar or sword.

The moment he stood on land the herald begged the first people he saw to conduct him to their master and, as he came alone and in peace, they immediately conveyed him along the steep, cobbled streets, through some fortified gates and finally into the castle itself.

In the great hall the herald was brought before the lord of Grimaud, the Baron Cadarache, his courtiers and his daughter. Bowing low he requested that his master, the Prince Taric, third son of the Alcayde of Seville, might be permitted to land with a score or so of his men. In this way they could fill their barrels with fresh water and afterwards, if the Baron agreed, come to the courtyard of the castle and trade with whomsoever might choose to do so.

The Baron, intrigued by the gorgeousness of the herald's robe and the dignity of his bearing, replied that Prince Taric might come ashore with twenty of his followers and twenty others could land also to see to the reprovisioning of the ships. But no more. He regretted that he was obliged to be so niggardly in his hospitality but, he pointed out, the territory of Les Maures had only recently been won back from the Saracens of Abd al-Rhaman and as the castle of Grimaud was the key to all the province, he, the Baron, could not allow it to be captured.

At this the herald smiled and said that the Prince came with but three galleys and only to trade. He knew that he was not strong enough to take such a well-defended town. All the Saracens of Spain, and Africa too, knew that Grimaud could be reduced by nothing less than a great fleet of ships and a great army of men.

The Baron Cadarache was flattered at this recognition of his power and he smiled and commanded that the Saracen be given a golden chain for his master. The herald received the gift and, as proudly as before, he strode from the hall, returning directly to the jetty where his retainers waited for him, hemmed around by a mob of peasants who had never in their lives seen servants so richly dressed as these.

From a window of his private apartments the Baron watched as far below the herald was rowed across the unmoving surface of the bay, the still wake of the boat pointing like an arrowhead at the largest of the three galleys. He spoke to his daughter, Princess Eleanor, who stood beside him, watching also. 'These moorish princes,' he said, 'are nothing more than pirates, trying to steal a kingdom wherever they can find one loosely guarded by a fool.'

The Princess gazed at the beauty of the ships on the dark sea and the haze on the purple hills towards Gassin. 'Yes,' she said, 'but how does anyone gain a kingdom? Would a Christian do any less?'

A little later, on board his flagship Prince Taric sat beneath an awning of thick silk and listened to the words of his herald. Although he was indeed the commander of a flotilla that took its chances where it found them it was also true that he was the youngest son of one of the greatest rulers of Moorish Spain. Unfortunately, like most younger sons, he had no expectation of inheriting his father's possessions, so rather than spend an idle and luxurious life at court he had set sail in three of his father's ships and gone to seek his fortune.

Though still young he was experienced and resourceful. He had sailed as far as Egypt and beyond, always accompanied by wise counsellors, and the closest to his heart was the friend of his youth and the companion of his manhood, the Lord Ozmyn, he who that day had acted as herald so that he might spy out the nature of the Baron and the strength of the castle of Grimaud.

'The castle is too strong for us,' said Ozmyn, and he took a seat near Taric and drank from a cup that was given him. 'The Baron is hospitable but wary, as any general should be. His soldiers are many and the walls of his citadel are stout. We will be allowed to enter it with goods to trade, twenty of us. But best of all, Prince, you will see the Baron's daughter, the Princess Eleanor. Ah, she is the most beautiful thing I ever saw. A flower. Much as I love you, master, I could leave your service for hers if she were to crook her little finger. Where there is love all other loyalties must take second place. "Amor vincit omnia."'

The Prince smiled at Ozmyn's Latin. 'If she is as graceful and full of charm as you say I shall see that the Princess is given some rolls of the choicest silk and I will make her a present of that emerald necklace we took in our last encounter. Let the men prepare.'

Early the next morning while it was still cool, Prince Taric, Ozmyn and twenty of their best and bravest soldiers, landed on the quayside under the walls of Grimaud and wended their way upwards through the town. Behind them came servants carrying bales of silk, caskets of jewels, bags of spices and a collection of swords and daggers fashioned from the steel of Toledo.

The Prince himself was dressed with all the elegance that Moorish warriors affected in those days. Under his long cloak he wore a cuirass inlaid with gold and silver. His boots were of the finest leather and his scimitar had been cunningly wrought by the best armourers of Damascus. Its scabbard, being richly enamelled, hung from a belt of golden filigree studded with gems. His dagger had been tempered at Fez and its pommel was ornamented with an enormous ruby. Ozmyn was no less dashingly attired and the guard of twenty each bore a light lance, upright, and from each point fluttered a banderole embroidered with purple thread.

Ozmyn went first into the courtyard of the castle and there, sitting on a raised dais close to a fountain and in the shade of a vast plane tree, sat the Baron Cadarache and his daughter. All around them stood the courtiers and the merchants of the town who had come to buy what they could. Word of the Moors had spread across the valley too and many people had journeyed in from the outlying villages and hamlets in order to see a Saracen at close quarters without the risk of being killed or sold into slavery.

Ozmyn bowed and presented his master to the Baron and his daughter. The Saracen soldiers stood to one side in a group, and the servants lay down their bales upon the cobbles.

The Baron smiled in the most friendly manner. 'Welcome,' he said, 'to my castle of Grimaud.'

In return Prince Taric touched his heart and kissed his hand. 'My lord Baron,' he said, 'even in Seville, the land of my birth, it is known that the castle of Grimaud is the most beautiful stronghold in Provence. We come in peace. Beauty and strength deserve respect.'

The Baron laughed with politeness at this sally and chairs were brought for the Prince and Ozmyn and while refreshments were carried forward the merchants began their trading. Goods were sold and bartered and, as the Prince ate a peach and drank a cup of wine, he had time to study the features of Eleanor, the Baron's daughter.

Ozmyn had not lied. Eleanor was surely the most beautiful woman the Prince had ever seen. Her hair was thick and fell to her waist in long and easy waves and it was the colour of the chestnuts that grow on the sunniest hillsides of the forest of Les Maures. Her skin was uncoarsened by the sun but was not pale or unhealthy. Her teeth were unblemished and her green eyes were bright with intelligence and kindness. She was dressed with simplicity in a long robe of light brown, and although she had not as yet spoken, she gazed about her with a fearless candour, and was not shy of observing Ozmyn and the Prince quite closely.

The two men were a revelation to her. The tales she had heard of Saracens – their cruelty, their warlike behaviour, their enslavement of women and children – had not prepared her for the grace and refinement she saw that day. The Prince seemed so gentle. Such Christian captains who landed at Grimaud could not compare to this. Prince Taric's garments were like something from a Persian legend, and the diamonds in his turban flashed flame under the broken sunlight that shimmered in the dark leaves above his head.

Eleanor was puzzled. Never previously permitted to see a Saracen this close she had always been led to understand that they were ill-featured, ugly even, with skins as black as a Nubian's. She could see for herself how false this was. The Prince's complexion was no swarthier than that of any man who spent his time on the deck of a ship. It was smooth and unlined too, and his profile was noble. She could not believe her father's assumption that the Prince was merely a pirate of the Barbary Coast.

Eleanor sighed. The suitors that had been presented to her in the past had all left her unmoved. Luckily her father had sons to secure his succession and would not force her to marry against her will. Neither would he allow her to marry anyone he did not consider suitable – and a Saracen, however handsome or well-born, was not suitable.

At this point the Baron leant forward in his chair, hand on knee, and smiled again at his guest. 'Your herald tells me,' he said, with more than a hint of irony, 'that you come of noble blood.' For the Baron a Moorish pirate was a Moorish pirate, never mind his clothes.

Prince Taric noticed the touch of sarcasm in the Baron's voice, but he shifted his eyes to Eleanor and kept them there. 'If Saracen blood can be good in your eyes,' he began, 'then I come of as good as any, and so does my herald. We are of families who date from the time of the prophet. Our ancestors conquered Africa and their descendants conquered Spain. My grandfather was Alcayde of Seville and my father is the Alcayde in his stead. His name is Ibn el Ghalib, the conqueror, a name that is not unknown, I think.'

The Baron's smile stiffened on his face and his daughter broke her eyes from

Prince Taric's stare. Ibn el Ghalib indeed possessed a reputation for valour that spread far and wide; his was the bravest of armies and the largest of fleets in all of Moorish Spain.

'So why,' asked the Baron, still doubting the Prince's word, 'is the son of such a renowned ruler sailing the seas and selling bolts of silk and barrels of spice like a common merchant?'

The Prince glanced at Ozmyn and laughed. 'My lord,' he answered, 'we Saracens have no disdain for what we do. Shepherd one day, prince the next. My father herded his father's sheep. With his own hands he helped to build his father's galleys and what he won at sea he gave to his father so that it became part of his own patrimony. I am not likely to become the Alcayde in my father's place, I have two brothers between me and that honour. My father gave me three ships. "There is always love for you here," he said, "a palace, servants, wives and wars to fight, but it will be better for you if you roam the world, take what you can and barter for what you cannot. Treat your men well. Keep your word and your religion and return only when you are weary."' The Prince smiled at Eleanor. 'My lord, and lady, I am not yet weary.'

The Baron slapped his leg and spoke again, without irony this time. 'To my own sons I gave the same advice,' he said. 'They serve the Count of Provence and fight with him in his wars. Here I preserve their inheritance, and will enlarge it too with the marriage of my daughter. My eldest son will return to the most beautiful of domains. Is it not a heaven on earth? The vineyards and orchards below, the river in the valley, the thick forest behind.'

'Yes,' said the Prince, nodding in agreement. 'If I could only be assured that paradise were equal to Grimaud then I would be happy to leave this world on the instant and say farewell to all its pleasures.'

The Baron was delighted with this compliment and insisted that the Saracens join him in a banquet that very evening. It was a splendid feast given in the great hall of the castle and the Prince sat at the Baron's right while on his left sat his daughter and next to her was placed Ozmyn the herald. The members of Taric's bodyguard, each one the son of a noble, were scattered here and there amongst the courtiers, eating and drinking with them at long tables.

The hours passed with great enjoyment on both sides, Saracen and Christian, and at the very end Taric rose from his seat and thanked the Baron and the assembled company. 'My lord,' he said, 'your hospitality has astounded me. I can never repay you, unless good fortune brings you to Seville. But now I must leave . . . and this very night too, for if I were to stay until dawn and saw this bay, these rich hillsides and this fine castle rising over all, I might never be able to leave Provence and my companions would chide me and be sad at the thought of never seeing their homeland again.' And with these graceful words the Prince presented the Baron with a fine sword and to the Princess Eleanor he gave a huge and heavy necklace made from the finest emeralds. 'To match your eyes, Princess,' he said.

The Princess acknowledged the courtesy but was uncertain about the gift. 'Was the necklace,' she enquired, 'stolen by a pirate?'

Taric was not dismayed by the question but responded frankly and without embarrassment. 'Princess,' he said, 'nothing is ours. When we die our possessions pass back into the world and become someone else's. As for this necklace in particular ... it passed into my hands through honest barter.' Eleanor was content with this answer and the emeralds were placed around her neck and Ozmyn smiled secretly to himself, saying; 'Aye, honest barter indeed ... a man's life for each stone.'

Fortunately these words were not overheard and once the ceremonies of leave-taking were concluded the Prince's bodyguard rose to their feet and escorted their master from the castle. And, sure enough, next day when the first rays of the sun spilled over the hills to light the sea, there was not one trace of the Moorish ships to be seen. When Eleanor awoke, as early as the dawn itself, she hurried to her window, wondering if Taric had been as good as his promise, and found that he had. As she scanned the wide and empty bay the Princess's heart felt desolate within her and she knew for certain that she had fallen in love with a Saracen prince.

Nor did the Prince survive this first meeting unscathed. Well might he order his flotilla to sail further into the Mediterranean but he could think only of returning to Grimaud. For six months or so he pursued a life of adventure, trying valiantly all the while to put every memory of the Princess from his mind. Nevertheless, when, at the end of his voyage, he discovered himself and his three ships within a mile or two of the coast of Provence, he knew he could not live a moment longer without a sight of the lovely Eleanor.

Ozmyn was only too willing to play the herald again. He donned his caftan and, accompanied by a handful of his noble friends, he landed on the jetty of stone, climbed through the town to the castle and was straightway shown into the presence of the Baron, the courtiers and the Princess herself.

It was a happy reunion and, completely at his ease, Ozmyn explained that he and Prince Taric had made a profitable voyage and, so agreeable was their memory of Grimaud, they had desired to anchor there on their way back to Seville; for although the Prince was not yet weary of adventure he longed to embrace his father. Furthermore the Prince wanted to present the Princess, and the Baron, with new gifts; gifts, said the herald, that had been bartered for honestly and which might be kept for a lifetime without any feelings of guilt.

The Baron was overjoyed to receive the Saracens while Ozmyn for his part, noticed a blush as hot as fever rising in the cheeks of Eleanor. After the audience was concluded he went, without loss of time, to his master on the flagship and told him of the Princess's confusion at learning of the fleet's arrival.

'I believe,' said Ozmyn, 'that your love is returned, but to enjoy it with the Baron's approval will not, I think, be an easy task.'

Later that day the Prince and his men landed and all was as it had been on the occasion of their first visit, except that the banquet in the great hall was even more splendid than previously. At the end of it the Prince clapped his hands and a huge chest was carried in by his servants. It was opened and out of it came long gowns of golden cloth for the Princess, together with bracelets of precious metal. For the Baron there were swords and armour, curiously inlaid, and a fine silken cloak said to have come from Cathay, on the very edge of the world.

The courtiers at their tables and the servants standing behind them gasped in wonderment. The Baron was astonished, awed by the luxury and variety of the gifts. Only the Princess Eleanor found words, though her voice was quiet.

'Oh, Prince,' she said, 'it is impossible for us to accept such things from a stranger and a . . .'

'Saracen,' the Prince finished the sentence for her. 'You have much to learn, Princess. I tell you our city of Seville is as lovely as this town of Grimaud, and ten times as large. There are turreted mosques and churches too, for we allow Christians the right to follow their own religion. My father's palace has cool retreats full of flowers and fountains and there are vines trained over our doorways to keep out the sun. Your Christian men of learning come from France and Italy to Cordoba and Seville, to learn from our scholars and read their books. We lead you in erudition and match you in holiness. We are as valiant in war and as generous in peace. To you we may seem below contempt – infidels and unbelievers. To us life is simple; we all worship the same God and live in the same garden. We come into the world through the same gate and leave it by dying the same death. Therefore, Princess, accept these offerings. All I ask in return is that the next time you hear a Christian knight tell you that all Saracens are heathen and uncouth tell him of Prince Taric and his noble friend and companion, Ozmyn al Hanaf.'

So wise and well-spoken was this speech that there was silence after it. All present in that great hall came to realize that the Prince was a prince of men indeed. Eleanor raised her head and was pleased, happy that she had not misplaced her love. The Baron waved a hand, regally, and laughed out loud. He had none of his daughter's scruples about taking rich gifts from a Saracen.

'My dear Prince,' he said, 'it would be churlish for us to refuse such magnificence so handsomely offered. My daughter's nobility of mind makes her too diffident, but I may command her in this. She will accept, as I do.'

The Prince inclined his head while the Princess lowered her eyes and the banquet continued. Ozmyn, who once again sat next to Eleanor, talked to her quietly while other conversations grew noisy around them. From time to time the Princess laughed, and from time to time she blushed and shook her head, but at last she nodded once and Ozmyn smiled and looked content.

The feast continued late into the night and when, in the small hours, it was over the Baron sent men with burning torches to light the Prince through the streets and down to the quayside. There the Saracens found a whole host of little boats loaded with fresh provisions, given by the Baron so that the Prince and his men might reach their destination without being obliged to break their journey.

The Prince was gratified with this gesture and commanded that the provisions be loaded immediately. Then he too went on board and, proceeding directly to his cabin, he removed his cloak and threw himself heavily into a chair. Ozmyn followed the Prince and sat opposite him. Taric looked up and shook his head.

'I love her even more, Ozmyn,' he said. 'I must somehow speak with her, alone. I must tell her what my heart says . . . but how? Her father would never allow it and she would not defy his wishes. What is to be done?'

Ozmyn took his friend's hand. 'Prince,' he began, 'do not fear. I, at table, spoke to the Princess, tonight, amid the noise and singing of the minstrels. I told her of your love . . .'

The Prince withdrew his hand from Ozmyn's and sat bolt upright. 'Was this wise?' he said.

Ozmyn clicked his teeth, twice. 'I was wary, my lord, wary. I simply told her of our six months' wandering and how you mentioned her name every day, every night; how you longed to return to Grimaud and how you wish to carve out a new country for the sole reason that she might be queen of it.'

'And what did she say, Ozmyn? And what did she say?'

'Why nothing, my lord. Nothing. What would you expect the good Princess to say? Had she said anything more than she should you would be displeased at hearing it. She looked away, my lord, but listened all the harder for that. She is no giddy fool your lady, but you would not want her if she were.'

'I would not,' answered the Prince, 'but little difference does it make. We know what Christians think of us. In Spain Muslim marries Christian and Christian marries Muslim and the world is none the worse for it.'

'Yes,' agreed Ozmyn, 'the Princess will know this, but she owes her duty to her father, like a daughter should. It is the Baron you have to convince.'

'This I know, too,' said Taric, 'but before I talk to him I must speak to her. A minute would be long enough.'

'Ah,' said Ozmyn, leaning back in his chair and chuckling, 'one little sip of the wine of love and we lose our sense of time. Listen . . . at table tonight I told the Princess how close our ships were moored to the sheer wall of the castle, where it plunges down into the sea . . . and how our tallest mast reaches higher than a certain narrow casement – a window that gives onto a staircase leading from the great hall up to the private apartments. Well, I think a certain Prince I know should climb into the crow's nest as soon as may be. While he does his lieutenant will edge the ship in under the wall, ever so gently, and the Prince may whisper to the window all he wishes and not be observed . . . though he will be answered.'

The Prince sprang to his feet. 'Ozmyn, is this true?'

Ozmyn laughed with the pleasure he was giving. 'It is true, Prince. You look to your task and I will look to the intricacies of the navigation.'

Most of the crew were fast asleep by that time of night, but as the Prince climbed eagerly to the masthead Ozmyn roused enough of them to pay out the anchor line and gradually, inch by inch, the galley slipped closer and closer to the wall of Grimaud. Soon the Prince was so close to the Baron's castle that he could lean over and touch the rough stones. Patiently he waited. There was no sound save for the lapping of the waters on the shore below and the creaking of the mast as it swayed this way and that in the dark. There was no tide and no moon; just the occasional rise and fall of the sea, breathing under the soft light of the stars like a huge beast at slumber.

After what seemed an age a smudge of white appeared at the tiny casement. The stars brightened and the Prince saw the Princess's face; her eyes were wide, her lips parted. Suddenly the mast reeled and threatened to bear the Prince out of earshot, but then it steadied.

'Princess,' whispered Taric, 'I am he who I say I am, noble of birth, son of the Alcayde of Seville. I have riches in my own right, a domain I shall surely have one day . . . I want you to know that my religion is not so fierce that it would deny yours, nor will it ever . . . but all this is as nothing, compared to the strength of my love for you. I beg you to forgive this candour but there is no time for me to speak otherwise. I mean to ask your father for your hand . . .'

The words broke off here for now a wave had moved the ship and the mast-top swung in a circle and the Prince soared away and out of sight. Taric cursed under his breath; this declaration of love was not to be as simple as Ozmyn had promised. The Prince felt both helpless and foolish; what sort of gallantry was this? But then the vessel lurched as the men on deck heaved against the anchor chain; the mast circled violently for a second time and the Prince came to rest near enough to the window to speak further.

'. . . because,' he continued, 'I must know your heart in this matter. If you return my love nothing shall keep us apart. If you do not then I swear that nothing shall force you into a marriage that offends you. I want you for my queen, not my slave, only answer me.'

Once more, and without warning, the ship moved and although the Princess crept closer to the opening of the casement, and even leant out of it, the Prince was not to be seen. In spite of the seriousness of the situation Eleanor could not restrain her merriment at the absurdity of this wooing from a crow's nest. Her laughter was loud and the Prince heard it and when he came swaying back towards the window he too was laughing.

'Oh, Prince,' said Eleanor, 'this is the strangest meeting and it little becomes a Christian princess to shout her affections from a turret top to a Saracen warrior who is flying through the night on top of a mast . . . but like you I see the time is now or not at all. Do not, above all, misconstrue my frankness as misconduct. I feel for you as you say you feel for me. This last six months you have not left my thoughts. I will be your queen whether you have a domain or not . . . but I shall do nothing that might distress my father and nothing that would harm my honour . . . nor should you ask me to. All that you may rightly demand of a woman I will give, but no more.' And here the Princess withdrew and the Prince climbed down to the deck of his ship with joy in his heart and embraced his friend, Ozmyn al Hanaf.

The next day the Prince and Ozmyn, accompanied by two of their noblest companions, were to be seen passing rapidly through the streets of Grimaud, halting only at the castle gates. There they were recognized and allowed to proceed to the entrance of the great hall. Inside they found the Baron, his daughter and most of the court engaged in their daily business.

As soon as the Saracens were announced the Baron looked up and smiled while the Princess reddened slightly and felt her heart race the faster. Once they stood before the Baron the two noble companions laid presents at his feet; a fine helmet for the father and another exquisite necklace for the daughter.

'These,' said Prince Taric, 'are to thank you for your hospitality and to mark my leaving.'

The Baron heard his daughter sigh and a doubt entered his mind but he smiled again nevertheless.

'I go,' continued the Prince, 'to put into my father's hands all those treasures I have won in a year of voyaging, and to ask him for permission to engage in the greatest enterprise I have ever undertaken.'

'I am sure,' said the Baron, 'that so wise a father will grant any boon to so deserving a son.'

Prince Taric bowed low and then looked directly at the Baron. 'The boon I shall request of my father,' he said, 'is that he allow me to ask you for the hand of your daughter in marriage.'

The silence of death fell in the great hall of Grimaud and each and every courtier there turned his head so he might see the Baron's face. The soldiers on guard along the four walls gripped the hafts of their pikes until their knuckles showed white. The Princess raised a hand to her throat and the Baron's smile went brittle on his lips, then broke and disappeared. He glanced at his daughter and fingered the pommel of his sword.

'Did I hear you aright, Prince?' he said.

'I wish to ask for the hand of your daughter in marriage,' repeated the Prince.

The Baron shook with anger and his features darkened with shame.

'I could have you killed for this,' he whispered, 'and see your blood run red across these flagstones. You are an unbeliever, Taric, a Moor. My daughter is a Christian. I will never give her to an infidel, by my solemn oath I will not.'

Prince Taric kept his voice calm. 'My father is a great king,' he said. 'He is as powerful in Spain as your Count of Provence here. He commands as many men, owns as many castles . . . has men like you subject to him.'

'Whatever your father is,' retorted the Baron, 'he is still a Moor and you are nothing but a pirate and a robber.'

'Like many a man who calls himself a Christian,' said the Prince. 'In my country we do not judge a man by his faith alone, only by the way he practises it.'

'Because you are not of the true faith,' shouted the Baron. 'I warn you to leave my castle this instant and never return or I will have my men throw you from the battlements like a common thief.'

Deeply insulted, Prince Taric fell back a step and his three companions came to his side, their swords half-drawn. 'I do not fear your threats,' he said, 'but I truly love the Princess and she me . . . it is wrong to keep us apart.'

The Baron signalled to his soldiers to come closer. 'What the Princess thinks or feels does not signify,' he said, the breath hissing over his teeth. 'She will marry a Christian and of my choosing. Again, leave the castle or you perish.'

The Prince went to unsheath his sword, intent on dying there and then, but his friend Ozmyn held him by the arm. 'Do not die today, Taric,' he said. 'She cannot be yours if you are dead; few marriages are made in the grave, at least not that I know of.' And with this the good friend drew his Prince slowly down the hall and the two companions guarded him on both sides. At the great door the Prince looked longingly one last time at Princess Eleanor and then he was gone.

Once the Saracens had departed the Baron turned on his daughter, his anger flowing beyond his control. 'You fool,' he said, 'do you not know that your marriage is in the gift of the Count of Provence? Do you not remember that we Christians fought for years to rid our land of these savages? Do you know nothing that you would abandon yourself to the first brigand who makes you a present of a silken handkerchief?'

The Princess raised her head, unrepentant and unafraid. 'I,' she began, her voice ringing around the stone walls so that all might hear her, 'I am in the gift of no one, whatever you and the Count may think. Prince Taric is a man of courage and kindness, a gracious man which is more than can be said of most of the Christian knights I have seen. I will not marry against your wishes, father, but neither will I marry against mine. I beg you to think again. I can have no faith without love.'

'Enough,' cried the Baron. 'I will not listen to an unformed girl who knows nothing of the world.' And with a sign he ordered his bodyguard to take the Princess to her chambers and commanded that she be kept there until the day of her marriage, a marriage that should be of her father's choosing.

***

The three galleys of Prince Taric left the Bay of Grimaud immediately and set sail for Spain. Their journey was uneventful and in spite of the fact that several ships were sighted on the way the Prince gave no orders to attack, having little stomach for adventure. He kept to his cabin, downcast and sad. Taric had hoped against hope that somehow the Baron would give permission for the marriage, but now he knew for certain that there was no prospect of such a thing. The Princess was lost to him forever. More than that the Baron had offended him at the very heart of his manhood, and though for Eleanor's sake he had not responded to those terrible insults against his faith, the Prince's shame was still great. The whole voyage long he said but few words and brooded alone on his aching sorrow.

Luckily the winds were fair for Spain and the Prince was soon obliged to think of other things. One day, after the briefest of passages, he heard the hail of the lookout and, bestirring himself, he went up on deck. There before him, shining like a strip of gold in the bright Spanish sunshine, with a frieze of silver peaks suspended in the sky behind, he saw the coastline he knew so well and his crew rejoiced, happy to be home.

As the three galleys manœuvred into the harbour that served Seville, which itself lay some thirty miles inland, a cannon was fired and a ball of smoke appeared, floating in the wind. At the same time a boat put out from the shore and was rowed with haste towards the Prince's flotilla.

'They are pleased to see our safe return,' remarked Ozmyn, 'it will be your brothers hurrying to greet you, or a messenger from your father.'

But it was neither the one nor the other. As the boat drew near, those on board the flagship saw that the person who was approaching so rapidly was the chief counsellor of the Alcayde, and he was dressed in mourning. The moment he set foot on board he embraced the Prince and tears sprang to his eyes. Then he bowed low, as if to his lord, and Taric felt a new sadness enter his heart.

'What is it, Celim?'

Celim lowered his eyes to the deck. 'Do not hate me, master,' he said, 'for bearing evil tidings. Remember when I tell you this that no one in your town of Seville had the courage to do what I am now doing.'

Prince Taric made a gesture and Celim told his story. 'Your father fell ill,' he began, 'several months ago and those beyond the mountains launched an attack believing that he was old and feeble and could not defend his kingdom. They reckoned without your brothers. They led your father's troops from the city and defeated their enemies, killing most of them and selling the remainder into slavery. They will not attack again.'

'My father?'

'Your father died, knowing that his sons had been victorious, but not knowing that they had died of their wounds, received valiantly in battle. We sent galleys to find you, Taric. You are the Alcayde of Seville now.'

The Prince shook his head, amazed by this great sorrow. In one moment he had lost father and brothers, all of whom he had loved. He needed to weep but there came a great shout from the men in the three galleys; the rowers in the counsellor's boat had whispered the news. Taric's soldiers now knew that their man had come into his inheritance and their prince raised his arms and accepted his destiny.

∞

During the months that followed the Prince, with the help of Ozmyn, and many others, made sure that his kingdom was in good order. Where necessary he repaired the fortifications, looked to the readiness of his troops and reassured himself about the well-being of his subjects. His work was quickly done for the Alcayde, his father, had been a wise and sensible ruler; the treasury was full and the land was as fruitful as a watered garden. There was soon nothing for Taric to do and so, one evening, he called Ozmyn to his side and led him out onto his private balcony where a meal had been prepared, and there the two friends took their ease.

Ozmyn raised a goblet of wine to his Prince. 'You have worked well, my lord. This kingdom is good. No one could take it now . . . and your people love you as they loved your father.'

Taric accepted the compliment. 'It has not been done without your help, friend,' he said. 'I should be happy, yet I am content and not content.'

Ozmyn raised an eyebrow.

'I cannot banish the Princess Eleanor from my thoughts,' explained Taric. 'To make my kingdom perfect I need a queen and she is the only queen I want. When I wake in the morning it is of her I think. When I sleep at night it is of her I dream. She is like a mist in my mind. What do you think, Ozmyn? Now that I am the ruler of Seville, shall we ask the Baron for his daughter's hand in a more regal manner?'

Ozmyn smiled. 'It is certainly worth asking again, my lord, but this time let him see how rich and powerful a man you have become. It may influence his thought.'

'Very well,' said Taric. 'Tomorrow we will begin to make ready. Leave behind enough men to keep the province safe, and three fast ships in the harbour to carry messages should the need arise. Apart from that let every fighting man and every warship come with us. This time we shall show the Baron that we are every bit as good as he.'

About a month or two later, one day at dawn, the Baron was roused from his bed and called to the battlements of his castle. When he got there he could hardly believe his eyes. The whole bay of Grimaud, from the horizon to the walls of the city itself, was covered in galleys, their sails furled and their ramming beaks painted in gold. The great oars lay at rest and the decks were crowded with warriors in armour, each figure clear and distinct in the early rays of the sun; and on each side of the bay the Baron could see that men and horses had already disembarked and were striking inland.

'By St James,' said the Baron. 'The Saracens. They have come to conquer Provence once more.' He turned to his Master at Arms. 'Quickly,' he said, 'send messengers to Draguignan, to Toulon and to Arles, let our friends send soldiers and ships as soon as they can, and let the messengers say that we shall defend ourselves to the last man . . . but let them hurry.'

These orders were executed on the spot and, as the couriers set out astride the swiftest horses the Baron possessed, the inhabitants of Grimaud were awakened so they might gather together their valuables and drive their flocks up the narrow streets and into the castle. As soon as they were inside the gates were closed, the battlements were manned and high on the walls the Baron waited for the onslaught that he was sure would come.

Strangely there was no attack and no explosion of cannon. Instead the sound of an enchanting music drifted across the still morning air and the ships stood as motionless as ships in a tapestry and, as the defenders watched, the sun rose higher and made the waters of the sea as blue as the sky so that it became impossible to distinguish where one ended and the other began, and across it all the gold and steel of the Saracen weaponry blazed up more vividly than flame.

The trees of the forest began to creak and crack in the heat of the day and the soldiers of Grimaud held their spears steady and continued to marvel, and soon they saw a splendid and beautifully ornate barge detach itself from the flagship of the fleet and pass, slowly and sedately, towards the stone jetty lying underneath the town walls.

Here, in all trust for they carried no weapons, about a dozen men in magnificent cloaks stepped onto the quayside, each one of them carrying an ebony casket in his hands. They were led by a man who was even more richly dressed than they were and without delay they began to climb the abandoned and silent streets of Grimaud, not stopping until they reached the citadel. On their arrival they found the Baron Cadarache, in full armour and with a naked sword in his hands, staring down from the fortifications of the gatehouse. The Saracens bowed and made no warlike sign at all. The Baron started in surprise as he recognized the leader of the group below him; it was Ozmyn, the friend and herald of Prince Taric.

'My lord,' said the Saracen, 'we did not mean to alarm you or your citizens. Believe me we come in peace and I bring these caskets of diamonds, all twelve of them, as tokens of my master's good intentions. He brings them, and these ships and men, to show you, and your daughter, the estate he now possesses. On our return to Seville we discovered that the old Alcayde and all his sons had perished. Taric is now the Alcayde of Seville and all his wealth and land and all his power he comes to lay at the feet of the Princess Eleanor and once again, in all humility, he begs her hand in marriage.'

The Baron's lips tightened at this speech of Ozmyn's and he leant upon his sword. 'Your speech is sweet,' he said, 'but so many ships seem like a threat of war, to chastise me if by chance I should not accede to the Prince's demands. My pride does not like to be threatened by Saracens, however great, however powerful.'

Ozmyn bowed again. 'We mean no threat, my lord. Prince Taric merely desires to show you the change in his fortunes.'

The Baron nodded. 'That's as may be,' he said, 'but a good general always fears an ambush. I shall have the postern gate opened and you will enter the castle so that we may talk of this matter. Let there be no treachery,' and with these words the Baron gave a sign and a small door set within the great gates of Grimaud swung open and the Saracens passed inside.

They were not kept long. Once the Saracens were in his grasp the Baron dropped all pretence of moderation. His soldiers laid rough hands on Ozmyn and his men and, despite the pleadings of the Princess, their fine clothes were ripped from their bodies and they were flogged without mercy, every one. Their diamonds were seized and the ebony caskets which had contained them were filled with dust and pebbles and returned to the Saracens as an insult to their master. Then, amid jeers and more blows, they were thrust back through the postern, near naked and with their backs bleeding.

'Let Taric know,' said the Baron, once more looking down from the gatehouse, 'that he may not presume to marry a Christian maiden, least of all my daughter. Tell him also that I will keep the precious stones he sent me for the trouble I had in whipping you, and bid him not to stay in the Bay of Grimaud too long. I have sent messengers to Arles and Toulon. Before many days have passed there will be soldiers and ships here, enough to send you infidels to roast in hell where you belong. Tell him that if he stays to fight I shall capture him and put out his eyes, this King of Seville, and hamstring him and tie him to my gates so that he may beg a living like a dog. Now go and take my message to your master.'

At the ending of this speech the Princess came to the gatehouse wall and leant over it, holding out her hands in pity and weeping for the gentle Ozmyn and his friends, but although this compassion touched those who saw it, it could not melt her father's heart. The Baron turned in anger against his daughter and demanded what she did there and cursed the servants who were meant to keep her in her chamber.

'You do not understand war,' the Baron cried, 'the beauty of it and the glory. It is for men alone. Say nothing for you know nothing. Once this is over you shall be given a husband, then may you war with him.' Still weeping the Princess was led away and the Baron crossed to the seaward side of the castle so that he might watch the disposition of the Saracen fleet.

As for Ozmyn and the messengers they made their way back to the barge at the jetty, helping each other to walk as best they might for their backs were torn with stripes and red with blood. On the flagship Prince Taric waited impatiently for the return of his men and, he hoped, good news. He leant back in his chair, willing the time to pass, lethargic under an awning that was kept moist by slaves to keep their monarch cool and protected from the sun.

Suddenly, breaking through the stillness, the Prince heard the call of a lookout and the noise of oars as the barge drew close. He raised his head eagerly but was not prepared for the sight that greeted his eyes as the limp and bloody body of Ozmyn was lifted over the side of the ship and laid at his feet.

Taric knelt by his friend and called for water and ointments and soft bandages. Physicians were sent for too, but the Prince bathed Ozmyn's wounds with his own hands and anointed them with medicines and salves. Tears sprang to his eyes, tears of grief mingled with anger, and as each of the nobles he had sent into Grimaud was brought into the ship the Prince's anger increased and drove the tender lover of Eleanor from his heart.

'Oh, Ozmyn,' he cried, 'to treat you thus when we came in peace. Where is this Christian's charity that he could use you in such a way. In all the laws of war and religion the herald is kept as sacred, he is holy and must not be touched. Yet you, my companion and the best of men, he whips and sends me dust for diamonds.'

Ozmyn gave a weak smile. 'You are an infidel my lord. You are unclean.'

Taric rose to his feet and, placing his clenched hands on his hips he stared across the waters of the bay and up to the silhouette of the castle, dark against the blue sky. 'Unclean,' he said, quietly, as if only to himself. 'Then I shall cleanse myself in Christian blood. I came here for a wedding feast but now there will be death. Has the Baron forgotten how infidels can fight. Ask him who drove the proud Charlemagne across the Pyrenees and slaughtered all his knights. Ask for his champions, Roland and Oliver . . . he will not find them. This land was our land . . . it could be ours again. At the very least that castle of Grimaud and all the beauty that surrounds it will be in ruins before I have gone. Owls will hoot where the Baron holds his court and lizards shall bask in his robing rooms. I promise it.'

Ozmyn raised himself on an elbow. 'Take care, Prince, and be swift. The Baron has sent couriers to Arles and Toulon. An army will be marching towards us and ships sailing in behind.'

The Prince looked down at Ozmyn and laughed. 'I am not my father's son for nothing,' he said. 'The horsemen I landed this morning, before first light, had special orders from me. They went to circle Grimaud, to guard all tracks and paths. You shall see, Ozmyn, that in a little while the Baron's messengers shall be here, standing on this deck. And then I shall give more orders. All who try to pass will die, killed in the forest itself and left to rot. The inhabitants of this castle will not be relieved, save by death or slavery alone.'

'Do not be too angry, Prince, said Ozmyn. 'Eleanor loves you and wept to see us beaten, but it may be that your rage could turn her love to fear and even hate. If you bring her father to the dust and ravage the country of her birth you may lose her. Her father deserves all this, and more, but she would be so full of shame that she could never take you for a husband. She would not wish to be a chattel won in war.'

'Ozmyn,' answered the Prince, 'what you say is always full of wisdom and I love you for it. But the Baron Cadarache has whipped my herald and a dozen of the noblest men of Seville like common criminals. I cannot let it pass. He shall pay for it and if, at the end of all, I cannot have my desires by asking then I shall have them by taking, and it will be on the Baron's head not mine, and he and his daughter will have to live life as it comes.'

And so in spite of Ozmyn's advice Prince Taric ordered his troops to land in their thousands and begin the seige of Grimaud. In his anger he commanded that the houses below the castle should be pulled down and anything of value given to the soldiers. And in the countryside round about it was the same story. The vineyards were trampled by the Saracens' horses and the trees in the orchards – the plum, the peach and the apple – were felled to make kindling for cooking fires, and all the hillsides and the valleys where it had been so pleasant to live were laid waste. From the walls of the castle the people of Grimaud could only watch and silently wish that their master had given his daughter to the Saracen, for it was obvious to them that their certain earthly paradise had been thrown away for the mere hope of a heavenly one.

These considerations were far from Taric's mind; now he thought of nothing but victory and urged his men to great efforts and fought by their side every day. As the time went by he directed that the ordnance from his ships be landed and pulled to within range of the castle. Then his gunners began to bombard the walls and turrets of the defences and, with all the leisure they needed to perfect their aim, their cannon balls soon made breaches in the stone citadel and those breaches became wider and wider and at last the Baron and his men prayed for their lives.

The Princess, meanwhile, was distraught that so many men, and women and children too, should suffer and die for her sake and for her father's pride. From her window she could see that the fertile valley of Grimaud was now a desert, covered by Saracen tents, and where all before had been grace and beauty there was nothing now but ugliness and death. Determined, she went to her father and, in the presence of his soldiers and captains, she knelt and begged the Baron to agree to her marriage with Prince Taric. She was sure, she said, that she could soften his heart for she knew he was not an evil man. What was more, he loved her and she was not indifferent to him.

It was no use. The Baron had sworn his oath that no infidel should marry his daughter and bring his grandchildren up to be followers of Mohammed. He was shamed before his soldiers that a child of his should love an unbeliever. He cursed the Princess and sent her back to her chamber, then turned to rally his men.

'We cannot be vanquished,' he said, 'this castle will not fall. Remember the messengers I sent to Draguignan, Arles and Toulon. The longer the Saracens stay here the more certain they are to die beneath our swords. Soon we shall see a Christian army marching over the hills and Christian ships sailing into the bay. Be strong and do not listen to my daughter's wailings. She is a woman and you are warriors.'

It was as if Prince Taric had heard this speech for the very next day the head of a man was catapulted over the walls of the city by one of the Saracen engines of war, and when the head had rolled to a standstill it was retrieved and shown to the Baron. It was the head of the messenger he had sent to Arles.

The following day another head landed inside the castle. This time it was the head of the man who had been ordered to Toulon, and on the third day there fell onto the battlements the head of the messenger who had set out for Draguignan. The Baron looked at his surviving captains. Their faces were as sombre as his. They knew now that they could expect no help from anyone, save God. Their provisions were all eaten and the breaches in the walls were wide. The Saracens could take Grimaud whenever they wished.

The Baron was no coward and he flourished his sword. 'All is not lost,' he told his troops, 'we shall live to fight again. In the bowels of this castle, and known only to me, is a secret tunnel which will lead us beyond the Saracen lines, far out in the forest on the highway to Draguignan. I know for sure that the road is guarded by only a few of the enemy, watching for messengers. They cannot stop us. The tunnel is high enough to take both man and horse

. . . we shall go silently and fall upon the guards and cut our way through. Before the Saracen realizes we have left the citadel we shall be at Draguignan, reinforced by friends. Then will Taric be made to quit our coast or leave his bones in Provence. My captains! I have these diamonds, my daughter's price he thought. They are more than sufficient to rebuild this castle and replant the vines and orchards in the valley. Grimaud will once more be what it was. Come my friends! Be not down-hearted. At the end of it all we shall escape and the Saracen will be defeated. We shall have a glorious victory.'

Word of this plan was brought to the Princess by her servants, fearful for their lives, and in despair she went again to her father and knelt before him. 'Father,' she said, 'if you and your soldiers leave the castle of Grimaud what will happen to your subjects, your peasants, their women and their children? Will you abandon them here, to slaughter and to slavery?'

'My first duty,' answered the Baron, 'is to save my fighting men, their weapons and my treasure. Do you not see, woman, that if my soldiers stay here to fight, even to the last man, your peasants will still die and I will no longer have an army. On the other hand if my men and I escape we shall return one day, rebuild Grimaud and raise an expedition to attack Taric in his own country. That would be a war worth fighting, that would bring glory to us all.'

'Oh, Father,' said Eleanor, 'let me go to the Prince. Let me become his wife. I know I can make him spare Grimaud and all within it, women and children and your soldiers too. He is a good man, I am sure of it. This war is not worth the fighting.'

The Baron's face turned dark and he swore a great oath. 'Have you no pride at all? Would you have me beg for mercy from a heathen? I would be shamed before the whole of Christendom. Speak no more. My plans are made and the peasants of Grimaud will have to live life as it comes.'

❧

Everything was done as the Baron ordered. With the briefest possible delay, and at the darkest part of the chosen night, the soldiers took their horses, their hooves muffled in strips of cloth, down the wide and sweeping steps that led into the arched cellars of the citadel. While the rest of the castle slept, there in a gloomy recess the Baron touched a hidden spring and a mighty door, high enough to allow the entry of a mounted warrior, swung back from the wall. Then a detachment of picked fighting men went into the tunnel and, after a tramp of a mile or so, they emerged into the night air well beyond the Saracen lines, just as the Baron had promised, deep in the woods and near to the Draguignan road.

Once this vanguard had established that it was undetected word was despatched to the Baron and the remainder of his men followed on through the secret passage. Last of all came the Baron and the Princess with a bodyguard to protect them. Eleanor herself was riding a horse which carried, all stuffed together in copious saddlebags, the precious stones belonging to Prince Taric, as well as all the gold and silver from her father's treasury. Everything the Baron held dear was borne by the one beast of burden.

The Princess went reluctantly into the passage. She could not bear to think of the people of Grimaud left in such jeopardy. When the Saracens discovered, at light of day, that the castle was no longer manned they would wreak a fearful vengeance on those who were helpless. The Princess knew many of the townsfolk. She had grown up with their children. Now they would become slaves in a foreign land, and so she wept.

Where the tunnel came out into the forest the Baron heard the weeping and seized the bridle of his daughter's horse and, edging close, whispered in her ear. 'Will you increase my shame with your tears, you fool? I cannot save the people except I flee this place to return more strong. There is no other way, so compose yourself while I lead my men. They have all left their wives behind them and you are the only woman to escape that fate. Again, I tell you there is no other way.'

'Oh but there is,' said the Princess. 'I can save you all if you'd let me, if it were not for your pride. I tell you I believe in my religion enough to sacrifice it,' and with surprising strength the Princess tore the reins from her father's grasp, wheeled her horse violently and cleared the path of soldiers. Before she could be stopped she had used her spurs and set off down the wide track that led towards the Saracen lines.

'My God!' cried the Baron, 'she goes to Taric.' He called to his bodyguard. 'Follow me,' he shouted. 'The rest of you make haste to Draguignan and fetch help as quickly as you can,' and with no more words the Baron went in pursuit of both his daughter and his treasure.

The Princess lashed her mount and leant forward in the saddle. An excellent horsewoman she was certain that no one could prevent her reaching Prince Taric. The saddlebags of diamonds and gold thumped against her horse's sides and its hooves thundered. Faster and faster she went and not once did she hesitate. This was a forest way she had ridden since her childhood, and she knew every inch of it.

Rapidly she approached the rear of the Saracen lines, and the ruins of Grimaud and the towers of its castle loomed high above her, black against the black sky. The Princess raced past the outlying sentries and drew near the tents of the troops that invested the town on the landward side. They were Taric's best men and had been given strict orders to let no one pass – and they did not. They heard the warning cries of their sentries. They heard the sound of a horse galloping; the outrider of an attack perhaps – how could they tell in the confusion of the night? They broke from their tents with strangely curved bows in their hands. Fifty – a hundred men – strung each an arrow and in an instant let the arrow go. Ten steel barbs struck the Princess's body and one pierced her throat. Her horse was struck. Its pace faltered. It screamed and stumbled and fell, lifeless, against a silken pavilion which collapsed in silent, billowing folds of white. The Princess was dead.

Then there came the sound of more horses and the Baron and his men reined in where the forest ended. The Saracen sentries rejoined their main force, now all awake, and formed in lines before their camp, bows restrung.

They could not see through the dark but they could hear the Baron speak.

'My daughter,' he cried, 'yield my daughter.'

'She is not here,' replied the captain of the Saracens who did not know who had been slain, and he gave an order and another flight of arrows left the curved bows and landed among the Baron's men, wounding some and alarming the horses so they reared and struggled to break away.

The Baron brandished his sword and urged his men forward. 'Come,' he shouted, 'I know she is here and we will take her.'

Bravely the Christians advanced and at first they forced the Saracens back past their tents and round by the southern side of the town, passing by and trampling over the body of the Princess as they did so. But soon more Saracen troops began to arrive, drawn by the noise and shouts of battle. The Baron's bodyguard were surrounded, dragged from their horses, and their throats slit so the blood might soak into the stony ground. In the end only the Baron was left alive, his sword broken, grime on his face and a deep wound in his shoulder. Ringed by spears he was kept safe for the coming of Prince Taric.

Prince Taric did not delay for long but rode across the battlefield with all his armour on and Ozmyn at his side. As he arrived his men, who were by now counting the slain and searching for booty, discovered the Princess where she lay, half under her horse, her body torn with arrows, all broken by her fall. Her face was covered in dirt and dust, blood ran from her mouth, her lips were twisted and her beauty was gone. Around her, spilled out in a huge swathe, were the diamonds of Prince Taric and the golden pieces of the Baron.

The Prince was called and when he came he gazed down and touched the diamonds with his foot and they shone as the night began to fade and the sky paled with the hard dawn creeping in from the other side of the world. Taric gave an order and his men lifted the horse from the legs of the Princess and her broken body was straightened and laid out upon a soft litter. Then water was brought and the Prince knelt and wiped the blood from the dead face and he wept.

When he had performed these tasks the Prince sat in a chair by the Princess's bed and the Baron was led to him and he saw his daughter's corpse for the first time. He cried out, a terrible cry of endless grief. He threw himself across the body and great sobs sounded in his throat. Then he raised his head and looked to where Prince Taric sat.

'You murderer,' he said, 'killing what you said you loved.'

'And you,' answered the Saracen, getting to his feet, 'have you not killed what you said you loved? This is where pride has brought you. Your castle at my mercy, your vineyards ravaged, your treasure captured and your greatest treasure dead . . . and all because we do not worship the same God.' He pointed to the corpse. 'Is your religion worth that? Is any?'

The Baron leapt to his feet and, his eyes blinded by tears, he attempted to grapple with the Prince, but Ozmyn came between them and the Prince's guards took the Baron and bound his arms behind his back.

'Oh slay me,' he cried, 'for all my fields have gone and all my hope.'

Taric ignored these words and gave commands and some of his soldiers scooped up the diamonds and gold that lay scattered on the ground, taking every last piece of the Baron's treasure. They went on to strike their tents and, by and by, a bugle sounded to warn the Saracen regiments to make ready to go aboard their ships.

While he waited for all these things to happen the Prince sat grim-faced in his chair and Ozmyn stood beside him. And the sun climbed upwards and shone like a shield, beating down on the death of Grimaud, and at noon it was time for the Prince to leave and the Baron knelt on the ground and once more begged to be slain.

'Slay yourself,' said Taric, 'for I will not. I leave you your daughter, just as you wished it. See her buried in a fine tomb and pray by it until you die, and there weep for your lack of wisdom. There is nothing else . . . no kindness . . . you scourged it from me when you scourged my herald and the nobles who brought you only gifts . . . and compassion died when your daughter died.'

With these harsh and bitter words the Prince mounted his horse and paced it slowly down through the littered and abandoned streets of Grimaud, down to the small stone jetty, boarding his ship immediately, leaving Ozmyn to carry out his last orders, and cruel indeed those orders were.

The Baron was left alive, as the Prince had said he would be, but he was hamstrung in both legs and left squatting like a beggar by his daughter's body. The castle walls were dismantled and most of the towers toppled to the ground. Worst of all, every inhabitant of the place, man, woman and child, was herded into the galleys and borne away to a life of slavery, never to see the land of Provence again.

Eventually the great fleet of the Saracens slipped across the horizon and a deep silence settled over the ravaged castle and its town, but it was the silence of pestilence and plague. Nothing moved in the landscape or above it, save for the birds of prey who wheeled in circles in the air and dropped to earth, now and then, to feed on human corpses, tearing at the soft flesh with their curving beaks of bone. And the smoke moved also, rising from the ruins in stately plumes of black to tarnish the painted sky with the gritty dust from a hundred Saracen fires.

Once the ships had gone a few peasants and soldiers crept from the forest where they had hidden themselves. They found their lord and tended his wounds, burying his daughter in a simple grave below the town and covering it with stones carried from the castle. Then they set the Baron on the litter where the Princess had lain and bore him to Draguignan.

This was the end for the Baron. He was but the shell of a man, tormented and crazed by an unbearable grief. He spent the rest of his days a penitent in a monastery, attending every mass and crawling from place to place like a child, praying first to one God and then another in the hope they could, between them, bring his daughter back to life and Grimaud back to its former glory. This heresy was tolerated by the monks because they knew of the Baron's great suffering and were convinced that the nobleman had behaved rightly and religiously, just as any true Christian should, and but for misfortune might even have won his battle with the Saracens.

As for Prince Taric he returned to Seville and its lands and ruled them wisely enough, but thereafter he was always a cruel man, both in peace and war, despatching evil-doers and rivals rapidly to their executions. After the passage of a few years he married a Saracen lady of great beauty who bore him many children, and the memory of Princess Eleanor soon faded from his mind. Ozmyn remained his friend until death, and that is the story of how the castle of Grimaud comes to be in ruins today.

# THE SQUARE AT BARGEMON

To sleep all night in the open air and wake to the smell of coffee and fresh bread from Bargemon was no mean pleasure, and I lay warm in my sleeping-bag for a while to relish it. To begin with I could hear the shepherds talking in low voices but soon those voices were gone and by the time I had pulled on my shoes and got to the fire I saw that the only person there was Paul Graziani.

In the order of march it was Paul who went first, walking at a slow and steady pace with a whip under his arm and trilling bird noises to entice the sheep forward. By tradition a flock is led by two or three giant rams who bear great curling horns on their heads and huge tufts of wool on their backs. Now it so happened that Paul was a tiny man and our rams liked him so much, and followed him so closely, that once we were on the move they loomed over him and he was completely hidden from those of us who came behind. At night we had the glow of his hurricane lamp to tell us where he was, but in the daytime, even if the road were straight and ascending, all we ever glimpsed of him was his corduroy cap bobbing this way and that above a sea of sheep. And this cap was no proper shepherd's garment but an outlandish cross between a beret and an Alaskan fur hat with flaps that should have been tied together on top of the head, though in Paul's case he let them bounce free like over-sized ears. He looked like a gnome with magic powers who had come from the deepest part of the forest to see that no harm came to us or our herd.

But cap or not, gnome or not, Paul was definitely odd in his appearance. His trousers had been cut down to fit him so although they were the correct length in the leg they were enormously baggy, and the crotch of them swung loose below his knees. His face too seemed the wrong shape for his body, being large and heavy with one eye drooping lower than the other.

Yet Paul was the most cheerful of all the shepherds and from the very first day, when we'd come together to eat at Gratteloup, he had taken notice of me, though his talk was not easy to understand. His mouth looked as if it had been kicked by a mule and when he smiled it disappeared into his face leaving nothing visible but a fold in the skin. I was told later that he had suffered, as a young man, from tuberculosis of the teeth and that this had deformed his jaw. When Paul Graziani spoke you were obliged to pay the strictest attention to what he said and even then there was a strange delay between sound and meaning – the sound registering in the brain at least a sentence or two before the meaning could follow it. It was like listening to a shout in a valley, hearing but not understanding until you heard the echo some seconds later.

Towards the end of the morning Jules appeared and took some food away for the others who had broken the flock into two or three small groups and dispersed with them into various pastures in the hills around. Paul and I lay in the shade and ate alone and at the distant edge of the field the cypress trees shimmered like obelisks in a mirage. In the noiseless heat of the afternoon Jules came back again and, on his way to reconnoitre that night's route, drove me to Bargemon so that I could buy a pair of boots. Paul came with me.

The square at Bargemon was as quiet and deserted as it had been at seven o'clock the previous morning. The fountain trickled with a gentle stream of water and the shade of the plane trees kept the water cool. For a moment Paul and I stood side by side, enjoying the peace of the place; one lanky youth, one old and stumpy man. Then he said something I didn't understand and strode away, rolling in his gait like they say sailors do. He led me into a steep street and after walking for a while we came to a door that opened directly into an over-hanging hillside.

As we opened the door a brass bell moved and jangled. After the brightness of the sun outside the interior of the shop seemed to be submerged in a dark, yellowish gloom, though that did not prevent me seeing a long counter made from uneven wood and some bare splintery shelves behind it.

I watched the bell bouncing on its coiled spring. Gradually its movement ceased and the shop became silent; as it did a man, no bigger than Paul, entered from our right and took up a position between the counter and the shelves – another gnome from the mysterious forest.

Paul began to speak in Provençal, tucking his whip under his arm so that he might gesticulate more easily. The boot-maker nodded and, when Paul had finished, he came back round the counter to look at my feet. His face showed no emotion but he clicked his teeth when he saw the state of my shoes. Then he left the two of us together.

'What did you tell him?' I whispered.

Paul sucked at his few teeth and the edges of his mouth folded inwards and then came out again. 'I told him that you have come from England to buy sheep and you will be taking them back with you and as it is a long road you want the best boots available, seven league boots even, and at the best price, because if they are good boots and inexpensive you will tell the shepherds in your country and they will all come here to get theirs.'

'He cannot believe such a fairy-tale,' I said.

Paul shrugged. 'We all believe fairy-tales,' he answered, 'and besides, he is none too sure where England is, and to tell you the truth, neither is Graziani.'

The boot-maker returned carrying only one pair of boots for me to try, boots that were truly magnificent with a special folding flap instead of a tongue and hooks on the outside instead of lace-holes so not the least drop of rain could penetrate to my feet. I knelt in the shop and put them on and they fitted me as if made by a magician. From that very first day the uppers felt as light and as soft as the skin of an antelope and the soles, ribbed an inch thick, gripped the ground and I knew there was no mountain they could not climb.

As I tied my laces the boot-maker bent behind his counter and brought up a large, black hat, just like Leonce Coulet's and just what I wanted. It was, as the boots were, a perfect fit. I left my old shoes on the floor and handed over the small amount of money that was asked of me. Then Paul and I stepped into the sunlight and the bell rang again as we closed the door and walked away, and although I was tempted I didn't look behind me once, being more than certain that the shop would have disappeared forever by the time the bell stopped ringing – and in any event, I thought, why should I give reality the chance to triumph over imagination?

In the square at Bargemon I sat, immensely proud, on the terrace of the café with Paul, and tipped my hat over my eyes and ordered pastis for us both. Waiting for the drinks the shepherd stared at me, leaning forward to rest his elbows on the table and his face on his hands. 'You know, Michèu,' he began, 'I think maybe you have been a shepherd before.'

'No,' I answered, 'never.'

Paul shook his head. 'What you say is difficult to believe,' he said. 'You do it well, you know, and if you hadn't said so I would have sworn that you had been a shepherd for years.'

This was high praise indeed and I was touched by it but I was totally unprepared for what was to follow.

'I have something to say,' said Paul as the drinks arrived and I poured the water, making the ice clink. 'You see, I am getting too old now to be a shepherd, walking the road, climbing the hills . . . but I have a good flock. I want you to come and keep the sheep with me this summer. In the autumn you will help me take them back to Grimaud. Through the winter I will teach you all I know . . . and next year I will give you my flock and you will take them to the mountains for me.'

Paul continued to stare at me and now I stared at him. I took a sip of my drink, astounded by the magnificence of this offer; but there was more to come.

'I also have a daughter,' said Paul, 'I will give her too, with the flock. What do you say to that?'

I didn't know what to say. I did not know if Paul's daughter was in his gift or not but I could see that he was sincere in what he said. I took another sip of my drink. Perhaps it would be a good idea to become a shepherd and spend all my summers on the clear mountains and all my winters down by the warm sea. I smiled at Paul and shook my head in refusal though many times since I have regretted it. 'I come from the city,' I said, 'and I don't know that I am capable of doing what you ask or even if I am ready to be a shepherd.'

By the time that Paul and I had returned to Favas the flock was all assembled across the field and Marius was hitching the mule to the cart and in a moment we were on the road once more. The dark came down like a castle gate that night and I soon saw Paul's hurricane lamp in the distance and as I walked I thought of him and the square at Bargemon and how quiet and full of shade that square is. Of all the places in Provence it is the one I think of most and it was the most difficult to leave. Whenever I remember it I see Paul opposite me at that table, his glass held in two rough hands, his eyes looking at me full of hope while all I could feel was a sadness at being unable to do what he asked; unable to become his shepherd and his son so that he might know that his sheep were on the mountains even when he was too feeble to take them there himself; and above all, unable, in the future, to help him remember the comradeship of the road and the ancient simplicity of the best days. Who, I wondered, would graze my sheep for me when I was old?

We stopped to rest at midnight some three or four kilometres before the town of Combs-sur-Artuby, near a ruined house that stood in a wild field by the bend of a shallow river. The mistral had got up but our fire soon cheered us and this time it was Paul's story and, in the light of the flames, his face was wise and gentle. And, what with my new boots and a day and a night of sleep behind me, I stayed awake and listened though, once again, I understood little of what was said.

The next morning, when we were breaking camp just after dawn, I asked Marius what the story had been about.

'It was about a black horse in the Camargue,' he said as I helped him lift the food box into the cart. 'More than that I cannot say. Paul is difficult to understand, even for us. You see, with him you think he has said one thing but he has really said something else. To tell the truth, with Graziani you never know where you are.'

# The Curse of Igamor

*T*he Lord of Aigues Mortes, the Marquis of St Gilles, came straight to the point. 'I need more money,' he said. 'This is the finest town in Provence, but our battlements and towers need constant repair, and that costs money. I have the finest soldiers in the world, and they cost even more money. Do my subjects not realize that but for me they would all be the slaves of some Algerian pirate. Do they not see that freedom costs money?' The Marquis stared at his Chancellor and squeezed his hands behind his back until the knuckles bulged; then he stared at the court Magician who was also present. 'There is no other way,' he continued. 'I will have to raise the taxes.'

The Chancellor moved his weight from one foot to another. All three men were standing in the Marquis's apartments and it was morning. The white sun of Provence shone directly in at the narrow windows and made patterns on the brown tiles that covered the floor. The Chancellor gave a weak smile. 'We have tried to increase the taxes,' he said, 'but the people murmur against us and refuse.'

The Marquis turned and looked out at the landscape that lay below and beyond the city walls. It was a strange landscape, one of the strangest in the world, for although only a few miles distant from the bright waters of the Mediterranean the town of Aigues Mortes was completely hemmed in by a trackless waste of marshland and salt lakes. In this wilderness were swamps that could suck a man down to his death. There were untamed horses too, thousands of them, white and strong. They could run like the wind those horses and no one ever caught them for, if pursued, they would swim deep into the rolling waves of the sea, swimming until their tangled manes were covered by an ivory foam and they looked for all the world like giant monsters of the ocean.

The people of the city were fearful of the horses and kept well away from them. They believed that the animals had been left behind by the Saracens when they had sailed away to Africa in the ancient days, after the wars. Some even said that the horses were bewitched and carried an evil poison in their teeth. 'Keep away from the marshes,' they would say to the stranger, 'especially at night . . . that is if you value your life.'

These matters never troubled the Marquis. He was above sharing in the superstitions of the ignorant and his only care was for his soldiers, the walls of the city and the amount of gold locked in the treasury. Without money he had no power and power was what kept him alive.

After a while the Marquis ended his study of the landscape and turned from the window, his face dark with thought and flushed with anger. 'I know how to deal with these peasants of mine,' he said. 'I will threaten them in such a way that they will be only too pleased to pay their taxes, however much I ask for. Chancellor, Magician, follow me,' and the Marquis left his apartments, crossed his private courtyard and went directly to the market square of the town, for he knew that there he would find most of the townsfolk setting up stalls and preparing for the day's business. The Chancellor and the Magician followed their master, step by step, and a handful of armed soldiers went with them.

The moment the Marquis and his companions appeared all noise and movement stopped and the townsfolk stood as still as statues and faced their liege lord. Satisfied, the Marquis raised an arm and pointed to the sky. 'You will pay more taxes,' he began, 'or you will suffer, everyone.'

There was silence for a little longer then a stall-holder standing nearby said: 'But, my lord, we pay our taxes regularly and in full.'

'It is not enough,' said the Chancellor.

'But,' said another stall-holder, 'if we pay more we shall not have enough to feed ourselves, or our children, and they often go hungry as it is. And if our children die there will be no one to pay taxes in the future, my lord. We shall all perish and so will our children's children.'

'Your children,' retorted the Marquis. 'What do I care for your children. I have other cares. If my soldiers are not fed and if the walls of this city crumble your children will be slaves in Barbary.'

'Slaves in Barbary at least eat well,' said someone bravely, 'even a Saracen doesn't like to see his money wasted.'

The Marquis flew into a rage at this insolence and commanded that the man who had spoken be flogged immediately. He gave a sign and his soldiers seized the culprit, tied him to the end of a market stall and gave him twenty lashes there and then. When the punishment had been completed the Marquis smiled and continued with his speech. 'You will see,' he said, 'that I am in earnest. One way or another I will levy more taxes this month and every month thereafter. If you refuse I shall take your children from you, nor will they be fortunate enough to become Saracen slaves, instead I shall command my Magician to cast a spell, a spell that will conjure up the curse of Igamor, and Igamor will take your children one by one, then your wives and, last of all, each one of you. If you give me nothing to defend this town with then I shall see that I have nothing in it to defend.'

The people of Aigues Mortes caught their breath and looked at each other in despair. The Marquis could not have pronounced a more terrifying name than that of Igamor. According to an ancient legend Igamor was a huge horse from the Camargue, but black with eyes of crimson flame, and teeth like sabres that clattered and clashed as he galloped. It was said that Igamor had a long long back that could stretch so much that he could carry many more riders than an ordinary horse. Igamor had hooves of iron and a coat of wire which clung to human flesh like burrs of steel and never let go. Once you sat astride him or touched him with a hand you were bound to him until death. Once he had you in his power Igamor bore you off across the marshes at a headlong pace, rushing with you to his cavern beneath the waves where he would devour you alive and your blood would rise to the surface and stain the blue sea red.

For generations the simple inhabitants of Aigues Mortes had believed this story; from age to age parents had warned their children against falling foul of Igamor and that was why they shuddered at the Marquis's words. Never before had they been threatened with such a fate.

The Chancellor and the Magician smiled to see the townsfolk so subdued and the Marquis spoke again: 'Now listen, you fools,' he said, 'Igamor is in the power of my Magician and my Magician is in my power. Should you not do exactly as I have commanded Igamor will come for each of you in turn. The first of you to disobey me will be the first to see his child take a ride on Igamor's back. Now swear to do my bidding, all of you.'

The people of Aigues Mortes did as they were ordered and swore an oath and their lord sneered at them. 'The tax-collectors will begin their task tomorrow,' he said, and pleased with his morning's work he stamped away, closely followed by his two henchmen.

As soon as the three men had returned to the Marquis's apartments they called for cups of chilled wine. 'Did I not speak the truth,' said the Lord of Aigues Mortes, toasting his own cleverness. 'There will be no more disobedience now. All you will have to do, Chancellor, is collect and count the money. As for you, Magician, just put on your magic gown, make a few passes in the air and speak some Latin backwards . . . then you will see those hag-ridden clowns of ours obey your every word.'

'How stupid they are,' said the Chancellor, 'to be daunted by a mere legend. Still, I suppose it is logical to assume that sheep were created so that wolves might feed off them.'

❧

The very next day every citizen was required to begin paying the extra taxes and they did. Month followed month and the people of the town grew sadder and hungrier. They lost their energy, their jollity and all the other qualities that normally come with living in the sunshine of Provence. They went about with a mournful air. No one joked, no one sang and the children, told by their parents of the danger they were in, no longer played in the streets or ran along the battlements. The black curse of Igamor hung over the whole town. Only the Lord of Aigues Mortes and his courtiers were happy; they had the money they wanted and the townsfolk were as subdued and as tractable as anyone could wish; never, it seemed, would they raise their heads again.

❧

Every now and then, generally once a year at the beginning of summer, it was usual for a troubadour to make his appearance at Aigues Mortes, arriving by sea and tramping along the causeway which joined the port to the city and ended at its southern gate. The year of the curse of Igamor was no exception, save for one thing only. Nearly all the troubadours who came to the town had been there at least once before and were known to courtiers and townsfolk alike. This man was a stranger.

He was dressed oddly too. He wore a long gown in place of the short tunic most frequently associated with troubadours, and from top to toe it was in two colours, half of it being in yellow and the other half in red. He carried, as was customary, a lute and a leather bag containing a few possessions, but, in addition to everything else, on his right shoulder sat a small, pale brown monkey, so pale that she was the colour of gold and her name was Heloise.

The troubadour went without hesitation to the great door that led to the Marquis's residence but he found his way barred, first by the soldiers of the place and then by the Chancellor.

'I don't take to you at all,' said the Chancellor. 'You are not like those who normally come here. I do not like your dress either, it is outlandish and foreign, and this animal – it comes from the East, no doubt, and could carry the plague. You are more like a tramp than a troubadour. See here, I will allow you to sleep in the square for one night, but you will not sing or tell stories, unless the Marquis says so, and tomorrow at dawn, you will leave the city . . . now be off.'

The troubadour, tired from his journey and footsore from the walk along the causeway, had no alternative but to do as he was told. It was already late afternoon and the shadows were lengthening as he passed into the town square searching for a corner where he might spend the night. All around him he saw numbers of townsfolk and their children, standing or sitting, but they were disconsolate and silent and did not extend the slightest word of welcome to the newcomer.

'By my stars,' said the troubadour as he sat by the fountain and pulled a piece of bread from his leather bag. 'Never have I been so received, and yet my brother troubadours told me that the people of Aigues Mortes were generous to a fault and loved a story more than life itself. They told a lie. I see that I might starve here before I received a smile, let alone a cup of wine.'

'And your brother troubadours were right,' said one of the townsfolk, 'but times have changed and us with them. We do not know how to smile now. We are hungry and our children are too, and yet we dare do nothing or say the merest word.'

The troubadour looked at his piece of bread for a second, as if it embarrassed him, and then put it back into his bag. 'Then tell me what is the matter,' he said, 'perhaps I can speak to your lord.'

'You will not understand,' said another of the townsfolk, 'our lord has cursed us with a spell and we fear it . . . sleep here tonight, friend, and be welcome, but when you leave tomorrow tell all those that you meet along the road that Aigues Mortes is the unhappiest town in Provence.'

'I see,' said the troubadour, and he smiled grimly and took out his piece of bread once more and chewed on it. 'Then I will not ask you to explain your troubles, but before I sleep here, on this hard ground, I will tell you a story, gratis, in the hope that it may lighten your hearts and lift this weight of gloom that lies over you. Sit down, and bring the children closer and let there be a man posted at each corner of the square to tell if those in authority approach for they have forbidden me to speak and besides my story is not for their ears.'

The townsfolk did as they were asked for although they were indeed down-hearted they, like the troubadour, hoped that the telling of a story might ease the burden they carried, and so, while the children made themselves comfort-able and the look-outs went to their places, the troubadour strung his lute and bade someone fill a pitcher of water and put it at his elbow so that he might drink when his throat became dry. Then he began and Heloise the monkey sat on his shoulder.

'Friends,' he said, 'my name is Mellano, Martinou Mellano, and I come from the mountains of the border country and I have never been anything but a troubadour and this story concerns another troubadour who lived a hundred years ago and it goes in this manner.

'There was once a lord of this very town who burdened his people with taxes that were beyond their means, saying that vast amounts of money were necessary to defend them against pirates and brigands. In fact most of the money collected was spent on the pleasures of the courtiers and on the whims of the lord himself. The people of the town resented this imposition but when they complained they were whipped and they and their children were threatened with the curse of Igamor.'

At the mention of this name there was a stirring among the townsfolk and they muttered to each other in fear and those who were sitting sprang to their feet and looked about them. But the troubadour ignored these disturbances and his listeners, remembering that look-outs had been posted, composed themselves once more and Mellano went on with his story.

'Now as you know Igamor is a huge black horse whose back can lengthen and whoever mounts him will never dismount save only beneath the sea, and there to be devoured. And so, rather than lose their children the good people of Aigues paid their taxes and went hungry, and the Marquis laughed at the simplicity of people who could believe everything they were told. Neverthe-less he was extremely gratified that they did and to make sure the townsfolk remained his dupes he occasionally had his soldiers steal a child and then sell it into slavery, afterwards giving out that the child had been taken into the marshes by the black horse, and the poor fools of Aigues believed this falsehood also and bowed down under their trouble and accepted it.'

Here Mellano took a drink of water from the pitcher that had been brought him and there was more murmuring amongst his audience and several individuals demanded to know where the truth of their predicament lay, but others argued that Mellano's story was only a story and, unless they did exactly as the Marquis had commanded, Igamor would certainly come for them. Again the troubadour made as if not to notice the disturbances and went on with his tale.

'Now the good people of Aigues did not know what to do until one day, as often happened at that time of year, a troubadour appeared and finding the town so cheerless he asked what the matter was, but so afeared were the people of their lord that they would not tell. Never minding this the troubadour gathered them together and began to tell them a story and it went in this way . . .

'"There was once a lord of this town," said that troubadour, "who burdened his people with taxes that were beyond their means, threatening them with the curse of Igamor if they did not pay. Now as you know Igamor is a huge black horse whose back can lengthen and whoever mounts him will never dismount, save only beneath the sea, there to be torn apart by the great teeth."' Again Mellano broke off his story and lifted the pitcher of water to his lips.

'But we are lost in your story, Mellano,' said one of the children during this interruption, 'what good does it do to go round and round in the same place?'

Mellano wiped his mouth with the back of his hand. 'It does little good,' he answered, 'so I will tell the story a different way, but you must listen to every word,' and the troubadour placed his pitcher carefully on the ground and, clearing his throat, he took up his tale once more.

'Now,' he said, 'while this troubadour of old was telling his story to the people of Aigues the little brown monkey that sat on his shoulder, for the troubadour in the story I tell was an ancestor of mine and always travelled with a little brown monkey the image of this one, a monkey that could talk, it was said, like a human-being, and carry spells like a magician . . . and so while my ancestor told his story the monkey dropped from his shoulder, climbed the nearest wall to the roof and disappeared into the gloom . . . because it was now night and the moon and stars were shining like silver, though every now and then a great soft cloud went floating across the sky and made everything dark.'

As Mellano was speaking these words the townsfolk shivered and drew closer together for Heloise had indeed slipped from the troubadour's shoulder and disappeared in precisely the way he had described. Again Mellano affected not to notice and went on speaking.

'And so the monkey scampered, as soft as a whisper, across the roofs of the town and clambered down to the balcony of the Marquis's apartments and there found his lordship leaning at his ease, gazing at the beauty of the sky and watching the clouds sailing in from the sea. The monkey did not hesitate but, clinging to the wall in the shadows, spoke gently into the ear of the Marquis, like a dream.

'"Oh, your lordship," she said, "bestir yourself, you are deceived by those who call you friend. Tonight a mysterious ship has dropped anchor in the harbour, a magic ship without captain or crew. How it came there is not known but its cargo is the richest ever seen. Jewels and silks there are, spices and sweetmeats and incense and wine . . . all are yours, but your Chancellor and your Magician have made a pact and have gone before you. They have set out in secret along the causeway, but your faithful servants have left a horse ready for you at the East Gate. Make haste and you will overtake your rivals. Go now, but go alone."'

At this point Mellano reached inside his bag and found another piece of stale bread. This time the townsfolk did not fidget or speak but waited patiently for the words to continue. Mellano finished his bread and smiled. It was night now and all he could see was the moon reflected in his audience's eyes and the glint of it on their teeth where their mouths gaped open. Again he smiled and went on.

'And so the troubadour's monkey, her story told, glided back up to the roof, soundless, like a lizard, but the Lord of Aigues came to himself and said; "I have been dreaming; a mysterious ship in the harbour, the Chancellor, the Magician, it would be like them to steal what is rightly mine. I must take horse and ride them down." And so, telling no one, he slipped from his apartments by a secret passage and made his way along the deserted streets to the East Gate, passing silently through the moonlight that came and went and rose and fell.

'Even though the Marquis acted immediately, by the time he had left his residence the monkey was halfway across the city. There she entered the Chancellor's villa and there too she found him taking his ease in the cool of the evening. Once more, unseen, the monkey spoke.

'"Lord Chancellor," said the voice, "you are deceived by those who call you friend. Tonight a mysterious ship has dropped anchor in the harbour, a magic ship without captain or crew, without sail or flag. How it came there is not known, but its cargo is the richest ever seen. Jewels and silks there are, spices and sweetmeats, incense and wine . . . all are yours but the Marquis and the Magician have made a pact and gone before you to take what is yours. They have set out in secret, along the causeway, but your faithful servants have prepared a horse for you at the West Gate. Make haste and you will overtake your rivals. Go now, but go alone."

'The Chancellor sat up straight and rubbed his eyes; "I have been dreaming," he said, "a mysterious ship in the harbour, the Marquis, the Magician, it would be like them to steal what is rightly mine. I must take horse and ride them down." And so, telling no one, he hurried from his villa and made his way along the deserted streets to the West Gate, passing silently through the moonlight that came and went and rose and fell.

'Now the monkey,' said Mellano, quickening the pace of his story, 'raced to the Magician's house to find him fast asleep amongst his potions and powders, lying flat on his back and snoring. You may well wonder why it was that his magic did not protect him from the monkey and the answer is simple . . . this magician was a charlatan and not really a magician at all. He did not wake up when the monkey came to his bedside to tell her story, he did not even blink his eyelids.

'"Magician," she said, "you are deceived by those who call you friend. Tonight a mysterious ship has dropped anchor in the harbour, a magic ship without captain or crew, without sail or flag. How it came there is not known, but its cargo is the richest ever seen. Jewels and silks there are, spices and sweetmeats, incense and wine . . . all are yours but the Marquis and the

Chancellor have made a pact and gone before you to take what is yours. They have set out in secret, along the causeway, but your faithful servants have prepared a horse for you at the North Gate. Make haste and you will overtake your rivals. Go now, but go alone."

'The Magician sat bolt upright in bed. "What was that?" he asked of the dark room. "Have I been dreaming? The Marquis, the Chancellor, it would be like them to steal what is rightly mine. I must take horse and ride them down." And so, telling no one, he scurried from his house and made his way along the deserted streets to the North Gate, passing silently through the moonlight that came and went and rose and fell.'

Now Mellano the troubadour rose to his feet so that he might tell the end of his story more easily, indicating at the same time that his audience should remain seated. The moonlight picked out the fine profile of his face and gleamed on the dark hair that swept his shoulders. He gazed at the faces gazing at him, at the children asleep in their parents' arms. 'We come to the last chapter, friends,' he said, 'and I will not disappoint you.' Then Mellano spread his arms as if to embrace the whole world, turning the palms of his hands to the sky, and once more going on with the story.

'And so it happened that the Marquis came hurrying to the East Gate, and the moon, like this one above us, raced through the clouds, making the shadows of the town leap and fall, dance and disappear. The mighty lord peered through the gloom and in the blackness of the great gateway he saw the shape of a horse, the outline of its back, the shine of a polished saddle and the glint of a stirrup.

'"By my faith," said the lord to himself, "some good servant has indeed placed a horse here. It was no dream I had . . . there must after all be a magic ship in the harbour, full of riches, and the Chancellor and the Magician have gone to it with never a word to me. So be it. I shall soon ride them down on this magnificent steed and all the treasure will be mine."

'With one leap the Marquis was in the saddle and he stretched his hands forward for the reins, but there were no reins and a cloud dropped down from the moon and suddenly his lordship could see and what he saw made his heart knock against his ribs.

'The horse on which he was mounted stretched away into the night, along the city walls, into the darkness. There was no head to the horse, and the Lord of Aigues Mortes screamed long and loud. Then he screamed a second time and tried to dismount but his legs were stuck solidly to the animal's side. He attempted to push his body free with his hands but they too had become glued to the horse's dark hide of wire. He could not move – he was helpless.

'"Igamor, Igamor," he cried, "who will save me from Igamor." But although many lying in bed that night heard his screams not one person ventured into the streets. The people of Aigues Mortes had been warned too often and their children knew that only a fool went out when Igamor was abroad.

'Now the Chancellor ran under the West Gate. In the gloom outside the city wall he saw a horse waiting patiently for its rider. He looked closer and saw the gleam of a saddle and the steel of a stirrup. "So," he said, "my dream was no dream, some good friend has indeed left me a horse here, and there will be a magic ship in the harbour and that Marquis and that self-seeking Magician have already gone to it with never a word to me. So be it. I shall soon ride them down on this magnificent steed and all the treasure will be mine," and with no more hesitation than that the Chancellor leapt up and into the saddle.

'He felt forward for the reins but his hands touched a rough spiky coat and a powerful magnetism pulled his hands downwards and held them there and his legs and thighs too were held fast to the horse's flanks. And the moon sprang from the heart of a black cloud and the Chancellor screamed in terror. The horse before him stretched away into the night, along the length of the city walls. There were no reins, there was no head. Again the Chancellor screamed and everyone in the town heard the scream. "Igamor, Igamor, will no one save me from Igamor?" But not one single person dared venture into the streets. The townsfolk trembled in their beds and their children told themselves that only a fool went out when Igamor was abroad.

'And at the same moment the Magician arrived at the North Gate. In the silver gloom of the archway he saw the fine head of a horse, the droop of the reins and the reflection of a bright stirrup.

'"Aha," he cried, "I do indeed have a friend and there must be a cargo of wealth in the harbour, meant for me, and while I dawdle the wicked Marquis and that greedy old Chancellor are on their way to steal what should be mine. So be it. I will follow after and ride them down and all the treasure shall be mine," and the Magician leapt onto the horse and seized the reins.

'As soon as he was in the saddle a strange power welded him to the animal. His hands felt fettered and his legs and thighs were sucked to the side of the horse and seized in a giant's grip. The moon thrust itself from behind a cloud and sped on to the next, and the Magician saw the bristling coat of the horse, the long black mane and the blaze of a wild and fiery eye. He twisted in the saddle, looking behind him and screaming in terror. The long, long back of his steed stretched away into the night along the black shadow of the city walls. The Magician pushed and fought against the power of Igamor but he was held fast and forever. He screamed again and the scream echoed across the roofs of the town and down into the square. "Oh save me, save me from Igamor, this cannot be. I am a Magician, save me from Igamor."

'There was not a single adult or child in bed that night who did not pull his blanket over his head and close his eyes when they heard the Magician scream, but no one tried to help him. The townsfolk bit their lips in fear and their children were sure and certain that only a fool went out when Igamor was abroad.

'Then the great horse snorted and shook his head, impatient to be running through the marshes down to his home in the sea, there to feed on the flesh of his victims. His teeth clashed in the night and the long body began to shrink and soon Igamor was the size of one huge horse only and the Marquis and the

Chancellor and the Magician came together and saw one another and realized they were indeed doomed. They whimpered and begged for mercy and they cursed, each one blaming the other two for what had happened, but it made no difference. Igamor stamped an iron hoof and galloped across the swamps, splashing the salt water high above his shoulders until at last he disappeared beneath the waves bearing all three men with him and, it is said, their cries can be heard to this very day all along by the sea's edge.'

There was silence for a while as Mellano drew breath; he sat and pulled a heavy shepherd's cloak from his bag and flung it around his body, for the cool of the evening had become the cold of the night. At the same time there was a movement on the nearest roof and the pale shape of Heloise glided down a wall and ran quickly back to her master and disappeared into the warmth of his garments. The troubadour was glad to see her return and said:

'And that was the story that the troubadour, my ancestor, told the people of Aigues Mortes all those years ago, and when it was finished those good people went to their beds, frightened, listening for screams and the iron tread of the horse, but there was nothing, though they could have sworn that during the telling of the story they had heard both those things. Eventually each and every one of them fell into a troubled sleep and the troubadour curled up on the hard ground.

The following morning the people of Aigues were awakened by the noise of music, something that had not happened during all the time of the curse of Igamor, and, opening their shutters they were able to see the troubadour sitting on the edge of the fountain, playing his lute and singing a song of Provence at the top of his voice.

'And the people of the town forgot the curse of Igamor and forgot the Marquis and they ran out of their houses, taking their children with them, and they surrounded the troubadour and sang with him. The troubadour would have been happy to sing and play forever but it was not long before the soldiers arrived on the scene, though strangely they came not to stop the singing but to look for the Marquis, for that morning they could not find him.

'And then servants came looking for the Chancellor and the Magician too for they also could not be found, nor were they ever though the whole town was ransacked from top to bottom. It was not until later that the sergeant of the gates came and said that outside the city walls that morning he had seen the hoofprints of a huge horse, so huge that it could only have been Igamor and the horse must have borne the three men away.

'The courtiers and the soldiers did not believe this story because, they said, Igamor did not exist and was only a legend. However, the people of the town thought otherwise and were grateful to the troubadour and thanked him sincerely, but he only laughed and would admit nothing, merely saying that those who used legends to increase their power might find legends used against them. In spite of this his heart was heavy, for he knew that it would not be long before the people of Aigues Mortes would be robbed by some other chancellor, falling under the spell of some other magician to the benefit of some other marquis, and this for the simple reason that they did not have the strength of mind to believe in themselves.

'Nevertheless, the people were happy for a while and when the troubadour left them they stood on the city walls and watched him until he had disappeared into the distance and the sound of his lute had faded also . . . and that is the end of the ancient story of Igamor as it was once told to me . . . and so, my friends, goodnight.'

With his story now finished Mellano began to settle himself as comfortably as he could by the fountain, making a pillow of his leather bag and wrapping himself round with his cloak. Without a word the townsfolk rose one by one to their feet and went to their beds, made silent by a mixture of terror and sadness; terror because Mellano's story had seemed so real during the telling; sadness because they knew that it could never become truth. The glimpse of a dream had only made the reality of their lives harder to bear.

But there was one citizen who had courage enough to speak to the troubadour, though he squatted down so that he might whisper his words. 'Mellano,' said this young man, 'I thank you for your story. Never have I heard anything so true and yet so exciting. I heard those shouts for help . . . I heard Igamor and felt the ground tremble under his hoofbeats. What a pity it is that Igamor is always used against us and never for us, except in legends, and what a pity that we shall not wake tomorrow and find our Marquis devoured like the one in your story . . . that would be too much to hope for . . . never mind . . . for a while you made us forget our misery and all I regret is that we are so poor that there is nothing to give you in return for the pleasure you gave us, no food and no bed either, for if we gave you gifts it would arouse the Marquis's anger . . . but one thing, Mellano, I can promise you, this story of yours will be told from generation to generation, we shall never forget it.'

The troubadour opened one eye, for he was already half asleep, tired by the exertions of the day and the effort of telling his story. 'Then, young man,' he said, 'that will be reward enough, for there is none better,' and he closed his eye and the young man stood and hurried away to his house.

The next morning, very early, only five or ten minutes after the sun had risen above the swamps and sent its first ray of light over the city walls, the townsfolk were awakened by the sound of music, loud music. Mellano the troubadour was playing his lute in the market square and singing a song to the sun at the top of his voice, while Heloise the monkey jumped up and down on his shoulder.

At first no one was brave enough to go to the window, but eventually the young man who had talked to the troubadour the previous evening went to his shutters and threw them open so that he could watch as Mellano sang in the sheer joy of being alive at the beginning of a new day. Soon more townsfolk appeared and some, with their children, came into the square and applauded, and others even gave Mellano some bread and some fruit so that he might break his fast. 'Perhaps,' they said, marvelling at the music, 'Igamor did indeed come for the Marquis in the night and carry him away, and the others too.'

It was not to be. The troubadour was given no opportunity to eat his food. Even before he could finish his song a band of soldiers, armed with pikes and led by the Chancellor, came running from the Marquis's residence, and while a small group of them arrested the troubadour the remainder beat the townsfolk from the square and forced them back into their houses.

'So,' roared the Chancellor, pushing his face right up against Mellano's, held fast as he was by two soldiers, 'so you did not hear me yesterday . . . did I not order you to leave this city before dawn, and did I not say there was to be no singing or story-telling unless expressly ordered by the Marquis, and have you not disobeyed me and told a story likely to disturb public order? Well then, troubadour or tramp or whatever you call yourself, let me tell you that if you ever return to this city I shall have you thrown from the top of the tower of Constance, but today you are fortunate and I shall be lenient. Soldiers! See that this man is given fifty lashes, then send him on his way . . . and break his lute so that he may not sing.'

The soldiers lost no time in carrying out the sentence imposed on Mellano, and the sound of the flogging reverberated through the deserted streets of the town and penetrated every house. The people of Aigues Mortes closed their shutters and their doors but that did not save them and they heard every stroke of the whip and every cry of the troubadour as he suffered in his loneliness and pain. These sounds passed through the open windows of the Marquis's residence also and he smiled to himself in satisfaction as he took his morning meal, and he gave a cup of chilled wine to his Chancellor and his Magician, who both attended him, and the three men raised their goblets and drank deeply.

When the soldiers had seen the punishment carried out they dragged the troubadour to the nearest city gate, leaving him in the dust at the side of the road where there was nothing to protect his bloody back from the full strength of the sun as it began to rise to the centre of the sky. For hours he lay without moving, Heloise the monkey sitting by his head, his broken lute beside him, and no one came to his assistance until, at length, creeping along the city walls from the direction of another gate, came the young man who was braver than the rest.

Quickly he seized the troubadour beneath the arms and dragged him to the shade of the nearest pine tree, unobserved from the city walls because it was now noon and the soldiers of Aigues Mortes had taken refuge from the heat of the day and were resting in the coolness of their stone-built guard-houses. From beneath his jerkin the young man produced a flask of water and a phial of oil. He began by quenching the troubadour's thirst and then went on to anoint his torn back, wiping away the clotted blood. In a little while Mellano was able to sit up and take some of the food that the young man had also brought with him.

'I came round by the city walls,' he explained to the troubadour, 'so that I would not be suspected, and everywhere along I saw huge hoof-marks, they were the hoof-marks of Igamor, I am certain of it. He was here, he came for the Marquis and the others, but why did it not happen as in your story? Why did we not wake this morning to find the story true?'

'Yes,' said Mellano, 'Heloise told her story and Igamor was here, but I can achieve no more than that. The real pity, my friend, is that the people of Aigues Mortes believe what they should not and not what they should. Until they change their ways their lot will always be the same. In the story the people believed in the story and so Igamor devoured the Marquis, the Chancellor and the Magician. It is so simple.'

The young man was puzzled. 'But why did you stay this morning and sing? Did you not know that you would be flogged?'

'I never know,' said Mellano smiling, 'I never know until my morning song is sung whether Igamor has carried off the Marquis or not. It all depends on how many people believe my story, and how hard they believe it too.'

'Are you often flogged?' asked the young man.

'Often,' answered Mellano, but he smiled again.

The young man drew a deep breath of amazement. 'I came here to help you,' he said, 'but also to ask you something. I want to leave this place and these people that have no courage. I want to follow you and learn your songs and your stories. I want to be like you.'

Mellano shook his head. 'You will be whipped like me if you do,' he said. 'Remember something else; you promised that my story would not die, that it would live from generation to generation. You must stay in Aigues Mortes and see that it does, for if the story dies how can the people of Aigues Mortes believe in it enough to make it true?'

'Is this the only way?'

'It is the only way for you,' answered Mellano. 'You must return to the city before you are missed. I thank you for your help and courage, but I do not want to see you flogged.'

'And you?' asked the young man, 'what will you do now?'

'Do not make yourself anxious on my account,' said Mellano, 'I have been whipped worse than this. Heloise and I shall wait until nightfall and take the road to Arles. I have friends there and they will look after me.'

'And your broken lute?'

The troubadour looked at the instrument which lay by his side. 'My friends will give me one,' he said, 'a better one. Come, you must leave me or you will be discovered.'

And with this the troubadour said farewell and in great sorrow the young man went into the shadows of the high fortifications and stole unnoticed into the city. That evening, at dusk, he returned to the spot where he had left Mellano but the troubadour had vanished and there was no trace of him under the pine tree, and even the broken lute had disappeared. Aigues Mortes never saw him again – he had gone to tell his story elsewhere.

# THE MOUNTAIN
# OF ROBION

After leaving Combs we entered a country that was empty and remote. From one horizon to the other the sky was hard and flat, scraped clean by the wind. What farmhouses I saw were small and distant and showed no sign of life. Every now and then the flock passed a holy shrine with flowers in a jar to decorate it, but the flowers were withered and dead and our sheep moved forward unhurriedly, heads down, grazing, as if the hands that had cut the flowers were dead too and the world had been given over to us entirely.

Jules and Joseph walked near me, just a yard or two in front of the mule cart, and I listened to them discuss how far we would go that day. Four hours later the road divided and we dropped down a little slope into the hamlet of Jabron and the way became so narrow that it barely separated the few houses and barns that stood there. Further on we came to a stream and the ground levelled beside it. We halted and ate and the talk was all of another flock that had gone by during the night at Combs, when, I suppose, I had been asleep for I had heard nothing. Jules talked more than anyone else, animated, his face bitter, and the moment he had finished eating he set out to retrieve his car, which he had left some kilometres behind us, halfway to Combs. I watched him stride up the slope from the river, his thick-set body leaning forward, the only thing moving in the whole landscape.

Because of the rival flock our plans had been changed and there was little time for us to rest; as soon as the heat of the day began to lessen we moved on. A little later Jules drove by us and did not stop to talk, being determined, said Marius, to go ahead and discover what was happening along the road.

Meanwhile our path advanced and led us through Le Bourguet and another stream flowed on our right, a tributary of the Jabron. Just beyond the village there was a tiny chapel, its yellow stones made gaudy by the strong colour of the afternoon sun. The turf here was short and springy, like the lawns of a château, and white stones and boulders burst through it as if escaping from imprisonment beneath.

Then we came up with the car and saw Jules sitting in the driver's seat, sideways, the door open, his feet upon the ground and his hat pushed to the back of his head in a gesture of despair. Above the road lay a forest, the place that Jules had chosen for our camp. Now someone else had taken it, taken the good pasture and the water as well.

I looked up but could see no sign of sheep; they would have been further back, in the shade under the trees. But I did see the figure of a shepherd, standing motionless, half hidden by a tree trunk, staring down at us. The sound of our bells brought his dogs into the open and they growled, baring their teeth. Another shepherd came to stand beside the first; they gave no smile of welcome.

Jules swore. He did not like to be beaten. What made the defeat worse was that the enemy was an ancient one and this was but the latest battle in a never-ending war. The other shepherds had deliberately broken the rules; when passing us at Combs they should have asked us where we intended to camp the following night, for we, as leaders on the road, had precedence over all flocks coming behind. Jules stood up out of the car and straightened the hat on his head. 'We cannot stay here,' he said. 'If their sheep and ours get mixed together during the night it will take a week of work to sort it out again . . . in the old days we would have gone up there with our whips.'

And so we continued our march, the road climbing in slow, sweeping movements and the land sprawling flat on both sides, confined only by two distant escarpments, with the one to the west – the Robion – high and sharp, its jagged edges picked out by the evening light. This plateau on which we found ourselves seemed unreal, insecure even, ready to tumble down into the deep gorges of the Verdon river. And further on still, to the north, I could see a terrifying jumble of mountains. Huge peaks and pointed ridges turning dark blue, indigo and black as they rolled away to the Alps.

I urged the mule forward and soon I saw Paul's hurricane lamp blaze up and I lit my own and in the dark we kept going for yet another four hours until suddenly Marius was beside me, seizing the bridle from my hands and we left the road and mounted a steep and dusty track, running hard, shouting at the mule until we had manoeuvred the cart onto a flat piece of ground carved out between two massive rocks. There was no water here and the grass was coarse but it didn't matter. All of us, animals and men, had walked too far that day and we dropped to the ground the moment we could, sighing with relief.

Except Jules. I watched him in the light of his lamp as he brought wood and made a fire, his face still angry. Then he washed his hands in water poured from a bonbonne, holding the wicker-covered bottle between his knees and controlling the flow of liquid by the movement of his body. There was such a solidity to the man, as if he himself had been hewn out of the mountain of Robion and erected by the roadside as a rough monument to inspire all travellers with determination and strength.

His face was almost always steady in its expression. For him the world was a harsh place and it rarely made him smile with pleasure. He expected no favours and if by chance he received one then that was simply a weakness on the part of Providence and Providence was a fool and ought to know better.

But I sensed, as I watched him, that he was a good person. His strength was massive but not evil and he would not go out of his way to do you harm just as he would not go out of his way for a fool. Some days later, at the very end of our journey, by the road to Argens, I shook his hand and thanked him before turning and going alone to Marius's village. Jules had been surprised:

'It is I who thank you,' he said, 'I needed someone.'

'Well, anyway,' I insisted, 'thanks for the food and the wine.'

Then Jules smiled a real smile and I have always remembered it. It was the smile of a man who knew the world inside out though he hadn't seen much more of it than the road from Grimaud to the mountains. 'If you'd been a shepherd,' he said, 'I'd have had to pay you as well. You are welcome to the food – after all, you worked for it. You can come again next year, if you like,' and with that he'd driven away.

❧

Under the long cliff of Robion we spent an uncomfortable night, looking down on the road and always with one man out listening so that we could leave at a moment's notice if our rivals attempted to steal yet another march on us. But they did not; the fire glowed red and we huddled down in our cloaks.

'We will leave before dawn,' said Jules eventually. 'In that way we shall be sure of the best place at Castellane, on the flat by the river, where the good grass is.'

This thought cheered Jules and he laughed, a short, coughing sound, and threw another piece of wood onto the fire.

'It's a hard old world,' he said, 'and a man must make his own luck, like Picabrier did . . . you know the story of Picabrier . . . now there was a world to live in . . .'

# The Perfect
# Garden

*T*o the north and east of Arles there is a range of bone-white mountains called the Alpilles and they lie, scattered like a broken rib-cage, in that corner of Provence which is bounded by the River Rhône on one side and the Durance on the other. Even in our day few roads lead into this lonely and barren land but more than a thousand years ago, as might be imagined, that same country was yet wilder and more dangerous, and only the faintest of mule tracks crossed it and only the most brave or the most desperate of men dared venture into it.

One of the oldest of these mule tracks ran south from the town of St Rémy and took the direction of Maussane, rising from the lowlands until, on the peak known as La Caume, it forked and one branch swung away eastwards, following the crests for a time before dropping down on the far side. Though it twisted and turned, it held its direction over many a mile, leaving the mountains only after it had passed beneath the cliff of Roquemartine. At that point it entered a well-watered and fertile plain and struck directly into it, disappearing at last in the place where it joined the main highway near the village of Eyguières.

Along this road, some score of years after the Saracens had been compelled, by force of arms, to flee their strongholds in Provence, on a day when the sky was so bright that it blinded the eyes and the sun burnt the ground so fiercely that it was a torture to walk on, two men were travelling, stumbling and limping as they went. Their clothes and their faces were whitened by the dust that lay everywhere and, disturbed by their feet, floated upwards as they moved. Under the dust their clothes were ragged and their faces were lined and hard. Such faces were the faces of men who defied life to deal them harsher blows than those they had already received; never would they be thirstier, nor wearier nor poorer. With their lips cracked and their eyes reflecting the bleakness of their hearts they journeyed on, looking what they were; soldiers without a war to fight in; mercenaries without a prince to pay them.

All that day the two men trudged on until at last the road brought them down from the hills and out into the little plain that lies before Eyguières. In that place, at no great distance from the road, they saw a peasant's hovel with broad leaved mulberry trees all around, a well nearby and a vineyard behind. There were two mules also, rendered insensible by the heat, standing motionless while the horse-flies sucked them empty of blood.

The travellers made straight for the habitation, barely able to walk now, and under the shade of the first tree they came to, they fell to the ground in exhaustion. After a while one of the men rose and went to the well. The shadows had begun to lengthen with the sun going down the sky but the air still scorched the skin and did not stir; too hot for the sound of cicadas or the songs of birds. At the edge of the well the man found a leather bucket on the end of a rope and he threw it down into the dark. Almost immediately he heard the echo of cool water splashing, then he leant forward and hauled hand over hand until the bucket was in his grasp and he could raise it to his lips.

As he drank a peasant woman came to the door of the hovel, a filthy child on her hip. She looked out from the gloom and into the sunlight but said nothing and the man at the well, though he was aware of the woman, said nothing either, contenting himself with one movement only, just lowering a hand from the bucket to thrust back his cloak so that he might reveal the brass pommel of a sword. Then, when he had drunk, he turned and carried what water remained to his companion who had lain all this time unmoving on the ground. There he crouched and poured the contents of the bucket over the dusty face and into the dry hole of a mouth. 'Come, Nardello,' he said, 'drink or die.'

Nardello's eyes flickered and opened and he raised himself on an elbow. He licked his lips. 'Ah, Picabrier,' he replied, 'I feel near to death indeed . . . I am not so strong as you . . . I beg you not to leave me.'

Picabrier laughed, the sound starting and ending abruptly. 'I'll leave you when it suits me,' he said. 'When you die you die and my being near or far has nothing to do with it.' And having uttered this wisdom he sat and rested his back against the trunk of a tree, calling to the woman as he did so; 'Bring me some food, I have not eaten for three days.'

The woman, well used to stern words and hard blows, went into the hut and reappeared after a short interval with some goats' cheese and bread and a jug of wine. The child was now tucked in the crook of an arm. She brought the food to Picabrier, showing no fear, returned to her position at the door and continued with her staring.

As Picabrier tore at his bread the sun began to sink more rapidly towards the horizon and a man, the woman's husband, approached from the direction of the vines and with hesitant steps went to the well and halted there, staring at the scene before him as fixedly as his wife.

Picabrier watched the man closely and, without interrupting his meal, drew his sword from its scabbard and stuck it into the dirt between his feet where it would be easy to reach. When his jug of wine was empty he held it up to the woman and shook it. 'Get me some more,' he said, 'and be quick about it.'

The woman did not hesitate and still carrying the child came for the jug and went with it into the hut. In her absence Picabrier turned his attention to the man and he nodded in the direction of the tall cliff of Roquemartine and said: 'Who is the lord of that castle up above?'

The peasant ducked his head and took a step forward, then he took a step backwards and said nothing. Picabrier swore. 'Answer me, you fool,' he said. 'Who is the lord of that castle, what manner of man is he and what is the castle called?'

At this point the woman returned. She gave the wine to Picabrier and answered his questions as he drank, her voice quite steady. 'It belongs to the Baron de Vallongue,' she began, 'a man past his prime. He used to rule his lands well and we were happy here, but as he has grown older he has become wary and suspicious. He trusts no one and the good days are gone. His wife died long ago and his two sons he has locked in his deepest dungeon for fear they may poison him for the succession. His own people he has turned away and takes on, for protection, only strangers and mercenaries, hard men, like yourself, and they rob and plunder this valley as they think fit. The Baron knows nothing and cares for nothing. He keeps to his castle in the belief that his people would kill him if he went amongst them . . . and we would, surely, if we could.'

Refreshed by the food and drink he had been given Picabrier stretched out his legs and studied the woman's face. He liked what he saw; he admired her courage. The child on her arm began to whine with hunger and she pushed aside her bodice to bare a breast.

'Why fear things so?' asked Picabrier, shifting his gaze and noticing how firm the woman's body was.

'What can I know about the great?' she answered. 'He fears the assassin's knife, his sons, his cousin, Boscabrun – a good man by all accounts – and it seems that more than anything he fears the Saracens too.'

'The Saracens,' exclaimed Picabrier, 'why, now they have lost their castles they do not care to venture far from the safety of their ships, not without good reason they don't. This Baron of yours is indeed timorous.'

'Like all who have much to lose,' said the woman, 'he cannot contemplate the thought of his own death, and so his grip on life grows tighter as he nears the leaving of it . . . meanwhile he makes certain that we live badly while his soldiers live well . . . and that is where you yourself should go. You can be no worse than those he has hired already and already you have been kinder. You see, my man and I need a protector. We live too near this castle.'

Picabrier swallowed a last mouthful of wine and then stood. 'I shall take your advice,' he said, 'now, while the evening is cool. If I prosper so shall you, for the food and wine I have had today.'

'And your comrade,' asked the woman, 'what of him?'

Picabrier laughed his laugh again. 'He is no comrade of mine,' he answered. 'The winds of misfortune blew us together as now they blow us apart. Do what you wish with him. There are coins in his purse and they may make it worth your while to care for him. If he recovers be wary, he is as crafty as a priest and has the same quicksilver in his tongue,' and with another laugh Picabrier prodded Nardello with his foot and then strode away in the direction of the castle of Roquemartine.

By the time Picabrier arrived at his destination it was nearly dusk and the captain of the Baron's soldiers had just given the order to close the castle gates. At that moment a shout was heard and when the captain turned to discover where the noise had come from he was astonished to see only one man in the road, a dark figure with a ragged and dusty cloak hanging from his shoulders and a broadsword in his hand.

'What did you say, fellow?' said the captain, stepping close to the stranger, 'what do you want?'

'I called for the best man here,' answered Picabrier, 'and what I want is first his life, then his place.'

'I am the best man here,' said the captain and he dropped a hand to his sword but he was not quick enough and, uttering a dreadful oath, Picabrier lunged forward and pierced his man to the heart.

The captain fell and, placing the castle wall at his back, Picabrier, with a stiff arm and a bloody sword, held the remaining guards at bay. They hemmed him round in a semi-circle, weapons drawn but not daring to attack, not knowing what to do.

'You fools,' said Picabrier, 'let one of you run to your master and tell him that a better soldier than your captain is here to guard his castle, hurry now for I am weary and need to sleep.'

For a moment the bemused sentries hesitated but then one of them did as he was commanded and within a very short time Picabrier was being escorted into the main room of the castle. There he found the Baron de Vallongue sitting in a chair; an old man with few teeth in his head and brown grave marks on his cheeks. He was wrapped in a warm cloak and surrounded by men at arms, yet his hands shook with fear and age.

'I could have you killed for this,' said the Baron as Picabrier advanced, 'I could have you flayed alive.'

'Yes,' said Picabrier, 'and what good would that do, and which of these spineless men of yours will be the first to attempt what their captain could not accomplish? Who will be the first to die?'

'You cannot kill them all,' said the Baron, 'you cannot kill me.'

Picabrier smiled. 'My lord, I have come to protect you, not to harm you,' he said, his voice softening. 'I have heard of your need; threatened by your sons, the evil Boscabrun . . . the Saracens even. Sire, I have been a soldier all my life. I have fought in Italy and Spain. I have fought against the Turk. There is no soldier who knows or loves the art of war like I do . . . and I am called Picabrier.'

At the mention of this name several amongst the Baron's soldiers gasped in surprise and they turned to their master, telling him that if indeed this man were Picabrier then he was the most ruthless mercenary in Christendom and exactly what was wanted as captain of the bodyguard.

The Baron was not reassured. 'If,' he said, 'you truly are this great Picabrier, why do you travel in rags, covered with the dust of the hills?'

Picabrier did not answer immediately but gathering up the hem of his cloak he used it to wipe his sword clean of the thick blood that stained it. 'This weapon is bright and sharp,' he said eventually, 'and it is all I need. I am a soldier, not a courtier. I have come, Baron, because no one can protect you as I can protect you.'

The Baron nodded. 'Very well,' he said, 'sleep here in safety and dine here too, we will talk more of this tomorrow.' And the Baron made a sign and, after making his bow, Picabrier was ushered from the hall.

So it was that Picabrier established himself as captain of the Baron's bodyguard. With the greatest ease in the world this newcomer played upon his master's fears and in less than a month had become the old man's most trusted retainer. He gained the confidence of the soldiers also, seeing to it that they were well paid, loyal to him rather than to the Baron. From the estates in the plain he took as much as he could get in food and taxes and soon began to amass a small but useful fortune. To the peasant woman, who had first succoured him on his arrival at Roquemartine, he kept his promise and his men never molested her or her husband. On one occasion, dressed in fine clothes and mounted on an elegant horse, he even visited her hovel to throw her a gold piece, partly in rough gratitude and partly because Nardello still dwelt with her, recovered in health but lacking the resolution to move on.

'You do right to stay here,' Picabrier said to him with a sly smile. 'I will have work for you in time. Soon I shall be lord of Roquemartine and all its lands. Should you help me to it your reward will be great,' and with this Picabrier had ridden on.

It was not many days after that meeting that the Baron called his captain to him and told him of a dream he had dreamt that night. 'I can never leave this room again,' he said, 'for in my dream a great army of Saracens battered down the gates and cut my throat at this very door. Tell me, Picabrier, how can we make this castle more secure. How can we make my safety more certain?'

Picabrier considered the problem for a moment, then he spoke: 'Sire,' he said, 'I am much too wily a bird to be caught out by Boscabrun or even by the ghost of Abd al-Rhaman himself. My men watch your cousin's farmhouse day and night and sentinels guard every approach to the castle. All that soldiers can do has been done . . . but if you desire to be beyond all harm for ever, more than any other mortal man, then there is only one way . . . you must send for Nardello, the magician.'

'Nardello,' said the Baron, his voice shaking with excitement, 'and who is he?'

'The greatest magician in Provence,' answered Picabrier. 'I have heard tell that he has travelled the whole world, he knows the secret of the pyramids and can understand the riddle of the sphinx. It was he who planned the fortifications at Les Baux and no one will ever destroy them.'

'Then he is what I need,' cried the Baron. 'With both soldiers and magic I shall be safe. Send for him, Captain. Promise anything if only he will come.'

'Oh he will come,' said Picabrier, 'of that I am sure and certain.'

And come Nardello did, appearing at the castle gates as if by magic only a week or so after the Baron had requested his presence. He had dressed for the part and looked solemn and stately. His gown had wide sleeves and fell to his feet and was covered with patches of gold and silver cloth, provided by

Picabrier, and sown in place by the peasant woman to represent suns and moons and a sprinkling of stars.

'Well, Magician,' said the Baron when his captain had brought Nardello before him, 'if you have the second sight you will know of my troubles and my pain.'

Nardello had been well schooled. 'Sire,' he began, 'your sons are disloyal, your cousin threatens you and the Saracens lurk in the night. Yours is a stony path.'

The Baron was impressed by this display of knowledge. 'You are correct in every detail,' he said, 'but do you not possess some magic that will protect me from my enemies.'

"I am monarch of all sorcery,' said Nardello, 'and now that I am beside you nothing can cause you harm. I shall straightway cast a spell and by it any foe who enters your domain will be seen in this magic crystal,' and here Nardello brought from under his gown a large piece of shapeless glass about the size of a melon. 'When an enemy approaches your borders this crystal will shine and show an image of him and the place of his incursion. With this device, my lord, you are beyond danger.'

The Baron seized the glass. 'Nardello,' he said, 'you are truly a great magician. I hereby create you a knight of Roquemartine, and Picabrier, I wish you to take this bag of gold to recompense you for the love you bear me . . . but for the moment you may go . . . I long to study this crystal in solitude.'

Picabrier was delighted with this day's work, so delighted that he presented Nardello with a gold piece for his pains, but he took great care to hide the bulk of his money in the secret spot where he kept the rest of his fortune, complimenting himself on his subtlety and foresight. The Baron too was content and passed all his waking hours staring at the crystal, hardly daring to take his eyes from it in case it glowed to warn him of an enemy. Nor did he sleep much either; he could not for he trusted no one to watch the lump of glass for him. As the months went by the Baron became totally obsessed by it and more and more reliant on his captain.

And that captain now rode out into the valley as if he were riding into his own estates, seeing to it that the peasants were kept at work, urging them on with whip and sword, while at the same time robbing them of everything they had of value. In less than a year he was a rich man, Nardello was his creature and only one thing lay between him and the realization of his ambitions: the continuing existence of the Baron's sons, locked away and forgotten in their dungeon. Picabrier knew that the ruler of Roquemartine, though still in good health, had reached his seventieth year and could not, in the nature of things, be expected to live much longer. As soon as the Baron died his sons would come into their inheritance and, aided by their cousin, Boscabrun, would muster their forces and rid themselves of the usurper who had stolen their birthright.

Given this situation it did not take Picabrier long to decide on his course of action – the heirs of Roquemartine would have to die. All that was needed, in order to satisfy the scruples of the castle's courtiers, was an order from the Baron. Having reached this conclusion Picabrier sent for Nardello, told him what was called for and, with no further delay, despatched him to the Baron's chamber and there the false magician bent to his task.

'Sire,' he began, 'as you know I have the second sight and I must tell you what it reveals to me even though such intelligence will distress you. It is this. Your sons, though still in prison, continue to harbour evil thoughts. Not content with conspiring with your cousin to end your life they are now planning to send messengers to the Saracens, begging them for assassins so they may achieve that which your wisdom has so far prevented. That is to say, your death.'

'Assassins!' shrieked the Baron, his fingers plucking at his throat. 'Surely the crystal will glow as soon as an enemy attempts to enter my domain?'

'Indeed, Baron,' replied Nardello, 'and so it will in all cases except this one. These assassins believe they cannot die and they have a great magic of their own and it enables them to shield themselves from the power of the crystal.'

'Aie!' moaned the Baron, 'may God protect me. That means . . .'

'That means,' continued Nardello, 'that they fear nothing. With their strange magic and their disdain of death they have been known to kill kings in their beds and emperors in their castles . . . and these are the men your sons wish to send against you.'

'Then what shall I do?' asked the Baron, 'I am once more in danger. How shall I protect myself?'

'I said I have the sight,' said Nardello, 'and so I have. I know that your sons have not yet sent their messengers, but I know also that they will. While they live they think only of taking what is yours, your life and your lands. I fear, my lord, they must be slain, only then will you be safe. You are still strong and will make other children.'

'Yes,' agreed the Baron, 'that is the way . . . but I would not want to have them suffer. Let them die easily.'

Nardello bowed but the Baron hardly noticed. 'Your tale of assassins,' he said, 'disturbs me. I thought I was secure but now it seems I am not. My cousin, Boscabrun, he could equally send a messenger to the Saracens, he may have already done so. You must think of a way to protect me and if you cannot I must find another magician.'

Nardello smiled as if he were superior to all magicians. 'Baron,' he said, 'I have already pondered this problem. I have the most wondrous spells in my books, greater than all the Saracen magic of Spain and Africa. Remember I know the secret of the pyramids and I know what keeps them safe.'

The Baron nodded like a child. 'Tell me,' he whispered.

'Behind this castle of yours,' went on Nardello, 'lies an area of ground protected by precipices. Here I will build you a garden, a garden as perfect as that which the Mohammedans call paradise, with water and flowers, trees and shade, grass and fruit and set at the middle of all will be a pavilion for you to live in, with an awning of silk.'

'Yes,' said the Baron eagerly, 'but how will this be made safe from Saracens and cousins?'

'By my powers, master,' answered Nardello. 'Around this garden I shall build a marvellous wall and it shall have no gates or doors and I shall lay a spell on this wall so that whatever lives behind it will be protected forever. This fortification will, by my sorcery, be too high to scale, too deep to mine and too strong to destroy.'

The Baron got to his feet, gripping the arm of his chair to steady himself, smiling with his few teeth. 'This is a miracle of ingenuity,' he said. 'At last I shall be out of danger and when I am safe the whole of my realm is also, for the head is the whole. Begin this work at once, Nardello, spare no cost for I am threatened on every side.'

Again Nardello bowed and he took his leave, well aware that the Baron, in his senility, had already forgotten the instructions he had given in regard to his sons. Nardello had not. Losing no time he went in search of Picabrier, told him his news and then watched while the captain laughed and gave orders that the Baron's heirs should be murdered that very night. The next morning, without a sign of remorse on his face, Picabrier went on with his plans in full confidence, directing that a large area of ground behind the castle be cleared and that a large number of peasants should present themselves within a day or two, on pain of death, so they might undertake the construction of a high, circular wall exactly as Nardello, who was placed in charge desired it.

So the peasants of Roquemartine were obliged to attempt this formidable task at the whim of their upstart lord, and the task was no easy one. Huge stones had to be dragged over several miles and then up to the heights of the castle. Rocks were quarried from the escarpment itself and then carved and cut into shape. For many and many a long day the Baron's subjects toiled in the dust and the sun, and when they faltered there was always a soldier waiting, ready to strike them down.

And Picabrier was there also, hounding the men on and praising the cruellest of the soldiers, for he was impatient to have the Baron behind his wall and to establish himself in that lord's spacious apartments; then he knew he would feel like a king and everyone would obey him without question.

After a month or two the wall was completed, save for a gap that would be closed once the Baron was inside. It was a solid looking structure and built in the bright, white stone of the mountains. It was crenellated at the top and a rough wooden ladder rose to the sentries' gallery, large enough to accommodate half a dozen soldiers and designed so that they could see whatever happened in the garden below.

Soon everything was prepared and the Baron was carried, with great solemnity, on a litter to the gap in the wall and passed through it, Nardello alone being permitted to follow him. Once within the Baron seized his magician by the sleeve and tugged at it. 'Make your incantations,' he said, 'until then I shall not feel safe.'

Nardello shook himself free of the Baron's grasp. 'Master,' he said, 'there is a spell in every stone that has been laid here, that is the secret of the Egyptians. You are already sheltered from danger. Come, I will show you this paradise . . . It too I have made with magic.'

And here Nardello took the old man by the arm and led him round the confines of the fortification, speaking as he went. 'Do you not see,' he began, 'how the water arrives by a strange device and how it flows everywhere in cool streams of clearest nectar. And do you not see these fruit trees and this trellis, covered by a vine where you may rest in the shade? In this arbour lies a silken bed, made secret with jewelled lattices. In this green garden the grass is a cushion underfoot and blackbirds and thrushes sing in every tree. And there, hidden from sight, a pavilion has been made ready with many rooms and comfortable divans. A breeze will follow your every step and the air you inhale will be fresh and untainted. Invisible hands will bring you all the delicacies you may need or desire. Oh, Master, is this not truly a great magic I have done you – is this garden not perfect?'

'Yes, yes,' answered the Baron, though he did not bother to look at what Nardello had shown him; instead he took something from his belt and thrust it into the magician's hand. 'Here is your reward,' he said, 'the key to my treasury, I have no further need of it, so leave me . . . I am in peril with this gap still in the wall. Go quickly, I beg you.'

'Goodbye then, Master,' said Nardello. 'Have no more fear. This wall will stand as long as the pyramids have stood. Should you desire my return you must call to the sentries and I shall visit you by sorcery, for now there is no other way,' and with these words the magician left the garden and ordered that the entrance be blocked.

As the masons did their work the Baron watched closely and only when the final stone was settled into place did he sigh with relief, and then he smiled an old man's smile and the saliva ran down his chin and stained his clothes. He was satisfied.

If the Baron was happy Picabrier was overjoyed. At long last he had taken complete control of the castle of Roquemartine, its land and its revenues. He had soldiers under his command and peasants to produce what food and drink he and his troops needed. For such an adventurer it was a great alteration of fortune. From being a penniless mercenary he had risen to become the ruler of a realm. He had the power of life and death over hundreds of men and women; he had also taken the Baron's key from Nardello and every coin in the treasury was his. Life had never been sweeter.

For his part the Baron knew nothing more of life beyond the wall nor even cared. This was the first time, since the onset of his anxieties at least, that he had ever felt entirely secure. Day after day he wandered aimlessly about the garden and picked his food up where he found it; nourishment placed before him he supposed, if he thought about it at all, by the unseen hands brought into being by the magic of Nardello. And so his life went on for many weeks and months, uninterrupted by care or danger, until at last a new worry came to assail the peace of mind he had imagined would be his forever.

It was true, he reflected, that he was safe in this perfect garden; and it was true that the wall was impregnable – but it was the magician who had made all this possible and it was he alone who controlled the power of the pyramids. It therefore followed that he could remove his protection whenever he fancied. All at once the Baron could see the danger of his position and he decided that something must be done. He lifted his head and called to the soldiers in the gallery.

It was not now an easy matter for Nardello to visit the Baron. First he was obliged to climb the rickety ladder that leant against the outside of the wall, and then he had to be lowered to the garden in a basket which swung on the end of a long rope. It was a dangerous and uncomfortable exercise but after a while, and none too pleased, the magician stood before his Master.

'Well,' he said, with no trace of politeness, 'what do you want?'

'Nardello,' said the Baron, his lips wet and his eyes full of guile, 'I am immeasurably grateful to you – I spend my time strolling in this garden with never a care . . . I bathe my feet in the fountain, I eat the magic food I find and I listen to the birds singing . . . life is truly a pleasure and death seems far away, but one little thing gnaws at my tranquillity.'

'Well,' said Nardello again, 'what is it?'

'The magic,' said the Baron, 'this power of the pyramids, what would happen to it if by chance you die? I do not desire it but you could fall from a cliff, you could travel to another part of the country . . . and what if I lost your trust, eh? What would happen to me then? I would be at the mercy of any passing vagabond.'

Nardello laughed. 'Is that all?' he asked. 'My lord, I have no intention of going anywhere, but even if I did nothing could harm you. The magic I laid upon this place will never disappear or wear away. Does not the great pyramid still stand and is its secret still not hidden? No, my lord, whether I am alive or not, whether I am here or not, this spell will last for all eternity. It is the greatest magic there is and none can destroy it.'

The Baron's face lit up. 'I am well pleased,' he said, 'truly your magic is great.' Then without warning he fell upon Nardello and, surprising him, he bore the magician to the ground.

Though old and past his strength the Baron had, in his youth, been a redoubtable fighter and he had not forgotten the art of dealing death. As the two men toppled over the Baron stabbed Nardello in the breast before he could defend himself and then held him down, face against face, so that he might watch him die. 'Thanks be to God,' he said when it was finished, 'I am truly safe at last.'

The soldiers on guard duty were witnesses to this murder and immediately sent to Picabrier to know what they should do. To the messenger's astonishment his commander only smiled and ordered the sentries to do nothing but to continue in their duties. Then, as soon as the messenger had left him, Picabrier filled a goblet with wine and drank to Nardello; another companion in arms who had served his purpose and gone his way.

And while he drank the new ruler of Roquemartine, overcome almost by a feeling of triumph, even considered doing away with the Baron himself but, on reflection, decided that there was no point in such a strategy. While the real Lord of Roquemartine remained alive Picabrier could always assert that everything he did was at the command of his master, despite it being quite obvious to those who lived in the castle that the mercenary had given up any pretence whatsoever of obeying the old man – for he was simply an amusement, a mindless prisoner in a roofless tower and nothing more.

None of this was apparent to the Baron. From the moment he had slain Nardello what little sanity he enjoyed vanished. The body lay where it had fallen and slowly decomposed in the heat of the sun; yet to the Baron the garden smelt sweetly of eucalyptus and mimosa and the buzzing of the flies was the chirping of cicadas; the food flung from the wall was still ambrosia, and the cistern that irrigated this paradise was still a silver stream that tasted cool. For him the garden was a haven of timeless magic that protected all within from evil and harm.

But harm was nearer than the Baron, or anyone else in Roquemartine, thought. During all this time the Saracens had not been idle. They had once occupied Provence for more than a hundred years and, although they had been forced to leave, they had left many spies behind them. Their galleys crept into the coast at night; men rowed ashore and talked to other men. In this way the Saracens learnt that there was treasure at Roquemartine, and they learnt also that Picabrier's soldiers had become lax in their duties, and that even the look-outs he had set to guard the approaches to the castle were negligent, carousing and sleeping through the night instead of standing their watch. Roquemartine was ripe for the taking.

❧

The attack, like all Saracen attacks, was sudden and cruel, planned with intelligence and care. The raiders disembarked as the night darkened and marched rapidly overland, led by local men who shared their blood. Only too easily did they overrun Picabrier's outposts and, butchering his drunken sentries where they lay, they came unopposed to the castle gates. These being lightly defended the Saracens soon gained possession of the place and slaughtered everyone they discovered. Picabrier himself fought bravely but, deserted by his men and outnumbered on all sides, he was wounded and, shouting that he would rather perish than fall alive into the hands of the infidel, was seen to run to the edge of the high cliff and throw himself over it, yelling defiance, down into the black night.

Once all resistance had been overcome the Saracens broke into the treasury and took what gold and silver there was, though they found little of value. Rushing on they ransacked the Baron's apartments and every other room in the castle as well. Again they were disappointed and this disappointment thrust them into a dangerous mood. They cursed long and loudly though in the end there was nothing for them to do but return to the coast. As they were about to leave some of their skirmishers came upon the walled garden behind the castle and reported it to their leaders. Perhaps, they said, this strange edifice, without doors or gates, contained the great treasure they were seeking.

Swiftly the Saracens went to investigate, setting about the sheer wall with their swords and battle-axes. In a moment they had loosened several large stones and before long, pushing and pulling with their hands, their torches held high and their faces ablaze with a dream of gold, they burst into the dark enclosure. They found nothing; the garden was empty save for a vile corpse and a crazy old man in rags, cowering in the dust.

The Saracens were enraged and gave no thought to pity. With yet more curses they brandished their scimitars and brought them down upon the Baron's body, cutting him to pieces. Then, without a second glance, they went back through the wall and, having thrown their torches into the castle to set it on fire, they descended a narrow track that led to the plain and disappeared into the dark.

When the pale dawn rose over Roquemartine the next morning it revealed a dismal landscape. Black smoke stood in columns above burnt-out ruins and corpses lay in every part of the castle, contorted, as in their last moments they had tried to escape the pain of death. As the morning passed a few survivors emerged from their hiding places, fearful and bewildered. After standing motionless for a while they bestirred themselves and began to arrange the bodies of the dead for burial and to pick through the discarded plunder. They were joined eventually, an hour or so short of midday, by Boscabrun; aroused before daybreak by his sentries, made anxious by the sight of red flames in the sky.

Boscabrun had brought his retainers with him and they came in good order; well armed and eager to fight the enemy. Along the way bands of peasants had rallied to him and although they only carried sickles and scythes they were ready to give a good account of themselves in the defence of their homeland.

It was all too late. Boscabrun stared at the corpses and the wreckage, hardly able to comprehend the desolation he saw. He ordered his men to search the castle from top to bottom, hoping that the Baron might still be alive, but all they found was a dungeon, its door beaten down, and inside it the remains of the Baron's sons; skeletons hanging in chains.

Then a servant came to Boscabrun and told him that the Baron had last been seen in a garden behind the castle, and Boscabrun remembered that he had indeed heard rumours of a paradise built by magic, and so he hurried across the courtyard and out by the ruins of the postern gate. There before him he saw a lofty stone wall, circular but less high and less solid than he had been led to imagine; only twice as tall as a man and encompassing only a small place.

As Boscabrun passed through the gap made by the Saracens and went into the enclosure a buzzard floated by on lazy wings to perch on the sentries' gallery. Boscabrun recoiled and covered his face with the edge of his cloak. Several of his men retched to their stomachs and leant against their companions for support. The stench of death and human excrement was all around them. The body of the Baron lay on the hard ground in a pool of congealing blood that was black with moving flies. Nearby was the rotting, half-eaten carcass of Nardello.

Boscabrun went forward, his men following. So this was the garden of perfection. He shook his head. All he could see was a scrubby piece of uneven land where tangled weeds grew between a pair of twisted trees. There was a shallow pool of foul water also, open to the sky and full of twigs and bird droppings. In the centre of all was a wooden hut, no larger than a large box; in this the Baron had slept, like a dog in a kennel.

With tears in his eyes Boscabrun commanded that the Baron and Nardello should be buried and then, while his orders were carried out, he returned to the castle yard. There he found a group of peasants and courtiers waiting, and they knelt and begged him to become the lord of Roquemartine and of all the lands that surrounded it. Boscabrun went to the parapet and looked down into the valley, at its orchards, its vines and woods. Then he turned and spoke to those who waited for his answer.

'I will rule you if you wish,' he said, 'but not from this place. Here there is nothing worth the defending. What there was the Saracens have taken and they will not bother to attack us again. Even so, we will keep look-outs on the high ground, always, and at the first sign of danger we shall assemble at the Mas de Gavots, and there we will be ready to defend ourselves, and all together. In this way we shall have little to fear, unlike the Baron, for, it seems, everything he feared came to pass simply because he feared it. His fear of death placed him in jeopardy: fear of his friends gave him into the power of his enemies and they gave him into the power of the Saracens. And, last of all, his estates have passed to me, the man he most feared would gain them . . . so come my friends, we will leave this castle and let it fall into ruins. In that way we shall be safe. By refusing to hide behind such fortifications we shall not excite the envy or suspicion of our enemies. We may then hope that if our foes are free of such sentiments then we might become free of them also.'

And Boscabrun said no more but walked out through the shattered gates of Roquemartine and went down the track to the valley, back to his farmhouse on the other side of the hills. A quiet fell over the ruined castle and gradually even the black smoke died and only the embers of some broken timbers glowed amongst the rubble. Then at last there was a noise and a hand appeared over the edge of the escarpment, followed immediately by another, digging its nails into the hard rock. Then a man pulled himself into sight and he stood and swayed. Blood stained the length of his sword arm, his clothes were torn and dusty and his face was lined with pain. It was Picabrier. Like the man of cunning he was he had long since prepared a place of concealment both for himself and his treasure. Now, with his gold slung in bags about his waist, he was ready to make his escape.

Slowly and carefully Picabrier went down the track that led to the plain and, making sure that he was unobserved, he headed directly for the dwelling where he and Nardello had rested on the day of their arrival. The woman might have been waiting for him. Her husband had ridden a mule to the market at Eyguières, she said, to sell it, and she took Picabrier in and undressed him and bathed his wounds, fed him and covered him with a counterpane so that he might sleep.

And when the mercenary departed two days later he rode upon the peasant's second mule and his gold was hidden under his cloak and his clothes were tattered and dusty for that was how he wanted it.

Not an hour after his departure the woman's husband returned and found his wife lying half-naked and dishevelled on the bed, her hair undone. The man could hear his child crying and he could see the wine spilled across the floor. In his anger he raised his hand to strike his wife but as he did so she showed him the purse that Picabrier had given her and her husband lowered his hand and sat at the table and began to count the coins. Here was enough money to make him rich forever; now he could buy land.

# THE CAFÉ AT
# CASTELLANE

**S**omewhere between the end of the night and the appearance of the morning mist we broke camp and resumed our march, creeping from the hillside like thieves. After an hour or so, as the daylight grew stronger, the flock struck off into rough country where I could not travel with my cart, up over long ridges and into a valley which would lead down to the wide river at Castellane.

I was meant to continue along the road alone but I was apprehensive, feeling excluded as I stood by the head of the mule and watched the sheep climb almost vertically away from me. As he was about to leave Marius must have noticed the fear on my face and he decided to keep me company. 'I won't let the shepherds from Frejus get you,' he said, laughing, and taking the reins he perched himself on top of the cart and invited me to do the same.

I rested comfortably on the mound of our possessions as we advanced and admired Marius as he made the old mule go. Travelling like this it was not long before we entered a deep gorge, a sharply falling valley that had been formed by a small tributary of the great Verdon river, which itself formed greater and more picturesque gorges to the west. Tourists came from all over the world to see those gorges but they never saw this one. It was narrow and choked with trees and bushes and the road dropped down it steeply, switching from side to side in tight hairpins. As the slope of the road became more abrupt Marius adjusted the brake on the wheels by turning a large handle at the front of the cart and the mule was allowed to dawdle, the weight of its burden only just pushing it forward. Around us all was silent, a world made gloomy by the early mist that was still trapped here and unable to escape. Above us on the mountain summits it rained, gentle and warm.

Halfway down the gorge Marius stopped the cart and we unloaded the two large bonbonnes which were used to carry water and there, by the side of the road, we emptied them. Not far from us was a cleft in the valley wall, a small cave, and inside it water sprang from the rock, clear and clean. Marius cupped his hands and began to drink.

'Try that,' he said, 'they say it is the finest water in Provence. Shepherds come from everywhere to taste it.' He winked. 'If you have enough of it,' he went on, 'they also say it will make you wise, though it will never make you rich.'

I knelt and drank in my turn, then we filled the bonbonnes and once more climbed aboard the cart. Marius flicked the reins and we got under way. 'I've got a feeling,' he said, looking sideways at me, 'that shepherds drink too much of that water. I should stay away from it if I were you – drink wine instead.'

Eventually we passed through the mist and came out at the bottom of the Verdon valley with high rocks on either side. The road now ran close to the edge of the river and as the mule drew us forward the sun rose in strength and warmed our bodies and the clouds became thin and then disappeared altogether.

At Castellane mid-morning arrived as we arrived and the river was just below us and there was a wide shore littered with stones. One or two boys were out fishing and above them dark cliffs climbed out of the shade and glittered in the sky. Straight ahead I saw the massive pinnacle of rock for which the town is famous. I leant back in the cart to see it all, more than five hundred feet high, and on the very top was the tiny chapel of Our Lady, its roof bright and new after the rain.

We went on but not far from the narrow bridge which carries the Route Napoleon across the gorge Marius drove our cart off the road and, passing along a faint track, we came into a fine meadow close to the sound of the rushing water. We unharnessed the mule and spread our cloaks and umbrellas out to dry.

'We will cook some soup,' said Marius, 'but while we wait for the others to arrive we will take an aperitif like civilized men do. It will help to protect us against the effects of the magic potion we drank at the spring this morning.' And with a slight bow the shepherd poured out two large glasses of vermouth and, leaning our backs against the cart, we solemnly drank each other's health.

∞

The sheep caught up with us at about midday and sought the shade of the over-hanging trees. Then Jules brought fresh provisions from Castellane, including a huge carton of pâtisserie, a gift for Joseph, and we lounged by the river like heroes of myth, taking our time as we ate, drinking our wine with pleasure. And when our meal was finished Jules curled up under his umbrella and went to sleep and Lucien, his hired man, offered to remain with the flock while the rest of us visited the town, tourists on a spree.

To begin with we flung off the tarpaulin that covered the cart and two or three suitcases were dragged into the open. In another moment we had rigged a piece of rope and our clean shirts were soon hanging in the sun, the creases falling away from them until they looked as bright as new butterflies. A cheap mirror appeared and we suspended it from a branch and it swung in the breeze as we took turns to shave, each one of us standing helplessly still as his reflection slipped away and was replaced by a view of cliffs and trees; and each one waiting patiently for the mirror to swing back in the wind so that he could once more examine his soap-covered face.

Joseph could not be bothered to shave himself, whether from laziness or because of an unsure hand I do not know, but sat on a rock by the river, his chin pointing to the sky, while Jean Martel, his son, did the work for him, lathering his father's cheeks with gentleness, scraping the skin with the razor and never cutting it once. All this time Milou watched us, a glass of wine in his hand. He had not changed his clothes, nor had he shaved. 'There are no cabarets in Castellane,' he said, 'and not many women who appreciate the smell of a shepherd either.'

Castellane, with its twelve hundred inhabitants, was the largest town on our route. In the old days it had been known for its fairs; shepherds from every part of Provence had gone there to find work. And on the vast market square, where flocks of twenty thousand had been bedded overnight, they had sold hand-carved staves, whips and wooden collars for sheep bells, all of them decorated with intricate patterns which their knives had made during the long lonely months on the mountains.

But none of us, I suppose, thought of these things as we crossed the old stone bridge that Bonaparte had used and went into the town, looking awkward in our clean clothes, self-conscious without sticks in our hands and a herd of three thousand animals to look after. In a straggling group we wandered, without speaking, from one small shop to another, while from beneath untrustworthy eyebrows Milou and I stared at every woman that passed as if we'd never seen one before. Then I purchased the huge blue umbrella I wanted and, tucking it proudly under my arm like I'd never done anything else, I followed my mates across the square to the terrace of a café-restaurant called 'L'Etape', and there we sat along the front row of tables, at our ease with our legs stuck stiffly into the roadway.

As we drank our drinks the noise of sheep bells sounded from the direction of the river and the flock that had stolen our place at Le Bourguet entered the square on the far side and, led by a tall old man, progressed slowly towards us. This shepherd walked superbly, like a king, his whip held behind his back in clenched fists, his beret low on his brow and his eyes gazing straight before him. Now all his sheep were in the town, filling the road and the bells grew louder, the noise of them redoubled by the high walls of the buildings around us. Then came the men of the rearguard and their whips cracked and with them came two or three mules bearing pack-saddles, and a score of long-horned goats as well.

This flock was larger than ours and it soon spread everywhere, stopping cars and isolating them in a sea of shifting bodies and forcing pedestrians to take refuge in shop doorways. The sheep were tired and covered in dust, their heads drooping. The men were tired also but, while we watched them in that amphitheatre, they would not allow their faces to show it. They raised their whips and shouted greetings and we shouted greetings in return. Like us the day before they would have to walk on, much further than they'd intended, because we had taken the place by the river. I stole a glance at Marius and the others, to see if their expressions registered triumph – they did not. To a man they knew what another four hours could mean on top of six hours already walked. They looked out from the café, unsmiling, simply enjoying the beauty of the sight, seeing if the sheep and dogs were good and nothing more.

In the end the last of the animals disappeared into the narrow street that led from the square, the noise faded and the dust settled. There was a shout and another shepherd joined us on the terrace; someone Leonce knew. He sat and smiled at us all and ordered more drinks. A woman had swaggered up with him; a woman who seemed to be as much a shepherd as he was. She was big boned with wide eyes and a loose-lipped mouth which smacked against her teeth, expressing appetite for everything. Under a shepherd's hat her uncombed hair hung free to her shoulders and she was dressed, like a man, in baggy trousers, boots and an old canvas jacket. Inside her trousers the hips were soft and vast and she laughed all the time with a rich vulgarity. She looked like a woman who could have eaten the world like an apple, pips, core and all. How many shepherds, I wondered, had she pulled into her embrace on the empty mountain tops?

She sat in the middle of our group, formidable, drinking her pastis and laughing: 'Couldn't bring sheep through here during the war,' she said, 'it used to be a real mutton trap. Every door of every house was left open and you could see little old ladies with bunches of grass in their hands, hiding round corners and making bird noises, cheep-cheep, cheep-cheep, like that. They'd have sold their virtue for a leg of lamb those days, though they all go to church on Sundays now. I tell you they only spend hours praying because nobody wants them for anything else.'

There was silence for a moment, then it was our turn to laugh though we stopped as soon as the woman began to speak again and even the café proprietor, who had come to the table to pour more drinks, sat down with us to listen.

'You see the rock,' said the shepherdess, pointing upwards to where the chapel still gleamed white against the blue sky, 'well, in the old days, before there was a chapel, there was a castle and a young girl grew up in it. You might have thought her fortunate to live in a castle but she wasn't . . . not even as fortunate as me, so if you have the time before our roads separate I will tell you the story of the Magician's Daughter, for she was born here in Castellane and only I know the story to the very end . . .'

# The Magician's Daughter

*L*ong ago, at the time of the troubadours, there was once in the mountains of Provence a many turreted castle. A pleasure to look upon it had been constructed at the very summit of a sheer pinnacle of rock. Along the base of this rock, in a deep chasm bounded by rough and craggy cliffs, ran a fierce torrent and the noise of it never ceased. The name of the river was the Verdon and travellers crossed it by way of a narrow stone bridge, from whose parapet they could perceive the township of Castellane, lying at no great distance to the north.

Now the people of Castellane enjoyed a much admired contentment. They were without envy and their lord, the Baron Joucas, was without greed or any unreasonable desire. Whenever a wanderer arrived at the castle he arrived knowing the Baron's reputation and he was received so well and so civilly that he embellished that reputation and carried it with him wherever he went on his journey. In this way the renown of Castellane spread far and wide and many songs were sung of it, right to the frontiers of France and the edge of the great sea beyond Navarre.

The Baron delighted in this life and so did his courtiers. Even the Baron's sorcerer, for all castles in those days had a sorcerer, did no harm and cast not the smallest evil spell. He was a good man and he loved his lord and all the peasants and shepherds of Castellane as well. Indeed, what powers he possessed he used entirely for the benefit of those who were weak and ill. He read and studied in many a learned book; experimented and made potions that alleviated pain and mended broken bones. Over the years he accumulated a great store of knowledge and, so that his knowledge would not die with him, he wrote everything he knew on sheets of parchment and had them bound together into great volumes covered in sheepskin. He knew which flowers to pick and what herbs to cultivate. He was a man who, in his youth, had travelled over the whole known world and, as a result, was convinced that no village or castle anywhere was happier than Castellane. It was as near paradise as this world can achieve – but happiness is as fragile as life and cannot last.

The Baron's wife had died not long after the marriage and she had left him one daughter and one daughter only; a beautiful and talented girl who was deeply loved by her father and who loved him just as deeply. She was graceful in spirit and mind and, at about the age of twenty or so, had been fully prepared for her inheritance – the government of her father's small fiefdom, an inheritance that she and her father hoped was many years distant. Unfortunately the natural order of things is not always the order in which things happen. One dark, sad day, the only daughter of Baron Joucas died suddenly. So suddenly that even the Baron's sorcerer and physician, the resourceful Casco, could do nothing. By the time he had been called to the princess's bedside her body was cold and still, her face pale.

In the castle of Castellane the singing was stilled and tapestries were drawn over the windows to keep out the sunlight. The troubadours put away their lutes and every room became silent with grief. In the village the inhabitants waited to see what the Baron would do. How long would his anguish last? Would he be able to live through the pain and endure into a new life; a life that would not be so complete as the life before but life all the same; a life chastened by the loss of so much love.

The sorrow of the Baron seemed at first to have no end. For many months he locked himself in his rooms and allowed only one or two favourite servants to attend him, and to these he hardly spoke. For the courtiers of Castellane, whose daily life had depended on the decisions of the princess and her father, this was a bleak time.

One or two of the more gifted troubadours composed sad melodies for the lady's death but as the Baron would allow no songs to be sung the unhappy minstrels journeyed on, taking their music to other castles where they might sing the story of the great misfortune that had befallen their master. Soon, as the Baron continued his mourning, courtiers began to leave the castle too, taking their women and servants with them. Gradually Castellane became less and less populated and less and less visited, until, after about a year, it was only a faded memory of what it had been before.

At last, when the twelvemonth was up, the Baron emerged from his chambers and stalked from end to end of his castle, now a desolate place. The tapestries still blocked out the sun, and dust and debris covered the floors. Discarded possessions lay on the stairways where they had been thrown, and those servants who still remained in the service of the Baron were listless and shuffled their feet stupidly as he went by, ducking their heads like slaves in a way they had never done before.

The Baron had altered out of all recognition. The dark hair and beard had turned grey. His eyes were lightless and the soft pouches beneath them were deep lavender in colour. His face was furrowed with bitterness, patterned by tiny lines like an oil-painting, centuries old. He gazed at his castle as if it did not exist, as if it were a dream to which he could never return. He stood motionless on the battlements and looked towards the high mountains of Provence and saw nothing; no sky, no peaks, no villages. He no longer saw goodness, he no longer saw beauty.

After meditating for some while in this manner the Baron went to the great hall of the castle and sat in what had been his customary chair. He ordered his servants to clean and scour the castle from top to bottom. He desired too that the tapestries be shaken free of dust and pulled back from the windows so that the sunlight and the fresh air could flood in at all points. Then, when he had eaten, he commanded that Casco, his sorcerer and physician, should appear before him.

During the time that the Baron had hidden himself from the world Casco had attempted to visit him many times, hoping that he might bring relief and comfort, not so much by the use of magic, though the sorcerer did have various potions to reduce melancholia, but rather by talking to his master and reasoning with him about the nature of life and death, for the magician felt that the Baron had one duty above all: to care for his estates and those that lived on them. But these opinions had made no difference; the Baron had spoken to no one and it was only now, when the mourning seemed to be over, that the magician was sent for.

Casco made his way towards the great hall with fear in his heart. Would the Baron hold him responsible for his daughter's death? Had he, over this long, long year, pondered on ways to revenge himself on a sorcerer who had been unable to save the princess from a sudden and mysterious disease? Casco wondered but then reassured himself. After all, the Baron had always been a gentle man, a man without extremes in his temper and one who had always chosen the middle way; the golden mean.

With these thoughts in his mind the magician entered the great hall and found the Baron waiting, sitting in his great chair at the end of his long table, attended by his guards and two or three servants. Casco walked slowly forward until he was close to his master. He folded his arms beneath his voluminous gown of black and silver and bowed his head low, raising it in a moment to study the Baron's face. What he saw shocked him.

A year previously the Baron had been a man in the prime of life. His skin fresh and clear, his eyes bright with intelligence. Now he was an old man with a face like parchment and there was a dark cloud on his brow. Where before the Baron's expression had been one of open honesty and delight in the pleasures of others now his looks were full of suspicion and cunning. He glanced about him like a frightened and savage animal. His lips curled back over his teeth as he waved the servants out of earshot.

'Casco,' he began, his voice sounding old beyond his age, 'Casco, you did not help my daughter. Was it one of your potions that made her die?'

The magician knelt before the Baron. He was a good man and this accusation hurt him sorely. 'My lord,' he answered, 'I loved your daughter as I love my own children. Had I been near when your daughter fell ill I might have saved her, but when I was called, it was too late. She was dead and my heart broke like yours, my lord.'

The Baron waved these words away. 'Someone wanted my daughter dead, to steal the succession . . . and they could not have killed her without your help.'

'My lord, I swear, never would I have done such a thing. Remember the days before, how happy and content all of us were, at Castellane.'

'I remember nothing,' sneered the Baron, 'except that I lost my dearest treasure and I want revenge.'

'Oh, my lord,' persisted the magician, 'do not let evil and rancour turn you from understanding. I am sure your daughter died of some strange fever, brought from some foreign land upon the wind, or by some bird perhaps. No one here would have done her any harm. Both she and you were too much loved.'

'See how love has served me then,' cried the Baron and he struck his magician to the floor and the magician lay there without stirring. Not because he was powerless, on the contrary, he had magic enough to defend himself, but because he loved his lord and understood his sadness and his suspicions.

'What do you want, my lord?' he asked eventually.

The Baron leant forward in his chair and whispered into the ear of the prostrate Casco. 'I could execute you this very minute,' he said, 'but I need you. All this year I have been thinking and now I know. You killed my daughter so that there would be no heir to my castle and my possessions, my lands and my estate, except perhaps you and yours . . .'

'My lord . . .'

'Listen, and do not speak. A wife I can easily find but I am no longer young and may not live to see a child of mine old enough to take my lands into its care. This is what you must do. You must prolong my life, find a potion that will make me strong and young, able to make good children and able to live long enough to see them tall and beautiful, rich and full of power.'

The magician raised a hand. 'This is devil's work, my lord. It is not right even to search for this knowledge. It is evil to discover it and a curse to bestow it. I will not do it. Seek out some vile wizard if you must, not me.'

The Baron threw himself back in his chair and laughed. 'Casco,' he cried, 'you will do as you are bidden. You too have a daughter – Beatrice – the only child still with you, the comfort of your quiet home, you told me once.'

'No,' shouted Casco and he leapt to his feet but the Baron gave a sign and his guards came from behind the throne and bound the magician's arms behind his back so that he could make no magic passes in the air and, in that way, protect his daughter from danger.

The Baron laughed again. 'It is no good, Casco. I have been planning my revenge for too long to be tricked by you. Your Beatrice is already in my dungeon, and there she will stay, surrounded by guards at all times, sleeping and waking. Should anything happen to me, even if I should die sweetly in my sleep, she shall die in the same hour. If magic takes me off she shall be maimed and then sold into slavery. Casco, you will do exactly as I say.'

And so it was arranged and the Baron forced the magician to swear the most fearsome and binding oaths he could devise. Casco was to devote the rest of his life, if needs be, to finding an elixir that would lengthen life, keeping whoever drank it young and vigorous beyond his allotted span. The Baron was content for now and he had his dearest wish. 'I shall take a new wife,' he said, 'I shall beget many children and live to see them grow,' and with that Casco was taken back to his laboratory and the door was locked behind him.

For seven years Casco was true to his vows but then he had to be for guards stood at his door every night and, in any event, he was not the kind of man to break his solemn word. Hardly ever was he allowed to leave his turret room and only rarely was he permitted to visit his daughter, and then always under escort.

During her imprisonment Beatrice grew from a fine cheerful girl into a stately woman, bearing her distress with as much patience as she could and, on those occasions when she saw her father, she always attempted to convince him that she was happy in her cell, although that was far from being the case. She missed the open air and the sunlight and the company of her friends in the village. Above all she missed the society and instruction of her father for he, being a learned man, had delighted in the idea of making his daughter as learned as he.

The Baron visited the magician regularly, demanding to know what progress Casco was making in the search for the elixir. On these occasions Casco would indicate the books and jars that lined the walls of his room and say that he was doing everything he could to make the discovery, but, he pointed out, it was a secret that had evaded all but the most gifted of sorcerers through many many centuries.

At each visit too the magician begged the Baron to release Beatrice from the dungeon but the Baron would never agree. 'The sooner you find my potion,' he argued, 'the sooner will your daughter see the sun.'

Casco found this assurance hard to believe. He knew from the servants who waited on him, and from the guards who stood at his door, that the Baron's character had become fixed in its wretched ways. No longer was Castellane renowned for its gaiety and charm. No longer did troubadours sing its praises, rather did they tell gloomy tales about its lord and the unhappiness that lived in the dungeon.

All these seven years the Baron had no pity and took no pleasure. Even the new wife he had chosen, a young châtelaine from a nearby village, had been unable to make him happy or alleviate his pain. She, like the magician, was kept in a turret room and saw no one but her waiting women. She went to the Baron only when he sent for her and she bore her lord not one child. As time passed the Baron's mind became more and more demented and his behaviour became more and more violent and malicious. Whoever could left the castle and spread its reputation for misery far and wide. Those peasants who could not flee remained in the village, fearing yet hating their liege lord. No longer were they tended by the kind magician. Disease became rife amongst them. They grew scrofulous and the boils on their skin were inflamed and poisonous. Castellane was in a sorry plight.

Finally, in the last month of the seventh year, the magician sent word to his master that he wished to see him. His studies he thought, were over. Again Casco entered the great hall and there sat the Baron of Castellane, and by him stood his guards in chain mail with their swords drawn for the Baron feared death in all its shapes and from every quarter. The magician looked at the Baron's face; once more it had changed. It was sly and wizened now, lined with wickedness and spite.

Casco raised his hands and the folds of his black and silver gown were rusty with age. He held a small phial between forefinger and thumb, transparent it was, containing perhaps a mouthful of dark green liquid.

'Well,' said the Baron, 'speak.'

'I believe,' said Casco, his voice devoid of any triumph, 'that I have discovered the elixir of life. I am sure that what I have is what you so desire. Drink this and you shall be young and strong and your children shall be many … but it may be that I have miscalculated its effects … it may give immortality.'

The Baron shifted excitedly in his seat. His eyes gleamed with a lust for forbidden things. His lips moistened with longing.

Casco shook his head. 'This is no good gift I bring you,' he continued. 'Neither man nor woman should live beyond their time. To live enough is enough. All else is greed, it is more than a man should have and immortality will only lead to madness, self-disgust and despair.'

'Give it here you fool,' cried the Baron. 'If what you say is true I shall inherit all wealth and all power. I will need no children to succeed me now and always shall I outlive my enemies.'

'And your friends also,' said the magician.

The Baron ignored the remark and snatched the phial from Casco's hand and removed the stopper. He held the liquid against the light and then sniffed at it suspiciously. 'It smells like gentian from the mountain,' he said, 'and crushed shells from the riverside.' He raised the potion to his lips as if to drink but then held back. He looked craftily around the great hall, at his servants and soldiers, and then back at the magician. 'Is this how my daughter died?' he asked. 'Was she tempted to drink a potion? You all desire to see me dead, Casco above all. Well, I shan't please you so easily.' He half-turned in his throne and spoke to the chief of his guards. 'Bring Casco's daughter here.'

Casco fell back a pace and lifted a hand to his throat and went pale.

'What,' smiled the Baron, 'do you fear for your daughter's life? Would you have me drink something that she should not? Is this the poison you gave my daughter, Casco? Well then, we shall see.'

'It is not poison, my lord,' said the magician, 'it will not kill you, nor will it kill her, but immortality is not a curse I would wish on someone I love so dearly as I love my daughter.'

'And did I not love my daughter?' shouted the Baron, his face dark with anger. 'Why was she not made immortal with the poison she drank?'

At that moment there was a noise at the door of the hall and the magician's daughter was led in. Everyone present fell silent, so tall and stately was the girl, so calm and self-possessed. The dungeon had not embittered her in any way, rather had it bestowed on her a grandeur and dignity that might have befitted a queen. She advanced with a smile towards her father and knelt to receive his blessing, then she rose and, joining her hands before her, she stared at the Baron as he might have stared at the lowest of his serfs.

The Baron returned the stare. 'This,' he said, holding forth the tiny bottle, 'contains a potion that your father has been making these seven years. I will not drink till I see you drink. If you live your father and yourself shall go free, wander where you will. If any harm should befall you, should you die then your father will die in the same instant for I will then know that he intended me harm and was the one who killed my own daughter . . . my daughter who was once no less beautiful than you.'

Casco stepped forward. 'No, my lord,' he said. 'Do not lay this curse upon her, let her go from here and live her life as she should live it. Remember the days when we were young and we were friends, let this evil go from amongst us. Let me drink.'

The Baron shook his head, determined, enjoying the power he wielded. 'That would be too easy for you, Casco. For all I know you have already taken the antidote, but your daughter has not. I want to see you suffer when she dies, as I once suffered. Come now, Beatrice, if the potion is harmless then there is nothing to fear but a never-ending life.'

'There is more than enough to fear in that, my lord,' said Casco.

But there was no more talking to the Baron. He made a gesture and the magician was seized and held by the guards and then the Baron came down from his throne and thrust the phial into Beatrice's hands. 'Drink,' he commanded, 'drink.'

'Nothing but a drop,' cried the magician, 'more than a drop may be too much.'

'Drink,' insisted the Baron, 'that is if you trust your father.'

'My father would not poison you or anyone,' answered Beatrice. 'Your daughter was the friend of my childhood, we grew up like sisters. My father loved her and she loved him, as I do. He is a good man,' and with a smile she raised the tiny bottle to her lips and drank half its contents.

'No,' sobbed Casco, and he struggled in the arms of the men who held him. It was too late. The smile died on Beatrice's face, the phial dropped from her hands and smashed to pieces on the flagstones of the floor. The girl clutched at her throat. Everyone in that room watched her, their faces strained and tight. Then the girl fell, her eyes wild, her lips flecked with the froth of madness. One cry left her lungs and then she was silent.

Quickly the Baron knelt by Beatrice's side. He felt her heart and the pulse in her neck. Nothing. She was as cold as death. The Baron shook with fear; he leapt to his feet and whirled to face the magician.

'So,' he roared, 'just as I thought, you planned to kill me. You poisoned my daughter and now you have poisoned your own. It is well done, villain, and I shall have vengeance.' And with these words the Baron drew his sword and thrust it deep into the breast of the unresisting Casco who did not moan or shriek as the sharp blade pierced him. All he did was reach out a hand as he fell, striving to touch his daughter's face as if that touch were some last and secret message to her.

The Baron snarled like a wild beast and sheathed his blood-stained sword. 'Take them away,' he shouted to the guards who stood staring at the dismal sight before them. 'Take them away. No burial, no tomb. Cast them from the battlements and into the river. Let the magpies and the wolves pick their bones.'

Tenderly the guards and servants placed the two bodies on long shields and bore them to the castle walls. There, summoning up all their courage and hardening their hearts to stone, they cast the magician and his daughter into the deep abyss and, as they plummeted down, the bodies struck time after time against the cliffs until, in the end, they disappeared into the white-flecked torrent far below.

'May the gods forgive us,' whispered the Baron's men to each other and then they returned to the great hall to tell their master that they had performed his bidding.

But one of their number possessed more courage than his fellows. A servant from the village he had, as a child, been saved from an early death by the efforts of the magician. Beatrice too had brought ointments and salves to his ageing parents and the servant remembered these things and crept from the castle.

Once in the open he made his way along a rocky path, not stopping until he reached that quiet place where the river of Castellane alters its course, just below the bridge, in a wide and leisurely bend. Here he began his mournful quest for he had determined, whatever the danger to himself, that he would see the remains of Casco and Beatrice properly buried. He had no intention of allowing their corpses to become the prey of wild dogs and scavenging birds.

The good servant found the father's body first but could hardly bear to look upon it, so mutilated had it been by the jagged rocks of the castle precipice. But then the man made himself think of the magician's past kindnesses and he covered Casco with his cloak and buried him in a lonely grave above the water line, marking the spot with a large, round stone. This task accomplished the servant set off again, wading through the shallows and searching everywhere as he went. At last he discovered the unmoving form of Beatrice lying half-submerged near a sand-bank, her sightless eyes staring at the sky, her hair floating.

Steeling himself for the sight of deep gashes and broken limbs the servant advanced but to his amazement he saw, when close to Beatrice, that she was unmarked. There was not even a scratch on her face, nor was she pale, and although she seemed lifeless there was a smile of contentment on her lips.

The servant knelt by the girl and touched her forehead. She was warm. Her breast began to rise and fall; a sigh came from her. The servant looked to the bank but saw no one. He shivered in the sun. This was magic of the greatest kind. No one could have survived being cast from the battlements, and then the chasm and the beating and surging of the fierce rapids where they rushed between the narrow cliffs – no one. But here lay Beatrice, breathing, her skin ardent with life, not a mark on her.

Quickly the man took the girl in his arms, passing through knee-deep water and entering a thicket not far from the river itself. There he lowered Beatrice to the ground and went as speedily as he could to his own hut in the village. Saying nothing to his wife or children he caught up what coverings and food he could spare and hastened back to the riverside. To his surprise the magician's daughter had gone. The servant searched the thicket and the surrounding undergrowth but could find no sign of her. He saw his own footsteps on the sandy foreshore and the crushed grass where he had lain the unconscious girl, but that was all.

Once more the servant hurried to his home and replaced the things he had taken. Then he went directly to the castle, saying nothing of what he had seen that day to anyone. Nor did he speak of it on any other day. All he wanted henceforth from life was to live his span and for the gods never to notice him or his family. With that fate he would be happy.

All through this dreadful time Beatrice had known what had been happening. She had felt the strength of the potion seize her. The chill of it had sped into the very centre of her heart. There had been surprise but no pain. Her body had become rigid but her mind had been alive. She had seen the slaying of her father and she had felt the touch of his hand on her face; his last farewell. She had seen too the open sky as the men had carried her to the battlements. Then there had been the rush of the wind as she had fallen, and afterwards, the water closing round her body in the river.

The blows of the rocks she had not felt, nor had she lacked for air beneath the surface of the torrent. Her father's physic had worked only too well – better than he could have imagined. Not only was it a potion that prolonged life, it also prevented death. Had the Baron been able to maintain faith he would have lived forever.

And so Beatrice had been swept downstream and when the servant found her she was quite calm. She could not move but she knew that her senses were returning. She felt unperturbed in a strange way as she stared at the sky. She was infinitely wise; all-knowing. She knew her father was dead, knew it with certainty, just as she knew that she was alive and could not die. It was this knowledge that left her unmoved. Today would soon fade into the past – and so would every day.

She watched the servant leave her. He would be going to fetch her dry clothing. A friend to help carry her perhaps. She hardly thought of him. As soon as he had gone the blood in her veins surged stronger. There was a great flush of warmth within her and she sat up. She must not be there when the man returned.

For seven years she and her father had been held prisoner in the castle but on the far side of the village, and only a little distant from it, the magician had, as a young man, built a small farmhouse and around it had planted an orchard to give fruit and firewood. It was to this place that Beatrice made her way, passing like a ghost through the outskirts of the village, walking silently on bare feet. She came unseen to the house and it lay deserted and open, the tenants being at work in the fields and in the vineyards. Quickly Beatrice passed into the chambers that had been reserved for her and her father all these years, and there she removed her wet clothing, rubbed her body dry and wrapped herself in her warmest cloak.

When she had done all this she passed into her father's private room, a room he had kept hidden from all but her, and sitting in his favourite chair she gazed at the books and parchments that he had left behind; documents that bore on their pages many of his thoughts and the results of most of his studies, and as she sat there she pondered her future.

She had no wish to stay in Castellane. Not that the Baron, or anyone, could harm her now, but, seeing her still alive, he might imprison her again and force her to renew the search for her father's potion. This she did not want. She must leave Castellane and go into the world. It would be dangerous. A woman, travelling alone she would be open to all kinds of perils on the highway. But her father's robes were in the house; she would dress in those, and from his library she would take the most erudite books and load them into panniers that she could strap to the back of the mule that was browsing in the shade outside. There was a store of gold too. Yes. She would leave that very day.

Beatrice took one last look around the room. How she yearned to possess her father's powers. How she desired to prolong the Baron's life so that she might torture him for ever. She sighed and put the Baron from her mind: as things stood he would doubtless die of old age years before she could learn enough to cast a spell upon him. There was no point in looking for revenge and so in this frame of mind Beatrice stole from the village. No one then living in Castellane ever saw her again for Beatrice had determined to wander the world and she did. Over a long period of years, and always dressed as a young doctor of philosophy, she visited every seat of learning, every university and school of medicine then in existence. In each place she dwelt as long as she could, reading her father's books and the books of other wise men, but more than a certain time she dared not delay, although she was often entreated. Beatrice knew that if she settled for too long in any one town her colleagues would notice that she did not age, that her face bore no lines and that she never contracted the slightest illness. And for this reason, whenever she considered that the hour had come, she would dress in her travelling cloak, load her mule with books and slip away in the dead of night to journey on to new countries and new knowledge.

At this time life and learning sat easily upon her and the sorrow of her father's death receded into the past, further and further. She was content at the prospect of eternal youth and sometimes doubted the wisdom of her father in seeing it as a curse, but she never forgot him and loved him always, only regretting that such a good man should die such a pointless death.

There are no records of Beatrice in history. Each time she moved from town to town or from kingdom to kingdom she changed her name, generally giving out that she had been born near Cordoba and schooled in the mysteries of the Saracens. For many years, for half a century perhaps, she travelled the world in this way: from the fabled lands beyond India as far as the rough black coasts of the Atlantic Islands; and from Ethiopia to the plains of Tartary. And no matter where she went she remembered the example of her father and she healed where she could, soothed where she could not, and where there was nothing to be done she held poor broken souls in her arms and helped them to die bravely and only sometimes did she wish that she could die for them. But she could not and all this time she talked to wise men and women and wherever she was, and under a hundred different names, she was revered and loved for the peace she brought with her in the seasons of disease and war.

This did not last. After many more years Beatrice grew weary and believed that she had learnt all there was to learn, and had seen all there was to see. She bore so much wisdom and experience in her mind that she felt she might burst asunder like an old cracked pitcher containing too heavy an oil. She had seen friends die horribly in battle. To some men she had told her secret and then lost these lovers to the plague. She had watched the rich treating the poor as cattle; gelding some to be their eunuchs while fattening others to serve in their harems. Children she had cherished and fed had been sold into slavery. She had toiled ceaselessly to do good but at the end of it all she had been emptied of will-power. There was too much evil in the world and the longer she lived the more of it she discovered. It swamped her. In spite of all she knew she was conscious of her insignificance, like an ant with self-knowledge. A hundred years now since she had walked from Castellane and she was weak under the weight of the world, enfeebled by her own disgust.

So for a lifetime or two Beatrice tried the ways of evil. She looked at her power and knowledge and, still disguised as a learned man, she put her magic and wisdom at the service of kings and potentates. She became proud and wealthy. She poisoned for pleasure, she gained lands and castles, riches beyond measure. She won battles and played with armies as with pawns on the board of chess, dashing them to the floor when she thought she would. Sometimes she revealed her womanhood and enchanted men by feigning weakness and, attracted by her fortune and beauty, kings came to take her and only discovered too late what a fearful revenge she exacted from them; slavery or death was not too much.

Then there was an end. Beatrice looked for her soul and found nothing but an empty husk. Her mirror showed her young, a face without a wrinkle. Her muscles were strong, her back was straight and her hair shone, but in her mind she knew there was a despair and self-loathing such as no one else had ever known. There was only one way for her now. She left her riches and her power and, donning her old black robes and taking just a few possessions on the back of a mule, she set out to return to the country of her real youth, back to the castle of Castellane.

It was a hard journey but Beatrice had known many a hard journey, and after all she had the whole of eternity to dispose of. There was to be more than a year of travelling for her on the roads of Asia and Europe before she crossed into Provence, and even then there was yet another month or so before she found herself on the track that led to her father's village. The Baron Joucas of course had died long since and his immediate successors also. In their place was another lord, no better or no worse than any of his kind ruling in Provence at that time.

Casco's farmhouse had disappeared too but it was not in that direction that Beatrice bent her steps. She knew that her father had sealed his turret chamber on the day of his death and since then no one had been able to open it. Beatrice was convinced that in Casco's room, amongst the papers and parchments, resided the secret of her death. There she hoped to discover the something that would untie the knot of life that bound her to the earth.

With no attempt at concealment the magician's daughter advanced into Castellane and strode towards the high pinnacle on which the castle was built. Those villagers who noticed the traveller stopped what they were doing, came to their doors and stared. Never had they seen anyone like this and they felt fear and pity all at once for this tall vagabond who strode down their dusty street. A face young but old; a gait that was tireless but without zest, and eyes that were piercing but dead. No salutation was offered and none was offered in return. In the bright sun of the early evening a breath of ice passed over the town.

Beatrice and her mule climbed the narrow track that wound upwards at the rear of the great rock, but at the gate of the castle the guards lowered their pikes and forbade her to enter. Beatrice simply clicked a thumb and a finger at this and the men dropped their weapons and everyone in the castle, and in the village below, came under the same fierce enchantment and fell, where they were, into a deep trance.

Then the magician's daughter crossed the castle courtyard where men and horses slumbered. Into the great hall she went, there where her father had died, and the great table was surrounded by courtiers as still as statues and some were sprawled across the floor, snoring, and proud ladies with their beautiful dresses awry, lay all ungainly, smacking their lips in their dreams.

Beatrice hardly glanced at them. She was in haste now to see if her magic was as strong as, or stronger than, her father's. She climbed the turret stairs, narrow and steep. She came to her father's door, a massive one of thick oak lined with beaten steel, held firmly closed by a huge and complicated lock as it had been for two hundred years or more.

Beatrice leant against the wall, her long journey over. She stretched out a hand and began to speak in the Saracen tongue, commanding the door to open. With an almost imperceptible noise the mechanism of the lock moved and all that remained for Beatrice to do was exert the lightest of pressures and the way into the room was unbarred. 'Truly,' she said to herself, 'my magic is greater even than my father's.'

The room itself was exactly as she had visualized it in her mind's eye all these years. Great shelves carrying hundreds and hundreds of parchments and palimpsests; rows and rows of glass jars containing oils and ointments of many colours, most of them dried away to nothing. There were talismans also, and over the ceiling were painted, in bright designs, the figures of the zodiac. On the walls were cabalistic numbers, and on the floor was circle within circle, decorated with magic beasts, for casting spells.

An old and comfortable chair stood before an ancient desk. Beatrice rested herself in it and the door to the room swung shut behind her. 'Here,' she said aloud, 'will I work. Here will I stay until I find the antidote to my father's potion,' and she swept a pile of litter from the table with her arm. 'Everything in this place will I read until I find the way out of this life I no longer desire.'

And so began Beatrice's longest and hardest task. The castle and village slept and the roads leading there carried no travellers and no beasts of burden. It was as if the thought and memory of Castellane had disappeared from the world's mind. For years Beatrice lived in her father's turret. She lost count of time for it did not touch her. Her food and drink was brought by magic, but she rarely touched it and hardly needed it. She read and wrote and copied. She mixed concoctions from the information written down in Casco's books. She tried anything and everything to end her life, but each year saw her as healthy and as strong as the year before until at last there was nothing more for her to read and no more potions to make. It was the end of her work; the beginning of a barren eternity. Beatrice lowered her head into her hands and allowed herself to be seized by a despair deeper than any she had ever known in the whole of her history.

As she stared, desolate, at the floor Beatrice noticed one small book protruding from under the mounds of parchment she had discarded during her studies. It was lying open and, like many of the other documents around her, its pages were covered with her father's writing. She stooped and picked it up, remembering how she had cleared it from the desk on the day of her arrival as being of no consequence. Now she examined it more carefully and found that it was a kind of day book, a record of experiments, a journal of jottings and idle thoughts. 'How sweet life was.' 'How good it was to do good and see good done.' 'The pain of beauty dying, the glory of beauty reborn.' The magician's daughter sneered. How many lifetimes had passed since she had left those thoughts behind her. She went to throw the book back into the rubbish but something held her hand and she felt a stab of excitement in her heart. What had her father written, if anything, on the day of his death.

She turned to the correct page and found a few lines there, scrawled hurriedly, untidily. 'The potion,' read Beatrice, 'there is no doubt this time. It smells of evil, it glows with evil. I want to destroy it but Beatrice lies in a dungeon from which I must free her.' Then there was a line drawn, then the words: 'The antidote.' Beatrice expected a formula but there was nothing like that, just another sentence, some more words: the remainder of the book was empty. 'The antidote,' Beatrice read again, and continued reading with the last sentence of all: 'If no one in this world loves you then weep here, and die.'

Beatrice read the words aloud and looked through the casement of her window, across the wild countryside, towards the mountains. Her father had meant something and these words were his meaning, of that she was sure. Was a formula for the antidote hidden in this sentence? It would mean more work to decipher it; more years alone in this sleeping castle. Alone. Beatrice repeated the word. Alone. No one in this world loved her; she had outlived them all; father, friends, lovers; her children, her grandchildren, even her great-grandchildren. A moan of heartbreak rose from Beatrice's throat and she shook her head in misery. She was loveless and alone for ever and the thought was, on this occasion, too much for her and the sorrow surged up in her breast and she wept for the loves that were gone and her own loneliness too, and the tears poured down her cheeks and fell onto the open pages of her father's last writing and mingled with the ancient ink.

At that moment Beatrice trembled and understood. This was the antidote. Her father had not known her fate, or his own, but the merest suspicion of their destiny on that day long ago had been enough and he had left her this way of escape. The antidote was the ink and the moisture was in her tears of pity; not only tears for herself but for the sadness of the world also. And a tremor of joy spread through Beatrice's body, so powerful that she knew she could not survive it. Her eyes were blinded with tears now, but they were tears of happiness and she could feel her flesh fading away, then her mind. It was over.

And on that very instant the castle woke from its sleep, and the village too, and the people of Castellane remembered nothing but they cleared the weeds and ivy from their halls and houses, replanted their crops and went on living. Years later some amongst them came to a room high in the turrets, Casco's room, and they found the door open where before it had always been locked. Inside they saw old books and manuscripts, every one turned into dust, unreadable, smelling of death and mustiness. Behind a large table, in a crumbling chair, lay a skeleton in tattered robes; the eyes had gone and the teeth had fallen.

On learning of all this the lord of the castle commanded that the human remains be gathered up and buried with due ceremony, while the books and potions should be thrown from the battlements. This was done and the people of Castellane thought no more of it, never noticing the great swathe of time the magician's daughter had stolen from them. Nor did they ever know of her existence or of the potion given to her by her father. Even today no memory of Beatrice is kept save for the shepherds who tell her story, though there is a superstition in Castellane which says that anyone drinking from the river at midnight will gain immense knowledge and live forever.

Those who are wise shake their heads and declare that however thirsty they might be they would never drink the smallest drop of water from below the rock. And yet there are others who say they would be happy to swill down huge quantities of it every night of their lives if they could bring themselves to believe such a ridiculous story – but then this earth has never lacked for fools who, because they understand nothing, are convinced they comprehend everything, and so, fortunately, the tale of the magician's daughter will never be more than just a tale to them. The rest of us may think what we will.

# THE LAKE OF CASTILLON

**A** few hours later it was our turn to march through Castellane and we whipped the flock from the field by the river, went over the narrow bridge and entered the wide square. At that time of day there was a great crowd ready to watch our progress for the cool of the early evening was settling in the valley and it was pleasant for the townsfolk to meet in the cafés and find their friends in the streets. On the terrace of L'Etape the shepherdess and her man were still taking their ease and other shepherds sat there with them.

As we passed across the square those shepherds shouted to us, pleased to see our sheep so white and dew-washed, and the shepherdess beckoned, offering to carry me away with her and I tipped my Bargemon hat in acceptance, though never doubting for a moment that I did not possess such courage. But the shepherdess only laughed with her big mouth and waved at me in farewell, knowing for certain that she would never see me again, not this side of death anyway, and she didn't care a bit because the sun and the shade were on the mountains above the town and the world was brazen and beautiful, like she was and like I was, and that was the reason we felt so proud; such a cavalcade and us part of it.

So I stepped out in my Bargemon boots, leading the mule cart as if my ancestors had been shepherds for generations, and the women of Castellane leant out of their windows and their children skipped along by the side of us. The sheep-bells rang and all our shepherds looked as proud as I did – each one wearing some new piece of finery bought that morning, a spotted kerchief or a new shirt, and all of us were strutting.

This feeling of elation did not last an hour. Soon we had left the town behind and even the most energetic of its children eventually deserted us. It was a dreary climb out of Castellane and all around were high and rocky ridges and broken peaks. As the light faded the prospect became wild and melancholy and the clouds were torn into shreds as they fled across the sky. Then the land flattened, laying itself open to the wind, and we made for the Cheiron pass, crossed it, and began to descend towards a man-made lake that had been formed by the dam of Castillon – a whole valley, fifteen kilometres long, flooded and drowned, and as we approached the edge of it the gloom seemed even more menacing for the sun had vanished behind the peaks and they soared above us now, even wilder and sadder than before.

Our road took us across the top of the dam itself and going over it was like entering an enormous cavern. It was dark by the lake and the surface of the water gave out a blackness and the wind whipped at the cold glitter of it. What light there was glowed strangely, like the reflection from some subterranean roof, and as we marched the wind grew fiercer and hunted the clouds overhead until there was nowhere for them to go.

The ghosts of the place made me fearful. I lit my hurricane lamp early, for comfort, and Jean Martel lit another one and walked near me, behind the cart, for the road was flat and fast and what cars there were came too quickly out of the night and threatened to run us down.

'It is always like this, along by the lake,' said Jean. 'It cannot be right to drown a village.' Our sheep stopped to graze and Jean gestured with his lamp. 'There was a flock in a thunderstorm, here, with the rain pouring down, the sheep all drenched and huddled together, too miserable and too frightened to go on, and the shepherd was in amongst them, trying to get them to move again, and then the lightning struck the flock and because they were so close, and so wet, it ran from one sheep to the other and killed every last one of them, and it killed the shepherd too.'

The sheep advanced a little and we paced after them. Jean Martel waved his lamp again, towards Blaron. 'And there was a shepherd who put his flock into the shade by a precipice and fell asleep, and as the shade moved through the afternoon so the sheep moved with it, bunching up and gradually forcing those sheep on the precipice over the edge until the shepherd woke and found that all but a few of his flock had perished. It is only by this lake that such things happen and I shall be glad to be away from it.'

We halted that night on a bluff overlooking the water, right by the hamlet of St Julien. It was past midnight and the clouds were rolling down the slopes and into the lake, making it blacker. Not a light shone in the houses nearby and the rays of our hurricane lamps barely penetrated the darkness. There was no comfort here; nothing but bare rock. Dispirited we sat and ate cold food, wrapped in our cloaks, gripping them tightly so they should not be carried away by the wind. But in defiance of this mood, Jean Martel gathered some stones together and made enough of a fireplace to protect our tiny paraffin stove from the wind. After a while he succeeded in boiling some water and he made us cups of coffee, lacing them with cognac, and we drew closer to one another and waited for the hours to pass.

'It's a terrible spot, all right,' said Jean, 'warming his hands on his tin cup. 'They shot eleven members of the Resistance here. No wonder it always feels so cold. Madness it was, madness.'

Jean Martel spoke with feeling and I knew why. I had watched him washing in the river at Castellane and just above his breastbone I had seen a livid splash of scar tissue where a bullet had torn through his chest. As a conscript in Algeria he had only just survived that wound and he always thought of it with bitterness. Perhaps that is why the story he chose to tell that night was the story of the Archbishop's Ransom. At any rate we others sat and listened to it in silence, sheltering in the lee of the cart without even a fire to keep us warm.

# The Archbishop's Ransom

*T*he city of Arles has always been one of the finest and richest in the world. The Romans, during the long years of empire, made it the capital of Provence and beautified it with numerous and splendid buildings, including a theatre, the baths of Constantine and an enormous arena which could contain more than twenty thousand spectators. As might be imagined such a place was universally envied and often attacked, and all through its history Arles made a tempting prize for any band of roving barbarians who considered themselves strong enough to capture it. Across the centuries Arles suffered many sieges but never was it in more danger than at the time of the Saracens. Those warlike men from Africa and Spain launched countless bold forays against the city, and its dependencies, in the hope of seizing both its treasure and its power. They could not succeed; they were thwarted by the single-minded determination of one man and the example he set. That one man was the Archbishop of Arles.

The Archbishop was a man possessed of a vision and he was fortunate in having the power to make that vision real. He ruled Arles like a king. It was he alone who decided when taxes should be paid and what they should be spent on; who should be a bishop and who not. Under his command was an army of soldiers whose duty it was to defend their country against any invasion by the Saracens, and this army was always prepared for the Archbishop hated the Saracens above all other enemies. They were Moors and Mohammedans, unbelievers and infidels, and the Archbishop's vision was to slay as many of them as he could and force the survivors to take to their galleys and return to the land of their birth beyond the sea.

A victory of that nature would not be an easy matter, for the Caliph of the Saracens was a brave and accomplished man, a fine soldier and general; valiant on the field of battle and cunning and cruel also. His name, known and feared throughout all Christendom, was Abd al-Rhaman.

The Caliph had sailed from Spain some score of years previously and had established himself far to the east of Arles in the broad sweep of the Bay of Grimaud. There he had made a safe harbour for his galleys and inland, on the steepest hill he could find, he had built an impregnable castle and he had named it Fraxinetta.

Since the day of his arrival he had ruled that part of the country in all security. Every army sent against him had failed; those advancing by land had been slaughtered in the wooded hills, and those going by sea had fallen prey to the Caliph's swift galleys. Abd al-Rhaman was invincible. He could roam where he wished and no one denied him. His pirates plundered the whole of the wide Mediterranean and his soldiers raided as far afield as the rich towns of the high Alps. The only treasure he could not take, so it seemed, was Arles.

This state of affairs was not good enough for the Archbishop. An ambitious man his vision gave him no rest; God's work had to be done. At every high mass in his cathedral he preached a crusade against the Saracens of Fraxinetta. He saw danger everywhere and wanted to prepare for it. The ramparts of his city must be repaired and the towers at the four gates strengthened. 'It is essential,' he argued from his pulpit, 'that we make the walls of Arles the stoutest in Provence, then, when we know our city is unassailable we can leave men to defend it while we set out to attack Abd al-Rhaman at his very heart. We must destroy Fraxinetta and slay the Caliph.'

The nobles and bishops of Arles agreed with these sentiments enthusiastically each time the Archbishop preached on the subject, but one day they were totally cast down when he announced that he was raising a special tax on property and, this time, was expecting the wealthy to contribute generously.

The nobles and bishops were not at all pleased with this news but, after some thought and discussion on the matter, they finally agreed to do what they always did when they were short of money – they would take it from their tenants by increasing their taxes and by demanding next year's tithes. In that way, they reasoned, they would delight the Archbishop, frustrate the Saracen, do good in the eyes of the Lord, and ensure not only their own salvation but that of their serfs and peasants as well. Nothing could be better.

For the ordinary people of Arles this was not too agreeable a solution. It was not the first time they had been taxed to finance the Archbishop's wars and it seemed that the more they toiled in the fields and in the vineyards the less they had to show for it. It was true that the Archbishop kept them safe from the Saracens and ready for the kingdom of heaven but, as they often asked themselves, could life be any worse under the rule of Abd al-Rhaman, and might not eternity be better in the paradise of the Mohammedans where, according to rumour, it was all wine, women and song anyway?

These doubts did the people little good. The amounts of tithes and taxes were doubled and everyone, without exception, was obliged to pay. Those who refused or were slow in settling were visited by mounted knights accompanied by men at arms carrying drawn swords. Any vassal who complained that he had no money or valuables had his hearth demolished and his hut half-destroyed as the soldiers searched until they found something of value they could sell.

Those who were deemed too poor to be able to give anything at all were made to sell themselves, or a member of their family, into slavery. 'For,' said the Archbishop, 'it is only right and proper that a few should be slaves so that they may secure the freedom of the many. It is a true Christian sacrifice and it will be remembered on the day of judgement. This I promise.'

Most of those being taken away in chains to a life of bondage did not question their fate, accepting it as part of the natural order of things, though some – the braver spirits – did wonder, quietly in their hearts, why theirs was such a hard way to heaven when the Archbishop's road to the same place did not seem as rocky or as perilous.

But the Archbishop had more pressing concerns and, having blessed the departing slaves, he set about the work that preoccupied him. For a year the building went on and the Archbishop supervised it in every detail. At the end he was satisfied; the fortifications of Arles were now much higher and stronger and at each gate the towers were massive. It was a great achievement and in celebration a magnificent banquet was given and all the nobles and bishops for a hundred miles round came to the feast. They climbed to the tops of the towers, they walked the perimeter of the walls and they toasted the Archbishop in quantities of wine, congratulating themselves on their good fortune in possessing such a city and such a man to lead them. He truly was their protector and, before taking horse for home, they stood on the steps of the cathedral and saluted him.

The Archbishop accepted their homage and basked in it. He was dressed, that day, in the richest of his rich robes. Purple it was and studded with diamonds and pearls. His great mitre, heavy with rubies, sat squarely on his head and caught the rays of the evening sun and turned them into blood. He lifted his hands in blessing and his fingers blazed with sapphires, the sign of his office. He smiled, certain that he knew God's will, all of it.

'Now,' he said, 'we are safe. This city is a sanctuary. We have done the work of God and God is glad, but the work of God is never-ending. There is more for us to do, my friends. There is no respite for us who would be together in heaven. Abd al-Rhaman still sits in his stronghold and laughs at us. The infidel ranges where he will. The greatest task of all remains. We must attack Fraxinetta and we must expel the Saracen from this land. I am an archbishop of deeds. I shall lead you, but I shall require soldiers and horses; armies cost money. You have been generous before, you must be generous again. This is for the Lord your God and for your salvation.'

With this said the Archbishop made the sign of the cross and the congregation accepted his blessing. They bowed and then made preparations for the journeys that would take them back to their estates. They hardly dared to look at one another; more revenues called for; more tithes to be imposed – where would the money come from?

On this occasion the levy was indeed harder to raise than previously. It seemed, especially to the poor, that the persecution would never end. And this time even the nobles and churchmen were compelled to open their purses, and quite a few of them were obliged to dispose of several small parcels of land. For months the scramble for money went on until at last the Archbishop was satisfied; his army was ready and his ships were built. All that remained for him to do was lay his plans and catch Abd al-Rhaman by surprise.

Catching the Caliph by surprise was no easy task; he had spies everywhere; within the city of Arles certainly. He even had men inside the Archbishop's palace, or so it was said. And why not? The Archbishop was not loved by those he had made the poorer by his schemes. So the Caliph knew what he knew and rather than wait to be besieged in his own castle he called his men to him and embarked them in his galleys. He would put to sea, journeying out of sight of the land until he was opposite the mouth of the Rhône and then, under cover of night, he would land his soldiers and their horses and attack Arles by stealth, just before dawn. If he gained entry he would do as much damage to the defenders and the defences as he could. That would cool the Archbishop's ardour for a crusade against him, and the Caliph laughed and set sail just as soon as his troops and his ships were ready.

A night of no moon was chosen by the Saracens and their plans were perfect. In the darkest part of that dark night the Caliph's galleys rowed silently in from the sea like huge monsters with countless arms and legs, their painted beaks grinning just above the surface of the black waters. Without hesitation they entered the River Rhône and made their way upstream. Soundlessly they dropped anchor and wide gangplanks were run out. The men wore no spurs; their horses' hooves were bound in heavy cloth and all their weapons were darkened with mud so that not a single spear glinted in the starlight. Neither was any lantern lit but none was needed; local fishermen waited to show Abd al-Rhaman and his soldiers the secret ways across the marshes of the Camargue. With the Caliph at its head the column marched on the sleeping city of Arles.

At the four main gates the Saracens sat and waited. They had no intention of storming the town; the new fortifications would have made that impossible without a long and costly siege. Moreover the Archbishop's army, though not quartered in Arles, was encamped at no great distance and when summoned, could have been on the scene within an hour or two. That would not have suited the Caliph at all. He had no desire to fight a pitched battle; his scheme was to be subtle and swift.

Earlier that month he had sent fifty of his best warriors, disguised as Spanish merchants, into the city. During those four weeks they had bought and sold in the market-place and had hidden their swords under their robes. Now they were ready and on a signal they overpowered the watch and opened the great gates which had made the Archbishop so proud. Unopposed the Saracens poured into the city from all sides.

In the narrow, gloomy streets the Caliph's men encountered little or no resistance. Those Christian soldiers they did meet were half-asleep and ill-officered and they were slaughtered without mercy. The Archbishop's bodyguard, strong and brave and well-disciplined, dared not leave the palace in case that too was ransacked and their leader taken. All they could do was send a messenger to the main army and hold their positions until help arrived.

It was a superb attack. While a third of the Saracens destroyed as much of the new defences as they could another third searched for booty. They put the city to the flame and the men to the sword, while the women and children were herded to the southern gate where more Saracens waited to convey them back to the galleys and into a life of slavery.

The Caliph sat in the Archbishop's chair on the steps of the cathedral and sipped wine from a cup of gold while watching his men in the light of the burning buildings. He could hardly believe his good fortune. In one night he had destroyed the power of this stately city; he had stolen a great deal of treasure, and he had run off the Archbishop's horses and killed hundreds of his soldiers. There would be no attack on Fraxinetta now.

The Caliph tossed his cup aside and gave a sign. A trumpet sounded and, their sad work done, the Saracens began to leave Arles, passing quickly through the broken fortifications, streaming southwards to their ships. The raid was over.

As soon as he could the Archbishop emerged from his palace. He mustered his bodyguard and those soldiers who had survived the onslaught and, calling together some officers to command them, he led his men in pursuit of the enemy. He had never been so angry. In the depths of his own stronghold he had been shamed; his treasures had been wrested from him; his battlements had been thrown down; his garrison had been decimated and hundreds of his people taken into slavery. When the news spread the whole of Provence would mock him, while in Islam they would admire the daring and the cunning of the Caliph, Abd al-Rhaman.

The Archbishop urged his forces through the night, hoping that he might come up with the Saracens before they could board their ships. Above all he and his men were determined to rescue the women and children that had been stolen from them. Their task was not easy. It was like fighting a will-o'-the-wisp. The main body of the Caliph's soldiers had made directly for the galleys, but a strong rearguard had been left behind and had separated into small groups, laying ambushes everywhere.

The land between Arles and the sea-shore was covered in swamps and streams and the ways were treacherous and uncertain. The advance of the Christians was slow and from the darkness sped clouds of barbed arrows and they took their toll. There was a terrible confusion in those marshes and many a brave knight in the Archbishop's army perished as black fingers found his throat; or drowned even, borne down by the weight of his own armour as his horse gave way under him, hamstrung by a Saracen skirmisher.

And as the dawn came up Abd al-Rhaman leant on his sword not far from his ships, watching the booty and prisoners being taken on board, and he laughed his laugh again and sent messengers to his rearguard, ordering his men to fight fiercely, promising that ships would wait to carry them off, back to Fraxinetta.

At the same time, and in the complexity of that broken country, the Archbishop observed the first of the Saracen galleys standing out to sea and, knowing this was a difficult time for the Caliph, he decided that it would be a good moment to attack, for the Saracen had half his men embarked and half of them still on shore.

The Archbishop had never lacked courage and, gathering his soldiers around him, he charged along the banks of the Rhône towards that place where the Caliph was himself overseeing the departure of his troops. The

Christians were convinced that they were on the point of gaining their revenge, at least in part, for the insult that had been done them – but Abd al-Rhaman had not yet finished with his enemies.

Before advancing on Arles, and in order to protect his ships, the Caliph had hidden a number of his finest warriors in a deep marsh. Now, at the blast of a trumpet, they appeared as if from nowhere and assailed the Archbishop's force in the flank. Such was the surprise and ferocity of this assault that most of the Archbishop's men turned tail at once and retreated out of harm's way. The Archbishop's own bodyguard was cut to pieces and, with more Saracens pressing forward, the Archbishop finally found himself alone and surrounded by his foes. A desperate charge of horsemen from the Christian lines attempted to rescue their leader but it was too late. The Archbishop was pulled from his saddle, his sword snatched from his hand and with no ceremony he was hustled on board one of the galleys and it immediately put to sea.

At this there were more trumpet blasts and the remainder of the Saracen troops circled in triumph on the battlefield and called in their rearguard. They repulsed one last Christian attack and then, leaving their horses behind, they suddenly scrambled onto the last of the galleys, waiting patiently at the water's edge, and were rowed to safety by their comrades. The Caliph had escaped.

It was only then that the Christian troops could come forward. They gathered on the shore and, dismounting, tended their wounded and watched the Saracen fleet moving towards the horizon. Their dishonour was measureless; their city had been sacked; their riches plundered and their loved ones stolen away. As if that wasn't enough, they had lost their Archbishop and their general as well. Many hardened soldiers lowered their heads into their hands and wept at the thought of it. Never had they known such a thing.

Not all the survivors, it must be said, reasoned in the same way. Some, in their private thoughts, hoped that presently, deeds of war could turn to talk of conciliation. A treaty might be made with the Saracen, boundaries defined, captives returned and the Archbishop given back in exchange for a promise of peace.

The majority, however, shook their swords at the departing infidels and screamed vile curses across the sea. They would never cease to fight, they shouted. This defeat would mean war to the death and continuing bloodshed until the Archbishop had been released.

The Saracens did not deign to answer these threats and insults but set their sails and rested their oars. There was nothing for the Christians to do now except return to their ravaged city, taking their wounded and the news of the Archbishop's capture with them.

∞

It was not long before messengers arrived from the Caliph. They were proud men of aristocratic bearing and they rode exquisitely caparisoned horses and wore cloaks of great value. There was no fear on their faces and they cared little for any treachery the Christians might visit upon them. Indeed they brought presents from the Caliph and a letter from the Archbishop, in his own hand, informing the city elders that he was unharmed and well-treated and was as content as he could be under the circumstances. It was God's will, he hoped, that he should soon be free.

There was also a letter from the Caliph which the messengers read to the elders, and the bishops, telling them that if they desired to see their leader again they would have to pay a ransom of a hundred thousand gold pieces, or its equivalent.

There was a long silence at this. A hundred thousand pieces of gold was a sum that could only be spoken of in a tale or in a fable. Where was such money to come from? The men of Arles could not answer the question. The Saracen heralds were asked to withdraw and a long discussion began, and many a city dignitary stood to speak his mind.

Some were for leaving the Archbishop where he was. Who amongst them had not been impoverished by the Archbishop and his dreams of conquest? Why not let him perish? He was a man of God and if he died a martyr then his fate would be assured. He would go straight to heaven and never suffer in hellfire like the greater part of ordinary mortals. There might even be peace! And in any event, how could they possibly find such a ransom? All the gold and silver plate from the churches would have to be melted down. The Archbishop's personal fortune, locked in the palace, would have to be used, and the nobles would have to dig deeply into their own coffers this time. Estates would have to be sold, or at the best mortgaged, and the poor would have to be taxed once again, that was if they had anything left to tax. From being the richest city in Provence Arles would be impoverished for a generation. And for what? Just to repurchase a zealot of an archbishop. It would be better to live in peace with the Saracens. They had a different religion, it was true, but they were cultured men from an ancient civilization and their schools and universities, at least in Spain, were second to none.

Most members of the council were outraged by the expression of such callousness. The Archbishop was the leader of the church, a brave man performing the will of God. The Saracen must be expelled from Provence and indeed from Spain too. A Christian could not and should not live with such people; he could come to no accommodation with them. They were dogs and unbelievers, and as for their much vaunted learning, well, that was merely the cunning of the devil and good Christians should beware of it.

There was no middle way. If the Saracen were permitted to become established along the coast then it wouldn't be long before the whole country was colonized. The heathen would intermarry and defile the good blood of Provence with his issue, but, more important than anything else, all those in authority should remember their duty to the poor. If the common people were allowed to fall under the sway of the Caliph they would be forced to change their religion and kneel to Mohammed. How would God, on the day of judgement, then treat those who had once held positions of trust if their serfs and their vassals were to be condemned to eternal damnation in the fires of hell?

There was no question of it – they had to fight on. They would defeat the Saracen eventually, to the greater glory of God, but not only that, there were lands to be won, estates to be shared and above all there was the fabulous treasure of the Caliph, hidden at Fraxinetta. It didn't matter a jot about the size of the ransom for in the end they would win this campaign and they would recapture everything they had lost, right down to the last diamond.

In this way it was decided. It was to be war to the death, but first they must show the world that they did not desert their leaders when in trouble. A special commission would be set up to investigate all properties and all fortunes, secular and ecclesiastical. The amount that each person should pay towards the ransom would be decided; precious stones and good farming land would be accepted in settlement. The townsfolk and the peasants would be taxed once more, to starvation levels if necessary, although it would be explained to them that some things were more important than life, and dispensations would be given to anyone dying because of the requirements of the time. They would be absolved from all their sins on earth, however great, and would be assured a haven in paradise.

After these weighty decisions had been taken the Saracen heralds were recalled and immediately informed that the ransom would be paid. The messengers bowed low at this news and smiled. In two months' time, they said, they would return with the Archbishop and the exchange could take place on the point of land near to where the Great Rhône meets the sea, there at the Pharos of Faraman. Then the Saracens bowed low again and departed from Arles and rode to their ship.

∞

Now began a time of great tribulation for the folk of Arles. Once more houses were ransacked and children made hostage. Even ecclesiastical land was sold and several large estates became smaller. This was a necessity that grieved the nobles more than anything and many of them complained bitterly. The bishops however would not be deterred from their course but joined their hands in prayer and lifted their eyes to heaven. The stand against the infidel had to be made somewhere, they explained, and that somewhere was Arles.

So it was that in due course the day of the ransom came and the Saracen ships were sighted off the mouth of the Rhône for it was but a short journey for them along the coast from the Bay of Grimaud. On the orders of the Abbot of Montmajour, second in command to the Archbishop, a great procession assembled outside the city. There were soldiers on foot and on horseback; the whole council of nobles and elders, the bishops and their clerics, hundreds of men at arms and knights on destriers, their lances pointing to the sky. Surrounding the two wagons which carried the ransom were the crowded ranks of the Arlesien archers, each with an arrow notched in his bow-string. And behind the pomp and display came most of the population of Arles, desirous above all to ensure that their treasure arrived at its proper destination, but also curious to see the Saracen leader, the famed Caliph, Abd al-Rhaman.

The noise rising from that company was deafening. There was music playing and the occasion was somehow festive, like the celebration of Mardi-Gras or a great saint's day, and everyone was impatient to be gone. So, at last, the Abbot raised his hand and the procession set forth on its journey, becoming longer and longer as it advanced for the tracks through the Camargue are narrow and bounded, very often, by water on each side.

After several hours the treasure and its escort reached a wide promontory beyond which was nothing but the enamelled sea and the azure sky, except that on the sea rode a hundred galleys of Abd al-Rhaman and another twenty or so were secured to the quayside, close to the stone lighthouse called the Pharos of Faraman. And on the open ground nearby were pitched sumptuous tents and pavilions of silk and cloth of velvet, and pennants and bunting of all colours were unfurled above them, and the blazing sun made everything shine and as the people of Arles arrived they spread to right and left so that they might gaze out their eyes for it was improbable that they would ever see such a sight again. It was like a vast and rich tapestry, with each detail picked out in threads of gold and silver and blue, and then hung in the halls of some extravagant and fabled king.

Foremost among the tents that day was one of great splendour, burgundy red and bedecked with stars, and before it, on a throne which stood high on a dais, sat the Archbishop. Above him, to give shade, was draped a voluminous awning, embroidered all over with yellow narcissi. The Archbishop himself was clothed in a magnificent robe of immense luxury and crowned with a huge jewel-encrusted mitre, all of which the Caliph must have provided from his stock of stolen treasure.

From a distance, certainly, the Christian leader looked as regal and dignified as he had always done. But behind him stood a Saracen soldier with a long lance and ready, it seemed, to plunge it into the Archbishop's back if there should be the slightest sign of treachery; and, as if that were not enough, keeping guard by the captive's side, waited two archers with their arrows prepared and strung against their bows.

The Abbot of Montmajour noted the disposition of the enemy troops and he and all his men went towards the lighthouse, their weapons drawn. Cautiously they advanced until, at about a distance of a hundred paces from the Archbishop's tent, a double line of Saracen horsemen rode out and blocked their way. Then, when both parties had come to a halt, a brass trumpet was sounded and the line of horsemen opened and the Caliph touched his horse with his heels and came, on his own and unafraid, to where the Abbot, the council and the bishops watched over their wagons of treasure.

The Caliph was dressed like the richest king of all the world. His slippers and leggings were of gleaming satin. His coat was flared at the waist and encircled by a belt that glittered with diamonds. The turban he wore was as high as the Archbishop's mitre, and it carried a plume that had been mounted in a ruby clasp as large as a man's fist. His cloak, trimmed with pearls, almost brushed the ground while his horse's bridle alone was rich enough to keep a peasant's family in luxury for five or six generations.

The Caliph halted and looked at the Abbot of Montmajour and that look struck fear into the heart of every man who saw it. 'My men will look at the ransom,' he said, and the Provençal was clipped and uncouth on his hard Saracen tongue.

'And the Archbishop?' asked the Abbot of Montmajour.

The Caliph smiled and, half-turning in his saddle, he waved an arm and the Christians saw their leader make the sign of the cross and they fell on their knees and did likewise, praising God for the safe return of the defender of their faith.

Then the Caliph lifted his hand again and four of his soldiers pushed their way past the Christian guards and pulled back the covers from the wagons and laid open the treasure to the eyes of the Caliph and those eyes glinted with a ravening greed.

A shout rose from the people of Arles. Never had they seen such riches, nor were they likely to again. Here was all the wealth of their city in two wagon loads. Here was their future and their past, all of it gathered into one place so that it might rescue the pride of one man and satisfy the greed of another. Here was gold and silver plate, diamond collars, brooches of emerald and ruby, opals and amethyst; golden daggers and garments of transparent silk; crowns of precious metals and reliquaries from the churches. Everything of worth had been taken from the city and the people of that city groaned at their loss. Soon their treasure would be borne away from them and hoarded in a secret cave on the far side of the country, for the benefit of one man only, and that man was Abd al-Rhaman.

The Caliph nodded. 'It is good,' he said. 'Now this is what shall be done. My men will place this ransom on board my ship, then my horsemen shall embark until there is only one ship left. Then I shall embark and the man with the spear and the men with the arrows will leave the Archbishop. If there is any treachery by you my archers will slay the Archbishop where he sits. You may possibly kill me but you will have lost both your treasure and your Archbishop. Do you agree?'

'We agree,' said the Abbot of Montmajour. He looked towards the Archbishop and the Archbishop raised his right hand again in blessing.

'Excellent,' said the Caliph and he smiled. 'You will find the Archbishop's mind changed by his experiences. He has discovered that we are not so barbaric as he thought we were. He and I had many long discussions and we have decided that henceforth we will respect each other's frontiers. He has abandoned his idea of attacking me at Fraxinetta, and I shall not attack Arles again. After all, there is nothing left for me to take, is there?'

The Abbot of Montmajour frowned. 'The Archbishop would never make a treaty with an infidel,' he said, 'least of all you.'

The Caliph ignored the insult. 'You will discover for yourself,' he said, 'what treaty we have made,' and turning his horse he passed through his line of horsemen and went towards the quayside.

All was performed then as the Caliph had said. Helpless, the Christians watched as the ship containing their treasure put out to sea. One by one the Saracen horsemen led their mounts up the wide gangplanks and, once each galley had taken its full complement of soldiers, it put to sea also. All tents, save the Archbishop's, were struck and stowed away until in the end only one ship remained by the land and only the Caliph stood by it. Under the Archbishop's awning the man with the lance, and the two archers, continued their watch, unmoving, weapons ready to slay their prisoner.

Now a servant led the Caliph's horse on board and Abd al-Rhaman gave a sign and the three soldiers left the Archbishop's side and ran quickly onto their vessel, their leader following. The long oars dipped once or twice and within seconds there was the length of a bow-shot between ship and shore.

The Abbot and the bishops and the nobles advanced only slowly towards the Archbishop's pavilion, behind them, at a due distance, came the townsfolk. The Saracen fleet drifted – and from it, across the water, louder than the sound of waves, came the noise of music and merry-making.

Still slowly, with no one preceding him, the Abbot went. A hundred paces were covered and he faced the Archbishop, then he knelt and bowed his head and a great cheer rose from the Saracens and the Abbot lifted his eyes and looked into the shade beneath the awning and understood. The Archbishop was dead.

The Abbot got to his feet and approached the throne. The nobles and bishops gathered together and said nothing. It was only too easy for them to see how they had been tricked. The Archbishop had been tied upright to his throne with golden cords and the thinnest, but the strongest, of horsehair had been fastened around his right hand, rising from there into the canopy overhead. In that place the Caliph must have concealed a servant and it had been but a simple matter for that servant to move the Archbishop's arm. That was how the blessing had been given. The Abbot touched the white face and the cold hand. The Archbishop had been dead a day or two at least. It had all been a charade.

The Abbot bowed and kissed the Archbishop's ring and then, while the Saracens fired their cannon and sang in celebration, he ordered that the Archbishop's body be placed, with all tenderness, in one of the empty treasure wagons. Thus the corpse would lead the populace back to Arles, and there it would receive a proper burial in a great marble tomb.

Hardly anyone spoke at that time, so downcast were they, but as the cortege began to move homeward one of the largest land-owners of Provence, a man known for his wit and irony, was heard to remark that there had probably never been, in the whole of the world's history, such an amount paid for a dead archbishop.

The Abbot of Montmajour reprimanded this noble and told him to hold his tongue and not set a bad example to the common people and soldiery who were within earshot. But it was too late. One of the soldiers, having heard the quip, topped it with one of his own.

'It is obviously a better bargain,' he said, 'to get the Archbishop back dead rather than alive, even at the price paid, for it is certain to work out cheaper in the long run.'

The rank and file laughed loudly at this sally but unfortunately it too was overheard by the Abbot and he ordered that the insolent soldier should be given ten lashes without delay. So he was and sentence was carried out against one of the wheels of the second treasure wagon and when it was over the wagon followed on at the tail of the column, bearing inside it the soldier who had been punished, his back all bloody.

This soldier groaned in pain as he was jolted along the rough road but after a while the noise stopped and he began to laugh quietly to himself instead. In the bottom of the wagon he had found a gold coin; more than he could earn in two years of hard work. Back in Arles that night he and his companions would drink the Abbot's health, yes, and the health of Abd al-Rhaman too.

# LA
# MURE-ARGENS

**W**e left St Julien without waiting for morning, setting out with the night sky still lying like a blindness upon us, while from the edge of the lake below rose the hard sound of the waves as they boomed against the shore.

When the light did come it was not a light that fell from the sun, there was no orange or gold in it. This dawn was just blackness at first, then a greyness turning to white, and thin layers of mist drove down the slopes and isolated each one of us from his companions and only by following the long line of sheep could we remain together and on the right road.

Above this low mist moved the larger clouds, always changing shape and dragging behind them their showers like great cloaks. On the surface of the lake the rain swayed up like a crop of tall weeds in the rough wind, and over the land there was but one uniform shadow. I bowed my head and tramped on, my feet splashing through puddles and my hand tight on the mule's bridle, the leather soaked and stiff.

After marching for an hour or two we passed through a tunnel and then, at a place where the lake was narrow, crossed a bridge and came over to the western side. At the end of the bridge I gazed back the way we had come and saw, on the horizon, looking exactly like another cloud, the long black hump of a mountain, flat along its ridge and rounded on the flanks. At this moment Joseph appeared beside me, struggling to hold his umbrella above his head. He greeted me with pleasure, as if we had been separated for days, and he pointed into the sky. 'That's mine,' he shouted, his words half-broken by the gale, 'that's my mountain . . . La Chamatte.'

Then suddenly the lake was gone, the mist had risen and our whole flock was visible again. One by one the shepherds reappeared, handing me the umbrellas so they could be folded away and thrown into the cart. We marched another hour and came eventually to St André les Alpes and, although it was still early, its inhabitants waited for us on their doorsteps, bowls of coffee steaming in their hands and chunks of fresh bread making their cheeks bulge.

These people were cheerful and talked to us as we trudged the length of their main street. St André was the nearest town to the valley of Allons, where the Martels came from, and so the shop-keepers knew every shepherd by name – every shepherd that was except me.

'And who is this?' they asked Joseph and Jean as father and son halted at every door to shake hands.

'Ah that,' they answered, smiling as if slightly ashamed of themselves. 'That is our Englishman. He is not as bad as he looks either, but be careful . . . he writes down everything you say in a notebook.'

Beyond St André we entered the upper valley of the Verdon, wide and flat now with a stony floor and tall pines on the hillsides above us. There was a single-track railway here too, running northwards by the shallow river and part of the line that joins Digne to Nice. And later, when we stopped by the lonely station of La Mure-Argens to water the sheep, the sight of it made me sad. Soon it would be time for me to leave the shepherds and this would be the way, standing alone at some desolate roadside halt with my duffel bag on my shoulder, waiting for the diesel-driven carriage, tiny as a toy, that would rattle me through the mountains and down to the coast, back into a life I was no longer sure I wanted.

Luckily this feeling of depression did not last long. The sun had climbed high and every shred of mist and every bank of cloud had disappeared. The crest of Joseph's mountain followed us as we walked and slowly our road fell away from the north and the hills began to close in on either side. After yet more walking we passed through a gorge, crossed a bridge and all at once found ourselves heading south in a soft-rimmed valley, protected from the wind. It was like going into a different country, all calm and quiet. This was the valley of Allons at last and the Martels were home.

All around us lay good grazing land and it climbed through trees to heights of between five and six thousand feet. By the wayside we rested and the sheep went no further than the nearest shade and we let them go for we knew they were too tired to wander. It was only midday but we had been on the road since four that morning and had covered at least eighteen kilometres.

Waiting for us when we stopped was Jean Martel's wife, Jeannette. A good-looking woman wearing a simple blue dress, she had shoulder length hair and fearless bright eyes. She had prepared a kind of celebratory feast for us and brought it down from Allons; now she unpacked it and spread it before us as we groaned with fatigue and sat.

Milou groaned the loudest and leant forward to unfasten the straps on his plastic sandals. 'It is the bastinado I have had today,' he said, and pulling off his socks he took from the pocket of his inside jacket a small bottle of Eau de Cologne that he had purchased in St André that morning. We all watched as he poured a little of the toilet water into the palm of his hand and began to massage the soles of his feet with cries of anguish and pleasure mixed.

Lucien sat next to Milou and took the bottle from him. He smelt it first, read the label, removed his beret, stiff as a dish with grease and sweat, turned it over and sprinkled a good quantity of the scent into it. 'There,' he said when he'd finished, 'the road is ended now and this Eau de Cologne will make me smell like a flower all summer.'

The meal I had that day was one that I could have wished to eat forever.

It came piping hot in black casseroles and there was soup with rabbit and pasta, slices of leg of lamb and cheese and fruit and wine. But it was not the menu that made that banquet so extraordinary. It was the company and the place, and the feeling that I had walked to Allons through a whole lifetime of experience and had seen all the world on my way, even though my notebook told me that I had been on the road for just one short week and that my point of departure had been no further afield than Grimaud. I know now that never again will I eat such food, because that is what the gods eat and only carelessness on their part had allowed me to be called that once to their table.

But even this meal came to an end and when it was over Joseph lit his pipe and Milou smoked a crumpled cigarette and thought aloud about the shepherdess of Castellane.

'I know that woman,' said Jeannette, 'and they say she is every bit as good with her flock as any man . . . and there is no reason why she should not be. Many a woman in the old days, and in these days too, had to do a man's work, and more, and got precious little thanks for it.'

'I told them the story of Pichounetta,' said Milou, the stub of a cigarette brown and extinguished in his mouth, 'the night we got to Callas.'

'There is another story,' said Jeannette, 'one that I heard from my own grandmother when she lived in the house where you live, Michel, where Bonne Maman Renoult lives. My grandmother told me that the families who lived there before believed that Rascas had been built from the stones of a beautiful château that once stood on the hill there and looked out down the valley. I don't know whether it is true or not . . . it is too long ago . . . but the story, that I do know.'

# *Malagan and The Lady of Rascas*

At the time of the crusades and in the land of Provence there were many beautiful castles and one of the finest was the castle of Rascas. High on a hillside it stood, built of golden stone and set against a sky which was as blue and as hard as the heart of any sapphire. At the foot of the hillside lay a village, its roofs shaded by broad-leaved plane trees and its streets cooled by the waters of a fountain that overflowed in the village square. All around stretched a valley and there the villagers raised sheep and laboured among the olive trees and vines for their sustenance and for the greater pleasure of their lord, the Baron Rascas.

Baron Rascas was a stern and selfish man who lived in great style and luxury and sought pleasure in all the good things that life had to offer him. He was not particularly cruel to his subjects but neither was he particularly kind. For him the common people did not exist. As long as his needs, and those of his courtiers, were satisfied then all was well; but if the Baron were thwarted in any way then he could become brutal and, like the violent soldier he was, he possessed the courage and the means to impose his will on anyone.

For the most part the Baron bore himself well enough and was content to live his life from day to day, gazing over his domain or seeking happiness with his courtiers. And thus he lived until the middle time of his life when, without warning, a royal messenger rode up to the castle and commanded the Baron to assemble his men at arms so that he and they might follow their king to Palestine, to deliver battle to the Saracens who occupied the Holy City, in an attempt to wrest it from them by force of arms for the glory of God.

The Baron had no alternative but to obey. Like any other feudal lord he held his lands under the king and was sworn to provide soldiers and service to his monarch whenever summoned and for as long as necessary. The Baron cursed but gave orders nevertheless and preparations were made.

Within three weeks all was ready and the day of departure arrived sooner than anyone could have thought possible. On that day there was a great noise and bustle to be observed both in the castle and the village. Pack horses were led from the stables and loaded; chargers were saddled and the Baron's armour, highly polished and reflecting the cloudless sky, was stowed away by his squires. The Baron too was busy and moved about his courtyard making sure that not one dagger or mace had been forgotten. From the battlements the courtiers, fine gentlemen exquisitely dressed in silken robes and velvet cloaks, gazed down and bit their lips. These were men too cowardly to follow their lord and desired only that the Baron leave so they might continue their endless round of amusement and dance.

The Baron was well aware of this state of affairs but had no wish to take his courtiers with him; they would have been nothing more than a burden and a hindrance. In any event his service to the king did not demand that he take all his followers. He had chosen only his bravest soldiers, about sixty in all, resolute men who knew that they might never survive this adventure, but who also knew that if they did they would live from the glory and holiness of it for the rest of their lives.

The Baron glanced up into the battlements; at least those he left behind would be there to protect the castle and the valley in times of danger. Though he could not trust them to fight well on a foreign campaign he was sure that they would defend their own lives and possessions to the last gasp if called upon to do so. The Baron sighed; would he and his men ever see this valley again? It was unlikely. The very journey to the Holy Land was full of hazards; there would be skirmishes at every frontier and drownings at every river crossing. On the high seas the army would be no safer. How many ships would founder beneath the waves and how many be taken by pirates? Even at the journey's end death lurked in every desert and waited at every oasis. Diseases that no physician could cure flourished in Palestine and when the king's soldiers reached the battlefield, those that survived, they would find in the Saracen an enemy more implacable than any in their previous experience.

The Baron shook his head and tried to clear his mind of such thoughts. He ordered the men at arms to lead their pack horses down the side of the mountain and to wait for him at the village, then he settled the sword at his waist and watched as the ladies of the court stepped aside in order that his wife might approach him to speak her farewells.

Of all the ladies in the castle the most beautiful was the Baron's wife, the Lady of Rascas. She was young and stately, but the most striking thing about her was the way in which the kindness in her heart showed through the features of her face. All through Provence she was renowned for her generosity and modesty. The Baron's courtiers could find no fault in her and the common people could not love her enough for the care she took of them.

Again the Baron sighed. He was a brave man, some said there was no man braver, but as he took his wife in his arms he felt his resolve weaken. His spirit quailed. He pressed his wife to him and closed his eyes. She was so beautiful; of all the things he possessed she was what he cherished most and the thought that he might never see her again tormented him. Perhaps she would weary of waiting for him and someone else, younger, more handsome, would come to the castle and charm her with his poetry, seduce her with a new song, laugh with her in the topmost towers as the sun went down the sky and turned the countryside to gold.

The Baron's face darkened; it was a prospect he could not face. Death and disease would be better.

'My lord,' said the Lady of Rascas, 'be not so sad, the day of your return is even now approaching.' She spoke gently and touched her husband's hand.

The Baron held his wife at arm's length so that he could contemplate her beauty.

'Can you love me this long time of absence?' he asked, his voice thick with feeling. But he did not wait for an answer and turned, forbidding anyone to follow him as he made his way into an arcaded gallery let into the wall of the castle and there he commanded that cool wine be sent to him and that Malagan, the sorcerer, should attend him instantly.

Malagan came, his soft shoes making no sound on the flagstones and he stood silently before his master, his arms folded beneath his scarlet gown. Malagan was young, tall and dark-skinned, there was Saracen blood in his veins. His hair was black and ragged and his nose was a hook in his face and the deep lines in his countenance were lines of suffering and grief.

There were those in the castle who said that Malagan was the most evil magician in Provence, in the world even, but they did not say it loudly. No one knew where he came from or what bound him to the Baron. Some courtiers said that the Lord of Rascas had, by accident, freed the magician from a spell and that in return Malagan had vowed to serve the Baron in everything for a certain number of years, and so far he had remained faithful to that vow.

What was known was that Malagan could change base metals into gold, imprison the souls of men in stone and make flowers bloom in the driest desert. He could also alter his form at will and like a maggot work his way into a man's brain and discover his innermost thoughts. In a word he could do everything that a god might do except restore life.

The Baron poured two goblets of wine and bade his sorcerer sit. 'Malagan,' he said, 'I want from you this day strong magic, magic to ease my heart of its jealousy and doubt. You will ensure that my wife is faithful while I am away.'

The magician put down his cup and spoke, his voice full of menace; 'This does not need magic,' he said, 'your lady is faithful and honest, this much I know for truth. No spell of mine can make her more or less so.'

The Baron looked hard into Malagan's eyes; 'It is a command,' he said.

Malagan spoke again; 'I can imprison her in a tree, a cliff. I can change her into a bird.'

'No,' said the Baron. 'There is danger there. A bird may be killed, a tree felled and a cliff struck by a thunderbolt. She must live in the castle, protected. she must see to my lands. I have considered it. Make her hard to look upon, so that no one will desire her, ugly, like a beast.'

'This is my lord's wish?' asked Malagan. He showed no surprise but he was hesitant.

'It is,' said the Baron, 'but I have no mind to see it. You will wait until I have left the castle. Then you will follow me on my journey. I do not want this spell to be undone during my absence.'

Malagan's eyes glowed at the Baron's words but he said nothing, only getting to his feet and bowing slightly as his lord left the gallery and went directly to the courtyard, back to his wife.

Once more he embraced her and urged her to be courageous and to endure faithfully the years of separation that lay ahead and to accept with humility whatever life might hold in store. For his part he swore to be brave and loyal.

'I am sure our love will survive,' he said. 'Now I go to join my king, leaving you in charge of my lands and fortune. You are to care for them as if they were your own children.'

At this the Lady of Rascas fell to her knees and watched as her husband, followed by his squires and his bodyguard, rode through the gate, across the drawbridge and into the narrow road that led from the castle and down to the valley below. The courtiers and their fine ladies watched too and waved their hands and handkerchieves, but their attention was soon caught by something other than their lord's departure. Bearing a great book of magic bound in Arabian leather and studded with silver stars, Malagan appeared in the courtyard leading his own savage horse and the sight of the magician rooted everyone to the spot where they stood. Malagan laid his book on the low stone coping of the castle fountain and, speaking in a curious tongue, he made strange passes with his hands while his dark eyes glared all the while into the horrified face of the still kneeling Lady of Rascas.

Malagan spoke for several minutes, his voice rising and falling in a dreamlike chant until at last his hands dropped to his book and he slammed it shut. Then, so sure was he of his magic that he turned without a glance behind him, mounted his horse and followed his master through the castle gates. And the courtiers, immobile, like statues in their fear, stared from the battlements and waited.

They did not wait long; a great moan of anguish rose from their throats as the effects of the magic became apparent. The Lady of Rascas touched her hands to her face and found that it was changing. Hair, close and stiff like fur, began to sprout there. Her eyes grew larger and larger, her lips thickened, her teeth widened and her jaw-bone became long and heavy. Under her fingers she felt her ears take a pointed shape and her nostrils spread and turn into voluminous purses of velvet. In a few moments it was over and her head was the head of a human-being no more; it was the head of a horse. This was the magic of Malagan. This was how her husband had chosen to keep her faithful, and with this fearful realization the Lady of Rascas screamed, leapt to her feet and ran to her apartments, locking the doors behind her and allowing no one into her presence. For many days her cries and sobs were heard all over the castle and the courtiers and the servants stood in the corridors and galleries in idle groups, unhappy and forlorn, not knowing what to do for their lady or for themselves.

But the Lady of Rascas was a lady of unusual courage. As the months went by she began to show herself again. First of all to her own servants and then, little by little, to the whole society of the castle. There were good reasons for this apart from her own strength of character. The demands of her husband's estate made it necessary for her to visit all corners of it; to see that everything was as it should be; to make sure that the fruit trees were pruned; the vines cultivated; the crops stored and the sheep counted. Gradually, as the months of the Baron's absence became years, the people of Rascas accustomed themselves to their mistress's appearance and as she went amongst them, still clad in her beautiful gowns, so pleasant was her manner, so calm her spirits and so quick her mind, that they hardly noticed that her face was not a human face. To strangers and travellers too she was so welcoming and gracious that after a few hours in her company they completely forgot the forbidding countenance of this stricken châtelaine. There were even troubadours and minstrels who composed songs and poems about the Lady of Rascas without mentioning her physical aspect. They sang instead of her composure and sensitivity; her good husbandry and learning, and the love and fidelity she bore towards her cruel lord.

And so life went on and the years passed, seven of them. The courtiers served their lady and accepted her judgements and her kindness with happy hearts. Of the Baron there was little news save occasional rumours of fierce battles in the Holy Land; death and disease; long sieges and forced marches; towns taken and cities surrendered. All that was known for sure was that the Baron still lived though many of his followers had perished, sickened by the plague or pierced by Saracen arrows.

But the Lady of Rascas bore her lot with patience and one day, in the eighth year of her transformation, while gazing from her window, she saw a plume of dust rising from the distant road near where it crossed the silver river. It was a dust that rose from the hooves of a messenger's horse and in less than an hour the breathless courier was at his lady's feet. The crusades were over, the Baron had landed in Provence and he and what remained of his retinue would be arriving at the castle within the week.

With haste and diligence the Lady of Rascas ordered everything to be made ready for her husband's return. The castle was swept, the store houses inspected, the accounts made ready and everyone dressed themselves in their best robes. So pleased was the Lady of Rascas and so delighted the courtiers that they forgot that the Baron had not seen his wife as she now appeared; he had not seen her since Malagan had wrought his evil spell, and they gave no thought to how the Baron would look upon her.

On the day of their lord's return the whole population of the castle assembled in the courtyard and waited for the Baron and his men to ride over the drawbridge and through the gate. They were shocked by what they saw. The Baron had aged more years than he had been absent. His armour was dented and tarnished, its leather straps cracked and broken by the sun. His face was furrowed by the terrible things he had endured, his eyes dulled by the blood of the men he had killed. His heart had grown hard in seven years of war and he remembered nothing of the ways of peace.

Like an old man he dismounted and leaning against his war horse he looked at his wife as she curtsied and offered him the keys of the castle. The Baron's lips parted in horror. When last he had seen his wife she had been the most beautiful woman in Provence.

He fell back a step and it was at that moment the courtiers recollected that the Baron had never seen his wife in this transformation and they searched with their eyes amongst the ranks of the Baron's followers and discovered for themselves what their master already knew – Malagan had been lost in the Holy Land and there was no one to remove the magician's spell.

So, with a roar of pain, the Baron covered his face and strode past his wife, thrusting his subjects from his path as he entered the castle. His lady pursued him and threw herself at his feet but the Baron would not look at her and commanded that she take herself off to the highest tower in Rascas and stay there until she died.

For many days the Baron was in the worst of tempers. He cursed his followers and cuffed his servants unmercifully. Most of his time he spent seated in a dark corner of the great hall, lost in sorrow and self-pity. The results of his cruel behaviour afflicted him deeply and when he learnt of his wife's irreproachable conduct and when he inspected his estates and saw evidence everywhere of her goodness, he regretted more and more what he had caused Malagan to do all those years previously. And he was shamed too by those courtiers who had learnt to love the Lady of Rascas and had the courage to say that her imprisonment was a crime, but although the Baron knew in his heart that they were right he could not bear to release his wife from her prison. He knew that every time he looked upon her his own shame would burn within him.

At last, and in despair, the Baron sent messengers across the length and breadth of Provence, offering a reward to any magician who could remove the spell from his wife and bring happiness to her. The reward was great and many strove to win it but there was no one whose magic was as strong as Malagan's and the Lady of Rascas stayed as she was and lived alone, and little by little her husband allowed the memory of her to slip from his mind.

Once more the long years went by and the Baron sought happiness in dissipation and his castle became renowned for luxury and merry-making, and troubadours hastened there from all over Provence to sing of its delights, and only a very few faithful courtiers and servants ever gave a thought to the sadness sitting lonely in the tower.

There came a time too when magicians and sorcerers no longer journeyed to Rascas for the Baron had ceased to send messengers in search of them. He had become more selfish than he had ever been. More cruel than in war and more foolish than in youth. The Baron and his flatterers thought only of themselves and the pleasures of the moment while his estates and his subjects, those possessions that this wife had cared for so well, began to suffer and decline.

But the Baron paid no heed to the state of his affairs, nor did he listen to those who begged him to change his ways. So it came about that one summer's evening, when the Baron was deep in wine at the head of his table, surrounded by the most beautiful of his ladies, a servant appeared at the door of the hall and, speaking with mirth in his voice, informed his master that there was someone at the castle gates who craved admittance. This man, said the servant, was aged and riding a spavined mule. He had no squire and was dressed only in a tattered cloak which had been torn by the winds and burnt threadbare by the sun. Tied to his saddle was a straw basket and that seemed to contain the sum total of his wordly goods.

The Baron laughed at this intelligence and held up his hand to signify that the traveller be received. He did this not out of a feeling of hospitality but in the hope that the newcomer might offer some entertainment. His ladies and courtiers were also intrigued with the idea and clapped their hands and called for some more wine, making a deal of noise as they did so.

But all this din came to a sudden stop and every voice was stilled as a dark shadow fell across the doorway to the chamber and in the yellow light of the torches a forbidding figure slowly advanced. The Baron and his courtiers stared. He was tall this traveller and his hair was long and grey and matted with the dust of travel. His face was sombre and its texture was like pitted stone which has been scarred by a thousand years of driven rain. The eyes were pale, like those of a dead man and the mouth was a gash with no lines of softness to make it human.

The Baron stirred in his seat and felt forward for his goblet of wine. The silence of the courtiers prolonged itself.

'Laugh,' commanded the Baron, 'do you not laugh when you see an old scarecrow?'

Dutifully a few of the courtiers made as if to laugh but the feeble sound soon died in their throats.

'What is it you seek here,' asked the Baron, 'a night's rest, money? Are you a beggar?'

'I am not a beggar,' said the stranger, and when he spoke his voice was sharp and strong and pierced the air like a lance. 'I bring you the gift of contentment. I have heard tell that there is a reward for whoever can bring your wife, the Lady of Rascas, to happiness again. This I can achieve.'

Now the Baron and the courtiers did laugh in reality. Could this scarecrow perform what the greatest wizards in the land had failed to do?

'Old man,' said the Baron, 'you do not have the power in your blood and the evil knowledge in your spirit to undo what has been done.'

The stranger at the door nodded. 'What you say, my lord, may be true, but old is not always bad and backwards is sometimes forward.'

The Baron laughed again, long and loud. 'If your magic is as strong as your words are foolish,' he answered, 'then my wife shall indeed be saved. You have amused me and I will strike a bargain. I will give you a room above the kennels for a period of fifteen days. If you achieve nothing in that time then I shall bind you backwards on your mule and the scullions will beat you down the valley. On the other hand if you should succeed in your attempt to bring me happiness then great riches shall be yours. Now leave me, I weary of would be magicians.'

'I want no riches,' said the stranger as he turned to go. 'My satisfaction lies elsewhere,' and he left the room.

The magician went directly to the place that had been given him and locked himself inside. Those who took him his food reported that he spent most of his time reading in a great book, which he carried in his straw basket, or staring from his window, unblinking, at the sun. Once or twice he had been seen drawing with a stick in the dust of the courtyard or talking to the animals in the stables, but not once did he address a word to any of the Baron's courtiers or servants. At last, on the fifteenth day, he climbed to the topmost tower, opened the door to the chamber where the Lady of Rascas dwelt, even though it was triple locked, and taking her by the hand he led her down the spiral staircase and into the Baron's presence.

There was a gasp from the onlookers. It had been years since anyone there had seen the Baron's wife. Many had never seen her at all, having arrived at the castle since the lady's imprisonment, and these cried out in horror. Even the

Baron turned his gaze away, shamed once again by what he had done. Yet the Lady of Rascas moved with such stateliness and grace that her ugliness was in some measure diminished and the courtiers calmed each other and ranged themselves all up and down the great hall to see what the magician should do.

Firstly he commanded the Baron's wife to sit on a low stool before her husband's throne. Then he stretched his arms in his tattered gown and began to speak, looking straight into the Baron's eyes while the Baron himself tried to look elsewhere but found he could not.

The language used by the magician was unknown to all there save the Baron. It was the Saracen tongue and he had learnt to understand it during his time in the Holy Land. Now, as he listened, he gripped the arms of his chair and trembled with fear.

'I tell the story of Malagan,' said the stranger, 'how he cast this fearful spell on the command of his lord because he too was under a spell at that time. I tell this story because I am Malagan and I have returned to undo the evil I did.'

The Baron roared as if under torture but still he could not turn his eyes away from the dreadful sorcerer.

'He bade me follow him to Palestine,' continued Malagan, pointing at the Baron, 'and he left me for dead on the field of battle nor bothered himself with my body or deigned to send messengers to see if I was really dead or no. I was sorely injured, captured, enslaved, made the menial of a subtle magician who drained all my power from me when I was weak, stole my books of magic, discovered the secrets of my charms and ointments, and then when he'd finished with me, sold me into even more abject a bondage. I became so weak that I was left upon the road to die. Somehow I survived as a beggar and was befriended at last by a man of Alexandria who took me into his house as a servant and saw to it that I was nursed back to health. He was a scholar, that man, and I studied with him and shared his knowledge and I regained some magic, but never was it as it had been before. After some years this man of Alexandria gave me my freedom and I journeyed back to Christendom, through many more years and many more adventures. Now I have returned to this castle to seek revenge for the years of slavery and toil, revenge on the lord who abandoned me.'

Malagan drew his breath and the Baron slipped low in his chair and his courtiers looked on, wondering at the words that had been spoken.

'They told me you were dead,' cried the Baron, 'we were hard pressed by the enemy, I could not return to give you burial.'

'You did not even think to try,' said Malagan, 'you did not consider me worthy. I am Malagan and I wish you harm . . . yet I would undo the evil you had me do and make your lady content . . . but, alas, my power is not what it once was. To reverse a spell requires more power than to make one.' And Malagan broke into a chant of ancient Arabic and now not one word of his language could the Baron understand. Malagan's voice rose and the summer air darkened and in the valley below the castle there was thunder and blackness. The courtiers fell to their knees and crossed themselves and prayed for mercy. Suddenly there was a cry from the Baron and he lifted his hands to his face and found that it was changing. Hair, close and stiff like fur began to sprout there; his eyes grew larger and larger, his lips thickened, his teeth widened and his jaw-bone became long and heavy. Under his fingers he felt his ears take a pointed shape and his nostrils spread and turn into voluminous purses of velvet. Then it was over and his head was the head of a human-being no more; it was the head of a horse. The Baron sobbed and fell senseless to the ground. Only his wife, amongst all those present, got to her feet and went to comfort him.

With his work done Malagan the Magician pulled his cloak around his shoulders and with his tattered gown flowing behind him he strode across the flagstones and passed through the high wooden doors of the great hall and left the castle, never to be seen or heard of again.

At first a vast sadness settled over Rascas and its inhabitants; there was an end to feasting, music and dancing. The Baron, ashamed of his appearance locked himself in his wife's tower room and would allow none to see him but she. Once more the Lady of Rascas was forced to take charge of the daily business of her husband's estates, and in due time this course of events brought many advantages.

The Baron discovered in his wife all those qualities she had developed during his absence and rediscovered those attributes she had possessed before his departure but which he had forgotten. She taught the Baron to accept his misfortune with patience and humility, showing him how to take a delight in the beauty of the valley and the simple life of its people. The Baron fell in love all over again and much more profoundly than he had the first time. He found in his wife the most loving and intelligent creature he had ever known and in the light of her husband's gaze the Lady of Rascas became happier than she had been in her youth. The people of the castle rejoiced in what they saw and they too learned to be happy, watching as a new love bloomed between their master and mistress.

So the Lady of Rascas was made as content as Malagan had wished her to be and her lord became wise and looked after his lands with care. Though they were never seen outside their estates they were renowned throughout Provence in song and in legend for the perfection of their love, the length of their lives and the beauty of their children and grandchildren. And over the castle gate the Lady of Rascas caused to be carved, before she died, the following words:

'Out of evil came good, out of ugliness, beauty.'

The Baron approved of this work but when the stone-mason had finished his task the Baron took him to the postern gate at the rear of the castle and there commanded him to carve once more. Today, many hundreds of years later, amongst the fallen stone and hollow walls of the place that was called Rascas, only that archway stands and these words may be read above it:

'He who turns to evil will, at the end, find it turned against him.'

# LA
# COURRADOUR

Later that same afternoon the flock was rounded up for the last time and then moved further along the valley. About a mile from the village we went down into a wide field and funnelled the sheep through a narrow gate that stood at the entrance to a large pen. At the gate was Jean Martel and as the sheep passed him, one by one, he moved a hurdle this way or that, according to the coloured dye that each animal bore on its back. Gradually the flock belonging to Jules and Leonce was set aside from the main herd and re-formed near the roadway, held together in a close and compact bunch by men and dogs.

As soon as this task had been completed two of the spare mules were loaded with provisions and Lucien led them away. Then, with his dogs to assist him, he began to urge the smaller, separated flock forward, back over the road and up the low slopes into the advancing dusk.

'He has to take them on to La Colle,' said Marius. 'He'll be on his own tonight, and so will the rest of us in a day or two.'

The village of Allons itself was nothing more than a group of about twenty small houses and sheds all tucked in against the curving side of the valley. Anyone might reasonably have wondered why we had come so far to find such a place, but there was good water and grass here and a track that mounted, Joseph said, to pastures of the richest kind. On the summit of La Chamatte was a lawn of several thousand hectares and there you could lie at your ease all day and watch the marmots playing in the open with their young, free after the long months of hibernation they had spent beneath the ground.

It was dark by the time we had secured the rest of the flock in its fold and when, grouped together, we entered the village street we were silent and our steps were weary. There was only one light in Allons and we followed Joseph to it. We sat at Jeannette's table and smiled with guilt at one another, as if it were a crime to be caught below a roof, hardly daring to believe that the transhumance was over. The shepherds sat with their hats on and ate their food slowly. If they spoke at all they spoke in a slow way about which pasture they would go to first and the quality of this year's grass. Nobody offered to tell a story or even referred to one. Story-telling was for outside.

I do not know where the others slept that night – the Martels in their own beds I suppose and the others in sheds or 'à la belle étoile'. For my part I slept in a stable, across the road from the house, cradled in a deep pile of clean straw. It was loose and soft, that straw, and my body floated in it, suspended in warmth. The night before I had lain on the rock of St Julien and by the morning the ache in my bones and the cold in my blood had reminded me how hard a bed the earth was. But now I was sleeping in softness and more pleased with myself than any man has a right to be. I was in a good place and to get there I had walked every step of the way. Never before and perhaps never since have I been so aware and so content – that much difference does a mound of straw make.

I was slow to wake the next morning though the street was still dark when I crossed it to enter the kitchen. Jeannette poured me a bowl of coffee and put bread and butter onto the oilcloth and told me that the others were already at work.

When I arrived below they were separating flocks again and I sat on the top rail of a fence and watched as the shadow of the hill behind me crept over the ground as the sun rose. Then it was done and there was no great flock any more and no more road to follow. Even the mule cart had disappeared into a barn. For the first time since leaving the Gorges de Pennafort I felt out of my proper place and awkward. Soon Joseph would take his sheep to the top of La Chamatte and Paul Graziani would move to the slopes opposite. Even as I thought about it Marius set out for the far side of the Verdon and Lucien was already halfway to the peak of La Courradour beyond Peyresq. There was nothing left for me to do but go.

All that afternoon, without any real purpose, I wandered. At first I followed a stream into the trees, then I climbed, up and out onto the vast and springy pastures that were Joseph's true delight and pride. I did not stop at that point but went quietly towards the summit and there I rested and gazed back down the country I had crossed, all blue and gold and much more to me now than just miles. After a while I lay on my stomach, propping my chin on my hands, feeling the coolness of the earth beneath me and the warmth of the sun on my back. And then of course the marmots came, whole families of them, playing outside their burrows, not knowing I was there or ignoring me because I was so still, half-hidden in the grass. Only eagles could disturb them in all that wildness and eagles are rare and when they do come the marmots whistle and are gone in the wink of an eye.

That night I slept on the straw again but this time my duffel bag was packed and lying near me. In the morning I dozed on into the daylight but when I woke and went into the sunlit street I saw Jules Martel standing by his car, the tail-gate open. He took my bag from me and threw it in, slamming the door. 'You might as well see La Colle before you go,' he said.

At La Colle I found myself in another high valley though much shallower than the one I had left. The village here was not a village at all but a hamlet containing fewer houses even than Allons, though they were solidly built with over-hanging roofs and set far apart. It was as if I had passed some invisible frontier and gone from France to Switzerland for now there were white mountain peaks all around me.

As we got out of the car Jules pointed above us and on the slopes of grass I could see Leonce and Lucien pacing grandly forward while behind them came the two mules and the obedient flock, browsing as they went. The men brought the sheep down to us and we met and shook hands, letting the animals wander as we drank wine and prepared the mid-morning meal. Lucien's face broke into a smile. 'You could come up to the cabin with me,' he said, 'and see Italy . . . La Courradour makes La Chamatte look like a pimple.'

Some six or seven kilometres above La Colle lies the deserted hamlet of Peyresq, a dark and scattered gathering of houses that had been abandoned years before by its inhabitants, leaving the place so dead that there is not even a ghost to haunt it.

It was in Peyresq that I was put to work again and told to secure a hurdle across a narrow street and make a gap so small that only one sheep at a time could pass. Then Jules Martel stood by the gap and counted the flock as it filed through, cutting a notch in a stick for every score of sheep that went by. Further away, on the hillside, Leonce and Lucien held the flock together and guided it slowly towards us.

At the end of it all the four of us stood in a group and waited while Jules counted; when he'd finished he threw the stick away, folded his knife and pushed it into his pocket. 'Just one missing,' he said, 'a good trip.'

Jules and Leonce only walked a little way beyond Peyresq, then they left Lucien and me to go on to the summit of La Courradour alone. 'Come down tomorrow,' said Jules, 'come to the house.'

I had not seen much of Lucien during the journey from Grimaud. Most of the time he had walked near the middle of the flock and when we had camped he had said little. He was a big man and his chin was dark with the stubble of a black beard and his eyebrows, black also, were thick and well-defined. He wore his beret flat on his head and under it his hair was shaggy. His clothes were ragged and dirty and his face was fat but in spite of his appearance there was something genteel about Lucien. As we went together up the mountain of La Courradour I learnt that away from the others his words flowed easily. He had been born in Arles, 'Where they speak the best Provençal,' he said, but he had been unable to live in such a big and busy city. He liked to be solitary and to sleep in the open air. He had become a shepherd as a boy and was certain that he would remain one until he died.

Halfway up the mountain we stopped to rest and from one of the mule packs Lucien took a bag and opened it in order to make me the gift of a sheep bell that he himself had fashioned and in that bag I glimpsed his small collection of books. 'This is all I own,' he said, and he made the statement proudly, as if this fining down of possessions was his greatest achievement. I turned the bell over in my hands, examining the wooden collar, the bone clanger and the metal bell itself.

'I make them,' said Lucien simply. 'I bring wood up here with me and carve it, then I steam it and bend it round my knee to get the shape. Leather to hang the bell on and bone from the sheep's leg to make the clanger. I make them as beautiful as I can. I can't do much more than carve but I make sure that I carve well.'

After half an hour or so, refreshed, we got to our feet again and marched on. I had hooked the bell onto the side of a pack saddle and it rang to the pace of the mule as we trudged along the ridge that leads to the top of La Courradour. Heads down we climbed, hands pushing on knees until one last step got us to the summit when it had seemed for an eternity that no step ever would, and then a different wind was suddenly strong on our faces and a new prospect was discovered. Looking up I saw the wildest country I had yet seen with peaks and ranges striding away into Italy, the ridges sharp, all mauve and dark blue like black with the sky as hard as diamond and lit from within by great splashes of sunlight.

'This is why I am a shepherd,' said Lucien, 'this is why.' And so saying he led the mules forward into a huge hollow that lay beyond the top of the mountain and we came out of the stiff breeze and the air was still and clear and on the far side of the great pasture I saw the stone built cabin, larger than I expected, with its eaves almost touching the ground, and we made directly for it.

'And the sheep,' I asked, noticing that we had deserted them.

Lucien smiled. 'They look after themselves now,' he said. 'They stay where the grass is. All I do is put a little salt on the stones for them to lick at. I could live in the village below for all they have need of me . . . but I never think of such a thing.'

The door of the cabin was unbarred and swung back lopsidedly on leather hinges. Inside I helped Lucien to clear the dust and debris left by the winter and then we unloaded the two mules and let them go free, afterwards stacking the provisions into a cupboard and throwing the pack saddles into a corner where they might lie until autumn. I brought water from the spring and scrubbed the table while Lucien lit a fire and made the meal.

'Why didn't you tell a tale on the way here,' I said and uncorked a bonbonne of wine.

Lucien spooned a pile of spaghetti and sausages onto my plate, then he sat opposite me.

'I will tell you the best Provençal story ever told,' he said. 'As you know, I was born in Arles, and this is the story that is always told there.'

And so, as the night settled on the mountains between France and Italy and the light of the fire flickered on the rough stones of the cabin wall, Lucien told me why two sides of the cloister of St Trophime are miracles of art and why the other two are not.

# The Cloisters of
# St Trophime

'The new cathedral,' said the Archbishop of Arles, 'will be a monument to the glory of God, and the cloister will be the finest in the world.'

The Archbishop's Deacon nodded in agreement. 'Only your Grace could have conceived of such a thing,' he said.

The Archbishop smiled, pleased with this flattery, and fingered the great silver cross that hung from his neck.

The two churchmen were standing amongst the labourers and stone-masons who were busy constructing the foundations for the cathedral of St Trophime. On all sides there was drudgery and sweat. Blocks of stone, some large and some small, were being unloaded from heavy wagons; carpenters hammered at wooden scaffolding; overseers were shouting commands through their cupped and horny hands and there came too the sound of saws as they bit deep into the marble. Everywhere a fine dust floated upwards and separated the golden air into hazy shafts of sunlight and made the blue sky seem pale and distant. The folds of the Archbishop's purple robe were thick with the same dust and his shoes sank softly into it so that he made no sound when he moved. Nor did his Deacon.

The Archbishop came to a low trestle, stepped onto it and pointed to a large flat area to the south of the cathedral's site. 'The cloisters will be there,' he said. 'In my mind's eye I can see them already. The coolest and the most beautifully decorated that Christendom has ever seen. The pageant of the Old Testament, and the Gospels, will come alive in eternal stone, Deacon, each capital carved by the hand of the Master Sculptor.

The Deacon looked up, squinting against the sun. 'Yes, your Grace,' he said, 'but will he come? His reputation has spread all over France. Kings and Popes call on him to beautify their palaces. His talents are so great – the rumours say that he bears himself like an emperor.'

The Archbishop held out a hand and was helped from the trestle to the ground. The dust rose in a cloud around his feet. A thud came from nearby as a square of stone was levered from a cart. 'He will come,' said the Archbishop. 'I have sent messengers with silver tongues and purses of gold. I have offered him as much wealth as he can spend in a lifetime . . . but for a man like the Master there are more important things. Every carving in the cloister shall be his, and then later there is the cathedral, the tympanum too. He will be able to create one vast work of art that will endure forever. I have also promised him that, at the end of it all, he will be permitted to sign his work, something that has never been done before. That is why he will come.'

The Deacon scratched his head. 'This is unheard of, your Grace.'

The Archbishop agreed. 'It is, but I am determined to be generous. After all, even if he is known as the artist I shall be known as the patron, the real creator.' He waved an arm. 'My name will live longer and shine brighter than his, Deacon, and all to the glory of God.'

The Deacon crossed himself. 'Of course, your Grace,' he said, and the two churchmen moved on, walking at an easy saunter, threading their way amongst the groups of toiling labourers, inspecting the work in progress and talking as they went until, eventually, they disappeared in the direction of the Archbishop's palace which stood at no great distance on the edge of a large and leafy square.

The Archbishop was to be proved quite correct in the judgement he had made of his man. Before many weeks had gone by the Master Sculptor was to be seen entering the city of Arles by the Avignon gate, dressed in the finest of clothes and riding a tall Arab horse that had been presented to him by a king. Behind him rode his two servants, almost as well-attired as their lord, and behind them came a pack horse.

The Master went directly to the Archbishop's palace and, calling from his saddle, he bade the guards inform the Major-Domo of his arrival. Then, leaving his servants to wait for his return, he dismounted and climbed the steps to the great door of the Archbishop's residence. By this time the Major-Domo had presented himself and, with the lowest of bows, he conducted the sculptor along the echoing corridors, past many a splendid painting and many a polished statue, until they entered the audience chamber of the Archbishop himself.

The Archbishop received the Master graciously. A seat was brought for him and a goblet of cool wine poured. 'We are pleased to see you safely in Arles,' said the Archbishop, 'for it is here that we want you to realize your highest ambitions. Tales of your great talent have preceded you and we are impatient to see the truth of them.' The Archbishop chuckled. 'There are even those who say that you are so gifted that you are no ordinary mortal, but rather a magician who achieves his effects by magic, casting spells and making pacts with the devil. What do you say to that, Master?'

The Master lounged in his chair and smiled. 'It is also said, your Grace,' he began, 'that all art has been touched by the demon, but I cannot tell where my talent comes from . . . what I do know is that these rumours of magic come from those who envy me. What gifts I have are the result of many years of study and of work, of years of travel. I began as a boy, I carried tools, I sharpened chisels . . . I followed a mason, then I cut the blocks of stone, I smoothed them with other blocks of stone. I lifted and levered them into position. Then I became a mason. I touched the stone, I fondled it and as I ran my fingers over it I fell in love with it and the stone loved me in return. My hands and eyes could see things deep down that no other person on earth could see and my chisel could remove all that was superfluous and unwanted and leave only the face and form that had been locked in the stone from the time of creation and known only to me. So my reputation grew and I became a

Master Sculptor. I worked with the divine Giselbertus, drew pattern books for him, carved life in marble with a finger. Much of what is called his – is mine. I do not mind this, I am better than he and my time will come for I am younger. Your Grace, there is no magic, only the magic of God's gift.'

During this long speech the Archbishop studied the face of the man before him. It was a handsome face but haughty and disdainful with no warmth or love in it, and although the Master was obliged, at that moment, to treat the Archbishop with deference, the Archbishop knew that he would deceive and scheme like the very devil for the benefit of his art. The Archbishop pushed the thought from his mind – a sophisticated priest, he was well aware that some of the world's most talented men had been the greatest failures as creatures of God: it was no concern of his, only the cloister mattered. He would make the devil dance to God's tune if necessary.

'Well, Master,' he said, 'you speak wisely. In the meantime you will tell me or my Deacon of your needs. A fine house has been prepared for you, there are servants who wait upon your bidding. Whatever you desire is close at hand and there is a mason's lodge on the eastern side for you to use as a workroom. My own steward will see to your provisions and whatever money you request. There are more than a hundred labourers ready and the best marble I could find has been shipped from Italy.'

'Good,' said the Master and he rose to his feet. 'Your Grace has anticipated all my demands save one. The sculptures for the cloister will be at eye-height. Prominent, they must be perfect. I like to carve my figures and my faces from life, not from pattern books as most sculptors do . . . therefore I wander the streets and when I see the face or form that matches my imagination I need the power of your authority to take that face or form back to my workshop, to use it as a model. These persons will have to attend me at my house or lodge for as long as I may desire them to. Will your Grace issue a proclamation so that all may obey me, in this one respect? Also I may, from time to time, request some archers to assist me in enforcing such commands.'

The Archbishop raised a hand. 'Master,' he said, 'you had my word that all you wanted should be yours and it will be so. Anything that builds my cloister and my cathedral the faster pleases me. The proclamation shall be issued,' and with this promise the audience came to an end.

◆◆◆

Whatever the Archbishop's estimation of the Master's character he could not tax him with laziness. On the very day after his arrival he appeared on the open site wearing rough workmen's clothes and began to marshal his men. And, as he did not spare himself, so he did not spare those that worked under him. He set the masons to cutting stone and polishing columns and the labourers to levelling the ground. In the days that followed he devoted himself to making sketches and drawings of both the general plan and the detail of the carvings that would decorate the capitals. As he proceeded with his task he discovered that one of the masons, a man of great experience who had helped build many a cathedral, seemed to possess an intuitive understanding of the great design. He could read the Master's drawings and could perceive his vision. His name was Faldo.

One day The Master took this Faldo into his lodge, out of the noise and bustle, and looked into the old man's face. 'I know,' he said, 'that you sense the beauty here. You can see already the cloister that will come into this empty space.'

The mason nodded. 'I can,' he answered, 'and though I have travelled all the roads of France and of Navarre I have never seen anything as good and true as that which you have in your mind's eye, Master.'

'Then you,' said the Master, 'will help me choose the marble that will go to form the capitals . . . you will know that it must have the shapes already within it. As time goes on you will study my drawings so that you can anticipate my needs, divining what my chisel will have to take from the stone. You will also watch over the preparation of the columns that will bear the capitals and the blocks that will support them. Can you do all this?'

'Yes, Master,' said Faldo, his face shining with joy, 'I can do it, and if I have to sweat like a galley-slave then I will.'

It was just as well that Faldo meant what he said for the pace of the work never slackened. The foundations of the cloister were dug and blocks of stone laid to support the outer walls. Then the columns rose and the carpenters carried in their timbers and the air shook with the constant noise of their hammers as they erected the centerings for the Roman arches, twelve to each of the four sides. And through all this confusion the Master hurried, swearing at his men, bullying them, cajoling them and all the time making rough sketches and throwing them down into the white stone-dust, and everywhere he went Faldo followed, rescuing the drawings and remembering every order given and making sure that it was obeyed.

So diligent was the Master that he took his meals where he worked, in the cloisters themselves, eating the rough bread of the labourers and drinking their wine. One block of stone was his seat, another his table, and always, nearby, there was Faldo, the mason, inspired, saying sometimes as he touched a piece of marble; 'Here lies the face of Herod the king,' and on other occasions, 'Within this block lie the heads of Balthazaar, Gaspar and Melchior.'

The Master would laugh at this, a hard cold laugh and would point at the row of columns on the east side of the cloister square; 'And there is The Last Supper,' he would say, 'The Flight into Egypt and The Flagellation.'

Once the ground plan of the cloister was complete The Master began carving his sculptures, working sometimes in his lodge on site and sometimes in a workroom he had made in the grand house given to him by the Archbishop. He seemed never to sleep and the sound of his chisel biting into stone was heard late into the night almost every night. When the chisel was silent it meant that the Master was wandering the streets of Arles, searching for models that suited his design. When he found what he wanted the archers who accompanied him would seize the person chosen and take them back to the cloisters, ignoring their protestations. The Master was ruthless in his art. He had no pity, dressing his models, men and women, in the roughest of clothes or stripping them naked to study their muscles and their bones. Often he made them pose for hours without rest or food, cursing them if they dared move without his express command, keeping them in one position until they swooned. He was like a man possessed and began to produce his sculpture so rapidly that many said the rumours were true, that he was indeed a magician, for it was impossible for an ordinary mortal to achieve so much so quickly.

As for Faldo, the mason, he did not believe these rumours, but he was concerned about the Master's health. He had seen gifted men before and watched many a one burn himself to death on the flame of own ambition. One day, when yet another model had fainted and had been carried away to recover, he approached the Master and begged him to rest. 'Sit on this stone,' he said, 'in the shadow of the scaffolding. Rest or you will kill yourself.'

Hardly noticing what he did the Master sat and took a cup of wine.

'You are too hard on them, Master,' ventured Faldo. 'They do not understand. They are ordinary people only, they know nothing of your vision of beauty, they cannot see what lies in the heart of the marble.'

'I pay them,' said the Master, 'and that is enough.'

'They do not understand,' repeated Faldo, 'and so they do not even care. They are interested only in their little lives. The labourers are the same, and you are hard on them too.'

'The people are fools,' said the Master, and he took another cup of wine, 'what is more they always have been. That is why their fate is irrelevant. They do not matter, but what I am doing in this cloister does. It will be standing here in beauty and wonder for all eternity. If the scaffolding collapses and crushes a score of labourers to death it does not signify . . . even you Faldo could be sacrificed. It is only the work that is immortal, and perhaps me, the maker of it, and that is the glory that is worth all my suffering . . . and all theirs. It is the only glory that lives forever,' and at this the Master stood, poured what remained of his wine onto a block of stone as a libation, and returned to his work.

The paired pillars of the east side were soon in position and the sections of stone which were to form the arches were shaped and ready. All that was needed for the work to advance were the carved blocks which were to support the arches as they sprang from column to column – the capitals – the Master's main work.

The first few of them were now complete and polished and one by one Faldo and his labourers gingerly set the sculptures where they were needed and lowered onto them the great slabs of stone which would carry the massive weight of the tiled roof. Arch by arch the cloister would grow: east side, north side and then the rest.

Faldo, who had seen much of the world, was overwhelmed by the beauty of what the sculptor had done. 'It is beyond praise, Master,' he said as soon as the first capital was in position. 'These figures live and breathe. I, who cannot read, know that these people have stepped from the pages of the bible as I have heard it read to me. Truly you are a magician.'

The Archbishop, when he was informed of the Master's progress, was much more circumspect in his comments. Followed by his Deacon he left the palace and picked his way around the piles of stone and through the groups of labourers and masons. They knelt when he passed, coughing a little as the fine stone-dust floated up from the prelate's feet.

At the first pair of columns the Archbishop halted. He stared at the sculpture, then moved so that he could see the second side of the capital. His heart soared within him, he clenched his hands behind his back and the flesh on the nape of his neck tingled. Never had he felt such joy. 'Surely,' he said to himself, 'this man is the divine Giselbertus himself. Look at the expression here, the fall of this gown, the turn of this leg. Is this not a miracle? Has he not made the marble soft in his hand so that he could mould it between finger and thumb?'

When the Master heard that the Archbishop and his Deacon were in the cloister he emerged from his lodge and going straight to the churchmen he knelt and the Archbishop gave his blessing, noting how the Master's hair was white with dust and the lines of his face were thick with it and the folds of his tunic also; he raised the Master to his feet and together, arm in arm, they walked a little way.

The Archbishop had at first thought that he might deliver a long and sincere commendation of the sculptures he had seen but he restrained himself. If this man could produce such work without the benefit of criticism what might he not do if vexed a little. The Archbishop gave a secret smile.

'Master,' he said, 'your work is exquisite and full of power. All that was said about you is true, including what you said of yourself. I feel, however, that you might, I am not sure how, infuse just a touch more life into your subjects. No . . . I beg that you do not misunderstand me, I am delighted, more than delighted, but I look for perfection, as we all must. Perhaps it is simply a case of choosing different models for your art. I do not know.' And looking once more at the capitals the Archbishop left the cloister and went to inspect the foundations of the cathedral, now rising above the level of the flat ground. Before following him the Deacon pressed a purse of gold into the Master's hand. 'His Grace is well pleased,' he said and then turned to follow his superior.

The Master smiled and watched the Archbishop move soundlessly across the dust. He continued smiling until the Archbishop was out of earshot and then his smile became a grimace of pain. He groaned and pressed his head against the marble of a pillar, tasting on his tongue the poison of faint praise.

Faldo the mason stood beside him, his heart near to breaking. 'Oh Master,' he said, 'he knows nothing, take no heed of him. I tell you your carving is the finest in the world. I tell you that, I who journeyed from church to church and from country to country. I who have seen more cathedrals than there are dishonest priests. Do not grieve, Master, do not listen to his words or let them spoil your work.'

Slowly the Master lifted his face and with a gasp Faldo recoiled. The face he saw was not one to reassure the mason; it was a face of cunning and resolve, an evil face.

'More life-like, is it?' said the Master, then as if dreaming, he pressed the purse of gold into Faldo's hand. 'Perfection he wants, perfection . . . so be it,' and saying no more the Master lurched away and disappeared in the direction of his house, leaving Faldo to blink a tear from his eye while at the same time slipping the purse into the pouch at his belt.

❧

After this encounter between the Master and the Archbishop, Faldo did not know what to expect. He thought it possible that the Master might lose his enthusiasm and abandon the cathedral, but it didn't happen like that at all. Instead the pace of work increased dramatically, and so did the quality of the sculpture, which Faldo had thought beyond improvement. He had been wrong; never had he seen such artistry. He was amazed by it, there seemed to be life in the very stone.

And so in this manner and in a very short while, the whole of the eastern side of the cloister was complete and there was even a pavement leading to it. Every day everyone was worked to the point of exhaustion, nor did the Master save himself although there was a distinct change in his activities. Faldo no longer heard the sculptor's chisel in the lodge or in the private studio of his house, yet the capitals were made, the arches glided on and over them rose the roof itself. It was a miracle.

Miracle or not the Master paid a price. He grew thin and gaunt as tirelessly he roamed the streets and markets of Arles, chose his models and returned with them to the cathedral site. He was relentless and gave himself no respite, but at the same time he seemed content, as if he knew that nowhere in the world was there a cloister like the cloister of St Trophime; no other sculpture as beautiful as his, not even that of Autun or Vezelay.

During this period Faldo often wondered if others had noticed these changes in the Master's behaviour. It seemed not and the mason was deeply perplexed and made doubly so by being unable to share his anxieties with his workmates. First of all, how were the capitals being produced if the Master was no longer carving the stone? Secondly, there was the question of the models. Not one had Faldo seen waiting in the cloisters as they used to do, or in the lodge either, at least not in daylight. And once a capital had been completed Faldo never again saw the person who had modelled for it, not even outside the Archbishop's palace where it had been customary for the models to wait for the money promised them.

There was another thing too which did not suddenly surprise Faldo but came upon him slowly as he placed the capitals in position and made sure that all was firm and solid. He began to notice how like their human models were the stone replicas. The talent of the Master was extending beyond any art

Faldo had ever seen. It was uncanny. It was beyond nature and it turned the mason's flesh cold, as if he were in the presence of some great evil. Then the idea came to him in all its starkness. These were not carvings at all, these were people. The Master was indeed using magic – magic of the blackest kind.

Faldo was terrified by these thoughts and he fought against believing the evidence of his own faculties, but in the end there was no denying it; face after face proved it. There was a piercing shriek of anguish imprisoned within each statue and Faldo the mason could hear them all.

This silent sound rang in his ears every time he entered the half-built cloisters. To him, and to him alone it seemed, the figures wailed and stretched out their arms. In his long years of travelling the stone-mason had been told many strange and outlandish tales of monsters and magicians, witches and hobgoblins, but never had he heard anything so weird as the tale his own mind was telling him. There was only one thing for it; he must satisfy himself that his suspicions were well-founded. He would have to watch the Master very closely – he would have to spy on him.

Once he had taken this decision Faldo acted on it immediately. At the end of every day's work he concealed himself behind a huge block of stone in the Master's lodge. There, evening after evening, he hid without success until at last, on the ninth or tenth occasion, late at night, the Master appeared in the workroom followed by a man that Faldo knew as a petty thief from the gutters of Arles: a thin and unlovely man with a twisted face and a shifty eye. He walked badly too with one shoulder sloping lower than the other; his bones were large and almost protruded through his scraggy skin.

Faldo caught his breath. Even from the distance of his hiding place and in the dull candlelight of the lodge the mason could see where this face was destined. Only that afternoon he had been admiring the Master's drawing of a statue of Judas carrying a purse with thirty pieces of silver in it. This thief who had come shambling into the lodge, bribed no doubt by the promise of a few copper coins, was that Judas in every detail.

The Master halted in the centre of the room and a servant awoke to light more candles and pour a goblet of wine. 'Leave us and go to your bed,' commanded the Master when these tasks had been performed, and as soon as he had been left alone with the thief, he handed him some money and the thief put it carefully into the purse he wore at his side.

At once the Master began to study his Judas, referring from time to time to his sketches, until finally he arranged the limbs of the man in the pose he desired and a cry broke from his lips.

'I have it,' he shouted, 'do not move again and do not alter your expression, this is exactly what the Archbishop wants . . . and soon you shall rest and earn a great reward.'

The thief was comforted by these words and obeyed, glad to learn that his task was nearly at an end – but his release did not come about as he might have wished. Docile, he watched as the Master donned a flowing gown all embroidered in suns and moons of silver and gold; and watched while a circle of chalk was drawn around him on the floor, enclosing him. And, as the circle was joined the thief felt the blood cease to run in his veins and all his will seeped from his mind and vanished.

Then the Master drew the secret signs of the Cabbal at the edge of the circle, though at no time did he step inside it. On the contrary, as soon as he was ready he stepped back, lifting his arms high in the air above his head, chanting in the ancient tongue of the Saracens.

The thief tried to call for help in his terror. He could not. He attempted to turn and run; he could not. He could not even fall to his knees to beg for mercy. His blood congealed and hardened into ice. His skin petrified, his flesh became hard and, in his eye, the light of cunning was seized in flight and stilled forever. No longer an ill-made villain of the streets who begged and spent and lived and died, he was a perfect statue, a work of art that would soon decorate the third main pillar on the cloister's eastern side.

Faldo, the mason, spying all this while from his hiding place, bit back a scream fearing that he too might be turned into stone. Was he not, after all, in the same room as a great wickedness? He licked his dry lips with a dry tongue – he was still alive, but struck motionless by wonder and fear. Such a transformation of ugliness into beauty, of life into death, he had not ever thought possible.

The moment the spell was complete the Master closed his eyes with exhaustion and sank into a chair. His face was narrow with pain, as if he had walked for many miles or fought the demon for many hours. Sorcery had taken its toll.

As for Faldo, he wanted nothing more than to escape, both from his predicament and from the memory of what he had just witnessed. As quietly as he could he inched along the rear wall of the lodge, behind the blocks of stone, and crept towards the door. Although terrified he felt confident of getting away unobserved. His feet were cushioned by the stone-dust that was everywhere and the Master, drained by the exercise of his magic, remained as if unconscious in his chair.

Faldo's optimism was misplaced. the Master was possessed of many powers and now that he was no longer concentrating on his spell it was easy for him to detect an alien presence in the room. Just as the mason reached the door he opened his eyes and half-turned his head.

'Master,' said Faldo, his tongue and his teeth getting in the way of his words, 'I came to see what orders you might have . . . for tomorrow. I found you asleep and was about to leave.'

The Master raised his arm as straight and as murderous as a sword. 'Do not lie,' he said, 'you have been here all the time. I can feel it.'

'I saw nothing, Master,' said Faldo, 'nothing.'

'Then do not deny it, fool,' said the Master with a weary sigh. 'I know what you saw.'

There was a long silence after this during which the Master closed his eyes once again. Faldo shifted his weight from one foot to another and wondered if he should go. Then, bravely, he spoke out. 'What you do is evil, Master,' he said.

Without opening his eyes the Master replied. 'Yes,' he said, 'but it is only a little evil and it is for a much greater good.'

'Those poor people,' insisted the mason, 'they have a right to their life, however miserable it is.'

Now the Master's eyes opened wide. 'Do they?' he asked. 'These scavengers, these lowest of the low. Were it not for me they would die of the plague or of hunger anyway. I save them from woe and misery, from witnessing the deaths of their sons and from the selling of their daughters into the bordellos of Algiers. I give them immortality and beauty.'

'But you are not God,' argued Faldo, 'they have a right to choose.'

'Ha,' cried the Master, 'choice, eh? What choice do they have? None! Only the rich choose. The poor are born poor, they remain poor, they die poor. There is no choice, only survival until the day of doom, a survival that is at the whim of whoever happens to be your liege lord or holy Archbishop. That is the life of a worm, Faldo. That is why I became an artist and why you became a mason. That is why I learnt the magic. That is where our freedom lies. We have something that the rich and powerful need and we are free only as long as we can do what the rich desire.'

'But to turn their bodies into stone,' insisted 'Faldo, 'that is crime enough, but what happens to their immortal souls? You are the magician . . . answer me that.'

'I do not know,' replied the Master, 'or much care. If they have a soul at all, these wretches, then I suppose it remains locked in the marble until the last judgement . . . if there is a last judgement.'

'By the Holy Sepulchre, of course there is,' cried Faldo, his fear falling away from him as the argument progressed. He advanced a little into the room. 'And these wretches do have souls. I hear them calling to me when I cross the cloister. Their voices drive me mad.'

'Yes,' said the Master vaguely. 'I hear them sometimes, but from afar.'

'It is their suffering souls,' said Faldo.

The Master laughed. 'Souls, eh? Or the wind moving between the columns. If God exists . . .'

Faldo drew a deep breath. 'What do you mean, "If God exists"? For whom then do you make this cloister?'

'I make this cloister for me,' answered the Master, 'then for the Archbishop and thirdly for God, if he is there. And if he is, how can he do otherwise than pity my victims and send them directly to paradise. If he isn't then they will have lost nothing from their lives but misery and death. It is quite a gift I have given them.'

'You are an unbeliever,' said Faldo, so shocked that his voice was a whisper. 'You could burn for this, if the Archbishop knew.'

'No, not an unbeliever, Faldo, rather am I a pagan, I believe in other things.'

'I should go to the Archbishop, tell him what you are, a heretic and a murderer.'

'I am nothing of the kind. I am a preserver of life, I turn it into art. As for my beliefs . . . they do not matter. If my art is good enough God will love me for it and send me to paradise. If there is no such place then I have done no harm and my name will be remembered for as long as man lives. My talents will protect me from extinction, Faldo. I shall be an angel in heaven or a fly in amber.'

'Your talents will not protect you against the holy wrath of Mother Church,' cried the mason. 'The Archbishop will have no alternative but to send you to the stake.'

'He will not lift a finger until I have finished the capitals,' replied the Master, 'and then there is the cathedral, the tympanum, the statues . . . I have more art than life in me Faldo, so go to the Archbishop, I will not stop you. He will dismiss your tales of magic, he will not want to believe you.'

Faldo hesitated. He had no wish to see the man before him die a heretic's death. He did not want the world to be robbed of such a gift, but then he looked at the statue of Judas that stood in the centre of the lodge – a man that was now stone. Faldo spoke again. 'Run away,' he said, 'you can escape, work somewhere else.'

'I have no wish to escape,' retorted the Master, 'never before has a sculptor been permitted to carve his name across a whole church. This cathedral is mine and I must finish it . . . and with that the Archbishop will agree. He will do nothing. He knows that it is the destiny of the simple to be sacrificed, in one way or another, to the demands of art. I will talk no more of it, Faldo. Leave me.'

The mason did as he was commanded, happy to escape so easily from the power of the Master, but, true to his word, he determined to inform the Archbishop of what he had learned at the very next opportunity. Consequently, as soon as the light of dawn showed itself above the streets of Arles, Faldo emerged from the tiny hovel where he slept and went towards the honeycomb of wooden scaffolding within which the walls of the cathedral were now beginning to rise. He knew that it was the Archbishop's custom to visit his cathedral every morning in order to see how the work was progressing, and there to say a prayer, a prayer that God might bless his life and all his endeavours.

Faldo waited at the west end of the church, the end where one day the steps would be and where the great tympanum would shield the entrance. He gazed up into the pale yellow sky and tried to imagine the great tower, the nave twenty metres high and the sculptures everywhere. How many more years would it be? Twenty, fifty, a hundred? Faldo sighed. He would never see it, except through his imagination. He was too old now.

While Faldo was dreaming in this manner he heard a noise and lowering his gaze he saw the Archbishop standing before him dressed in a splendid robe. Behind him stood the Deacon in black. They had come from behind a pile of cut stone.

The Archbishop raised an eyebrow. 'The mason, Faldo, are you not? An industrious fellow. What you do in the cloister does not go unnoticed by me . . . or by God.'

Faldo fell to his knees and kissed the Archbishop's hand. 'Forgive me your Grace,' he said, 'but there is something that goes unnoticed by you and at the least unpunished by God, for although I am a simple man I know that he sees all . . .' and in little more than a whisper Faldo went on to tell the Archbishop what he had suspected and what he had seen.

The Archbishop frowned when he had heard the story. He bade the mason rise from his knees and taking him by the elbow he led him a few paces away from the church so that his Deacon might be left behind and out of earshot.

'My son,' began the Archbishop when he had the privacy he sought, 'what you say is not possible. You must be exhausted by what you do. You suffer, but then man must, we cannot live without suffering and we certainly cannot build to the glory of God without it. As we go higher I know that men will fall from this scaffolding and die. Walls of stone will collapse and more men will die. Should I then not build my cathedral because of this?'

Faldo lowered his head. 'I do not know, your Grace, I am an ignorant man.'

'My son,' continued the Archbishop, 'trust me. I am your father in Christ, learned in the laws of this world and instructed in the ways of the next. This is some evil vision that has come to you out of your fatigue, a trial of your devotion. Be firm and pray. I will send my own confessor to you. Remember, my son, the Master is a man of many talents – dedicated and cruel perhaps, but he is no wicked magician. God would not allow his servant to use the black arts to construct a place of holiness and grace. Evil is ugly and yet you can see that the cloister is a thing of beauty. Believe me, my son, pray and rest, but pray more.' With this the Archbishop indicated that the audience was ended, and Faldo knelt again in the dust while the Archbishop made the sign of the cross over the mason's head and then walked away, his Deacon scuttling behind him.

Faldo watched them go. The Master had been right. The Archbishop had not wanted to listen to anything that might impede the building of the cloister or the cathedral; for the churchman that came first. Faldo trembled and wept in terror. He was trapped.

❦

Very much later that same day, at the end of the afternoon, the Archbishop reappeared at the cathedral and went into the cloisters. Here, in the slanting shadows of evening, Faldo and a group of his workmen, supervised by the Master himself, were struggling to place the figure of Judas Iscariot into position.

At first the Archbishop said nothing, but stared intently as the men sweated and grunted like beasts of burden, pulling on ropes and levering with scaffolding poles to move the statue inch by inch along. The Master was everywhere, swearing at his men one moment, only to beg them the next not to crack or chip his carving.

197

Eventually the Judas stood in its destined place, the ropes and poles were removed and all the workmen fell back so that the Archbishop might approach and examine the cloister's most recent adornment. The Archbishop advanced until he was close to the statue, face to face, and he studied it. Behind him was the Master, behind him some clerics, and to one side, panting, Faldo and his labourers.

The Archbishop half-turned and smiled. 'You improve,' he said to the Master, 'from day to day, from statue to statue. This Judas is life itself, as if he had been surprised by your chisel. See how he carries his purse. How can I put it? You seem to have imprisoned the living flesh within the marble.'

The Master glanced at Faldo but the mason stared before him and did not move. 'You are kind, your Grace,' he said, 'I thank you.'

'Yes,' said the Archbishop. 'You are nearly at the end of this east side now . . . then there is the north. I hope you will not suffer from a lack of ideas . . . or models.'

Once more the Master glanced at his mason but again Faldo did not move. 'I will not find myself without ideas, your Grace,' replied the Master, 'or models for those ideas, that I promise you.'

The Archbishop nodded. 'I cannot praise this Judas too much,' he said. 'So like life,' and with an expression of irony on his features he left the cloister and, picking his way with care over the dust and between the white blocks of stone, he returned to his palace, followed as always by the black-clad Deacon.

The moment the churchmen had gone the Master ordered his labourers away and then turned on Faldo, grabbing him by the shoulders. 'So, my little Christian,' he said, 'you saw fit to tell the Archbishop of your suspicions. You fool! Now you see that it has come out just as I said. He did not believe one word of your preposterous tale.'

'Certainly he believed,' cried Faldo, struggling to free himself from the Master's grip, 'but he is as wicked as you are. He recognized that Judas there, but he thinks more of his cloister and his cathedral than he thinks of his immortal soul, or your punishment.'

'And he is right to do so,' shouted the Master, 'for we are engaged in a work too important to be halted by a simpleton like you. Art is not for insects – that is why many of the finest sculptures are placed on the highest pinnacles . . . God sees them . . . and if there is no God to look it does not matter . . . I know they are there and so does the Archbishop. We understand each other, that is why he says nothing and why he never will. He would remain dumb even if he saw my face on one of these capitals.' The Master removed his hands from the mason's shoulders and stared at him. 'Or even yours, Faldo, even yours.'

The mason's face went white with fear. 'Pity, Master,' he said, 'pity.'

'Do not try to run away, Faldo. If the Archbishop's men do not find you on the road my magic powers will. I can conjure the birds of the air and they would discover you whichever way you took. So leave me for the moment and say no more. There is nothing here for you but hard work, perhaps years of it, but only if you obey.'

To obey was all that was left for Faldo and he performed everything that was desired of him, hoping that a zealous attention to his tasks might eventually gain freedom for him; a freedom from a master whom he now loathed and feared. He made the labourers work harder too, and they heaved statues and corner stones into position with a will. The Master's models came and went and Faldo saw them reappear in stone, but he kept his terror and his pity to himself, not daring to voice his knowledge in case the sparrow that perched nearby was the magician's messenger.

Meanwhile the Archbishop and his Deacon visited the site every day and smiled and nodded and gave the Master purses of gold. The cloister marched on and swung to the left at the north-eastern corner and the north side was begun and the figures and the faces were more lifelike than ever; the Ascension, Moses receiving the tablets of the law, Doubting Thomas and the resurrection of Christ. Even the common workers, those who hauled and split the stone, were much impressed and knelt before these sculptures and crossed themselves and wept to see such beauty. And Faldo wept too, in secret; not for the art but for his fellow men who had been transformed into marble by the occult powers of the Master.

Yet the Master continued in his purpose and seemed never to rest. In just one year the north side was complete, right to the north-west pillar, and all the capitals were in position save only the last – the one for Lazarus. And Faldo cut the stone for it and that evening, when the dying sun threw long shadows across the cloister's flagstones, as the mason went towards the hovel where he slept, he felt a great power turn him in the direction of the Master's lodge. Faldo fought against this power but it did no good. He could do nothing – the Master wanted him.

The moment he entered the lodge Faldo could see that the magician was resolved. Already he wore his necromancer's robe of gold and silver and had drawn his circle on the floor. Candles stood on blocks of stone around the room and spread a shifting yellow light over the whole scene. Hope faded within the mason's breast.

Barely looking at his victim the Master spoke; 'Stand in the circle,' he said, and Faldo did as he was told, powerless to disobey.

'I have been searching,' continued the Master, 'for someone to grace my last capital on the northern side. Lazarus rising from the grave. For weeks I have been wandering around this city of Arles, looking for the face, and yet I could not find what I needed. Well, Faldo my friend. The face was here all the time, next to me – yours. You will never die, Faldo, imagine that. A humble ignorant fellow like yourself who can do no more than cut stone straight and work hard. Imagine.'

Faldo found his voice at last and begged for his life. 'Master,' he said, 'I do not understand these high matters of art like you and the Archbishop. Master, I ask your forgiveness . . . in threatening you I went beyond my comprehension. I do not want to be immortal. Leave me my tiny little life, insignificant as it is, do not turn me into stone. I will work for you the rest of my days and never breathe a word of what I know . . . only let me die in my bed and go to the Lord in the way I should. Let me not live forever in the cold prison of this marble.'

The Master laughed. 'You fool. Have you not learnt, with all your travelling, that life uses us as it will and then forsakes us. In spite of your promises I know that you will talk and the labourers will gossip. Then, when the murmuring becomes strong enough the Archbishop will be forced to act and it will be the stake for me. No Faldo, you are to be sacrificed, not I. It is your turn to go into the stone and you will dwell there until the last day.'

When Faldo saw that there was no pity in the Master's heart he wept and wrung his hands but in his fear he spoke out with a terrible curse. 'May you lose all your powers,' began the mason, 'both natural and magic. May you be spurned by those who admired you, and may you spend the remainder of your life like a slave, working all your days but without the comfort and pride that your art brought you in the past. And may you always know what you have lost, and may your heart always be empty so that you suffer as your victims suffer. With this curse I curse you.'

Again the Master laughed and raised his arms to prepare his spell. 'Your curses cannot touch me, Faldo. You have no magic. I am beyond harm. Even if your God could hear us he would not undo what he has done for I shall make more beauty in his name. Farewell, Faldo, you are doomed and see, no angel comes to save you.'

Then the Master moved his hands through the air and said his Saracen words and the candle flames quivered and shook and Faldo took the attitude and shape his Master desired. The blood left his skin and his skin went grey; his body stiffened and his garments became as one with his flesh. Faldo was marble; Faldo was Lazarus.

∞

When the Archbishop heard of the completion of the north side of the cloister he was overjoyed. The walls of his cathedral were high now and all was proceeding as he wished. He would, so it seemed, live to see his ambitions fulfilled and, as the Archbishop who had devised and then executed such a vast scheme, a great deal of the glory, if not all, would be his. He walked past the cathedral, gazing upwards, his breast swelling with pride. When he came to the cloister he inspected every column and every statue, putting his face close to the face of each carving, gesticulating with pleasure at what he saw.

'There will be no better cloister in Christendom,' he said. 'The Bible is alive here. Even the most ignorant will be forced into contemplation as they walk through this arcaded garden. Master, never have I seen a sculptor to equal you, and I have seen many of the great churches in the world.' The Archbishop signalled to his Deacon and yet another purse of gold was placed in the Master's hands.

The sculptor reddened. 'Your Grace,' he said, 'your praise is reward enough.'

The Archbishop ignored the remark. 'There will be work for us here forever. Once you have finished with the cloister you will begin on the cathedral's tympanum. I warn you, Master, I shall work you until you die.'

The Master bowed low and tucked the purse of gold into his belt.

'You have my blessing for evermore,' said the Archbishop and he stepped up to the newest sculpture on the northern side, the figure of Lazarus. He examined it closely and coughed. 'I do not see your mason, Faldo,' he said, 'is he ill, or injured?'

'He has left me, your Grace,' answered the Master. 'He needs to tread the roads of Provence from time to time, so he has gone. I shall miss him, he was a good man.'

The Archbishop gestured at the Lazarus. 'If I did not know it was impossible,' he said, 'I could swear that this figure was him to the life.'

The Master assumed a look of concern and moved closer to the carving. 'I did use him as a model, your Grace, but you flatter me. The likeness is only slight.'

The Archbishop laughed in his most urbane manner. 'You are too modest. I was reliably informed, remember, before your arrival, that you were a veritable magician in stone, and now I believe it. No normal man could carve like this without the aid of magic, or a divine gift of some sort . . . but who could conceive of such an idea – an eternity imprisoned in stone.'

'Infinitely more restful, your Grace,' answered the Master, 'than a life imprisoned in poverty – an existence so full of toil that it allows no knowledge of the finer things of life.'

'Perhaps,' said the Archbishop, 'but at least the peasant has no awareness of what his life lacks,' and laughing again he left the cloister and returned to his prayers.

As soon as he was out of sight the Master touched the Lazarus with his finger. 'You see, my Faldo,' he said, 'there are things much worse than imprisonment in stone, so be not sad and think on those who are less fortunate than you, those who work and sweat and die and never once see beauty. Think on them my friend.'

◈

Now that half the cloister was done the Master, with the Archbishop's full agreement, permitted himself a little breathing space and set out to enjoy some of the gold he had earned. He bought fine clothes, sat with the best company and visited, for a while, the women of the town.

After a few weeks, however, this mode of life began to pall on his senses and the Master decided to return to his work. He sent away his fair-weather friends, and dressing himself once more in his labouring clothes, he went back to his lodge, ordering a model to follow him. There, putting his magic aside, at least for the time being, he took up his mallet and chisel, chose a block of stone and looked deeply into it for inspiration.

There was nothing there. The Master felt no excitement, neither in his blood nor in his imagination. He peered again into the stone; it was empty – no line, no shape, no form. He saw a block of stone only and only the outside of it. He could not see its heart although he knew a heart was there, and a misery such as he had never known seized him. It was like a torture and he was on the rack of it. And the Master let out a sudden cry of pain and threw his tools to the ground, while the terrified model crouched on his haunches like a cat and shivered with fear.

Then the Master swore a great oath and strode to the place where the wretch cowered, lifting him and dragging him forward. 'Stand there,' he commanded, and taking out his gown of magic he pulled it round his shoulders and drew his circle and his signs upon the floor. He made his passes in the air and sang his words of Saracen. The model cringed and wept and prayed but he remained safe. His flesh, though poor and scraggy, stayed flesh.

This was only the beginning. In the days that followed the Master tried and tried again. The more he looked at stone the more opaque it became and the more stone-like was his mind. The more he attempted to cast his spells the more nonsensical did they sound, so much so that one of his intended victims, a hazy-minded drinker from the taverns, listened to the Master's magic for a while and then fell to the floor, laughing uncontrollably at the gibberish he heard. The sculptor's powers had gone. At the very end he sat, lonely and morose, in his empty lodge and all around him the noise of the work in the cloisters died away to silence. The workmen stood and sat in listless groups and archers came for the Master and escorted him to the audience room of the Archbishop's palace, and there he stood, dusty and unkempt, pathetic and forlorn.

The Archbishop laid down the letter he was reading and leant forward on his throne.

'Master,' he said, 'your fame preceded you and recommended you. What you have done has impressed me . . . but it has made me exigent too. I have seen so much beauty issue from your hand that if I do not see more I shall become angry. My glory is to reside in this cloister and in this cathedral . . . you were to adorn them both with your work. What is half a cloister to me? Where are your promises and your idle boasts? Perhaps you live too well, amid too much luxury . . . your house will be taken from you, and all your gold. You will return to the cloister, now, and you will be kept under guard. I will give you a month to find your art again, to sculpt another capital. If you fail I will use you as you have used others . . . with callousness and contempt.'

The Master was given no opportunity to answer the Archbishop but was marched away and stripped of all his possessions and fine clothes. Then the soldiers chained him by the ankle to one of his own columns and just enough length was left on the chain to allow him to reach his tools and stand by a work bench where a block of stone was placed. Not even his masons were left to him but instead were put to work on the cathedral walls, and so, apart from the two or three archers sent to guard him, the Master was alone.

He made no attempt to break out of his lethargy. Most of his time was spent sitting on the low wall of the cloister with his head in his hands. Occasionally he would shamble to the work bench and touch the stone that stood upon it.

He would stare at it too, as if trying to release what was imprisoned there, but not once did he pick up his chisel or mallet.

He knew it was pointless. His talent and his magic were lost for ever. The fearful curse that Faldo the mason had laid upon him had worked, and yet Faldo had been no magician. How then had such a thing happened? There was only one answer. The Master's magic had worked against the Master's art. When Faldo had pronounced his curse he had been within the Master's enchanted circle; he had spoken under the influence of the Master's own spell. The Master had made the magic and the mason had said the words.

And every part of the curse was coming true. The Master was suffering like those he had maltreated. He had taken life from others and now life was taking from him the only thing that gave his life reason. He felt cold and empty inside, with a heart of marble. There was no flame, no fire. His imagination was extinguished and yet the Master could remember the warmth of it. For an artist it was a living death. The rest of his life lay before him and he could see the statues he might have made stretching away into infinity, statues that would have astounded the world and made his name live forever. Now there would be nothing and the world would never know. The Master would fall into a nameless grave.

For the whole month he suffered and, when the month was up, the chain was struck from his ankle and once more he was taken before the Archbishop. This time, so weak and ill did the sculptor look, that a chair was brought for him and he sank wearily into it.

For a while the Archbishop was silent, shocked by what he saw, but at length, prompted by the remembrance of his own ambitions, his pity left him and he began to speak.

'I am told you have done nothing,' he said, taking up some of the Master's drawings from a table at his side, 'why not?'

'My art has died, your Grace,' said the Master, 'I am a husk, a shell.'

'Why?'

'I have been cursed, and it is the worst curse of all. To have had a great talent and then to have lost it. To be aware of beauty and not to be able to reproduce it when once you could. It is a torture more scorching than hellfire, more crippling than the breaking of bones.

'Is this not,' asked the Archbishop, 'a punishment for what you did to others? Did you not scorn virtue? Are there not human lives imprisoned in the stone of the cloisters?'

'I gave them immortality and beauty, your Grace. I took them out of misery and out of suffering.'

'Yes,' answered the Archbishop, 'and I shall send you into it. You have committed murder, you have performed black magic, here in God's house. Blasphemy, heresy and sacrilege are punishable at the stake, but that would be too merciful. I shall send you to the galleys, there you may toil for as long as you live, remembering what you once were and what you could once do.'

The Master groaned. 'Why are you so cruel?' he said.

'Because,' cried the Archbishop, 'you showed me perfection and then stole it from me. My cathedral and my cloister were to be the most beautiful in Provence . . . now that dream is dead. My name would have lived forever in this glory and now it will not,' and the Archbishop threw the Master's drawings to the floor and raised his right hand and his soldiers laid hold of the prisoner and prepared to take him to his punishment.

The Master did not struggle but rose to his feet and looked at the Archbishop, showing a face that was like one of his own carvings where the lines were deep. 'Your Grace,' he said, 'men strive hard for glory because it is the one thing they may take out of this world but perhaps, after all, beauty should have no name upon it, neither yours nor mine. It is the world's beauty and should pass from generation to generation. Would it not be the greatest irony of all if the only people remembered in this affair should be the villains I turned into stone, remembered not by their names but by their humble faces? You and I will be forgotten but they will remain, staring out into the world as you and I crumble into dust. You, your Grace, will have nothing, but at least I possessed the golden gift, if only for a little while, and I will not mind following it, wherever it has gone.'

The Archbishop could suffer no more of this and rose from his throne in a fury and ordered his soldiers to escort the prisoner from the chamber at once. So the Master bowed low and, surrounded by his guards, walked proudly from the room to begin his long years of slavery.

And the Archbishop watched him depart, his anger still seething in his blood, but the Deacon came close to his superior and, with due deference, whispered to him. 'Your Grace,' he said, 'should I not initiate a search for a magician with the power to dissolve these spells, someone who might be able to free those wretched victims from their prisons of stone?'

The Archbishop turned on his acolyte, his lips white as he held his temper in. His voice, when he spoke, was hardly to be heard. 'You fool,' he said, 'rather find me a magician who has the art to do what the Master did, and as beautifully. I have a cloister to finish and a church to build. Remember that, Deacon, and nothing else,' and the Archbishop strode from his palace and went directly to his cathedral to see how far the walls had climbed since the previous day.

# LE
# CORDEIL

**E**arly the next morning I left Lucien and, with my umbrella slung over my shoulder and the sheep bell in my hand, I went down the mountain on my own, passing through the empty street of Peyresq and going on to Jules Martel's house in La Colle. He was ready for me, leaning against the side of his Peugeot estate, his arms folded. As I walked towards him Leonce Coulet came out of a shed where he'd been slaughtering a sheep and I shook his huge hand for the last time.

'You did well,' he said, 'for an Englishman. Perhaps you'd better marry Graziani's daughter and stay with us after all.'

I went off in the car with Jules who was on his way back to Allons, and he stopped to let me out at the station of Thorame-Haute, a tiny, unattended halt by the roadside in the valley of the Verdon. I sat in my seat, unhappy, not moving. 'Perhaps I will go up to Marius's mountain,' I said, 'I don't feel like going down to the coast.'

Jules nodded and drove on past the station. 'You might just as well see all three pastures,' he said, 'each one is worth the journey.'

A few kilometres further on he left me where the road to Argens begins to climb up from the valley. The last I saw of him was his big face looking towards me out of the open window of his car. 'You'll be at the village in an hour and a half,' he said. 'If he's not there he'll be somewhere on the mountain. You can't miss him, just go to the top and make for the cabin, or the sheep, he'll see you.'

The road to Argens was barely two or three metres wide and rose abruptly, following the contours of a wooded hillside where the undergrowth was wild and impenetrable. Below me, on my left, the vegetation was no less dense and fell away down a steep slope that led, according to my map, to the bottom of a narrow ravine.

After walking for a while the weight of my duffel bag began to annoy me and so, after only a moment's deliberation, I hid it and all its contents in the undergrowth near the road, marking an over-hanging tree with my knife and placing a large stone at the edge of the wood where I could not fail to see it on my return.

Now I strode out in earnest towards my destination and as my path rose my spirits rose also. I saw no one; no one passed me on foot nor did I hear or see a single motor-car. All around me was silent and dark green with just one great band of blue above.

And then came the eagle, stopping my heart with the sudden beauty of its flight, its wide wings motionless and all its body poised on the air as if the air were solid. I was still some distance from Argens, the road a mere shelf in the mountainside, when it appeared before me. Perhaps it had been disturbed by the sound of my steps as it perched in the shade of some tree, or perhaps the bird had been drifting down the shape of the sky, searching for its prey. I do not know. All I do know is that for a moment it was close enough for me to smell, swooping within the stretch of my arm, and for a split second I saw every detail of it; the bright clean plumage and the imperious head; the curving beak and the hard eye which stared at me as if I lay in its power, body and soul, reminding me that eagles could kill whenever they chose. Then it skimmed away and for another moment I could look down on it as it soared below me, over the tree tops of the valley – contemptuous – then it was gone.

❦

When I came to Argens I discovered it to be the smallest of the three hamlets I had seen; just five or six tiny houses built on an outcrop of rock and using for their construction the rough stone of that rock. Arriving there was like arriving at the ruins of a castle keep that had been left to decay, its walls worn down by the wind and rain of a long past.

It was midday when I walked into its short and crooked street and found no one there but an old man sitting on his step and leaning back against his door with his eyes closed, warming his lizard skin in the sun.

I woke him and though he hardly understood French he showed me Marius's house; two little rooms with a stable below. The door was open and I went inside and found the bare rooms cool and restful after my long march, the slatted shutters casting striped shadows on the dark, tiled floor. There were some signs of Marius's passage – unfinished food in the small refrigerator and a saucepan on the gas stove.

I removed my clothes and made myself a meal, eating naked. Afterwards I threw open the shutters and warmed two large casseroles of water. Then I stood in a plastic washing-up bowl and scrubbed myself clean, splashing my body all over. It was the first thorough wash I had managed since leaving Grimaud and I sang with the joy of it, although the English songs I sang must have sounded barbarous in the ears of the old man outside for when I left the house a little later, to begin the climb to the summit of Le Cordeil, he was nowhere to be seen.

Le Cordeil is nearly seven thousand feet high and, for me, a good two hours' climb. At the end of it I came out onto a wide ridge about eight kilometres long and I followed it northwards until I spied Marius's cabin just below the summit on the eastern side. It looked totally vulnerable in all that emptiness and as I advanced towards it I saw myself from a distance also – just a small figure walking in that same great space.

I came to the cabin silently over the grass, so silently that the dogs did not bark. The door lay open. Inside the earthen floor was uneven. There was a table, two stools and a double bed made from rough planks. On the wall were some sloping shelves and nothing more.

I went to the rear of the hut and there was Marius lying in the sun, his head resting on his rolled up cloak and his eyes staring up at a silver aeroplane that was scratching a vapour trail across the enamel sky. The dogs growled and he looked at me, then he pointed above his head.

'I was thinking about them up there and me down here,' he said, 'and whether I ought to be with them in that flying box, breathing chemicals out of a canister and on my way to Paris or Rome . . . but then I thought that here I've got air as fresh as mountain water and mountain water as light as mountain air. You know, when all is said and done, I bet their days don't even compare with the nights we have in Provence.'

∞

I stayed two of those nights and one complete day on the summit of Marius's mountain. We watched the sheep from afar, through binoculars, and ate together lying on the grass, talking of everything. But then, on the second morning I awoke and knew that it was time for me to catch the train to Nice, and from there another train to Frejus and then the bus to St Aygulf and Grimaud; names that now sounded like names from a foreign country; words that felt strange and awkward on the tongue.

Marius walked with me until we came to the faintest beginnings of the path that led down to Argens and we sat on the grass together and looked into the valley. After a moment he opened his leather bag and brought out a bottle of vermouth and two glasses; he polished them on a napkin and then filled them to the brim.

'Your health, Michèu,' he said, 'and do not slip on the turf going down, for it is smooth and once you start rolling there is nothing to stop you.'

I raised my glass. 'I promise not to slip,' I said.

Marius took a mouthful of his drink and went on. 'I never thought you would get here at the beginning,' he said, 'when your shoes fell apart and your feet were all blistered . . . but you have done more than just get here. You have seen La Chamatte, La Courradour and now Le Cordeil. You have even made Jules Martel laugh and that is rare, and you have heard some stories too . . . but above all you have seen the marmots and the eagle . . . and with those you have seen everything.'

'Yes,' I answered, 'I have been lucky.'

'What story did Lucien tell you?'

'The Cloisters of St Trophime . . . he said it was the best.'

Marius smiled and refilled our glasses, placing his own carefully against his bag so that it would not spill. 'Ah,' he said, 'did he? Well, before you go I will tell you mine. I was going to tell it at Bargemon because it is about Bargemon, but it will do just as well here . . . and in my opinion this is the best story of them all.'

And so, on top of his mountain kingdom, lying back on his cloak, Marius Fresia the shepherd, laced his fingers across his chest and told me the last of the Provençal Tales.

# The Plane Tree and
# The Fountain

'**W**hat the populace would like to see,' said the steward, 'is a fountain and a plane tree in the centre of the town square. Then, so they argue, they would not be obliged to fetch water from the stream below the hillside and, in addition the ladies of Bargemon, and the gentlemen of course, would have somewhere agreeable to congregate in the cool of the evening. Well, my lord, I have given this matter a great deal of thought but have come to the conclusion that it would be too costly . . . therefore, sire, I have delayed my decision.'

The Lord of Bargemon, the Baron de Barjaude, looked from his window and sighed. It was not worth his while answering the steward for the man was used to ordering the estates on his own authority. He would go on prattling, quite unperturbed, through the whole of that morning's business; it made no difference whether his master intervened or not.

The Baron sighed again. He would have to abandon this dreary servant and his droning voice. Instead of standing there trying not to yawn he would command his groom to bring his best horse from the stable and take himself off to the hillsides. He would go into the wild forest and wander at will along the deserted tracks, hiding from the sun under the green shade of the green leaves, absenting himself for a month or more.

The castle which the Baron desired to quit so eagerly was in fact a delight to look upon. It stood halfway up a range of wooded hills and stared southwards over the curved roof-tiles of a town where scores of houses clambered carelessly onto each other's backs. It was an enchanting castle, built for pleasure rather than conflict, and it was furnished with fine carpets and soft couches. Without realizing it the courtiers of Bargemon had been born into one of the most easeful places on earth. Minstrels played to them: troubadours told stories of distant lands and the ladies of the court listened and embroidered those same stories into tapestries. In Bargemon everyone was happy. Everyone, that was, save the Lord of Bargemon himself.

As the long years had passed over him the Baron had found himself increasingly possessed by a powerful melancholy. At first it had puzzled him; his peasants worked hard and provided all that he needed; his courtiers sought enjoyment and found it readily and Bargemon flourished almost without supervision. Indeed his lands were so well-regulated it appeared that all the Baron had to do to secure the continuation of his own and his subjects' happiness was to play his part and do nothing. It was only gradually therefore that he came to understand how it was this very feeling of indolence, winding into his heart like a worm, that made him sad.

To counter this sadness he had thought, once or twice, of marriage but the idea of sharing his life with another frightened him. Besides he had left it too late and was too set in his ways. At fifty years of age, as he now was, what woman young enough to bear children would take him as a husband? His neck was wrinkled and his back was stooped. In any event the problem of the succession did not worry him. There was the son of a cousin somewhere beyond Fayence who would be only too pleased to step into his shoes when the time came. 'No,' said the Baron to himself on the frequent occasions when he pondered the subject, 'there is nothing to be done.'

So it happened that, despairing of ever being as content in age as he had been in youth, the Baron took to riding alone in the savage country towards Brovès, roaming even as far as la Bastide and idling along by the banks of the Artuby. He came to admire this country with its abrupt hillsides and fierce sunsets. He respected too the rugged people he found there. He did not know them or they him but he was accepted without affectation and always given shelter for the night when he needed it. Somehow these people, their solidity and simplicity, seemed to help the Baron retain his hold on life; sometimes he even thought that it was only their existence that reassured him and kept him alive.

In the beginning these absences of the Baron had worried his courtiers and several of them had gone for advice to the astrologer who lived in Bargemon, near the main square, in a dwelling that was half house and half cave. According to common rumour this man, who was dark-skinned, had come originally from the East. It was also said that he was ageless, knew all things and was master of great magic. The learned scoffed at this foolishness and pointed out that no one had ever seen the old man do anything more amazing than mend an arm or set a leg; all the rest was idle gossip.

So much then was in doubt but it was known for certain that the astrologer was very short-tempered and disliked being disturbed at his books. 'You are idiots!' he cried at those courtiers who had come to seek his opinion. 'You lead a perfect life in an earthly paradise and yet you cannot let things be. As long as the Baron is content let him wander as he will . . . perhaps he finds your company as tiresome as I do. Now leave me to my solitude and my studies or I shall turn you all into snakes.'

With this answer the courtiers were obliged to be content and they left the astrologer's house with great speed, trampling on each others' heels in their eagerness, and after that one attempt to understand the Baron's melancholy they made no more. It seemed, on reflection, wiser to leave things as they were.

⁜

In this way did life go by at Bargemon and on the day that the steward had talked to his lord about the plane tree and the fountain the Baron left his subjects, mounted his horse and rode northwards, not pausing until he had reached the banks of the River Artuby. There he allowed his mount to drink and, as the animal quenched its thirst, the Baron noticed a young man lying in the flowered grass on the far side of the water.

There was something about the young man that caught the interest of the Baron and he studied him closely. Obviously a troubadour he wore a loose tunic embroidered all over with blooms as bright as those he lay among, and so colourful were they, and so cunningly fashioned, that it was impossible at first glance to tell where the tunic ended and the meadow began. By his side was a lute and a large goatskin bag containing his few possessions and his songs and poems. With his eyes closed this wanderer lay flat on his back, protected from the heat of the day by the shade of the low branches above him. His legs were crossed at the ankle and both arms were flung out from the body as far as they would go. Round his shoulders curled his long black hair and his breathing was light and even. He was a man who looked perfectly at peace with himself and in total harmony with the spinning planet at his back.

The Baron dismounted and, the Artuby being little more than a stream at this point, he crossed it and stared down into the sleeping troubadour's face. Such was the beauty and contentment of what he saw that, although he kept his voice low, he could not refrain from speaking to himself aloud. 'Ah,' he said, 'this man sleeps as innocently as a child. Here indeed is a happy mortal. He has no cares and he goes where he will, blowing where the wind listeth. There is no melancholy for him.'

A voice answered the Baron immediately and he started in surprise, realizing in the same second that the troubadour was speaking although he hadn't moved and nor had he bothered to open his eyes.

'What I do,' he said, 'any man can do. It may be certain that not everyone on earth has the talent of the troubadour, but anyone can learn to love the poems of others and learn to sing a song well enough. That will cast melancholy aside. What do you need in life but sufficient food and a rough roof for the winter?'

'As for that,' answered the Baron, squatting down on his haunches, 'I have more than I need. There are servants to do my bidding, peasants to grow my crops and courtiers to serve and amuse me. Even so, I am not happy as you are happy. Happiness is a gift and it is a gift I have not been given.'

Here at last the troubadour opened his eyes and sat up, his face flushed with the anger of argument. 'Since when,' he demanded, 'has happiness been a gift? Do you think it comes to you out of the sky, like rain? Have I not searched for years? Did I not follow other troubadours and listen to their every word. Did I not seek out remarkable men and sit at their feet. Happiness! I tell you, stranger, a life is like a work of art and must be fashioned as a poem is fashioned – throw away all that is dross and keep only that which you need. For all your fine clothes I can see that you have wasted your life on the wrong things and you know nothing. Well, know this, fool, you will never turn a bend in the road and find happiness waiting for you at the end of the journey as if it were a city . . . happiness is the road itself and you must walk it.'

The Baron sprang to his feet, enraged at being admonished in such a forthright manner by a mere troubadour. 'Hold your tongue,' he cried. 'Why, I am the Baron de Barjaude, Lord of Bargemon, and I could have you whipped for this.'

To the Baron's astonishment the troubadour laughed, long and loud, rolling over in the grass, helpless with mirth. 'In this wilderness you are lord of nothing,' he replied as soon as he had recovered himself, 'and if your life compared to mine in its wisdom and pleasure you would know it, and you would not be threatening me with talk of whippings. I suspect, my Lord of Bargemon, that in this life there has been no love for you and that even your courtiers only serve you out of custom. You are their master and you keep them in idleness – that is the only tie between you.'

The Baron bit his lip and remained silent. He knew that the troubadour had spoken no more than the truth. Though much younger than the Baron his experience of life was wider and deeper, and he did indeed seem to carry wisdom and pleasure about him in equal proportions. The Baron swallowed. He meant to be angry but could not. There was something in the troubadour's words that eased the melancholy around the Baron's heart. He smiled. 'Perhaps what you say is correct,' he said, 'but it is too late for me to learn your wisdom now.'

The troubadour rose to his feet and brushed the grass from his embroidered jerkin. 'Wisdom has no date,' he said, and then: 'Only a mile or so from here, on the road to Jabron, there lies a woodcutter's shanty. I have half a loaf in my sack, you no doubt have something better in your saddle-bag, and I know the generous woodcutter will give us a cup of wine or two and the loan of his shed to sleep in. Let us spend the night there and if you wish it you may journey a little of my way with me and we will talk together until the path divides. What do you say, you Lord of Bargemon?'

The Baron laughed at the troubadour's impertinence as he had not laughed for many a year. 'I agree,' he said, 'wholeheartedly, but tell me your name for you know mine.'

The troubadour bent for his lute and struck a chord on it, afterwards making a reverence like a courtier. 'My name,' he said, 'is Mariu de Montepezet, and there will be a time when my songs are known by all those who speak or hear the golden words of Provençal.'

∞

The Baron was transformed by the troubadour's company and the two men spent more than a month wandering the roads together.

The nobleman's melancholy disappeared so completely that he could hardly remember it. He slept in the meanest huts and ate the roughest fare, even selling his horse and saddle to keep himself in funds. His clothes became worn and dusty and he laughed at it. His hair and his beard grew tangled and he combed them with his fingers. Never had the Baron felt so fulfilled or so attached to life. He learnt the songs and poems of the troubadours just as quickly as Mariu would teach them and he and his companion talked endlessly as they journeyed. At night they sang ballads to shepherds for food and told stories to peasants for wine.

For the Baron such a way of life was a revelation and he never wanted to leave it, but it could not be. One day Mariu halted on the banks of a great river and, staring across it, he laid his hand gently on the Baron's shoulder and spoke, his voice trembling with affection.

'Lord of Bargemon, my friend,' he said, 'this is where our roads part. This is the Durance, beyond it is Manosque and now I must go on alone.'

The sadness of this announcement struck the Baron like a blow but he had learnt enough about the calling to realize that a troubadour was obliged to follow his own path through life; it was in the nature of things. In spite of this the Baron allowed his feelings to show and a tear moistened his eye. 'It is like death to leave you, Mariu,' he said, 'but I am grateful. You taught me much and cured me of my grieving.'

Mariu nodded and both men rested on a rock and shared a last meal. 'I am content for you,' said the troubadour, 'but it was not really I who taught you . . . you learnt to be yourself, that is all. For years you did not know what you wanted and were disgusted by what you had. From the chasm that lay between rose your melancholy.'

'Can I be happy and wise now, if I am myself?'

'Perhaps,' said Mariu, 'but be on your guard. You are still the Lord of Bargemon. To lead the simple life is not simple. Every day you will have to open your eyes and ask why you are alive, and every day you must also ask, "If my life is a poem am I writing it well?" Think of your time on earth as a wine which is already leaking out of the pitcher drop by drop. It is a wine beyond price. Do not spill it carelessly and do not pour it out before fools.'

Here the two men finished their meal and put away what remained of their provisions, then they stood and embraced in farewell.

'Adieu, my friend,' said Mariu. 'Remember that the lion and the goat must live side by side. You must keep the lion tranquil while at the same time you graze and milk the goat. Once more, adieu – we shall never meet again,' and so the troubadour turned from the Baron, waded into the shallow river and then struck out for the distant shore. Not once did he look back.

※

On his arrival at Bargemon the Baron went directly to his castle and, without changing his clothes, washing his body or combing his beard, he commanded that all his subjects – courtiers, men-at-arms and servants – should attend him without delay in the great hall. There, in straightforward terms, he explained his long absence and told his people that from that moment on he was determined to lead a simpler life, one that was closer to nature and one that he hoped would lead him, in his last years, along the philosopher's road of self-perfection.

On the other hand, insisted the Baron, his decision would alter nothing in respect of his subjects. Those who lived in the castle, or elsewhere for that matter, should continue exactly as before. Anyone who wanted might use the Baron's private apartments. His horses were at everyone's disposal, as were the contents of his cellars and the produce of the valley. 'Share all there is amongst you,' he cried.

As for the Baron himself he would not be far away but he made a point of ordering his vassals, under pain of his utmost displeasure, not to interrupt him in his new life. There was an old and abandoned farmhouse in the hills towards Montferrat and there, accompanied only by the servant who had been his companion and friend since childhood, he would live.

The people of Bargemon who, to be truthful, had hardly missed their lord during his travels, watched with equanimity as he and his servant left the castle. Over recent years they had become quite used to the Baron's moods and changing whims. This, they considered, was just another example, a little more extreme but that was all. To their minds it was obvious that he was going mad; tramping the countryside with common troubadours; sleeping in ditches and eating with shepherds, now he was going to live as one. Well, it did not matter, nothing would change. From the very day of the Baron's inheritance they had always directed their own affairs. The Lord of Bargemon had thought to govern them, especially at the beginning, but that had never been the case and certainly not since the onset of his melancholy. So let him go into the hills towards Montferrat, and let him stay there till he died.

∞

In this manner were things arranged and for many months the life of Bargemon hardly seemed any different. The peasants toiled in the dust of the fields and the nobles took their dues. The sun shone, the wind bent the trees and the birds sang, but all was not well – jealousy and hatred began to grow in people's hearts. Great quarrels arose amongst the courtiers. First one and then another moved into the Baron's apartments, for to occupy them and issue orders became the desire of every petty noble in the castle. They squabbled over the horses and they fought over the wines. From day to day the situation worsened, blows were struck and swords were drawn. No one was content and everyone took sides; cabals were formed until at last one of the most powerful of all the courtiers died under mysterious circumstances – suffocation said some, poison said others. Whatever the truth of the matter life in Bargemon had become not only unpleasant but dangerous also, and that was not the end of it.

The peasants, seeing that the courtiers fought amongst themselves, began to fail in their duties. They neglected to pay their taxes and they refused to bring their produce to the castle, keeping everything for themselves and selling what they did not need in the markets, hiding their money away in secret places.

Alarmed, the courtiers tried to forget their differences, banding together to threaten the peasants with the soldiery but the threat was an empty one. Most of the Baron's soldiers had wandered away to serve other lords and those that had not were peasants themselves and had returned to their families and their farms. It was not long before the courtiers grew ill-fed and unkempt and the peasants mocked them, nor would they bow when they went by or raise their hats. The castle itself fell into disrepair. Piles of dust rose in the corners of every room. Rats nested in the rafters and the tapestries fell from the walls. Bargemon was dying and it seemed that nothing could be done.

∞

Fortunately not everyone still living in the castle surrendered to despair. The man who had once been the Baron's steward gathered together a few like-minded courtiers and, after a long and violent discussion it was decided that the Lord of Bargemon had, by default, relinquished all his rights to sovereignty. In consequence a messenger was sent to the Baron's cousin at Fayence, telling him what had happened and begging him to present himself at the castle without delay so that he might claim his inheritance and become the rightful lord of all.

The cousin received these tidings with delight. For many years, though he was still a young man, he had been waiting to seize Bargemon and its domain. Now his waiting was over. Gathering about him his friends and sycophants, and as many armed men as he could pay for, he set out across country and within a very short time was riding into the courtyard of the castle. Here he was welcomed with great warmth and, dismounting, he quickly inspected every room and chamber of his new residence.

He was very much dismayed by what he saw and, with oaths and blows, he set the servants to scrubbing the castle clean and re-hanging the tapestries, and as for the courtiers, he told them to prepare for a great ball that very evening.

'A ball,' cried the steward, hardly able to believe his ears. 'But there is no food in the castle, no wine.'

The new Lord of Bargemon sneered. 'Let that be my care,' he said. 'While you make ready I shall take my soldiers to visit the peasants . . . just to show them that times have changed.' And with a laugh he strode to the courtyard and leapt into his saddle.

That day the peasants did indeed learn that the times had changed for the soldiers burst into their farmhouses and took everything they wanted. Fruit, meat and wines were loaded into stolen wagons until the axles almost snapped under the weight, and anyone who dared dissent was tied to a wheel and whipped until the blood ran down into the dust. 'This is no more than you deserve,' said their lord, 'for months you have not paid what you owe . . . now the time has come to make it good.'

The ball was a great success and the courtiers were overwhelmed by the alteration in their fortunes. The castle shone in its cleanliness and there was more food and wine to be had than ever before. Everyone agreed that inviting the cousin to be their lord was the best thing they could have done. They smiled and danced and raised their goblets, praising each other all night long and not one of them felt weary until many many hours after the sun had climbed into the sky.

The peasants woke to a very different day. For them the world had changed also but not one jot for the better. In the briefest of moments all the provisions they had laid by and all their wealth had been stolen from them. And, as if to mock their predicament, down from the castle floated sweet music and the shouting of the revellers as they drank and danced. There was worse to come. Over the next few months, to make sure that the peasants had truly learnt their lesson, the new lord sent his soldiers everywhere through the estates, giving them full licence to behave like the troops of a conquering army and to beat senseless anyone who offered resistance.

The peasants and the farmers had no way of defending themselves against this onslaught. They were ignorant people and had little experience in the ways of the world, but, in spite of this, some of them began to meet in secret, coming together at night so they could discuss their troubles and attempt to find a way out of them. It was not an easy undertaking and, finally, after several meetings and many hours of talking, they could think of nothing better than to go to the astrologer and ask him for the benefit of his wisdom and erudition.

The astrologer was as angry with the peasants as he had once been with the courtiers, perhaps even angrier. 'I might expect such foolishness from flunkeys and parasites,' he said, 'but from good peasant stock I at least look for some degree of mother-wit. Isn't that what living close to nature is supposed to teach a man . . . isn't such a life meant to lead directly to common-sense? Had you but kept your so-called masters happy in their castle, supplied with as much food and wine as they needed, you could have lived your lives as you wished and would not be suffering today from the outrages of this upstart lord and his soldiers. I do not even pity you in your stupidity . . . you wallow in it. I can think of nothing for you to do save one thing only . . . persuade your rightful lord to return to his duty. Now begone, all of you. If you bother me again I shall turn you all into the oxen you already resemble.' And with this threat the astrologer drove the peasants from his door with a heavy stick.

It did not take long for the peasants to implement the advice they had received and within a day or two a few of their number set off to present themselves before the Baron. These men found that their one-time lord had established himself, and his servant, in a sturdy, stone-built farmhouse. It was a beautiful place and well sheltered from the bite of the mistral: there was a deep well in the hillside that never ran dry; shade from the sun in summer and a huge stock of sawn wood for the fire in winter. On every side, and in amongst the trees, a small flock of sheep and goats grazed and their bells sounded now and then, drowsily, as they moved. Keeping watch over the animals was a girl, a shepherdess who went barefoot across the grass and wore a simple dress.

The Baron was simply dressed also and his subjects found him sitting in a comfortable chair on the shady side of the house, a book in his hands. He looked well, both in body and spirit and, although jealous of his contentment and seclusion, he received the peasants well enough for he had always been kind to his bondsmen. His solitary wanderings, as well as the time he had spent in the hills with the troubadour, had only served to strengthen what in him was a natural inclination.

His pleasure was short-lived. On hearing what had happened at the castle during his absence, especially in regard to his cousin's behaviour, he flew into a mighty rage. He rose from his chair and threw down his book. 'Why is it,' he exclaimed, 'that men cannot live together? It is such a simple thing. You have done wrong in not sharing your produce with those who live in the castle, but they have done worse by ill-treating those whom they should protect. As for this kinsman of mine, this heir, he overreaches himself and he shall find that he has roused a sleeping lion. My courtiers should have had wisdom enough to govern themselves – now they deserve punishment. You are simpler and will receive my help. What is more I am angry and touched in my pride . . . leave me to ponder my revenge . . . I shall stand by you.'

The peasants were delighted by the Baron's response to their petition. They thanked him and bowed and went on their way. As soon as he was alone the Baron dressed in the best clothes that remained to him, girded on his sword, mounted his horse and set out for the castle. Once there he rode to the door of the great hall, swung from his saddle and strode directly through the throng of courtiers and soldiers until he came to his cousin who sat, lounging, in a huge chair which stood raised a step or two on a wide dais like a throne. Silence fell and every face turned towards the centre. The Baron, impressive in his anger, raised an arm and pointed at his cousin.

'Usurper,' he cried. 'You have come here without my command and against my wish, you have taken my castle and my lands like a robber in the night. You oppress my subjects and steal their goods, you wrong their women and whip those who dare deny you. Never have the people of Bargemon suffered so and they will suffer so no longer. Get you gone and wait your appointed time, you imposter. Crawl away to your hovel and take your men with you,' and here the Baron drew his sword.

Immediately after this speech there came another silence, extremely short, broken as it was by the cousin's sneering laughter. After a moment's hesitation the courtiers laughed too and the soldiers and the servants followed suit. They realized that, brave though the Baron was, there was nothing he could do. The cousin clicked his fingers above his head and his soldiers advanced; lowering their pikes, they ringed the Baron with sharp steel. One word of command and he would have been slain.

'You buffoon,' said the cousin. 'What foolishness brings you here? You abandoned your inheritance and you deserted your courtiers . . . there has already been bloodshed. Had it not been for me your peasants would have starved the inhabitants of this castle to death, they would have taken our lands and our wealth. Who could live in such a world? Not these people, not I, not even your peasants. You are an old man now, so go back to your garden and your goats, live in Arcadia and live in peace. Go sing songs with your shepherdess and let her stroke your grey hair.' And the cousin laughed again, uncontrollably this time, and the whole assembly laughed with him.

The Baron was struck dumb. Not for a moment had he imagined that he might be treated in this manner. Rather would he have died fighting, but even that escape was not allowed him. Instead the soldiers moved forward, striking the sword from his hand, and they beat him about the shoulders and hustled him from the great hall, out to the very gates of the castle where the servants heaped dust and kitchen refuse on his head. And when they had done, and still laughing, they bound him backwards on his horse and led him down into the town. There they left him for the townsfolk to see but the townsfolk turned away from the man who had once been their master and the peasants, who had been waiting to discover the outcome of the Baron's encounter with his cousin, turned away also, realizing that they, in the end, would have to accept their lot and make the best of what life brought them.

Only the shepherdess, who loved the Baron and had followed him to the castle, did not flinch but went to him and cut his bonds and wiped his face. 'Be wise,' she said as she helped him from his saddle. 'Do not be angry. Remember the happiness we have together. Come, let us return to our home. Forget your people, you can do nothing for them. Come.'

But a great anger had now arisen in the Baron's heart and although he knew the truth of what his shepherdess had said his pride was too strong and he pushed her away.

'I will have revenge,' he cried, 'and I will not rest until I see this cousin's blood running into the castle drains and every courtier who laughed at me today will kneel in the mire and kiss my shoe.'

'But how,' questioned the shepherdess, 'will you accomplish this? You have no soldiers, you have no riches.'

'I will go to the Count of Provence,' said the Baron, his eyes flashing madly, as if anger had robbed him of reason. 'He will give me soldiers, and then there's my astrologer,' added the Baron suddenly. 'I have kept him in idleness for years, as did my father before me, and his debt to my house is great. Never have I asked him the smallest service. He will know what I should do. He can read the future and he has the magic. Let him turn my cousin into a pig to eat the swill that lies below the castle walls . . .'

By now the Baron, who had been walking this way and that in his excitement, found himself at the astrologer's door and, without pausing to reflect, he knocked and strode into the house like one who owned it. The astrologer was at his books and as irritable as always.

'Well Baron,' he said, hardly looking up, 'here you are in a sad muddle of your own making, and, by the stars, you smell very like the pig you desire that I would turn your cousin into.'

'You heard . . ?'

'Humph,' snorted the astrologer. 'It would be a sorry state of affairs if I had studied magic all these years without being able to do something occasionally.'

'That's it exactly,' said the Baron. 'I know your powers, I know you can read the future . . . tell me what I must do . . . and tell me what will be best for my subjects also.'

The astrologer folded his arms, hiding his hands in the wide sleeves of his gown. 'Do as your shepherdess tells you,' he said. 'Return to your garden, your flocks and your books. Your peasants will be no worse with your cousin than they were with you . . . not in the long term they won't.'

'If you do not help me,' retorted the Baron, 'I shall go to the Count of

Provence and he will give me a great army. I promise you there will be bloodshed and men will die, though I also promise you that there shall be a peace and contentment afterwards that my peasants have never dreamt of. Bargemon shall be blessed.'

'Humph,' said the astrologer again. 'You seem to be looking into a future that bears no resemblance to the one I see. I tell you, Baron, I have seen many a war and though I once thought them amusing I do not now want one on my doorstep with both sides disturbing my solitude.'

'This is ridiculous,' cried the Baron, 'with your gifts you can do anything, even alter the course of events if you wish. You could help me save the peasants .'

The astrologer shook his head. 'It is a bad idea to interfere with the natural order.'

'Natural order,' shouted the Baron, shaking with rage. 'There is no such thing as a natural order when you may change it at will. Listen to me. When my parents gave you this house to live in did you not promise that you would assist their child in every way? I am that child. Help me in this war. Help me to punish my courtiers and kill my cousin.'

Again the astrologer shook his head. 'Your courtiers are too ignorant to change and your peasants do not understand what you offer them. I can tell you that even if you have your war it will all come back to the same thing in the end, so you might as well save yourself, and me, the trouble. Go home, back to your life of contemplation.'

'You charlatan,' hissed the Baron between his clenched teeth. 'If you have the gift of second sight, if you possess the magic then why did you not warn me that all this was going to happen? Why did you let me suffer the melancholy? Why allow me to fall under the spell of the troubadour? Why bring me to this fall and why set my cousin up to make a mock of me, covering me with offal from the kitchen. Why did you not help me?' And the Baron sobbed from his heart and hid his face in his hands.

The astrologer sighed and closed the book he held in his hand. 'My son,' he said, his voice strained, 'how you would curse me if I made magic all the time and did not allow you to direct your life. You would hate me even more than you hate me now.' Here the astrologer rose from his seat and a bitter smile flitted across his lips. 'I too would like to live the tranquil life but I know I never shall. Very well, Baron, this once, and this once only, I shall go against my own laws and aid you.'

The Baron uncovered his face and stared at the astrologer. 'You are truly as kind as my parents told me,' he said, 'and I swear to you that as soon as I have righted these terrible wrongs I shall desire nothing more than to live as the troubadour taught me to live, never wasting my energies in vain pursuits but simply to live and to love.'

The astrologer half-turned his head and studied the features of the shepherdess. He raised an eyebrow. 'That is a wisdom given to few,' he said. 'Now come with me and bring the girl.' And the astrologer smiled his bitter smile once more and, with his robes flowing behind him, he led the Baron and the shepherdess out of the house and into the open square that stood at the centre of the town. There he halted.

'See Baron,' he said, 'how calm and quiet everything is. Your courtiers have accepted your cousin, as have the townsfolk and the peasants too. Bargemon is as near perfection as your subjects deserve. It is pointless to struggle further. I know.'

'Help me as you promised,' said the Baron, 'and restore me to my rightful place.'

'I will,' said the astrologer and, closing his eyes, he began to chant in a strange and incomprehensible language, first raising his hands in the air and then laying them on the Baron's head.

To begin with the Baron smiled, as if he were convinced that he was about to see the realization of all his dreams. He was perhaps, but not in a way he expected. Slowly his body grew taller and taller, his feet spread and sprouted into the ground and became great gnarled roots and his arms rose gracefully above his head and multiplied and became long branches, heavy with wide green leaves.

A terrible moan broke from the Baron's lips. 'No,' he cried, 'this is not what I meant, I beg you, release me.'

The astrologer ignored this entreaty and moved his hands through the air again. More branches sprang from the Baron's body and his skin turned mottled and hard, like bark, thickening until it was bark and the Baron had disappeared altogether, and in his place stood a lofty plane tree giving a cool shade where before there had been none.

The astrologer was pleased with his work and although several white faces looked out from neighbouring windows no one came to challenge him. There was silence and only a light breeze stirred in the leaves of the tree until, all at once, there came a loud scream and the astrologer turned, surprised. He had forgotten the shepherdess and she, distracted at seeing the man she loved transformed like this, shrieked again and fell to her knees, sobbing like a wild thing.

The astrologer wrinkled his nose in distaste at this outburst of emotion. 'Come woman,' he said. 'I thought you wiser than that. He has found the tranquillity he said he sought for, and his people will be as happy as any alive. Take your own advice and return to your flocks and be content, as he is content.'

The shepherdess lifted her stained and reddened face and, between sobs, answered the astrologer. 'Love is not philosophy,' she said, 'have you not learnt that, you who know everything? I wanted to spend my life with him and would have followed him to war if that had been the only way.'

The astrologer stamped the ground in irritation. 'How I forget things,' he said, 'even that love is foolish. Would you follow the Baron now?'

Through her tears the shepherdess smiled. 'I would,' she said, 'I would.'

The astrologer shook his head in disbelief but at the same time he spoke once more in the strange tongue and moved his hands over the girl's head. Now it was her body that altered and grew taller, and her flesh solidified and becme stone and in the same second she was transformed into a fluted pillar of marble and from it poured clear water to form a fountain at her feet, a fountain that was bound in by a solid coping, high enough to sit upon.

'It is done,' said the astrologer when his task was complete, 'there may you weep for your love, little shepherdess,' and, throwing his gown across his shoulder, the astrologer made his way back to his house and the comfort of his study. With a sigh of relief he settled into his chair and opened his book. 'And now,' he said, 'perhaps we shall all be happy.'

Outside on the square there was, at first, no movement, but gradually the more adventurous of the inhabitants of Bargemon emerged from their houses and, their faces blank with wonder, they came to the tree and the fountain and touched them with their hands, unwilling as yet to believe the evidence of their own senses. They looked up also and saw where the branches of the tree swooped down as if to embrace the fountain, and they were amazed and frightened.

And to this day in Bargemon, just as the shepherdess had wept for the Baron in life, so from time to time the waters of the fountain overflow and moisten the roots of the plane tree as if in love and pity. There is also a second tree which stands nearby – it gives a smaller shade than the first – and some say this is the Baron's servant who loved his master and grew so lonely without him that he too went to the astrologer, and the astrologer, angrier than ever at being disturbed now that he had convinced himself at last that all disturbances were at an end, changed the servant into a tree even before the poor wretch could give a reason for his visit.

Luckily the transformation was exactly what the servant had desired and if, as it was said, the astrologer had the gift of second sight then he was only anticipating what he had no doubt foreseen. But of course we should beware of stories that tell of astrologers who know all and see all; such tales are suspect, often being nothing more than the light-hearted inventions of a vagabond minstrel singing for his supper. There is certainly no record in Bargemon itself of such happenings and if, by chance, you should stop someone in the street there and ask for the truth of the matter, they will look at you in a strange way and tell you what they believe – that the trees of Bargemon are merely trees and the fountain just a fountain – and then they will hurry away, not in the least eager to prolong such a conversation with a stranger.

# THORAME-HAUTE: GARE

I had been out of the world for what seemed like an age but I had no desire to re-enter it. I was not the slightest bit interested in rediscovering buses and trains or hotels and their ambitious managers. I felt different and set apart, marked even, and I said as much to Marius as we drank the final, farewell toast.

'Is that why people think shepherds have the magic,' I asked, 'and think them so wise, because they live out on their own?'

Marius shrugged. 'If we have wisdom,' he answered, 'it is only because we spend so much time watching the stars and the sheep. That's how we fill our lives, thinking and remembering.'

'I don't know what to do,' I said, 'or where to go.'

'Yes,' said Marius, 'when I return to the coast I am like a savage. I cannot talk to anyone except the other shepherds. The air is so hot and heavy down there, and sleeping under a roof is like sleeping with a rock on your chest. We have a saying for the autumn . . . we say that each man must follow the "flocons". The flocons are those three clumps of wool which remain at shearing, high on the backs of the big rams that lead the herd. They are to remind us of the stones that were laid, a thousand years ago, across the peaks to show us, and those who come after us, the track that goes from one pasture to another . . . all you can do is follow them.'

I left Marius lying on the grass, arms outspread like the troubadour in his story, his hat flattened on the ground behind his head like a halo. I was still unsure of my destination. Back to Grimaud for a while, yes, but never back to the life I had lived before. I had always wanted a pure adventure and now my wish had been granted. As I went down the mountain I had no idea what, if anything, I was taking with me, but I did know that I wanted to keep in my heart – forever if possible – the elemental simplicity I had seen and admired along the way.

Most of the shepherds had been born to their trade but still had understanding enough to appreciate their good fortune. Not that their lives were easy or romantic, nor did they think they were, but there was little or no dross in them and they had no truck with the Garreaus of this world – and what was more, they each had a mountain to live on.

I walked slowly towards the station at Thorame-Haute. I found my bag in the undergrowth where I had hidden it and the bell Lucien had given me clanged as I picked it up. The noise saddened me and sometimes, even now, it still does. That day I felt sure I was going in the wrong direction. It wasn't until many years later I realized that what I had brought down the mountain with me were the stories, and they were not given to everyone, but once you had them not even death could take them away.

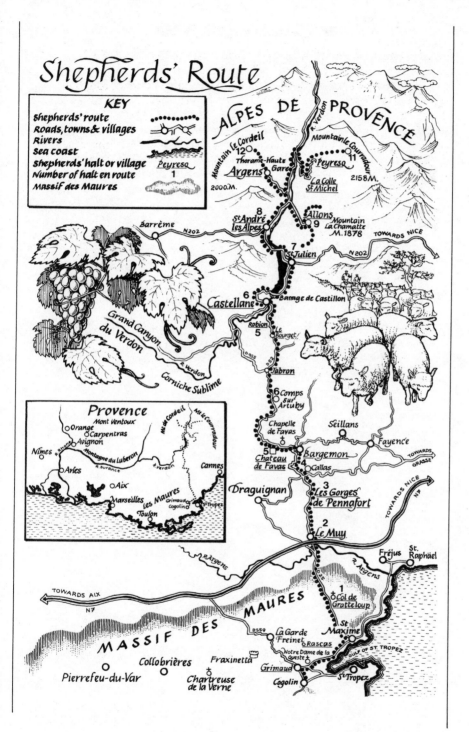

# Shepherds' Route

### KEY
shepherds' route
Roads, towns & villages
Rivers
sea coast
shepherds' halt or village    *Peyresq*
Number of halt en route    1
Massif des Maures

**ALPES DE PROVENCE**

R. Verdon

Mountain le Cordeil
2000.M.

Mountain le Couvradou
2158M.

12 O
Thorame-Haute
Gare

11 O
*Peyresq*

*Argens*

*La Colle*
*St Michel*

8 O
St André
les Alpes

*Allons*
9

Mountain
La Chamatte
M.1878

TOWARDS NICE

Barrème    N202

7
St Julien

N 202

6
*Castellane*    Barrage de Castillon

Grand Canyon
du Verdon

R. Verdon

Robion
5
*Le Bourget*

Corniche Sublime

Jabron

6 Comps
sur
Artuby

Chapelle
de Favas

Séillans

### Provence
Mont Ventoux
Orange
Carpentras
Avignon
Montagne du Luberon
Nîmes
R. Rhône
R. Durance
Arles
Aix
Marseilles
Toulon
Les Maures
Grimaud
Cogolin
St Tropez
Cannes

5 Château
de Favas

Bargemon

Callas

Fayence

TOWARDS
GRASSE

*Draguignan*

3
Les Gorges
de Pennafort

TOWARDS NICE    N7

2
Le Muy

R. Argens

Fréjus    St.
Raphäel

R. Argens

TOWARDS AIX

N7

R. Argens

1
Col de
Gratteloup

**MASSIF DES MAURES**

D559
La Garde
Freinet

St.
Maxime

Rascas
Notre Dame de la
Queste

GULF OF ST TROPEZ

Collobrières

Fraxinetta

Grimaud

Pierrefeu-du-Var

Chartreuse
de la Verne

Cogolin

St Tropez